CASTO

GODS OF WAR

XENIA MELZER

DSP PUBLICATIONS

Published by
DSP PUBLICATIONS

5032 Capital Circle SW, Suite 2, PMB# 279, Tallahassee, FL 32305-7886 USA
www.dsppublications.com

Casto
© 2016 Xenia Melzer.

Cover Art
© 2016 Aaron Anderson.
aaronbydesign55@gmail.com
Cover content is for illustrative purposes only and any person depicted on the cover is a model.

Author Photo
Photographer: Andreas Eirainer, bildwerk.
Makeup: Kathrin Fuchsenthaler.

ISBN: 978-1-63476-837-5
Digital ISBN: 978-1-63476-838-2
Library of Congress Control Number: 2015918979
Published June 2016
v. 1.0

Printed in the United States of America
∞

This paper meets the requirements of
ANSI/NISO Z39.48-1992 (Permanence of Paper).

To Michael. Thanks for loving me.

ACKNOWLEDGMENTS

I HAVE to thank a lot of people for this book and since it is always hard to determine who contributed most, I will just list them chronologically.

First, I wish to thank my wonderful husband Michael, for never giving up on my dream even when I myself doubted the wisdom of hanging on.

I would also like to thank Dr. Richard Marranca, my professor from university days and dear friend, who has always supported my writing and egged me on when I thought about giving up.

Thanks also go to my sister, for being a very critical and, most importantly, honest proofreader who always points out my flaws to me—story- and character-wise.

And, of course, everybody at Dreamspinner Press for welcoming me into the fold and giving my brainchild a chance to see the light of day.

I'm very grateful for the best editors a newbie writer like me can get. Sue Adams, Liv, and Jonathan Penn have shown great patience with the countless mistakes I made and have given the story a wonderful final polish. You guys rule!

If I have forgotten somebody here, I will make sure to mention them in my next book.

AUTHOR'S NOTE

DEAR READER,

For an author, it is always hard to determine how much fantasy there should be in their work. I'm not talking dragons, elves, unicorns, or dwarves here, but something a lot simpler and yet infinitely more complicated: measurements.

As a devoted reader of fantasy, I first thought about "going all the way" and creating my very own system of measurement. Unfortunately this didn't work out (there's a reason I'm a writer and not a mathematician). I didn't want to be stuck with ordinary miles and feet either, so after some intense thinking, I came up with a solution that I hope will make everyone happy.

I went and researched ancient, mostly medieval, means of measurement, some of which I think readers will be familiar with, thus avoiding the confusion that comes with a completely made-up system. So here I proudly present the list of measurements used in Gods of War:

Measurements of Length

1 hand = 4 inches = 10.2 centimeters (1 hand is the unit still used
    to measure the height of horses.)
1 span = 9 inches = 22.9 centimeters
1 ell = 45 inches = 114 centimeters or 1.14 meters
1 pace = 5 feet or 60 inches = 1.5 meters
1 league = 3 miles = 4.8 kilometers

Measurements of Mass

1 ore = 0.85 ounce = 24 grams
1 clove = 6.4 pounds = 2.9 kilograms
1 quarter = 2 stone or 28 pounds = 12.7 kilograms
1 hundredweight = 8 stone or 112 pounds = 50.8 kilograms

As to readers who are familiar with the various measurement systems during medieval times, I would ask them to kindly turn a blind eye on any inconsistencies they may find.

GODS OF WAR

HOW THE world came into being. Excerpts from the Books of Lore, written down by Brosilanus the Younger.

How the Mothers Created the World

In the beginning there were Magic and Chaos, the eternal siblings. They filled the void, but no life could spring from them, for these two break any vessel they pour into. The Mothers tamed Magic and Chaos and directed the power toward fruitful outcomes.

Ana-Isara, the Empress of the Dead, and her sister, Ana-Aruna, the Source of Life, left their own realm, the Green Lands, to establish life in this newborn universe. They used the raw magic to force chaos into rules and formed a world: Ana-Darasa, the New One.

To enlighten their world, they sent two moons, Isara and Aruna, as well as a sun, Eltam, the Bright Star. Soon Ana-Darasa was covered in forests and seas, but Magic and Chaos were still strong. Their power burned part of creation, and the Hot Heart, the merciless desert, was formed.

When they saw this, the Mothers decided to create something that would be able to dip into the source of magic and use its powers. This way, they would tame the stream of magic further until it was no longer a threat. They called their new creation La'ides—the humans.

Thus the First Aeon began.

The First Aeon

In the beginning of the First Aeon, the La'ides were like small children, barely able to look after themselves and certainly not fit to use any magic at all. With their limitless patience, the Mothers taught these naive creatures how to survive in their own world. They gave them a language, today known as the language of the Ancients, and taught them how to write and make music and the basics of mathematics.

Soon it became apparent that the talents of the individual La'ides were very different indeed. Some were very good at making tools, others excelled in singing, or building houses. The Mothers fostered all these talents, proud of their creation.

It was at that time that the witch clans were established. They consisted of people who could easily make a connection to magic and use it to perform certain tasks. Unlike the Mothers, for whom magic was the raw material from which they formed whatever they pleased, the talents of the witches had their limits. One line was able to step behind time, others had command over the elements, or could see the future, or change their shapes, or make plants grow. One clan was able to use magic for healing, but those blessed with this talent paid a high price: the more patients they cured, the faster their own lives came to an end.

This changed when the snakes came to Ana-Darasa. Like the Mothers, they were from a different world, one that had already ceased to exist. They are nomads without a home, who are always drawn to life.

With the blessing of the Mothers, the snakes formed a pact with the healer clan, enabling the healers to use their power without being killed by it. In return, the snakes were given a home in the hearts of the La'ides. It was a good pact, which benefitted both sides.

For many years, the La'ides lived happily under the reign of the Mothers. It was a golden age that found its end when the witch clans realized that their power was dwindling with every passing generation. The wild stream of magic had turned into a tamed river whose waters could no longer be manipulated easily. The order intended by the Mothers started to take over.

But the La'ides were filled with fear. Without the witches' powers, life became harder. They also thought the Mothers would leave them as soon as the magic was completely tamed. In their misery, they turned to Ana-Isara, who thought about the pleas of her and her sister's creation for a long time.

When she had made up her mind, she wandered over the surface of Ana-Darasa, her heart and spirit wide open to take in the essence of the world. Heaven and earth, fire and water, soil and air, everything that was her creation, every pulsing of life she and her sister had called into being was taken in. From this material, the Empress of the Dead formed two children who ripened inside her pale body.

2

The Second Aeon

After Ana-Isara had promised her creation two leaders, she took in the essence of Ana-Darasa and returned to her sister in the Green Lands. There she carried two sons: Canubis, the Wolf of War, and his brother, Renaldo, the Angel of Death. When the boys were born, they were as pale and lifeless as their mother, since the Empress of the Dead cannot bring forth life. So her sister stepped forward, kissed the boys, and gifted them with the essence of life.

Ana-Isara made her firstborn, Canubis, into an absolute ruler. His word would be law, even for his brother, and the power of his commands was irresistible.

Renaldo charmed the Mothers with his beauty. Never had a more perfect child seen the light of day. Underneath that perfection, however, a fire burned—one so powerful even Canubis had to be wary of it.

The Mothers raised the boys in the Green Lands, taught them everything they needed to know as future gods of their world. When they turned sixteen, Ana-Isara took them with her to introduce them to their people.

Unfortunately, the hearts of the La'ides are fickle, and time runs differently in the Green Lands. For Canubis and Renaldo, sixteen years had passed, but for the humans it had been almost a thousand.

During that time, when the Ancients had felt betrayed by the Mothers, a new goddess had appeared. She called herself the Good Mother and came from a world of chaos. Her intent was not to tame magic and use it for the general good; she only wanted the power. She promised the witch clans she would give them back their powers if they assisted her in destroying the shackles the Mothers had applied to the stream of magic in order to tame it. Some of the Ancients betrayed the Mothers, to whom they owed so much, and swore fealty to the Good Mother.

When Ana-Isara became aware of this, she was so enraged she decided to take the lives of her sons back. It was only thanks to Dweian and Dria—siblings and seers—that this did not happen. They begged the Empress of the Dead for mercy in the name of those who had stayed loyal to her. Ana-Isara listened to their pleas and they soothed her fury. Not wanting to let the betrayal go unpunished, though, she decided to take her son's hearts, the seat of their power. She entrusted the essence to chance, sending it out into the world. Only when Canubis and Renaldo had found their hearts again, each in the form of a human, would they be able to redeem the La'ides.

Thus the gods were demoted to demigods and the Second Aeon ended.

The Third Aeon

It was not only Ana-Isara who was furious about her creation's betrayal. When her sister heard about it, she, too, was enraged. She decided that the punishment her sister had exacted was not enough. A people who had betrayed its Mothers so shamefully had to prove it was worthy of serving its demigods.

She commanded that Canubis and Renaldo would only be able to use their full power once they had gained eight worthy souls among the La'ides in addition to their hearts. Those eight future demigods were called "Emeris" by the Ancients. Dweian and Dria foresaw them all in a vision, and gave them the names we still know: *Ana mearo La'id*, the spirit man; *ana rieto La'id*, the unbending man; *ana regena anoso*, the queen of time; *ana doromo ansi*, the one wreathed in shadows; *ana skretoro La'id*, the wise man; *ana regena raktol*, the queen of nightmares; *ana lareno La'id*, the taming man; and *ana ligtos wanda*, the one walking in the light.

Once they had proven their worth, Ana-Isara would welcome them with her kiss and mark them as members of her family.

Still, it took another thousand years, to the end of the Third Aeon, until the divine brothers were able to welcome the first Emeris at their side. Until then, they chose a valley in the North as their home and led countless battles against those who had decided to follow the Good Mother.

ARANA

1. CAPTIVE

"RENALDO, YOU won't believe what we just found!"

The desert brothers, Kalad and Aegid, approached their god with broad smiles on their faces. He looked at them expectantly.

"If I won't believe it, then you better hurry up and tell me before I run out of patience."

"A caravan! And right now it's taking a break at the oasis we discovered yesterday. You know, it's not even an hour from here. We could go there, get the quarry, and be back before anybody misses us."

Lost in thought, Renaldo observed their camp, set up in a dip beneath the hill where he had waited for Kalad and Aegid. Renaldo's brother, the powerful Wolf of War, had sent them on patrol to make sure the area was entirely safe. So far, they had not come across any danger, which meant that it was all right for them to have some fun. His brothers-in-arms looked at him eagerly. "Well, there's no harm in having a look, is there?"

Kalad's lively brown eyes overflowed in happy anticipation. "No, definitely not. We'll show you the way."

The other members of the patrol led by Noran—like Aegid and Kalad, he was an Emeris, a chosen counselor of Renaldo and Canubis—were ten of the best and most experienced mercenaries in the service of the warrior gods, and they lined up behind the desert brothers. The group rode sharply toward the oasis that had quenched their thirst only a day ago.

Between the trees there was indeed a caravan with thirty camels, every beast burdened high with merchandise. It was not only the traders who delighted in the fresh water from the spring; the warriors also spied some heavily armored men patrolling the goods. Renaldo shot Kalad a slightly poisonous look. Kalad had obviously forgotten to mention this small detail, but the desert warrior just shrugged. There weren't enough enemies to get them into any serious trouble.

At that moment the people at the waterhole stirred. A man wearing a floor-length cloak led a pitch-black stallion to the spring. Although the stranger was clothed in white, as was sensible in the heat, he radiated an intimidating arrogance that surrounded him and the steed like a shield. The traders, as well as the mercenaries, hastened to make room for the exceptional pair. Renaldo's eyes lit up. Never before in his long life had he seen a horse like that: its mane and tail sparkled in the sunlight like polished blackwood; the noble head with the big, intelligent eyes sat on a muscular, proudly held neck; the long, clean legs with hooves as hard as flint carried the powerful body with elegant, elastic movements despite its mass. The long silky tail trailed like a banner behind the proud beast. Then the stallion bent down to drink, and the man leading him followed his example.

Renaldo watched this scene in fascination, purposely ignoring his fighters' imploring looks. He had to have that horse, no matter the cost.

The horse's small ears were nervously flicking back and forth, and then suddenly the noble head reared up and snorted a warning.

The hooded man jumped into the saddle, drawing his sword in one strong, fluid movement while his eyes scanned the oasis, searching for intruders. "Danger!"

His voice echoed through the loosely scattered date trees like a melody, causing panic among the traders and priming the mercenaries to fight. Renaldo couldn't suppress a satisfied nod. Those men were highly professional and definitely worthy opponents.

He turned to his men. "Let's go!"

They left cover in a semicircle, each attacking their chosen mercenary. Renaldo had planned to go after the hooded man and his steed, but two of the enemy bore down on him from the sides. On his periphery he could see one of his men going against the stranger and being swept out of the saddle for his trouble. Then Renaldo lost sight of the man and the horse he so wanted.

CASTO SWORE under his breath. He had been feeling uneasy since they reached the oasis, but the leader of the caravan, Elan, had ignored his warnings. The place was perfect for an ambush, and the attackers used the terrain to their advantage. They had positioned themselves in a semicircle, preventing escape into the desert—anyone who wanted to flee had to fight his way through their lines. At the caravanners' back was the oasis with its countless trees that made it difficult to organize a counterattack. Not that it would have been of any use. Casto recognized the signature of experienced fighters, and the ambush was perfectly executed. He already knew the caravan was lost to these men. All he could do now was try to manage his escape and kill as many enemies as possible on his way out. As soon as they reached the open plains they would be safe, as Lysistratos could use his superior speed to escape, but among the trees anything beyond a careful canter was simply too dangerous. His brother snorted indignantly. He, too, was furious about the ambush.

"It's okay, Lys. We're almost there."

At that moment a bulky man on a sturdy gray horse blocked their path. His face was grim and he held his heavy broadsword as easily as if it were made of cloth, not steel. The long blade gave him the advantage over Casto, whose sword was a lot lighter and probably would not withstand a direct blow from this fearsome weapon. Terrifying as it was, though, it also had a massive drawback: it considerably slowed down the person wielding it.

Lysistratos did not hesitate. With a shrill whinny, he attacked the gray, turning around at the last possible moment and shattering the other horse's ankle joint with one powerful blow of his hoof. The horse went down with a pained cry, pinning its rider underneath. Lys ran on, light-footed, only to be stopped in his tracks again.

A slim warrior, with countless braids hanging to his upper arms and a curved blade in his fist, attacked them from the side. Casto parried the first blow while Lys bit into the other horse's neck. Squealing in pain, the horse retreated with hasty, unsteady jumps, blood oozing from the wound Lys had inflicted. Without mercy, Casto used his opponent's moment of weakness to deal another blow with his sword, making the warrior bend backward. Then Casto sliced the girth in one graceful movement, dealing the horse yet another wound in the process. Since his enemy's weight was already too far back, he slid down with a colorful curse on his lips. His horse fled in panic from Lys, who jumped over the fallen fighter, hitting him full force on the shoulder as he landed. The creaking sound when the bones were shattered to a pulp made Casto shiver.

Now he could see the ravine that led out of the oasis and to freedom. With his ears perked up, Lys started to gallop and could only evade the giant who threw himself in their way by a hair's breadth. The big man's sword ripped through the air over Casto's head and caused him to bend sideways. Two fast, powerful leaps gained Lys and Casto enough room to give them a chance to counter. In one fluid motion, Casto righted himself in the saddle. He wasn't even completely upright when his left hand extended like a snake ready to bite. A wet, thumping sound indicated the dagger had sunk its claws into his opponent's shoulder. At the same time, Lys smashed his hooves into the other horse's rib cage, forcing it down with the sheer power of the blow. Casto pressed his upper body tightly against his brother's neck, to better avoid another surprise attack, and rode toward the ravine.

They had almost reached it when there was a sough in the air, and Casto felt something heavy against his head. He did not have time to curse his misfortune before darkness claimed him.

AFTER MAKING sure that his enemies were defeated and his men had gained control of the situation, Renaldo followed the path of destruction the stranger and his stallion had left in their wake.

He passed Noran, who had drawn a dagger to put his whinnying, struggling horse out of its misery. Then he found Kalad, sitting in the sand, one hand pressed against his deformed, bloody shoulder, his face contorted in pain. With his outstretched hand, Aegid indicated the way the stranger had taken. He, too, was smeared with his own blood.

When Renaldo realized how close his target was to the ravine— and to freedom—he drew his dagger without hesitation. He didn't want to hurt the man, because a warrior like him was always welcome in the Pack, but he couldn't let him get away either. With a singing sound, the weapon flew through the air and the hilt hit the rider on the back of his head. Almost in slow motion, the man tumbled down, not trying to stop his fall in any way—a sure sign that he had already lost consciousness.

Renaldo anticipated that the stallion would panic and run for it once his rider was gone, but the powerful beast stopped, skewed around with flying hooves, and positioned itself protectively over its fallen rider, teeth bared and ears flattened.

Deeply impressed by this display of loyalty, Renaldo reined in his own stallion at a respectful distance. Not for one moment did he doubt that the black one would kill him without mercy should he get the chance. Renaldo dismounted, then slowly edged toward the horse and the unconscious rider. At the corner of his peripheral vision, he saw movement.

Kalad's strained voice reached him. "Be careful, Renaldo. He's dangerous."

"I'm aware of that, Kalad. And now put away that bow. I want both of them alive."

"Just as we do—you can bet on that." Aegid's voice had a threatening undertone. He did not like being defeated, and he appreciated it even less when his desert brother got hurt.

Noran, too, had come to join them, his face twisted in anger, his clothes drenched with his horse's blood. Renaldo threw them all a warning glance before he took a few careful steps toward the stallion. The beast gave a warning snuffle and turned sideways so that it could use its hooves as well as its teeth as weapons should it be necessary.

The fallen rider stirred. Whimpering, he dragged his head up, and his gaze met Renaldo's.

Renaldo froze. Never before had he seen such piercing blue eyes. They were as blue as the sky above the Valley on a clear summer day, as deep as the lake when it was fed by the glaciers in spring. And they were so full of unwavering arrogance that Renaldo had to fight for breath.

The man's gaze wandered around then. He must be still dizzy from the blow to his head. He finally lifted his hand and caressed the hair on the leg of his exceptional steed. "Lys, *alan.*"

Renaldo didn't recognize the language the man had used.

The stallion snorted, outraged, his threatening gaze turned to Renaldo. The fallen man repeated his words, this time with slightly more conviction.

"Alan, Lys, *alan.*"

The stallion's neck whipped round with snakelike speed; his teeth closed with a snapping sound, and then he suddenly skewed on his hind legs and disappeared through the ravine before Renaldo or his men could react. The piercing blue gaze followed the stallion for a moment, but those two sentences seemed to have taken all the strength the man had left. The eyes rolled up, the lids fluttered like a caged butterfly, and the stranger lost consciousness again.

Renaldo approached him carefully, because even though he was lying motionless, it did not mean he was actually helpless. He turned the limp body around, disarmed him with practiced movements, and took away the turban-like hat that had also covered a lot of the stranger's face. Renaldo gazed at noble but also incredibly young features. The warrior who had managed to beat three Emeris was about sixteen, perhaps seventeen. He had a distinguished, elegantly curved nose, high cheekbones, and full, sensual lips. His wheat-blond hair was like a crown of light, and his skin was slightly tanned and shimmered golden in the desert sun.

"Beautiful brat. He'll make an excellent plaything once he has paid for his actions," Kalad growled.

Although Renaldo had known him for more than eight hundred years, Kalad's suggestive tone now irritated him to no end. He sized up his brother-in-arms with narrow eyes. "He's mine. I was the one who caught him."

"But he has harmed us all. We all have a right to him." Even Noran seemed determined to stake his claim.

Renaldo picked up the limp body. "We can talk about this later, when we are back at the camp. Go and get everything ready. Canubis will surely be pleased when we bring such rich booty home."

Somewhat reluctantly, the three Emeris followed their leader's instructions. Together with the other mercenaries they lined up the camels, killed any traders who had been too stupid to run away, and then organized the journey back to the camp.

The beautiful prisoner sat in the saddle in front of Renaldo, his head resting against his captor's shoulder. He was still unconscious, but the man holding him was a demigod who wasn't bothered by the additional burden at all.

BACK AT the camp, Renaldo took his catch to Noemi, his brother Canubis's wife, after which he went to talk to Canubis himself.

Canubis, the powerful leader with the amber eyes and the shoulder-length black hair, was pleased by the outcome of his brother's expedition.

"You captured plenty of booty, Renaldo. That's a promising start for our campaign."

"Please, brother. Arana isn't a city that justifies the term 'campaign.'"

Predatory amusement sparked to life in Canubis's eyes. "You're right. It's been some time since I've last seen such a childish system of defense. It's bordering on open insult, but Duke Markon is paying us quite a nice sum for erasing this city, plus we can keep everything we salvage. That's a refreshing change compared to the last two years."

"It's welcome, I agree. We just have to see to it that the men don't get bored."

"An opportunity will present itself, I'm sure. How's your prisoner?"

"Still unconscious. Noemi says it's not only the blow he received. He seems to be completely exhausted."

"I heard others claim him as well?"

Renaldo did not try to conceal his irritation.

"Yes. Aegid, Kalad, and Noran, as well as four of our mercenaries. My brothers-in-arms have problems dealing with the fact that they were defeated by a mere child."

"You have to be good to get three Emeris down. This boy could become a valuable member of our Pack. What a pity that the stallion is gone. Such well-trained horses are rare."

"I haven't given up on him yet. Once the boy wakes up, we might still be able to get the steed back."

Canubis nodded. "You know you have to fight for him?"

The answer was a broad smile that seemed to illuminate Renaldo's perfect features from within. "I'm aware of that. My brothers will have to face their second defeat in such a short time."

"That's not so bad. It's always a good idea to remind a warrior that he's not invincible—except for us."

The brothers laughed at the joke that was only funny to them. Canubis and Renaldo were gods of war, and there was nobody in this world who could hope to defeat them in a direct confrontation.

The Wolf of War placed a hand on his beautiful brother's shoulder. "What are your plans for the boy once he's yours?"

"I'll go according to custom. First, I'm going to make him my slave, since I doubt he'll stay with us of his own free will even if we try to bribe him. Then we watch him, and if he's as good as we think, and as soon as he's gotten used to living with us, we offer him a place in the Pack."

"Unless you scare him away before. I know you, Renaldo. You want him for your bed."

"What if I do? Perhaps I'm not his type."

"You're everybody's type, brother, as you well know. Nobody can resist your charm."

"It's not my fault that I'm beauty incarnate."

The words sounded arrogant, but Canubis knew only too well that his brother was simply stating a fact. And the experience of countless centuries had taught him how heavy a burden such perfect looks as Renaldo possessed could be. He had long ago stopped envying him.

"Promise that you'll hold back. If he's as good as you claim, we can't afford to lose him."

"Please, I always hold back."

"You know what I mean. Now go and prepare for the fight tomorrow morning. I doubt our brothers-in-arms will make it easy for you."

STARTLED, CASTO woke up. He had had a bad nightmare in which the caravan had been assaulted by mercenaries and he had been taken prisoner by one of them. His gaze darted through the tent he was in; he did not see anything familiar, which could only mean that his dream was a memory, not an illusion. He concluded that the place had to be a healer's domain, because he saw several beds on which patients could rest, glass bottles filled with potions, and three shelves with bandages to treat wounds.

When Casto sat up to leave the bed, a petite woman with astonishing emerald eyes and a mass of flaming red hair falling down her back in a braid stopped him.

"Easy. You've received quite a terrible head wound. It would be better not to move too fast for the time being." She wore a simple green dress that was cinched at the waist with a small belt. The sleeves were tight on her arms, not getting broader at the seams as was the current fashion.

13

Casto could understand her, as she was talking in a northern dialect that did not quite fit her looks, which placed her origins more in the direction of the Eastern Kingdoms. For the time being, he deemed it wise not to show his understanding, so he shot her a well-calculated, imploring look.

The healer tried three other languages, all of which Casto understood but feigned ignorance about, until she returned, somewhat frustrated, to her own dialect. With gestures, she made clear that he was to stay, before she hurried away to get him some food.

While Casto was eating, her green eyes watched him sharply. When he finished, she sighed. "I've got a feeling you won't like what's going to happen today, but I can sense that you're bound to stay with us for quite some time. I just hope this doesn't turn into some disaster."

The cryptic words left Casto puzzled, but before he could ponder them further, a tall man entered the tent. The way he moved already gave away that he was a warrior and leader even before he opened his mouth to speak. The healer got up and kissed him on the mouth as a greeting. She did not seem intimidated by his presence, which led Casto to the conclusion that they were close in rank.

The man's voice was dark and filled the whole room. "So, our guest has finally woken up? Just in time—the fight's about to begin."

The healer shook her head. "Canubis, I'm begging you. He doesn't understand a single word we're saying. There's no chance to explain to him what's going to happen. Can't you just leave him here?"

The amber eyes drilled into Casto, who looked back defiantly.

"No. The suspense is a small price to pay for abasing three Emeris. He surely can do with some humility."

"They attacked him. It was his right to fight back. It's not his fault that their pride has been hurt."

"No more discussion, Noemi. He comes with me."

With that, the warrior turned to Casto. A few forceful gestures told him to get undressed. A salacious smile appeared on Canubis's lips as he held out a small loincloth. He obviously wanted Casto to wear the offending piece of fabric. The young man shook his head vigorously. The leader's gaze darkened. It was apparent that he was not used to insubordination. He gestured at the fabric with more emphasis, implying that he would force Casto should he not comply.

After a long, thoughtful glance at the man's powerful physique, Casto grabbed the cloth. He looked pointedly at the healer.

She blushed. "I'm sorry." She turned her back; a favor her husband did not grant Casto.

After a last moment of hesitation, Casto started undressing.

Canubis watched his brother's prisoner like a hawk. He agreed with Renaldo that the stranger was still very young—he had not reached his twenties yet, that much was sure. His features were beautiful and distinguished, the eyes indeed piercing and somewhat intimidating, which was surprising for somebody so young. The young man's body was well muscled, and it was evident he hadn't spent his life in idleness. His movements were smooth and graceful, like a dancer's. Canubis could understand why Renaldo wanted him so badly. He wasn't only a precious addition to any army but also an ornament for any bed he might choose.

With angry movements, the young man fastened the loincloth around his slim waist. When he was done, he glared at Canubis, openly challenging him. The Wolf of War had to suppress a smile. He liked humans with a strong will.

His heart pounding loudly in his chest, Casto followed the dark leader out of the tent into the blazing sunlight. He was in a military camp, albeit an unusually orderly one. The tents stood in file and were surprisingly roomy. Everywhere he looked slaves were attending to their chores. Here and there Casto caught a glimpse of groups of warriors all going in the direction the leader, Canubis, was indicating. By now Casto had realized who had captured him so brutally. It had taken him some time to place the name Canubis, but he was glad now that he had followed the man's wishes in the tent. Lord Canubis was by far the most powerful and dangerous mercenary on the continent. He and his brother, Lord Renaldo, conquered cities—and even whole countries—in exchange for money. The stories about their atrocities knew no end and were added to every year.

And Casto had fallen into these men's hands. The only reason he did not despair was Lys's presence nearby, which he could feel clearly.

His brother had followed him, and together they would escape from this place.

Canubis led Casto to a small arena where a pole had been rammed into the ground at the southern end. About two hundred men and women had gathered at the sidelines. Most of them were warriors, but he could also see some slaves wearing collars in different colors, all of them measuring him with their stares. All of a sudden, the young man felt very naked, but he would be damned if he would show a single sign of weakness.

Canubis raised his arm and silence ensued. "Sisters, brothers, this is the prize of today's fight."

He gestured toward Casto, who fought to keep a neutral expression so as not to endanger his cover. Among the spectators an appreciative whisper rose. Casto could hear phrases like "beautiful," "nice body," "magnificent," and "definitely bed material."

His back muscles tensed. Not because of shame about the obvious remarks—he was used to being treated as eye candy—but with anger. Casto had grown up in a society where intercourse was a kind of currency to accomplish one's goals and where the partner's gender was of no importance. Only two things mattered: how much power the partner wielded, and how attractive they were. Power could make a person more attractive than a beautiful face. Because of his own beauty, Casto had received invitations from both men and women from an early age, but he had always declined for numerous reasons. One of them was that he had never met anybody he deemed interesting enough to be worth more than casual attention, not to mention something as superfluous as affection.

Being reduced to a sex object made bile rise in his mouth. He could feel his anger overflowing but managed to control it at the last possible moment. He knew only too well that even with Lys by his side, he wouldn't stand a chance against the Wolf of War.

Canubis now grabbed his wrist, led him to the pole, and chained him there. Then he gestured to the opposite side of the arena, where seven fully armed warriors had taken position. "These are the ones fighting for the prize."

Heralded by thundering applause from the audience, Canubis introduced the warriors. "Elua, Belnor, Xi'an, and Reenua. The Lords Aegid, Kalad, and Noran."

One after another the fighters entered the arena, and Casto was shocked to recognize some of his opponents from the oasis. None of them looked as though they had been wounded. Even the one Lys had trampled did not show any signs of the terrible injury he had suffered.

While Casto was still trying to figure out how this could be, the last fighter stepped into the arena.

He was tall, about eight spans, and he moved with such relaxed grace that he immediately dominated the place. He was also astonishingly beautiful. His gray eyes stood wide in his regal face, his nose was a noble arch, his lips so full that they were sensuous but not effeminate, his chin chiseled, and his shoulder-length, dark brown hair tied in a band of leather. The fighter's whole body was packed with muscles, but he did not appear cumbersome. He gave the impression of a big cat dozing in the sun, yet ready to strike at any minute. But it was not only the beauty of this haughty, overbearing man that fascinated Casto. He could also feel an inner fire, hot and all consuming, that the warrior gave off, and it attracted Casto like a moth to a flame.

"And, of course, my precious little brother, Lord Renaldo."

After this rather playful introduction, Canubis gave the fighter a friendly pat on the shoulder before he explained the rules of the fight.

"As usual in a fight involving more than two warriors, anything goes. You can pair up with whomever you like, abandon them as you please and strike when you prefer to. A direct hit means you're defeated, leave the arena and you're disqualified. Now go and show us what the members of the Pack are made of!"

Clearly amused, Canubis left the arena so the fighting could begin.

The other warriors drew their weapons and took position in front of the good-looking one, Renaldo.

Terrified, Casto realized that they all wanted to attack Renaldo, who didn't seem to be very concerned about this fact. After a short, calculating glance, Casto decided that he would set his hopes on him. All the others had been hurt and humiliated by Casto—as Canubis had remarked with such painful accuracy. Casto could imagine quite vividly what would happen to him should he become the possession of the one with the braids. He doubted the man would let go of the fact that a stranger had beaten him, and on top of that, one as young as Casto.

The two dark-skinned giants did not look too friendly either, and Casto had no inclination to test the limits of their patience. At an early age, he had learned to assess and judge people with one look, because his survival had depended on it. One of the two had countless tattoos that made his body look like a living painting, and milky blue eyes and white hair in stark contrast to his dark skin. He might have looked frightening at first, but he surely wasn't as bad as the other one, whose massive body was wrapped in an aura of impending darkness.

The other four fighters were less intimidating but emanated danger as well. Especially the two women, each wielding two short swords, who moved with the elegant grace of those trained in close combat. To successfully use two blades at the same time, one had to be as quick as an attacking snake, flexible like a cat, and fearless like a bird of prey. Casto had received training with the short sword as part of his education, but he had never gotten the hang of it. He was able to defend himself when he had to, but his forte was definitely the long sword, especially on horseback. He gritted his teeth. A whole lot of good it had done him so far. Captured and bound like chattel for the market by probably the most dangerous warriors on the planet, his future seemed bleaker than it had in a year. He had heard too many stories about the brutality and cruelty going on in the army of Canubis for Casto not to know he was in deep trouble, no matter who won him. Still, his intuition forced him to set his hopes on the Angel of Death, and so he prayed for a miracle that would allow the good-looking warrior to defeat seven opponents at once.

Now Canubis gave the signal, and the seven warriors started circling Renaldo like a pack of wolves. The men moved like hungry predators who couldn't wait to kill, while the two females gave the impression of hunting falcons, advancing in feigned attacks and then retreating quickly in order to lure their prey out. It was a nerve-racking, if elegant, dance that must soon lead to Renaldo's defeat.

Renaldo, on the other hand, did not seem too worried. He easily evaded the attacks from his opponents, no matter how fast and well orchestrated they were. To Casto's utter surprise, Renaldo remained in defense, although he had the chance to strike once or twice. It looked like the warriors were indulging in some relaxed training and not a deadly serious fight over a valuable prize.

18

As if there had been a silent signal, the body language of all the warriors suddenly shifted from playful teasing to deadly concentration. Belnor, Xi'an, and Noran charged at Renaldo at the same time from three different angles, forcing him into the waiting swords of Elua and Reenua. There was no way he could evade them, for the females went at him with the speed and ferocity of hungry hawks.

And yet he did.

Renaldo somehow managed to dodge Elua's swords, but that maneuver brought him dangerously close to Reenua, who didn't waste her chance. Her right hand came up for a direct strike that would divert her opponent's attention while her left arm snaked forward to deal the final blow. The Angel of Death bent his upper body sideways at an almost impossible angle, barely avoiding the first blade that swished past his face so closely it stirred his long hair. There was a scream of pain, and the second blade, which had been directed at his lower body, clattered to the ground. Reenua staggered backward, pressing her left wrist close to her abdomen. The red marks of Renaldo's fingers shone angrily on her skin where he had squeezed so hard that she had to drop her weapon.

She was an experienced fighter, and almost immediately regained her composure—only it wasn't fast enough. Renaldo went after her, sweeping her off her feet in one graceful movement. The tip of his blade rested on her throat for the blink of an eye, during which a victorious smile flashed across his perfect features. Then he spun around and forward, his sword describing a perfect circle around his body, and fenced off Aegid, Kalad, and Elua, who had tried to get to him while his back was turned.

Casto sighed. He hated himself for it, but he was drawn into the fight against his will and had to admit that the fencing skills of all the warriors involved were superb. Now that they were short one fighter, the challengers retreated a little to regroup. Renaldo allowed them to do so, though this would have been a perfect chance for him to get rid of another one of his opponents. Casto decided that the man was either overly self-confident or mad—or possibly both, given the way he seemed to enjoy the whole matter.

Since Renaldo was still heavily outnumbered, the warriors tried a similar tactic again. This time it was Elua and Xi'an—a man of slender build with the bronze-colored skin of those living in the Eastern

Kingdoms—who executed the fake attacks. At the same time, Belnor and Noran started forcing Renaldo in the direction of the fence surrounding the arena. Casto was sure the warrior didn't stand a chance against this new ruse. Noran's blade was a little more than eight spans long, a distance that would be hard to counter even without the added attackers.

When Renaldo reached the fence, he leaped into the air and onto the railing without apparent effort. With this outrageous action, he at once gained double advantage over the other warriors. He was now situated higher than his opponents, giving him a much better view, and they could no longer attack from behind since that would mean leaving the arena.

Like a tightrope walker, Renaldo danced along the fence, his challengers trailing behind him with determination but lacking his grace and a tactic to deal with this new development. Out of the blue, Renaldo jumped down. His sword made a *swoosh*ing sound and turned into a blur in the air. Two colorful curses and a high-pitched clatter marked the elimination of Xi'an and Belnor, who had tried their best to get Renaldo down.

Renaldo danced back a few steps, his gray eyes trained on Noran, Kalad, and Aegid, not seeing the crouched figure of Elua, whose muscles were tensing like a cat's as she got ready to bring her leader down. At the last possible moment, Renaldo took a small step sideways, grabbed her wrist, and forced her down in midjump. Against all probability, she managed to turn and stabilize while still in the air. Her free hand shot forward to deal a winning blow, but Renaldo tossed his sword high into the sky, deflecting her blow without breaking his movement, and then sent her flying over the fence. Elua let out a huffing sound, but there was no doubt that she was defeated.

Noran, Kalad, and Aegid had learned their lesson. They did not take the time to regroup and give their leader a chance to assess the situation. Without reluctance or mercy, as befitted such skilled warriors, they surrounded Renaldo once again. This time they did not settle for fake attacks to create an opening for one of them, but went after their target seriously, each man trying to bring him down. It was an exhausting, lethal dance that gained momentum every time the swords clashed. Soon the movements of the warriors were so fast it was almost impossible to follow them. Casto wondered how he had managed to defeat the three desert men now that he witnessed their skills at such close range. But then again, he had been with Lys, which always tipped the balance in his favor.

A roar tore Casto from his musings. With his unbelievably big blade held high over his head, Noran went straight for Renaldo's back while Aegid and Kalad both tried to make use of the opening he had created. Casto bit his lip to stifle the groan that tried to escape from his mouth. This could not be. Renaldo could not be defeated after showing such impressive swordsmanship.

To call the body language of Renaldo patronizing was seriously downplaying the impact his obvious carelessness made. As languidly as if he were taking a stroll, Renaldo evaded Aegid's blade, which hit the ground so hard it stayed stuck. At this, Renaldo knocked the giant's feet from under him and touched his throat with the tip of his blade, just as he had done with Reenua at the beginning. Aegid lifted his hands to admit defeat, a gesture his leader accepted with a small nod. Then Renaldo turned his attention to Noran and Kalad, seemingly oblivious of their furious determination. For a couple of blows, Renaldo indulged his challengers, even allowing them to come quite close, but it was obvious he was merely playing now, teaching his men a lesson for even thinking about taking his prey from him. Casto had had his part in enough power plays to understand this all too well, and could not help but feel resentment against him.

Finally, Renaldo had enough of the whole affair. His sword swished in a complicated arc, disarming Noran and sending him to the ground in one go. Again the tip of Renaldo's blade found its mark and pure triumph made his features glow. Almost casually, his sword arm turned, the tip of the blade stopping right at Kalad's throat. The spry warrior froze instantly and his sword clattered to the ground.

Kalad's voice was hoarse. "Damn. I always forget that you've got eyes in your back."

Renaldo gave a broad grin. "Lucky me, bad for you."

He lowered his sword, and the two shook hands to the thunderous applause from the audience.

The other challengers reentered the arena to congratulate their leader. None of them appeared to be miffed about the outcome of the battle, as if they had already anticipated it—a fact that surprised Casto since they all had fought so grimly only moments ago. The white-haired one with the tattoos glanced in Casto's direction, making him the focus of attention again.

"We had to try it. He's simply too adorable."

Renaldo patted Aegid's shoulder in a friendly, only slightly patronizing manner. "It's okay. I understand."

Then he went to Casto. Renaldo's gray eyes bored into those of his new slave, and what he saw there made his blood sing. The young man was definitely hotheaded, and the way his gaze ignited showed him to be strong willed. He would not back down easily. Like his brother, Renaldo had a weak spot for humans with courage, a gift his beautiful new slave seemed to possess in abundance. Even better, that wasn't all he could read in Casto's heated gaze. There were also determination, ruthlessness, and an arrogance that made Renaldo's breath come raggedly. Whoever this man was, Renaldo looked forward to getting to know him.

Casto had to hold back his disdain for his new master. It surely wasn't a wise move to pick a fight with this man unprepared. Renaldo's power surrounded him like a shield and he emanated a wild, animalistic aura that drew Casto in and repelled him at the same time. Before him was a man who did not have to obey any rules or conventions, because he could bend and break them at his leisure. Renaldo had to be a man who always got what he wanted without apparent effort.

The rational, calculating part of Casto wanted to get as many leagues as possible between him and Renaldo, preferably right now. He instinctively knew this man was bad news, but another, more ferocious aspect of his personality immediately realized that Renaldo was his future. The larger part of Casto was simply furious to be at the mercy of a barbarian.

Now Canubis approached his brother, handing him a dark blue collar made of leather. With great effort, Renaldo withdrew from the clear blue depths that had been taunting him with their untold secrets, and he closed the sign of humiliation around his angry slave's neck. The golden latch snapped shut with a foreboding tone, and Casto looked as if he wanted to throttle his new master with his bare hands.

With the audience's roar of approval ringing in his ears, Renaldo led Casto away.

2. TOURNAMENT

CASTO'S CHEEK rubbed against rough stone, his fumbling fingers touched an artful ornament, and the dreaded clinking of chains assaulted his ears. He looked up, only to realize that the sound was made by the shackles that fastened him to the ground. It was freezing, a cold draft swirling through the crypt, and the flickering light of a single torch illuminated the expressionless faces of kings long gone. His mother, too, stared down on him, her disdain and disappointment obvious. Casto knew she had despised him for his weakness and would punish him severely for his cowardice had she still been alive and able to do so.

But she was cold and dead, like everybody in this mausoleum of former splendor.

Casto got up and the chain rattled, the sound thrown around in the crypt like the cry of a vengeful ghost. The light of the torch started to dwindle, and in the shadows that slowly thickened into night, the spirits of the dead began to stir. Frightened to his core, Casto backed away, against his mother's coffin, his hands held up in a gesture of denial. The cold seeped into his body like a curse. He could feel himself slowing down, losing the battle. A hand like ice fell on his shoulder.

With a scream, Casto got up. Panting, he shot panicked glances around the tent.

The crypt of his ancestors was gone, the freezing cold only a fading memory. On his skin he felt the penetrating heat, which was almost unbearable here at the outskirts of the desert. Without making a sound, he got up and slid out of the Barbarian's tent, something he had been doing every night for the last five days. He was grateful that Renaldo had a surprisingly deep sleep for such a seasoned warrior and did not want the man who thought he could own Casto to witness his pain. Not that those nightmares were anything new; they clung to him like tar and never left him, probably never would. Nor would the Barbarian care if he left the tent. This was about principles. Casto would never show any signs of weakness to anybody. Never.

The night air was a little more tolerable outside. A gentle breeze brought at least the illusion of relief. For Casto, more important was the fact that he could feel his brother out there. Lys stayed near the camp, and during the night he came close to console his rider. Lys was impatient to get him out of there, but Casto knew they could not hasten things. The pack of wolves traveling with the army was very large. Casto had counted more than forty beasts, all of them healthy-looking, bigger, and more intelligent than normal wolves. They also seemed to share some strange bond with both Renaldo and Canubis, and until he knew more about it, Casto hesitated to make his move.

Regarding speed, Lys could easily outrun them, but first he had to get Casto out of the camp, which was not an easy task. Casto still hadn't thought about a plan that he was sure would work, so he asked his brother for patience. Hesitantly, Lys gave in, not without reminding his rider of the other option they still had.

Casto sighed. *Of course.* Lys could call a storm anytime he liked, and then their escape would be quite easy, but here in the desert, without any restraints, the risk of turning it into a catastrophe was simply too great. If things got out of hand, the whole camp could be eradicated, and although he had been here for only five days, Casto had already met enough people to know that he didn't want them to die miserably in an out-of-control storm.

Apart from that, his situation was not unbearable. The nightmares and his growing loneliness set aside, he could count himself lucky. Because Renaldo thought Casto could not understand his language, Casto had only had light chores assigned and was free to roam the camp at his leisure. The Barbarian had gone to great pains to find a dialect Casto could understand. In the end, Casto had talked to a slave from the lower plains, an area relatively close to Ummana, the city where he had spent most of his life until now. Since a good lie always contained a grain of truth, Casto had told the slave, an older woman called Yran, that he came from a family of merchants who had fallen into poverty due to various misfortunes. Yran had believed him without hesitation, since this kind of fate was not big news in the vicinity of the proud center of all trade on the continent.

She had also told Casto some details about life as a slave in Canubis's army. Casto had been surprised to find out that he was protected by a series of laws that, for instance, forbade forcing him into bed or torturing him for fun. Where he came from, a slave, especially a good-looking one, had only one right: to bend his knees and serve his master's will. Obedience was rarely rewarded, insubordination heavily punished. As liberal as the laws in the Pack sounded, though, the punishment for an attempt at escape was far more brutal than anything Casto had encountered before. A slave who dared to run away was flogged with a glass whip—an instrument that could skin a delinquent completely. Then the slave had their legs broken and was exhibited for three days and nights as a warning to others. If he or she was still alive after this ordeal, the master decided if they were allowed to live. And even when that mercy was bestowed upon those unlucky creatures, they remained crippled. Casto had been repulsed by this truly barbaric practice, but Yran had stayed surprisingly calm. Unrelenting punishment like this held up the discipline in an army that was famed for it.

Yran had also roughly explained the hierarchy within the Pack so that Casto would not make any mistakes and shame his new master—not that Casto cared for such petty details. As Renaldo's personal slave, he outranked all other slaves, and even the mercenaries would respect him accordingly.

The hierarchy among the serving class was quite complex and often distinguished by nuances. First there were the normal slaves—they were public property and responsible for all the chores an army this big required. Cooks, cleaners, farmers, carpenters, and all other kinds of professions, who lived their lives quite peacefully. As long as they fulfilled their duties, they were free to do whatever they wanted. They formed the lowest rank among the servants.

Above them stood the slaves who had managed to gain a master's benevolence. These servants received small presents on a regular basis and often developed a growing bond with their masters until they eventually rose to the rank of personal slave or even favorite. When this happened, they were marked with a collar in the colors of their master and usually started living with him or her in a domestic relationship.

Although Casto deemed it humiliating to live like that, most of the slaves in the Pack considered being chosen by one of the masters a worthy prize. Casto would have preferred being a lowly, faceless servant, but in that opinion he stood alone.

If a relationship between a master and a personal slave proved stable, it could even lead to the slave being freed—though Casto doubted that Renaldo would ever let him go.

Among the three main ranks of slaves were countless layers, determined by various circumstances such as the rank of the owner, their age, and, of course, a slave's network of friends and allies.

The only group lower than the normal slaves were the traitors. They wore an iron collar to show their inferiority and were the only ones not protected by the laws of the Pack. Everybody, even the slaves, could do with them as they pleased. A slave fell to this state when he affronted his master in a serious way or showed negative behavior. Traitors were rare, since they did not survive the ordeals linked to their low status for long.

After explaining all these things to him, Yran had dared to gossip a little bit and had given Casto more intimate information about his new master.

"He can be quite intimidating, but Lord Renaldo, although he is called the 'Angel of Death,' is never unjust. If you serve him well, he will reward you, but don't try to oppose him. He loathes disobedience."

Casto had taken the advice with a shrug. The Barbarian might be fearsome, but Casto had faced worse and survived. As long as they couldn't communicate, there was no problem. Renaldo did not even know Casto's name yet, since Casto had refused to tell it, which had caused Yran to tremble with fear. Renaldo had taken it in stride, seemingly unfazed by Casto's obstinacy. During the last few days, Casto had rarely seen his master; Renaldo was too busy conquering the pitiful rat hole of Arana, which could only be called a town because it served as a station on some minor caravan route.

Full of longing, Casto looked up at the star-covered sky. If only the nightmares would stop. Ever since his escape a year ago, they had gotten worse, torturing him with their intensity. It had been right to leave. All that had waited back home was death.

Casto listened to the comforting whinny of his brother. Lys could feel his distress and tried to help him as best he could.

"I wish you could understand me. Then I'd tell you that everything is going to be fine."

Startled, Casto spun around.

26

Renaldo stood behind him, his gray eyes, not unfriendly, fixed on his slave. "I'd tell you that you can call him, your demon. He won't be harmed."

Casto was so angry at this distraction of his thoughts, so furious that the Barbarian had seen right through him, that he snapped back without thinking. "I doubt that, Barbarian."

Renaldo's gray eyes widened in astonishment, and at the same time a smile rose on his sinful lips. "So you do speak our language."

Dismayed and angry that he had given up his cover without thinking, Casto challenged Renaldo further. "Your brutish way of talking isn't that difficult to master."

"But you didn't tell me, for tactical reasons. Not bad, not bad at all." The Angel of Death seemed rather pleased. "And you can believe me. When I give you my word, you can rely on it."

"I don't rely on anything you give me, you brute. You have imprisoned me!"

Suddenly anger sparked in the eyes of the warrior. "Are you calling me a liar?"

"I don't know you. Why should I trust you?"

"Because you hardly have a choice in the matter."

Angrily, they stared at each other, Casto's blue eyes shooting deadly sparks into the irritated gray gaze of Renaldo. It was a first direct confrontation, a careful weighing of opponents. Suddenly a hot wind awoke, sweeping over them and then vanishing as if it had never existed.

When it became obvious that neither of them would give in, Renaldo started talking again.

"I promise you by my honor that your stallion goes unharmed. Nobody will touch or ride him without your permission, and I won't use him to bring you to heel."

Casto was torn. Renaldo's offer was alluring, and having Lys in the camp would make his escape that much easier. On top of that, Casto would no longer be so lonely. But should the Barbarian lie, he would have endangered his brother without reason. He hesitated for a long moment. In the end, his sense of loss won over rationality. "Well, then, Barbarian, I'll take you at your word."

He was just about to call for Lys when he remembered something. "What about the wolves? I don't want Lys to be harmed."

Renaldo grinned as if Casto had just passed another test, something that only served to heighten Casto's irritation.

"But of course." He made a strange barking sound that was answered by a high-pitched howl, then smiled at Casto. "You're good to go."

Lys, who felt that something had changed, was already on his way, which was why Casto put his two index fingers between his lips to give a shrill whistle. He had no intention of showing Renaldo how deeply connected he and Lys were. Should the Angel of Death ever find out, his mighty words would surely crumble to dust and be as worthless as the dirt between Casto's naked toes.

The ground shook when Lys appeared, a shadow of the night, his black coat melting into the surrounding darkness as if he were a part of it. In front of Casto, he came to an abrupt halt, his gaze trained on Renaldo in open threat.

"Lys, this is Renaldo, the man who has captured me. He promised me that you would go unharmed, which is why I called you."

Casto could feel his brother dealing with this information. Their connection gave Lys the details and exact reason why Casto had called him. He snorted reproachfully.

Fascinated, Renaldo watched while his beautiful slave communicated with the powerful stallion. He had been surprised when Casto suddenly revealed his knowledge of the northern dialect, and almost dumbfounded when he realized Casto was going to trust him.

Now Casto shook his head vigorously. "That's out of the question, Lys, no. I refuse."

Lys nudged his rider in a none too friendly fashion, an action he followed by stomping the ground with his right front hoof as if in threat. Casto rolled his eyes like a reprimanded child and murmured something—that sounded suspiciously like a colorful curse in a language Renaldo didn't understand—before turning back to his captor. Casto had a defiant look that showed clearly how much he disliked what he was about to do.

"Since you gave me your word, Barbarian, it would be shameful if I didn't do the same. I promise by my honor, I won't try to escape as long as this campaign is in progress."

A graceful nod was Renaldo's answer. "I accept your vow, slave." He hesitated for a moment, then added, "Out of curiosity, when does a campaign end, according to your definition?"

An amused twinkle was the reaction to this first, careful joke. "A campaign ends when the army is back home safely."

"That's good news for me. The Valley is absolutely safe." The blue eyes darkened again, but before Casto could voice his anger, Renaldo distracted him. "You haven't told me your name yet. Of course, I could keep on calling you 'slave,' but that gets old pretty soon, don't you think?"

Casto hesitated for a moment, unsure whether he should tell the Barbarian his true name—or any name at all. He was inclined to keep it a secret, if only to defy his captor, but then again, Renaldo was right. "Slave" was not a name he wanted to hear too often in connection with himself. Grudgingly, he said, "My name is Casto. And this is Lys."

Renaldo nodded, pretending not to have noticed Casto's hesitation. His new slave had obviously more than just one secret, and Renaldo, though eager to discover them all, knew better than to corner him. So he changed topic again, this time to safe ground.

"Let's get your stallion to the stables. I'm sure he's hungry."

With a happy snort, Lys made his consent known.

"SINCE YOU can understand me perfectly well, it's only fitting that you serve me like a good slave should."

The Angel of Death regarded his exceptional slave with mild curiosity. After they had taken the black demon horse to the stables, the rest of the night had been spent in peace. Renaldo was well rested and refreshed, but his prisoner looked as if his sleep had been less rejuvenating. Still angry, Casto had started to serve his master, his pride prohibiting him from performing badly. That was why Renaldo could enjoy the perfect manners, efficiency, and, above all, grace of his new acquisition. After his own plate was filled, he beckoned Casto to sit down as well.

"Take some and eat. After this, we'll go visit the stables. I want to know if you are as good a fighter as my brothers-in-arms claim."

Warily, the young man sat down, took some of the bread and cheese laid on the table, and helped himself to some water. Renaldo furrowed his brow.

"Don't be shy. You can take some of the wine as well."

The blue eyes showed their disdain openly. "Thank you, but I'll pass. If you like to drink this swill, it's up to you, but I prefer water over something as disgusting as this."

"What's wrong with this wine?"

"It's from an awfully bad year. You can smell that the grapes didn't get enough sun before they were pressed. To balance, or better, to mask this failure, the winegrower has added another wine, which unfortunately doesn't fit the bouquet. Whatever you paid for this brew was surely too much."

"And how do you know such things?"

"I already told you, I come from a family of merchants. Even though we weren't among the big players, business wasn't bad. My uncle specialized in wine before he died during one of his journeys."

"So you're basically telling me that I was overcharged."

"Definitely. Wine like this is either disposed of or, perhaps, if you don't want to be wasteful, turned into vinegar. But only for cleaning purposes. Everything else would be a waste of time, money, and storage room."

The Angel of Death smiled. "Thank you for telling me. From now on, you'll be in charge of selecting my wines."

"Aren't you afraid I could take measures to get rid of you?" The challenge in Casto's words was punctuated by his fierce gaze.

Renaldo took it in stride. "No. At least not like this. You're a man of honor, Casto. You would never sink so low as to stab me in the back, figuratively speaking."

Casto avoided his eyes. "How can you be so sure?"

"The same way you're an expert with wine, I'm an expert with people. You may be many things, surely as complicated as hell, but you're neither a coward nor a murderer."

"Don't bet on it."

Renaldo gave an amused laugh that did not improve Casto's mood at all. They finished their breakfast in loaded silence.

AT THE stables, a small crowd had gathered at Lys's paddock. The reverential murmurs died as soon as Renaldo stepped toward the fence. Lys immediately sauntered to Casto, greeting him with a soft nose kiss. Casto fondled Lys's broad forehead, and his voice was friendly, almost playful.

"Good morning, Lys. Are they treating you well?"

A satisfied snort was the answer. The stallion was obviously content.

From the crowd, Kalad emerged and took his place next to Renaldo. His brown eyes glittered. "Your plan has worked?"

"Which plan? Are you talking about my meager hopes that the stallion would stay close by? If so, then yes, I was lucky."

"As lucky as your slave when he sent me off my horse. You're well matched."

"I don't need luck to get you on the ground." Casto's voice was as cold as ice.

Kalad spun round in utter surprise. "He speaks our language?"

Renaldo flashed a huge grin. "Yes, he does. And not too badly, as you can see."

"What a happy coincidence. I stick to my words. It was your lucky day when you beat me."

Casto's chin went forward, his blue eyes boring into Kalad as if he was an interesting insect that had just shown some curious behavior. Surprised, Renaldo realized that despite his youth, the slave was able to defy Kalad. Casto did not show any fear challenging a man who had every reason to resent him and who definitely ranked higher than Casto himself. This self-confidence, which had nothing to do with desperation but was clearly born out of habit, showed another piece of the jigsaw puzzle that was Casto.

Casto's next words just served to emphasize this impression. "As I said, luck had nothing to do with it. Your riding skills simply aren't good enough to make you a serious opponent for me."

Everywhere around them were sharp, shocked intakes of breath. Never before had a slave dared to give back talk to one of the lords in such an insolent manner.

Kalad's eyes narrowed. It was hard to tell whether he was amused or annoyed by the blatant insolence his leader's slave was showing. "You can, of course, always say so. Show us some proof."

Renaldo shot his brother-in-arms a warning look. "That won't be possible, Kalad. Lys hasn't got a saddle yet, and by the look of him it'll take some time to fit one for him."

"I don't need a saddle to defeat the likes of him."

Renaldo was indecisive, and his gaze wavered between Kalad and Casto, who were both now clearly angry and agitated. It did not seem as if either of them would give in. He sighed. There was only one solution to situations like this one.

"Okay, you can duke it out. After that, I don't want to ever hear a word about it again, am I understood? And nobody is to get seriously hurt, which means blunt weapons. When I call an end to it, you will both comply without any back talk, are we clear?"

Both men exchanged a glance before showing their consent with nods. Kalad ordered a slave to bring his horse. While they were waiting, he turned back to Casto.

"Three rounds. The one to first score two hits wins. We fight within the training area. Leaving it means instant defeat."

Casto shrugged. He did not really care about the fine detail because there was no way he would lose against Kalad. "Agreed."

Kalad's horse was a lively chestnut stallion with an elegant head and long legs that screamed runner. Kalad got in the saddle and looked expectantly at Casto.

Lys appeared next to his rider, looking unappreciatively at their opponents. In one graceful movement, Casto mounted the bare back of his horse, shooting Kalad a challenging look over Lys's ears. He knew he was acting recklessly, that the most important thing at the moment was to keep a low profile, but Kalad's careless arrogance rubbed him the wrong way when he was still angry about the weakness he had shown to Renaldo the night before. He simply could not, and would not, let that braided desert dweller get the better of him.

He patted Lys's strong neck in an attempt to reassure them both. The stallion was not happy about this fight that could so easily expose them, but like his rider, he would never avoid an open challenge such as

32

Kalad had presented. They just had to be careful not to arouse too much suspicion.

At the entrance to the training area, Renaldo handed each man a blunt sword. They received them with grim expressions and took position facing each other. The news about Renaldo's new slave and Kalad having a match had burned through the camp like wildfire. Canubis himself had come to the stables to witness the outrageous event. The air around the training area was buzzing with the whispered comments of the quickly growing audience. The tension, between not only Casto and Kalad but also among the spectators, was palpable.

When Renaldo gave the signal, the two men on their eager horses charged without hesitation.

Kalad, who did not intend to give Casto time to think for even a moment, tried to distract him with a quick blow to his head, but Casto ducked gracefully under the swishing sword. In the same movement, he let himself fall down on Lys's right side, causing the audience to hold their breath and Kalad to perk up, since it looked like Casto had lost his balance while riding without the aid of a saddle. Instead of falling, Casto's feet only touched the ground lightly before the momentum of Lys's movement catapulted him back up. Lys spun around with surprising speed, enabling his rider to counteract Kalad's next attack.

When he realized that the slave had not fallen off the horse but instead executed a standard maneuver, Kalad reacted quickly in order to get him off-balance. But Kalad had gravely underestimated the speed with which Lys shot forward. Casto pressed his body against the stallion's neck, avoiding the wide swing of Kalad's sword. He thrust his own sword straight forward and was satisfied when the blunt edge made contact with his opponent's rib cage. It wasn't a serious thrust, not one that would cause any damage, just hard enough for everybody to see that he had won a point. There was no use pushing his luck any further than strictly necessary.

"One!" Renaldo's voice rang out like a bell.

Kalad's eyes narrowed in anger. He had not expected a quick victory, not after he had witnessed the young man's riding skills firsthand back at the oasis, but the determination with which Casto fought took him by surprise. He knew that he had egged the slave on, forcing him into this confrontation at least partly against his will. Kalad loved to tease, especially arrogant, conceited people like Casto, and if he was honest with himself, he also wanted to get back at the man. Being defeated twice in such a short time did not sit well with Kalad's pride as an Emeris, and this seemed like a perfect opportunity to let off some steam. Although it was not very nice or honorable, Kalad also calculated that a slave would not dare to go all out against a high-ranked member of the Pack such as him. It had seemed like a safe bet, but now it looked as if he had miscalculated. In front of so many witnesses, he did not want to lose face again, and so he forced his own horse to bump into Lys.

This time Casto was unable to dodge him because his leg was caught between the two horses. Kalad tried to stab him, aiming for Casto's chest. He missed the first time, but managed to score when he drew his sword back. A triumphant light gleamed in his eyes. This would show the boy what it meant to go against an Emeris!

"One!"

There was no mistaking it! The Angel of Death was clearly enjoying this little fling between his new slave and his brother-in-arms.

The stallions danced nervously around each other then, each waiting for the other to make a mistake and determined not to disappoint their riders. Lys was angry that Casto had been hit.

Casto tried to calm him down. "Easy, Lys. You heard the Barbarian: no serious wounds. We'll get into trouble if those two get killed."

The stallion shook his head in indignation. He was in full battle mode now and had a hard time controlling his temper. Suddenly he made a huge leap sideways, causing Kalad's surprise attack to fail, and this time Casto didn't wait until the warrior gathered himself again.

With his ears pressed flat against his skull, Lys rushed after the chestnut stallion, urging him against the fence with his powerful body, thus forcing Kalad to lift his leg so that he wouldn't be smashed between the angry horses and solid wood. This gave Casto the opportunity to send him to the ground with one well-aimed blow.

Unable to regain his balance, Kalad landed right in front of Lys's hooves, forcing the stallion into a bizarre maneuver to avoid trampling the fighter.

"Two!" There was a hint of malice in Renaldo's voice while he watched two men catch Kalad's stallion.

Casto, still mounted on Lys, looked down on the fallen warrior with an impenetrable gaze. There was no telling what was going on behind those clear blue eyes, whether the young man was happy, or shocked, or afraid of the consequences of this unthinkable deed. Any sensible slave would have allowed Kalad to win, just because he was a master and had the means to make their life hell if he so wished. But then again, any normal slave would not have had a chance of defeating the warrior in the first place.

Silence descended, and it was almost as if all the spectators were holding their breath at the same time. Nothing like this had ever happened before. It was so unbelievable that most of them had difficulty comprehending it. A slave beating an Emeris in open combat. People's minds reeled.

As if unaware of the sudden change in atmosphere, Casto jumped down from Lys's back, went to Kalad, and offered him his hand. The warrior took it with a broad grin that shattered the tension.

After a moment's hesitation, Casto smiled back. "I told you, I wasn't just lucky."

"And now I believe you. You're a dangerous fighter, Casto." Kalad had never been one to deny credit when credit was due.

"You're one to talk. You're pretty dangerous yourself."

"Enough with the gawking! Back to work, all of you!" Canubis ended the spectacle in his usual dominant manner. With Aegid and Renaldo in tow, he apprehended the two combatants.

"Pretty impressive, both of you. In close combat your stallion is hard to defeat." The compliment sounded rather grudging and was clearly directed toward Lys, but it was nevertheless honest. Before Casto had a chance to react, Canubis fired his next question: "How about his endurance?"

It was obvious that their little display had woken Canubis's curiosity, something that could easily lead to serious problems should it go any further. Casto shuffled closer to Lys. His cheeks made light contact with the stallion's warm coat. His brother's presence gave him the self-confidence to weave the net of lies that was necessary to protect them both. In order not to kindle the warlord's interest even more, he tried to be as vague as possible.

"Lys is fast and ardent."

Renaldo's brow furrowed. This was not a satisfying answer at all. He did not like the way his slave avoided his brother's question. "We're positive about that. We want to know how fast he is. Would you be willing to race against Canubis and me?"

The clear blue eyes flamed in suspicion. "What happens if I win?"

Canubis started to laugh. "That's not going to happen. *If* you win, you get the fame. We surely won't punish you, if that's what you are afraid of."

Casto had indeed suspected something like that. He knew enough masters who delighted in playing cruel games with those who were at their mercy. After everything he had heard about these two warlords, it was entirely possible they wouldn't go easy on him. Although he didn't trust them, he had never been one to let a provocation go. Besides, there was no way he could back out now, not after he had so readily accepted Kalad's challenge.

"Let's do it."

Slaves brought two stunning stallions, one of them purely white, the other one the color of a stormy sky. Aside from their different coloring, it was obvious that the two were brothers, for they resembled each other like mirror images.

"Casto, these are Ghost and Demon, our horses."

With respect, Casto bowed to the steeds, a gesture he had not bestowed on their riders yet. Canubis and Renaldo got into their saddles. Casto, too, mounted Lys again. He already had a plan in mind, because one thing was for sure, although the two barbarians were not to know how fast Lys really was, he would not let them win either. He just couldn't bring himself to do that, although it would surely be wise to exhibit some humility.

Canubis stated the terms for the race. "We start here, inside the training area. Our goals are the three date trees on top of the dune west of the camp. They're hard to see from here, but very distinctive once you get closer. I'd say it's about one league there and back, enough to get a clear picture of Lys's abilities. That is, if you don't back out now?"

Like Kalad, Canubis loved to tease and Casto was a prime target. The young man pointedly ignored Canubis. His eyes were already trained on the date trees in the distance. Canubis grinned. "Kalad, you're our starter."

The warrior nodded, raising his arm. The three riders waited impatiently, and as soon as Kalad's bare hand touched his thigh, they started off at full speed. Ghost and Demon were faster than any horses Casto had ever met, but they weren't able to outrun Lys, who stayed glued to their heels all the time, forcing their own murderous pace on them. When they reached the dunes, the stallions had already started to foam. Their riders hadn't spared them, trying to get rid of Casto right from the start. Now they realized that had not been the best tactic to choose, but it was too late to back out. Ghost and Demon had no intention to budge either. They were the horses of powerful warriors, gods even. There was no way they would simply give up, especially not when facing an impudent stranger. They kept their pace until the camp came back into sight. A quarter of a league before the finish, Casto gave Lys free rein. Without apparent effort, the stallion overtook his opponents and reached the training area at full speed. He even found time to turn around so that his rider could greet the barbarians. After reining in their agitated horses, the two warriors stared at him with a mixture of awe and anger.

"Well done, Casto." Renaldo's smile betrayed his pride. He had definitely won himself a rare gem here, and he was pleased with himself about it.

Canubis fixed the young man in a repressive, assessing gaze. What exactly went on behind those enigmatic amber eyes, Casto could not tell, but the following words surprised him. "The tricks Lys showed during the fight with Kalad in the arena—would you be able to teach them to other horses?"

Casto shrugged. He was dimly aware of what Canubis was getting at and was not at all sure he liked it. He phrased his answer very carefully. "Depends on the horses. They have to have the right traits."

It seemed that Canubis had anticipated this answer, because his retort came swiftly. "You can have your pick from all the horses available, including Ghost and Demon. How many do you think you could train at the same time?"

"Alone? Ten, perhaps twelve. But only when I don't have other chores." He looked pointedly at Renaldo.

Canubis and Renaldo exchanged a long glance that Renaldo ended with a shrug.

Canubis flashed a satisfied smile. "That's a good start. Of course you'll receive help. Renaldo and I are going to talk about the details later." He was about to turn away, but then the intimidating gaze homed in on Casto one more time. "A very good race. I cannot remember ever being defeated in such a competition by anybody other than my brother."

Casto bowed on Lys's back. He deeply respected that the powerful leader admitted his defeat so easily in front of a slave. It required a huge amount of confidence and character to do so.

3. ENEMIES

"THAT ARROGANT, shameless bastard!" In his helpless rage, Jeran thumped a heap of horse blankets. "If only I could, I'd smash his beautiful face."

"I gather you're talking about Lord Renaldo's latest acquisition?"

Sindal shot his friend an imploring look. Ever since he and Elwan had managed to reach the rank of overseer they had lost contact with their peers in the stables, but not to such an extent that they wouldn't visit now and then. During their current meeting, they had started talking about the young twerp who had been working for the Angel of Death for a week now. According to Canubis himself, the boy was allowed to do as he pleased in the stables. He could even push around such a seasoned stableman as Jeran. Not that he would sink so low as to do something like that, oh no—Casto went even further. He simply ignored the haulers. Only when he needed something did he talk to them. His arrogant, cool attitude aroused the other slaves' disdain as much as the fact that he obviously knew what he was doing. Nobody could deny that he was indeed an excellent rider, and his behavior showed that he knew it all too well. Jeran hated Casto's guts with all his heart.

Sindal and Elwan shared a glance. They had not had much contact with Casto yet, but Jeran was a friend.

Jeran looked at his friends with burning eyes. "What that little busybody needs is a lesson in humility, don't you agree?"

"A lesson in humility? He needs to be thrown into the deepest gutter!" Elwan grinned maliciously. "And that's our cue. Isn't he riding that mare of Lord Wolfstan's?"

"You mean the crazy one? Yes."

Jeran did not understand what his friend was implying, so Elwan spelled it out for him. "What chances do you think he has of staying in the saddle when she experiences one of her... little moments?"

Jeran thought about this for some time. The conclusion he came to was a satisfying one, that made his lips split into a gleeful grin. "I guess it's nobody's fault when she gets terrified. Everybody knows about her bad temper." He stared at the tent's ceiling in silent contemplation.

"She doesn't like noise. Perhaps there's something I'll have to transport tomorrow. Something heavy."

Elwan patted Jeran's shoulder. "I can see you're a faithful slave who can't wait to do his work tomorrow. When does the bastard train? Sindal and I would like to pay you a visit."

"Always at sunrise. She's the first horse he rides every day."

"We'll be there. Have a good night's rest. Tomorrow, exciting things are going to happen!"

Roaring with laughter, the two overseers left the tent. Jeran was alone with the warm feeling of revenge soon to be fulfilled.

DEEP IN concentration, Casto led the mare through an exercise that would strengthen her hind legs. As expected, she had immediately understood what he wanted from her and was now eager to please him. If it were not for her weak nerves, paired with a tendency to go into full panic at the slightest disturbance, she had the potential to become his number one pupil. She was teachable and had an excellent build with perfectly set muscles and legs as clear and straight as Lys's. To top it off, she was fast and brave. Unfortunately she was also jumpy, and even a small noise could send her to high alert. It was a real pity.

Casto was just about to change hands when suddenly a deafening rumble, followed by a high-pitched clatter, filled the air. At the edge of his vision, he saw a slave with an overthrown cart full of pottery fragments. The slave had lost control of the vehicle and half the clay was now on the ground.

The world around Casto exploded into flitting shadows. The mare's head shot up like an arrow while she jumped into the air with all four legs at the same time. When her hooves made contact with the ground again, she started to buck. Agile and flexible as she was, Casto was more than once in danger of losing his place in the saddle, but somehow he managed to stay on the crazed animal's back. Slowly the mare started to calm down. Just when Casto thought the worst was over, the rumbling started again.

While trying to steer the cart away from the heap of clay, the slave had managed to tip it again, sending the rest of the cargo down as well. The mare's eyes rolled up until only the whites were visible, her nostrils opened wide, and she stuck her tail between her hind legs. With a grunt that would have been more befitting of a pig than a horse, she threw herself around and started to run.

It was the kind of run that could not be stopped easily, or anytime soon. Here was a horse determined to get as much space between itself and danger as possible. Casto only needed a quick glance ahead to see that he could not afford to jump off. His steed was completely out of control and headed right for the fence, which was about one pace high, that surrounded the training area. It was impossible for the inexperienced mare to manage the jump on her own. Even with a rider, it was still dangerous because of her uncontrollable speed. There was a high risk they would both break their necks in the process, since the fence was built with heavy timbers that would not give much even when hit by the heavy body of a warhorse.

Casto didn't hesitate. He pressed his knees hard into the soft leather of the saddle and fixed his eyes on the fence, trying to determine the perfect moment to start the jump that would send them safely over the hurdle despite their breakneck speed. The secret was to exercise just enough pressure, at exactly the right moment, which would cause the mare to react to him even though she was in such a panic.

Casto concentrated. His whole world shrank to that one, crucial point that would decide both their lives. The blood was roaring in his ears when he dug his heels into the mare's sides with all his might. With a shrill whinny, she was airborne. The horse's jump was so high it almost threw Casto off. Unfortunately it was not high enough. He heard a splintering sound as she hit the top rail with her hind legs, scraping them open on the rough surface. Upon landing, the mare almost lost her balance, and for a moment she looked as if she were about to crash down. But then she managed to get up again, the movement so rapid that Casto was almost shaken off. The time it took him to regain his balance was enough for the crazed beast to remember why she had been jumping in the first place. Her head reared up again and the whites of her eyes shone ghostly in the pale morning light, then she left the camp at full gallop and raced into the desert.

"Damn! How did he do that?"

Stupefied, Jeran, Sindal, and Elwan watched Casto's retreating silhouette.

Jeran trembled visibly. "Did you see that? Although that crazy beast acted like a demon from the other realm, he managed to stay in the saddle. And then he made her jump the fence!"

Sindal could only stare with his mouth open, but Elwan started to laugh. "He's good, I give him that, but it won't benefit him." His friends looked puzzled, and he raised a forefinger. "My dear Sindal, I don't know what you're thinking, but I've got the impression that we just witnessed an attempted escape. As overseers, we do have the duty to catch the fleeing slave and hand him over to his rightful owner in the usual fashion so that he can decide about his fate."

Finally Sindal understood. "Of course you're right, Elwan. It's my honor to help you hunt him down."

Elwan turned to Jeran. "Don't worry, old friend. The bastard will pay. Just a word to the wise. If I were you, I'd see to it that this place gets cleaned up fast in order to avoid unnecessary questions. Sindal and I've got to go."

"Thank you. You're true friends indeed."

The two overseers bowed mockingly. "It's our pleasure. Don't forget, you owe us one."

SLOWLY CASTO led the still-trembling, utterly exhausted mare through the desert sand. He could not tell how many leagues she had run before he had managed to finally stop her. He only knew it would be a long journey back to the camp, since riding was completely out of the question. The brown mare was foundering; the sinew in her right front leg was thick and hot, and blood trickled down her hind legs where some splinters had embedded so deeply it was impossible to get them out. Her breath was still ragged from exhaustion. Time and again, Casto stopped to let the horse rest, trying to keep further damage to a minimum.

Casto did not dare to imagine what Lord Wolfstan would have to say about this. He didn't know most of the owners of the horses he was training, but Lord Wolfstan had introduced himself after Casto had chosen the mare as a possible candidate. Wolfstan was the armorer of the Pack and had given the impression of a levelheaded man, but Casto also knew that Wolfstan really liked the horse. If Wolfstan decided to blame his leader's slave for her recent condition, Casto would be in deep trouble—again.

It was around noon when Casto finally reached an area close to the camp. Only about half a league more and they would be back home. From a ridge, he saw two riders drawing near, and he assumed they were guards. When they approached, Casto stopped in order to greet them. They were overseers he had seen in passing once or twice in the stables, and though Casto resented being a slave, he was not stupid enough to challenge them openly.

Casto assumed that they had witnessed the incident and were coming to help him. Their sudden attack took him by surprise. They grabbed him brutally by his arms and kicked him in the backs of his knees, forcing him to the ground. Before he could say anything or react to this brutal treatment, they had already ripped his shirt off, given him two nasty blows with a whip, and bound his wrists with rope. Then they dragged him back to the camp, despite his furious protests. The sand chafed his skin and made him feel like he had fallen into a tub of stinging nettles. The mare followed the other two horses on unsteady feet. Casto was deeply worried that she wouldn't make it.

Back in the camp, his captors forced him down in front of Renaldo's tent, not listening to his vehement protests and angry demands. While Sindal hammered two wooden poles into the ground till they were only one hand above the earth, Elwan was keeping Casto down by forcing his knee into his back. Still dizzy from being dragged, he wasn't able to fight back. Casto was aware of more and more spectators gathering, but one look at their blank, uncaring faces told him that any pleas for help would fall on deaf ears. Not that he would ever sink so low as to beg strangers for help. He got the impression that this scene had played out numerous times before and that he would not like the outcome at all.

With even more brutality, Sindal and Elwan positioned him between the poles, spread his arms apart, and chained him down, forcing him into a humiliating kneeling position he could not escape from. While they were doing this, verbal abuse poured from their lips, dripping like acid into Casto's ears.

"I'm sure you've been told what happens to those who dare to run away. You're in for some serious pain, pretty boy. Lord Renaldo is known for his short temper and brutality."

"What do you think he's going to do with him, Sindal?"

"Oh my, I don't dare to imagine. Guess it will be the glass whip. All that smooth skin hanging in shreds and the blood staining the ground. I can hardly wait."

Sindal clearly enjoyed frightening his helpless prisoner. He bent down to bring his lips closer to Casto's ears.

"And that's only if the lord feels merciful. But don't get your hopes up, so far he has never pardoned a runaway slave. I can already hear your bones cracking. They use an iron bar for this, so it'll be fast. After that, all you have to do is endure another agonizing two or three days until you're allowed to die. Isn't that nice?"

Outraged by this brutal and unjust treatment and the stinging words, Casto wanted to tell Sindal and Elwan what exactly they could do with their cruelty and where to stick it, but before he could utter a single word, the leather whip cracked again and he had to concentrate not to scream in pain. While Sindal hit him repeatedly until a dozen welts covered his back, Elwan went to inform the Angel of Death. To the overseers' delight, Lord Renaldo was out and would not be back until the evening. It filled them with glee when they imagined how much the arrogant newcomer would suffer until his owner was back to torture him even more.

The rest of the day, Casto was stuck in the mercilessly burning heat. Even when the sun started to move westward, there was not the tiniest shadow to bring him any relief. The two overseers had chosen the place with meticulous care. Casto had not eaten or drunk anything since early morning and soon started to feel dizzy. A growing headache was accompanied by a painful stinging in his back where the sun burned his raw, damaged skin. His rage about this treatment, as well as his own stupidity, soon gave way to desperation and then delirium.

When Renaldo finally returned to the camp, Casto was already way past caring. He was not even able to lift his head, let alone plead his case to his owner.

Speechless with rage, Renaldo stared at the bound, huddled figure of his pitiful new toy. The formerly velvet-soft skin was burning red, the blood from the lashes had turned almost black and was crawling with the shimmering, repulsive bodies of numerous flies. The voices of the overseers washed over him from a place far away.

"He was attempting to flee."

"He was riding Lord Wolfstan's mare, because she's the fastest."

"Jumped over the fence...."

"...far inside the desert—"

"Enough!" Renaldo held up his right hand. "I've heard enough. You may leave now. We'll talk tomorrow. I wish to be alone with my slave."

Bowing deeply, the men left him.

Renaldo made haste to loosen the knots on Casto's wrists. Disgusted, he stared at the fiery red markings that marred the once flawless skin. When he picked the young man up, Casto made a whimpering sound. His eyelids fluttered and he tried to say something, but only stertorous breathing escaped his throat.

Renaldo tried to soothe him. "Shh. Don't push it. I know. Be still. I'll look after you."

With Casto still in his arms, he turned to a passing slave. "You! Run and tell Lady Noemi to come to me. It's urgent. Hurry!"

The slave dashed away.

In his tent, Renaldo put Casto down gingerly on a divan bed, trying hard not to add to his injuries. When Casto whimpered hoarsely, he offered him a cup of water. "Drink this. But slowly, otherwise you'll get sick."

With a frustrated grunt, Casto obeyed. He drank the precious liquid in small sips. He had finished almost half the cup when Noemi finally entered the tent.

Her eyes widened in surprise when she saw him. "What has happened?"

"I don't know yet. Please help him."

The healer nodded. Carefully, with her eyes closed, she placed her cool hands on Casto's cheeks. Casto felt a warm tingling along his spine, as if somebody had poured honey all over him. The pulsating pain in his back, as well as the splitting headache, decreased until both were gone. He stared at the redheaded healer in silent wonder.

"I'm very grateful, my lady. How did you do that?"

A sad smile appeared on Noemi's lips. "I'm a witch, Casto."

From her somewhat agitated body language Casto deduced that she was used to all kinds of extreme reactions to this fact. It was a feeling he was deeply familiar with, and he treated her to his most dazzling smile.

"A witch? Impossible! You're way too beautiful!"

For a heartbeat, silence descended, then Noemi kissed him spontaneously. "You're very charming, Casto. I guess it's me who's grateful." She glanced at Renaldo, who had followed their exchange with furrowed brows. "I'm going to send somebody with broth and a special tea. Casto needs as much liquid as he can get, but he shouldn't overdo it and should take his time. And, by the way, they didn't stop at the whipping, they also dragged him. Underneath the whip marks, I could sense deeper bruises and there was also some internal damage. Nothing too bad, but let me say this, he's a tough one."

There was a dangerous glow in the intense gray eyes. "Thank you, Noemi."

The witch left the tent, and for a moment the two men remained silent before Renaldo started to talk.

"Are you going to tell me what happened?"

"Are you going to believe me?"

"I already know that the version of those two tricksters is wrong."

"How come?"

A thin, knowing smile was the answer. "That was easy. You gave me your word, and as I already said, you may be many things, Casto, but liar is not one of them. Besides, if you attempted to flee, you sure as hell would do it with Lys, not some unknown horse."

To buy time, Casto took another sip of water. He was not sure how to handle this situation, so he decided to stick to the truth.

"I was training. The mare panicked because somebody overturned a cart full of debris. She bolted, and it took me some time to calm her again. We were pretty far into the desert by then. Upon my return, those two captured me and bound me in front of your tent. They didn't even listen when I told them to get her to a healer. I'm worried—those wounds were serious."

Renaldo sighed. "I'll find out what has happened to her, but I'm sure she's all right. Not all our underlings are useless, I can assure you. Do you happen to know who handled that cart?"

"No. It was a slave from the stables, but I don't know his name."

"Would you recognize him?"

"Of course."

"I think it's best if we deal with this tomorrow. Have another sip, then go wash yourself. You look horrible."

Casto was about to come back with a sharp retort but thought better of it. The day had been too taxing to waste his energy on another fight.

OVERFLOWING WITH malicious expectations, Sindal and Elwan entered Renaldo's tent the next morning. They were sure to be rewarded greatly for their diligence and could not wait to see Casto's tortured body. One of the best things about Lord Renaldo was his ingenuity when it came to punishment. To their dismay, the boy was nowhere to be seen. Instead, the Angel of Death was waiting for them with a face like a thunderstorm.

"Explain to me in detail what happened yesterday!"

The two overseers shared a quick glance. The oppressive atmosphere did not escape them, and they were glad that they had practiced their story, just to be on the safe side.

"But of course, Lord Renaldo. We'd been on our tour through the stables when we saw that slave of yours jumping over the fence with Lord Wolfstan's mare. We immediately knew it had to be an attempt to escape. That's why we decided to follow him."

"Interesting. Where did you catch him?"

Oblivious to the sharp tone in Renaldo's voice, Sindal pretended to be thinking about this question. "I'd say almost a league south of the camp. He had to stop because the mare was injured. And of course we didn't waste that chance."

"Of course. And then you brought him back?"

"Yes. He resisted, that's why we felt it would be a good idea to drag him behind the horses. For educational purposes. We proceeded as usual."

Renaldo had heard enough. His voice was an angry hiss. "How dare you lie to me in such an offhand manner? How dare you misuse your position like this? What has my slave done to you to merit such animosity?"

Sindal could feel the hair on the back of his neck rising. Not for a second had the two of them thought Renaldo wouldn't believe them.

Elwan was a little more collected than his friend. He tried to bluff their way out of it. "I don't know what you're talking about, my lord. Whatever the slave has told you, he's trying to protect himself."

A dangerous light crept into the gray eyes. "Casto doesn't lie! He's given me his word not to flee, and he's a man of honor. And even if I shouldn't believe him, all the proof is in his favor. Do you really think he would leave the camp with another horse than Lysistratos? Without weapons, supplies, or gold? That is a grade of stupidity only you two would show. I really don't know what is worse—that you have mistreated your position like this, or that you honestly thought you could fool me. This is your last chance to tell me the truth."

Confronted with their master's unmasked fury, the two men fell to their knees. They knew their game was lost, and they were desperate to keep the damage to a minimum.

"Please forgive us, lord. It was a misunderstanding. A stupid mistake. It won't happen again."

"About that you can be sure, because I hereby take your rank away from you. From now on you're back in the stables as ordinary slaves—assuming you survive the punishment I have in store for you. Your accomplice is going to keep you company. For laying your filthy hands on what is mine, you'll be whipped and exhibited for a day. Then you'll be dragged. I'm sure it'll prove healthy for you to have a taste of your own medicine. I do not allow anybody to touch what I have chosen. May your punishment be a warning to all the other slaves. There is only one will in the Pack you have to obey—that of your masters. And now get out of my sight! Leave, before I decide to punish you this instant."

Frightened to their cores, the former overseers fled from the tent.

48

Renaldo heard a rustling behind him and turned around.

Casto stood at the rear entrance of the tent, his arms crossed, his irritatingly blue eyes darkened by rage. "I'm not your possession!"

Taken aback by the young man's fury, Renaldo's answer was indignant. "Yes, you are. And I had expected a little more gratitude from you since I punished your tormentors quite harshly."

"Please, don't make me laugh. You didn't do that for me but to protect your authority. Besides, I couldn't care less about what happens to those idiots, they're insignificant. But I'm not your possession, and I hate it when you treat me like a thing."

"Well, I don't like it when you call me a barbarian. I resent your provocative tone and your whole brazen attitude. I've won you in a fair competition; you're my possession. Should you doubt it, let me remind you that you're wearing my collar."

"That means nothing, nothing at all. You'll never own me, never!"

By now they were standing so close, the tips of their noses almost connected. Both of them were trembling with rage, and neither was willing to give the least bit of ground.

Renaldo suppressed a growl. "You'll learn to serve me, slave. Believe me, it'll be easier for you once you give in."

"Never! I hate you, Barbarian! You took my freedom from me! Don't expect me to ever give in to you!"

Renaldo took a deep breath. Reining in his irritation was not easy, but he managed to force himself to retreat a step.

"Put your clothes on and get out of my sight. I had planned on letting you rest today, but somebody who acts as cheeky as you can surely do his work as well."

"As you wish, Barbarian." Without a second glance at his master, Casto dressed and left the tent.

Deep in thought, Renaldo stared at the entrance Casto had just passed through. He could not remember when somebody had last dared to talk to him like that, but it stirred something inside him, this knowledge that Casto was indeed not afraid of him. He knew it would be for the best to discipline the young man without mercy, but for reasons only partly rooted in fascination, Renaldo could not bring himself to punish Casto. The laws governing the Pack protected slaves from sexual harassment and despotism by their owners, although when confronted with Casto's unruly behavior, nobody would deem his punishment arbitrary. And normally Renaldo was among the first to punish disobedience severely and without any mercy. He wondered why, when it came to this special slave, he was hesitating. At the thought of marring Casto's beautiful skin once again with whip marks, Renaldo felt bile rise in his mouth.

Made uneasy by his own gloomy thoughts, the powerful warrior shook his head and resumed his duties.

SINCE LORD Wolfstan's mare could not be trained due to the injuries she had suffered, Casto found time to visit the tent in which Noemi was treating her patients, to offer her his thanks.

The witch welcomed him with a smile. "Good morning, Casto! I'm happy to see you up and about. How are you feeling?"

"Splendid, thanks to you, my lady. I've come to thank you in person for your help. I'm in your debt."

"That's a place you shouldn't go to. My power means that everybody is in my debt. If anything, you should thank your master for allowing me to heal you."

Casto grimaced. "Perhaps I'm going to do that."

"I know it's not my place to say, but I'd advise you to be a little politer to the Angel of Death. He's powerful, proud, and easy to anger. I don't want anything to happen to you."

"You're very friendly, my lady. I'll think about your advice."

Noemi sighed. "But you won't heed it, will you? Don't even try to deny it—I can see it in your eyes. You're as stubborn as he is, and that's not a compliment!"

"Why are we talking about the Barbarian when there are so many other, more pleasant topics?"

Noemi's smile was ironic. "You're aware that I'm a barbarian too?"

"Never, my lady. You're too beautiful, too well-read, and definitely too graceful."

"You're flattering me. How does the son of a merchant know such perfect manners?"

Casto bowed slightly. "It's always a good thing to impress your trading partners. Good manners have often proven the crucial ingredient in otherwise hopeless negotiations."

"So you're trying to win me over?"

Casto appeared to think about this for a moment. His striking blue gaze wandered through the tent as if searching for a suitable answer before returning to the witch. "Perhaps a little bit. It's kind of a habit, I have to admit. But first and foremost, I'm here because I'm really grateful for your help. Plus, I had the impression that your life isn't always easy. A little small talk can do wonders sometimes."

Noemi's cool fingers touched Casto's cheek; her voice was dark, thoughtful. "You're right. It's not always easy for me. I'm a witch, and although I use my power strictly to do good, people are often afraid of me. It's lonely sometimes. How come you don't fear me?"

Casto took her hand and kissed it reverently. "Why should I fear somebody as good as you? In my lifetime I've already met some true monsters, and I've learned—the hard way—to recognize them. You're most definitely not one of them."

The vulnerability showing in Noemi's question, as well as Casto's heartfelt answer, left them in awkward silence for some time.

Then Casto flashed her one of his dazzling smiles. "This sure is a sore topic. Why not forget about it and talk about more pleasant things? For example, where you got that wonderful tea I'm smelling in the air."

Noemi exploded with laughter.

"That 'wonderful tea' is a concoction of some really nasty herbs and meant to treat festering wounds. But you must have been aware that it's not a beverage!"

"I am. It was my sneaky way of talking you into offering me some real tea."

Noemi gave in to the boyish charm. "And it just so happens that I have a really good blend at hand. Would you honor me by being my guest?"

Gracefully, Casto bowed. "It's my pleasure, my lady."

IN THE southern part of Arana, Canubis and Renaldo inspected the destroyed and still-smoldering remnants of the depot. Desperate to escape the mercenaries, the citizens of Arana had decided to give up their most precious assets—the warehouses in which all their goods were stored—in the hope to somehow soothe the powerful warlords' wrath. The brothers were amused by so much ingenuousness. They ordered their men to seek out the most valuable pieces and burn down the rest of the merchandise, together with the warehouses. After getting a clear picture of the damage they had caused, the two demigods got on their way back to the camp.

Renaldo sought out his brother's opinion. "Shall we take their defensive walls and end this tragedy?" Even though he was equal to the Wolf of War, he usually left tactical decisions to him. It was an arrangement that dated back to the time when his fire and his temper had both been equally uncontrollable.

Canubis contemplated the question for a moment, scanning the hastily heightened walls in the northern part of the city where the citizens had fled, turning themselves into rats caught in a deadly trap. "No. Let's give them a few more days. Their supplies are low. Soon they'll start to fight for the remaining bits of edible material. When they tear each other apart over the last scraps, we'll attack. Until then, our men should get everything ready for departure. Once the town is destroyed, I want to leave as quickly as possible."

"What do you think? Two weeks to go? Or three?"

"I'd wager on three. People can be surprisingly determined when their own survival is at stake. Not that it makes any difference in the end, but that's how they are."

They laughed at this, which was only funny to those whose life knew no end. Although the brothers had been reduced to demigods when their hearts had been stolen, they still showed the natural arrogance of those born to rule. To them, even the men and women fighting in their army were hardly more than useful pawns in a game where the outcome was still undetermined. Renaldo pointed toward the tents in which the booty was stored.

"I'm going to look for a present for Casto."

"It has evaded my attention that your slave's obedience already merits a present."

"It doesn't, believe me. But I'm hoping to make him a little more compliant."

Canubis's look was stern, and he did not try to hide his consternation. "A good hiding would make him compliant as well. He's a slave, brother. He has to obey."

Renaldo shrugged. "It's not that I don't agree with you, but I'm afraid a hiding would be counterproductive. He's tough—physical punishment would only serve to harden his attitude."

"And that's why you want to bribe him?"

"I don't see your point."

Canubis's eyes narrowed. His brother's behavior was highly unusual. When realization finally dawned, he started to grin. "He's giving you the cold shoulder, isn't he?"

Renaldo was clearly annoyed, but he did not answer.

"What is it, Renaldo? Is your legendary charm dwindling in your old age?"

"No, surely not. For that, Casto would need to be aware of me trying to seduce him. But he's simply not interested. If he rejected me outright, I'd know how to react, but he doesn't even realize my intent. You could almost think he doesn't care."

"Perhaps he favors women?"

The brothers shared a look, then shook their heads simultaneously. Nobody, neither man nor woman, could withstand Renaldo's radiance. It was part of his power.

Canubis articulated the unthinkable. "Or could it be he's simply not interested in *you*?"

"It seems so. But I'll be damned if I let this pass. I'll get Casto into my bed. It simply can't be that he doesn't care for me."

Now Canubis was laughing openly. "Could it be you feel insulted as a professional seducer?"

Instead of an answer, Renaldo smashed his fist into his brother's upper arm with full force.

The laughter only grew in intensity. "I like this. Casto's value has just gone up as far as I'm concerned."

"Just shut up. I'm going to select a present."

"Don't overdo it. You know, less is often more. And, brother, should you need some advice or my help, my door is always open."

Renaldo made a bawdy gesture, accompanied by some colorful slurs in the language of the Ancients, then he turned toward the tents to find a gift for his stubborn, effervescent, arrogant slave.

4. ARGUMENT

TIRED AND dusty, Casto entered the Barbarian's lodgings after a stressful day. He longed for a bath, some food, and sleep. Renaldo was already there, lounging on one of the couches, a challenging grin on his lips.

"You look horrible."

"A good day to you too, Barbarian. It was pretty hot today."

"Perfectly normal for this time of year. Hurry up, wash yourself. I've got a surprise for you."

Warily, Casto went into the back part of the tent where he and the Barbarian slept. Behind a curtain stood a tub filled with fresh water. The Angel of Death was a great fan of cleanliness—one of the few things on which Casto agreed with him. He, too, loathed nothing more than having to cut back on his personal hygiene. He hurried to get washed because even his love for spruceness was somewhat diminished by the cold of the water. Dressed in a simple, dark blue tunic, he emerged from the back.

Renaldo had helped himself to a cup of wine. He gave Casto a friendly nod. "Have a seat. I assume it's in vain to offer you some wine?"

Casto gave a derisive snort. "What you're drinking at the moment is slightly better than the swill from last time, but I still don't want to affront my taste buds with it."

"Calm down and stop questioning my taste and discernment in such a rude manner. This is for you."

He offered Casto a bundle wrapped in linen. The young man stared at it as if it contained a nest of poisonous snakes.

"Open it. It's a present, so it won't bite."

"Why would you give me a present?"

"Oh, so you *are* aware how inappropriate your behavior is?"

A venomous glare was the answer to that taunt.

"I take that as a yes. Regarding the present... I do know how much you dislike being here." Renaldo held up his hand to stop Casto from giving another furious retort. "But you'll have to put up with me for some time. This little something should make your situation a little more palatable."

"The only palatable thing for me would be my freedom."

"That's the one thing I can't give you. You're too valuable."

Hearing these words, Casto's eyes widened, but luckily for him, Renaldo misinterpreted his reaction.

"Before you throw your next tantrum, you'd better open the package."

For a change, Casto obeyed without further discussion, a fact that should have spurred Renaldo's suspicion, but he was too eager to see how his difficult slave would react to the gift to pay much attention. The young man now held up the trousers that had been wrapped in the linen. They were a gorgeous, vivid blue with a golden belt fixed to the waistline and made of the finest silk Renaldo had ever seen. It was the kind of silk he would never have expected to find in a rat-infested place like Arana. A present fit for a king—which should justify a not-too-small amount of gratitude, if not infatuation.

His beautiful slave didn't seem to be in the mood for such reactions, though. He threw the precious cloth to the ground as if it had burned his fingers, his blue eyes shot deadly sparks, an angry heat reddened his cheeks, and his breath heaved.

"*This* is your idea of a present? Do you really think I would ever wear something as despicable as this? If this is your way of being friendly, then I'll refuse any further presents in the future."

The unexpected tantrum took Renaldo by surprise, but he quickly regained his demeanor. Deep inside him, the angry fire that always slumbered there awoke to a sudden, blazing flame. He seized Casto's arm and shook him hard. "That's your way of thanking me? Despite your willfulness and arrogance, I stoop to give you a present every other slave in this camp would pine over, and all you do is spurn me?"

"What else should I do? You're a damn barbarian, keeping me against my will!"

"I might be a barbarian, but first and foremost I'm your master and owner. You don't seem to understand what that means."

"I fully understand! But you don't have the slightest right over me. I would never wear something as repulsive as this. I'd rather go naked!"

"Damn it, slave! You'll be begging me on your knees to wear whatever I deem fit. You're my possession. Everything you get—food, clothes, even the roof over your head—you get through me. It's time for you to remember that.

"You'd rather go naked than wear what I choose for you? As you wish. Until you apologize in a suitable and, above all, honest manner, you won't get any clothes. From now on, you'll have to do your work stark naked, and you will only be fed once a day. That should teach you some respect toward your master."

"Respect is something that has to be earned, Barbarian, and you're far from gaining mine."

Renaldo pushed Casto away. His inner fire burned hot, urging him to kill the little vermin that dared to defy him, but he stopped himself. He wanted to subjugate Casto first, wanted him to come to heel. After that, he could still enjoy the pleasure of taking his life.

Trembling with rage, Casto ripped off the tunic he had been wearing. The Barbarian seemed to think he could humiliate and force him. Nobody had ever succeeded in that, and it had not been for lack of trying. Casto would rather die than let a mere barbarian from the North do what even his own father had not been able to accomplish.

Unnoticed by the two angry men, the scorching heat they had built up escaped into the night. The water in the jug next to Casto stopped boiling, and the wine started to cool again as master and slave went into the bed area to rest.

WITH EYES like saucers, the small boy followed the movements of the dancers who swayed their bodies to the enchanting sounds of foreign instruments. The two women and one man belonged to the visiting queen who was now enjoying the show together with the woman who ruled over this country. The two powerful queens smiled with benevolence at the slim, limber bodies of the attractive slaves, who looked like they were wearing nothing besides golden cuffs around their ankles and wrists. Indeed, they were clad in silk so fine it served as a second skin to the bodies it was supposed to hide.

Although the boy was only five years old, he already understood the purpose of the clothing. It was there to expose its wearers like cattle in a market. Their only reason to live was the pleasure their bodies, in whatever form their owners desired, were able to give. The boy shuddered at the mere thought of being degraded like that. With burning eyes, he witnessed the end of the performance and watched as the dancers sat down at the feet of the two queens, seemingly unfazed by the hungry looks thrown at them from everywhere around the hall. Unable to bear the unbecoming spectacle any longer, the boy sneaked back into his rooms, his head full of thoughts he was still too young to comprehend.

LOST IN thought, Casto wandered back from the stables to the Barbarian's tent. Almost two weeks without any clothing had made him immune to the taunting looks, the scorching sun, and the rough ground. His once lightly tanned skin was now a rich bronze tone that glowed from within and made him even more alluring to the casual observer. If the Angel of Death really thought the ridicule of the other people in the camp and the deprivation of food would break him, he was in for a surprise. Never would he bow to the Barbarian's will; not one step would he take toward him. Casto knew that Renaldo was hoping to get him once they started their journey back to the North. Renaldo thought the cold would defeat Casto, but he would rather freeze to death on Lys's back than beg Renaldo's forgiveness for trying to humiliate him like that. He would—A sharp pain stopped his angry train of thought. Irritated at the interruption, he looked down at his right foot. A large clay shard from a broken pot was driven deep into the sole. The pain pulsated with the rhythm of his heart, growing in intensity. Casto knew his body well enough to realize this was serious. Now the lack of food made itself known as well. Casto felt unconsciousness creeping up on him. Trying to ignore the momentary weakness, he grabbed for something to hold on to, then felt for the shard to remove it from his foot.

"If I were you, I wouldn't do that."

The voice was as cheerful as ever. Casto did not have to turn around to know it was Kalad standing behind him. And where Kalad was, Aegid could be found as well.

"That looks nasty. Removing it here means a big mess. Wouldn't you rather have the excessive bleeding in Renaldo's tent?"

"Leave me alone. I'm fine." Casto's voice trembled slightly. He did not feel well and was furious at having these two witness his weakness.

"I'm going to carry you." Aegid grabbed Casto's shoulders without waiting for his consent. Indignantly, Casto tried to shrug him off.

Kalad seized his wrists. His voice was calm. "We're well aware of how much you resent being dependent on anybody, especially barbarians like us, but believe me, right now you need us. You're as white as a linen, which means your circulation is just kissing your brain good-bye. And this shard is stuck deeply. Allow Aegid to carry you to Renaldo's tent while I get Noemi. Please." A broad grin lit up Kalad's youthful features. "Otherwise we'll have to wait until you lose consciousness, and that could be boring. Tough as you are, we could lose interest, and then you'd be lying here all alone."

Against his will, Casto felt a smile stretch his lips, but it was instantly cut off by the growing pain. "As you wish. I thank you."

Without further ado, Aegid picked up Casto while Kalad went to get Noemi.

Inside Renaldo's tent, Casto was carefully put down on one of the couches, then Aegid got a blanket and covered him. After that, he offered him a cup of wine. Before Casto could voice his disdain at the drink, Aegid had already proffered the mug to his lips. His voice was soft as if he were trying to talk to a wild animal. "Drink. Wounds like that do require the drinking of alcohol, trust me. Even Noemi won't be able to spare you any further pain, and at moments like these, I prefer to be as drunk as possible. Makes it easier to be brave." He winked conspiratorially.

Casto gave in and started to drink. "I bow to the wisdom of your words."

"You're not half as dumb as I thought!"

Casto was ready to give a snotty retort, but at that moment Kalad and Noemi entered the tent.

The witch bore down on Casto like an avalanche, her features agitated by a mixture of anger and worry. "What have you done this time, Casto? And since we're on the topic, why haven't you visited me for so long?"

"My lady. I haven't done anything—I never do. Concerning my visits, I didn't want to insult you with the sight of my naked flesh."

"You idiot. I'm not easily insulted—especially not by flesh as beautiful as yours."

A hint of color returned to Casto's pale cheeks. Compliments on his looks always made him uncomfortable, as Noemi had already observed. With her cool hands she inspected the wound. Her expression became serious. "This looks bad, Casto. The shard is pretty long and, above all, bent. When I get it out, I'll damage a tendon. Of course, I'll be able to heal it, but the pain will be severe. I'm really sorry, but it's a miracle how this thing could get in so deep without causing even more damage."

She turned to Kalad and Aegid, to give Casto time to get accustomed to the news.

"You two will hold him down. The less he can move, the better. Kalad, get me a blanket we can place under his foot. This is going to be messy."

Kalad nodded and vanished into the back of the tent. He returned with a blanket he hoped Renaldo would not miss too much.

Noemi nodded to the desert brothers. Aegid's massive hands rested heavily on Casto's shoulders, pinning him down forcefully while Kalad took hold of Casto's ankles. Just when Noemi was about to start her work, Renaldo entered the tent.

"What's going on here?"

Noemi was annoyed by the disturbance and did not waste time with long explanations. "Your slave is wounded. Help Kalad and Aegid hold him down."

Without asking further questions, Renaldo went to the lounge. Aegid let go of Casto's shoulders and made room so his lord could take his place at Casto's upper body. Renaldo sat down behind Casto and pulled him toward his massive chest. His right arm snaked around Casto's torso like an iron bar.

Aegid grabbed the wounded leg. Casto was no longer able to see Noemi; she was obscured by the broad backs of the two warriors. Since Aegid had brought him to the tent, the pain had steadily increased, but now that Renaldo was holding him, it seemed to dull a bit. It was strangely comforting, lying in the Barbarian's strong arms. All of a sudden, Casto felt secure and pampered, as if no pain in the world could ever reach him again. Without thinking, he rested his head on Renaldo's chest and closed his eyes as he started to relax for the first time in a long while.

Noemi's voice drifted to his ears from a place far away. "I'm going to start now."

Then there was a terrible pain, only bearable because the Barbarian's warmth engulfed him so soothingly. Casto could feel his blood gushing out of the wound in a thick stream.

"I'll let it bleed for a moment to cleanse the wound."

All Casto's remaining strength seemed to flow out of his body with the blood. He felt unbelievably tired. He hardly noticed it when Noemi healed the wound. Through a thick fog, he heard Renaldo thanking Kalad and Aegid. The two warriors left the tent, and Noemi started to scold her brother-in-law in a voice high-pitched in anger.

"Whatever he's done, I'd strongly recommend feeding him properly again. He's so weak, the only thing that's keeping him upright is his stubbornness."

When Noemi had finished speaking her mind, she left as well, and Renaldo sat down next to Casto. He made Casto drink some water, then started to feed him soft white bread steeped in sweet oatmeal.

Slowly, the fog surrounding Casto's thoughts vanished. He watched Renaldo fetch a big bowl of warm water and a sponge. First, Renaldo cleaned Casto's bloodied leg with surprising gentleness. As soon as all the blood was gone, he got fresh water and started washing his body.

Renaldo was surprised that Casto did not resist when he started to sponge off the grime. He decided not to question his luck and to make use of the moment. Carefully, as if Casto had already given his consent to share his bed, Renaldo let the sponge caress Casto's skin in an attempt at foreplay.

The material fitted perfectly with the contours of the muscles it cleaned. Single drops of water shimmered like diamonds on Casto's belly; a small trickle ran down from his neck through the taut pattern of his abdominal muscles and into the valley of his navel. Renaldo followed that path, letting the sponge circle once, twice, and then dipped it into the small puddle. He looked at Casto's face. Casto had closed his eyes and his lips were slightly open—usually an invitation for kissing, but Renaldo knew he had to resist. When he glided the sponge over Casto's left hip, his thighs, and then his penis, Casto arched his lower body, shuddering all over. With a satisfied smile, Renaldo placed the sponge in the bowl. His fingers followed the track he had just made, then mingled at the young man's balls. He was just about to bend forward, ready to kiss the still-inviting lips, when Casto opened his eyes.

The electrifying blue never ceased to fascinate Renaldo. By now he had learned to read a little in those mystifying depths, and what he saw there made him stop dead. His beautiful slave was not only aroused, but confused and full of fear. As much as Renaldo longed to finally make Casto his, he would never force himself on him. Renaldo was skilled enough to have the young man lusting over him to the point where he did not care what was done to him, as long as it was done by the Angel of Death. Right then that would mean taking advantage of Casto's weakness. Renaldo loved getting the upper hand, but he also preferred winning in a fair contest. Seducing Casto now meant reverting to dirty tricks before the time was right. With a sigh, he retreated.

He was rewarded by a relieved, grateful look, before Casto raised his walls of defense again.

"I'm sorry you were hurt like this," Renaldo said quietly.

Taken by surprise, Casto opened his mouth, but before he could muster an answer, Renaldo went on.

"I'm responsible for your well-being and safety. I've neglected my duty in a shameful way. I do apologize for that."

Renaldo braced himself for the acid comments that would surely follow after this open display of weakness, but once again, Casto managed to astonish him.

"I, too, have to apologize. My behavior toward you lacked respect and was ungrateful. I'm really sorry about that and ask your forgiveness."

Renaldo had trouble believing his ears. He probably resembled a stranded fish as he gaped at Casto in wonder.

Casto made a face. "I overreacted. But I sure as hell won't beg you to wear what you choose for me."

Renaldo grinned. "That, I never expected. Why do you apologize? After what I put you through, I thought you'd never talk to me again."

"Don't get me wrong, I won't forgive you for this anytime soon. But you just apologized sincerely and I'll never allow a mere barbarian to show better manners than me."

Both men shared a smile, a first, careful gesture, a confession that they could be more than just opponents.

After a long internal battle, Renaldo decided to take a risk. "Are you going to tell me why my present made you so angry?"

The blue eyes clouded, but only for a moment. "You really don't know, do you?"

"I don't know what?"

Casto sighed. "I should've known. I mean, you don't know anything about good wine either. I'd better show you."

He got up to fetch the trousers Renaldo had hung over his bed as a constant reminder of Casto's wrongdoing, and slipped into the humiliating piece of cloth.

Renaldo started gaping again. "Holy Mothers! I didn't know that! I mean, I've heard stories about such silk, but I'd have never guessed that I was actually holding it in my hands."

His gaze traveled over Casto's lower half with barely concealed hunger. Naked, the young man would have been a lot more decent than with the cloth he was wearing. The blue silk was like a second skin, caressing his body, sketching every muscle and, of course, his penis, in glorious detail. It was no wonder the young man had resented the gift so much.

Casto's voice was soft. "It's very rare for such a piece to make the journey from the Eastern Kingdoms into the West. My father was once lucky enough to get his hands on a panel of this silk. He made a fortune with that alone. The kings of the East are very avaricious when it comes to trading this silk. It's usually exclusively reserved for the dresses of favorite concubines and slaves in the harems of the ruling class. Whoever was meant to wear these trousers must have been held in high regard by their master or mistress. I mean, it's not only the silk—the belt is made of solid gold."

"It really is very charming. But you don't have to wear this. Please believe me when I tell you I didn't have a clue what it really was."

Casto lowered his gaze. His voice was still soft, almost hesitant, as if he could not believe what he was saying.

"I believe you, Barbarian, and I do apologize for my reaction. I thought you wanted to humiliate me on purpose."

"Casto." Renaldo's voice was soothing. "You know the laws of the Pack protect you. I'll never ask anything of you that you aren't willing to give—at least when it comes to matters of the bed. The decision of what is to happen with your body, whom you grant the honor of touching it, is yours alone."

Casto looked up. "I've never thought I would ever say this, but I thank you, Barbarian."

Renaldo grinned.

"You'll have to thank me for a lot more in a second. I hereby annul your punishment. From now on, you can go back to eating as much as you want and wearing whatever you fancy."

Casto bowed graciously. "How very kind of you, Barbarian."

It was not entirely clear how seriously Casto meant his thanks, but Renaldo was in too good a mood to pick another fight, so they spent the rest of the day in rare domestic harmony.

"Is LORD Renaldo here?"

A young man with short-cropped light brown hair and laughing blue-green eyes peeked into the tent. He was about Casto's age, perhaps one or two years older. Like most people in the camp, due to the heat he was only wearing light trousers made of linen, and simple leather boots. He was very brawny. Casto could tell he was used to tough manual labor. As he looked closer, he detected a web of fine, thin white lines covering the young man's body like a spider's web. At some point in his life, he must have endured terrible things. On his arms were a couple of fresher, darker scars like tiny dots, perhaps caused by flying sparks.

He offered Casto his hand. "I'm Sic. My master, Lord Noran, sent me to return some jewelry to Lord Renaldo."

It was difficult not to be touched by the young man's warmhearted openness. Contrary to his usual behavior, Casto returned the smile. "I'm Casto. The Barbarian isn't here at the moment. I don't know when he'll return. Ever since Arana fell, I don't see him too often."

"That's okay. I'm allowed to give the item to you." Sic gave Casto a small box. "Everything is repaired. My master hopes Lord Renaldo will be pleased."

"I'll tell him."

The young smith was about to leave, but at the entrance of the tent he turned around again, his laughing eyes sparkling with curiosity. "Did you really throw Lord Kalad off his horse?"

Upon hearing Sic's tone, a mixture of awe, admiration, and a hint of horror, Casto had to laugh.

"Yes, I did. Even twice, counting our first meeting when I was taken prisoner."

"And you weren't punished?"

"No. Since it was he who challenged me. Besides, Lord Kalad is a man of honor who can own up to being defeated, although I would never tell him that to his face."

Sic laughed, a comforting, warm sound that hit Casto hard. He couldn't remember the last time somebody had laughed with him.

Before an uncomfortable silence could grow between them, Sic began babbling. "You've given the gossip in the camp quite the fuel. Nobody has managed to put up with Lord Renaldo as long as you have."

Casto furrowed his brow. "What does that mean? I've been with him for barely two months."

"Which makes you the all-time winner. Compared to your predecessors, you already have endured a lifetime. As far as I understand, the prize was lost this time."

"What prize? What are you talking about?"

"Oh, you don't know?"

"What should I know?"

Casto was starting to lose his patience. Sic seemed to sense this, because he hurried to explain things.

"There is always some betting going on here in the camp. It's like a national sport. And everyone loves to bet on Lord Renaldo's actions because he's so incredibly unpredictable. When he won you, everybody with enough money placed their bet about when he would sell you. Last week the bet ran out and you're still here."

"So nobody won. What happens with the money?"

Sic grinned. "It sits there mocking them all. No, it'll be the basis for the next bet, which makes it all the more attractive."

"You barbarians sure are an interesting people."

Sic bowed, still laughing. "I'm glad I could entertain you a little. But now I have to go. My master doesn't like me being lazy." He winked at Casto. "I'm curious how many bets will be lost because of you in the future."

He left the tent, and Casto, who was brooding over their conversation.

Casto had already mused upon the reasons a warlord as powerful as the Angel of Death did not have any personal slaves in his tent. All the necessary work was done by servants Casto rarely saw. He could verify that Renaldo was not easy to deal with at any time, but he wasn't capricious enough to be a hopeless case.

While Casto was still deep in thought, Renaldo entered the tent. "Casto! You're already here? What a fortunate coincidence. Come with me."

In silence, Casto followed the Barbarian. Renaldo led him through the camp to the store tents.

"Where are we going?"

"I could tell you that this is a secret, but since my last attempt to surprise you was such an epic failure, I'll play with open cards. Arana has fallen, so we're going to leave in a few days. The big packing has already started. Before that, I want to give you a present, and to avoid another argument like the one before, I've decided to let you choose."

Casto lifted an eyebrow. He hated to admit it, but it was fun when Renaldo interacted with him in such a relaxed manner. "Where's your sense of adventure?"

Renaldo broke out in roaring laughter. "You probably won't believe me, but since you've come here, I've had enough adventure. I thought I'd try boredom for a change."

"A barbarian longing for boredom? You never cease to surprise me."

Still grinning broadly, Renaldo led Casto into one of the tents. Inside, various lamps cast their warm shine on rows of trunks, boxes, and rolls of fabric. Renaldo made a sweeping gesture.

"Feel free to take whatever you like."

Casto stared at him in disbelief. "Are you serious? Whatever I want?"

"Of course. I'm sure it's better than anything I can come up with."

"You might be right about that, Barbarian."

Renaldo monitored every movement as his slave wandered along the rows of stolen goods. He was curious about what his capricious prisoner would choose. The trunks with the jewelry were left untouched and the crates with elaborate clothes were discarded as well. Casto strolled past boxes filled with shoes made of the finest leather, and he ignored all the other riches Renaldo knew any other slave would have homed in on like a hungry vulture to some carrion.

Not that such behavior affronted Renaldo—he was way too realistic for that. He knew very well that a slave lived in a world defined by possession. The slave was nothing but merchandise that could be sold or bartered at any time. Jewelry and other trumpery were proof of the unwavering affection of an owner, cementing the possession's status. Renaldo himself never failed to give his slaves regular feedback of their worth in the form of little presents. This helped to maintain stability among the servants. Although Renaldo was sure Casto understood this concept, he neglected the practice—a fact that made him all the more interesting in the eyes of Renaldo.

After about an hour of thorough searching through the vast amount of goods piled in the tent, the young man finally found what he wanted. He returned to Renaldo with two books in his hands.

"I'll take these two. Thank you, Barbarian."

Although he had anticipated an exceptional choice, Renaldo was still dumbfounded. "You're surrounded by such riches, and you choose two books?"

A smile of genuine joy lit up Casto's noble features. "Not just some books. This one is the poems of Brosilanus the Elder, and this one is a collection of fairy tales I haven't read since I was a child. Both carry warm memories, which makes them the most precious items in here."

Renaldo smiled. It was the first time Casto had allowed him a glimpse of his inner thoughts. Wisely, he refrained from digging any further.

"Then so be it. I've noticed that your breeches are falling apart. Let's see if we can find some replacement. The way back into the Valley is long."

At the mention of the Valley, a shadow crossed Casto's features, but he caught himself. And the Barbarian was right—his breeches had expired some time ago.

THE VALLEY

1. BEGINNINGS

THE JOURNEY back to the Barbarian's home was tiresome and boring. The army itself was quite nimble despite its numbers, mostly due to the superhuman discipline carried out by all the mercenaries. What hindered the progress were the freshly caught slaves and the heavy carts with the booty. Casto more than once played with the image of those wretched things going up in flames. It would have made the journey that much faster.

Their pace slightly increased after they had sold the slaves in Eliam, a small town east of the Umman. The never-ending whimpering and wailing had been grating on Casto's nerves. He did not spare any sympathy for people who gave in to self-pity instead of changing an unwanted situation with their own strength. He himself thought more than once that it would be easy to escape during the trip, but unfortunately Renaldo had been right: he was a man of honor. He could hardly do less than the Barbarian, who stuck to their agreement down to the last letter. Nobody, not even Renaldo himself or his brother, had tried to get close to Lys. As much as Casto resented it, Renaldo, too, was a man of his word.

Although it was not fall yet, it got chillier the farther north they went. Casto was not used to defending his body against the cold; he came from a country where even the winters were so warm people could still go out in short-sleeved tunics in the evenings. He reacted to this unfamiliar weather with an even worse temper than usual, which finally caused Renaldo to get him a complete new outfit: boots, lined with the silky hides of snow rabbits; warm underwear made from the finest wool; and a coat heavy with the winter fur of mountain deer. Equipped like this, Casto was able to bear the unfamiliar weather and wonder about the barbarians who still went around with their chests naked.

Only Aegid and Kalad had some sympathy for him. Both warriors were clad in thick fur similar to Casto's and even helped him sometimes when the teasing from Renaldo got too much. Not that Casto could not defend himself, but it was nice to know that he was not alone in his cold-induced misery—although he still felt a chill down his spine whenever he looked at Aegid. He knew he was being silly. If anything, the gigantic warrior was softer and more in control of himself than his lively, lethal brother, but the white hair, the seemingly blind eyes, and the tattoos that snaked under Aegid's dark skin like some kind of obnoxious disease touched a part of Casto's soul he wanted to ignore.

After almost six weeks on the road, they finally reached the Valley. The closer they got to the mountains, the narrower their path became. Casto could not shake a growing feeling of confinement while the wide-open plains slowly turned from hilly to mountainous. The massive walls of stone seemed to crush him, and more than once Casto had to suppress the urge to turn around and flee back to more open space. He hated every form of physical restraint, and every step taking them deeper into the mountains fed his unease.

The Valley itself was well hidden. To get there, the convoy had to pass a ravine that opened into a small clearing. A guardhouse made from massive stone protected the entrance to the Valley. The passage was narrow enough to make it possible for even a few men to defend easily. The walls of the small fortress were thick and without ornament, reduced solely to its grim purpose, making it even more intimidating. Casto could vividly imagine how the view of this hostile dwelling alone could make potential intruders back off.

After passing this deadly chokepoint, the way in front of the wanderer quickly widened and became inviting. The Valley was basically a big cauldron, surrounded on all sides by high mountains whose steep and barren flanks prevented surprise attacks from even the most adventurous enemies.

Since fall had by now claimed the world, the trees in the Valley had colored their leaves in shades of gold and red, welcoming the army with an explosion of tints. As far as the eye could reach, small hills alternated with forests full of deer and fields golden with wheat.

The rich beauty, in stark contrast to the surrounding rocks, reminded Casto of a clam protecting the precious pearl within by means of a hard, unwavering exterior. He estimated it would take a horse about five days to go around the basin once. The place was the ultimate hideout, since it provided everything an army of mercenaries needed: protection from enemies, enough space to accommodate everybody, and fertile soil to grow food. The Valley was some kind of paradise, created for the sole purpose of protecting and feeding those living in it.

Their way led them directly into the heart of the cauldron where the main house and great hall were seated on a rise. Both buildings were made from the same massive stone as the guardhouse at the entrance, and they clearly were some of the oldest houses around. The other compounds had been built with reddish bricks that looked sturdy enough but were far less intimidating. Casto's trained eye told him that the architects of this place had been very capable, with a preference for utility. Nowhere could he find the needless ornamentation, statues, or richly decorated fountains that towns usually displayed. Despite the spartan exteriors, the buildings exuded a certain charm that managed to intrigue him.

South from the main house was a large square building that Casto identified with no small amount of surprise as a bathing house. The mercenaries' compounds and the barracks of the slaves were scattered around it. The stables and the smithy formed two additional central points in the otherwise seemingly chaotic scheme.

On the other side of the hill were even more houses—some small like huts, while others resembled the more mansion-like buildings of rich farmers.

Later Casto found out that each mercenary was allowed to build the kind of house they preferred. Sometimes they would form groups to build spacious housing, while others went for smaller accommodation alone. The personal slaves usually lived with their masters in the same house, those entrusted with important tasks had their own lodgings, and the others stayed in the barracks. The barracks were quite spacious, meticulously clean, and pleasant to live in.

While Casto was taking in all these new impressions, he had to change his preconceived ideas about the mercenaries more than once.

The rooms of the two leaders and their counselors were in the main building, together with a huge kitchen. Casto was impressed by all the luxury he found so far away from civilization. The Barbarian's quarters were spacious, and the ironclad door at the entrance opened right into the main room. Three unobtrusive passages branched off the room, one leading to a smaller room that became Casto's sleeping place. The second led to Renaldo's generous bedroom, but the third passage opened into a world of wonders.

The bathroom was about as big as the main room, with a pool a little more than one and a half paces long and almost as broad. A golden spigot in the form of a fish constantly provided fresh water into the blue marble basin. Two stone lounges were embedded in the water, just waiting for somebody to relax on them. At the front end of the room was a washbasin carved from the same material. The taps and the big mirror hanging on the wall were richly embellished with golden ornaments. The floor and walls were of expensive white marble, with frescoes showing the creation of the world by Ana-Isara and her sister, Ana-Aruna. The ceiling was arched and hewn from the same blue marble as the pool, but hundreds of diamonds had been embedded into the stone. Just one candle was enough to turn the whole room into a fiery explosion of light. Never before had Casto laid eyes on something so splendid without it being vulgar at the same time. The design of the ceiling was perfect and existed solely to serve the beauty it created.

Casto loved the bathroom and enjoyed spending time there, unable to get enough of the intricate design. Renaldo was wise enough to let his slave be. Indeed, he was happy that the shrewd young man was so openly fascinated by a place under the control of his master.

SINCE ESCAPE over the mountains was impossible, Casto was allowed to roam the entire Valley freely. As soon as possible, he used this concession to get a feel for his surroundings. Casto and Lys quickly decided that it would be quite easy to leave the Valley despite the guards—human and beasts alike—but Lys also suggested that it would not be a bad idea to spend the winter there. They had heard stories about how extreme the weather could be in the North. The Valley was safe; none of those who were still hunting Casto would dare to come here. Casto and Lys had yet to experience how dreadful the winters could be in the North, and it would be a wise move to get accustomed to the weather before leaving the Valley for good.

At the northern end of their new home, Casto found a small lake fed by the same subterranean stream that provided the water for all the wells in the Valley. It was a calm, tranquil area that Casto immediately fell in love with. His instincts told him there was no more peaceful place in the whole world, and he was curious about the secrets slumbering in the impenetrable depths of the shimmering waves.

Close by, they found a small plateau, which no ordinary horse and only a few people would be able to reach. Where the plateau ended at a steep stone wall, they discovered a narrow cave in which Casto hid some clothes and the weapons he had used when he was riding with the caravan. It had not been difficult to get his hands on them, since they were inferior to the quality the barbarians were used to. Nobody cared about such mediocre equipment, but Casto knew that should they leave the Valley, these items would come in handy.

The plan itself was easy. The biggest danger came from the wolves, with their superior sense of smell, but not even the fine noses of the predators would be able to follow a trail laid during a storm. That was the heart of their plan: that Lys would call a powerful thunderstorm that would disguise their escape. Before their persecutors would be able to follow them, they would already be far away, and the Barbarian could go and find himself a new slave to humiliate.

Casto was looking forward to the day when he would leave Renaldo. His only regret was that he would not be able to see Renaldo's sour face once he realized his slave was gone for good.

When the first storms of fall shook the trees in the Valley, Casto was already better acquainted with the forests and meadows than most of the mercenaries. Although he would never admit it, he even felt at ease. He liked working with the horses, and the regular fights with his master held their own—sometimes tiring—charm.

In the rare relaxed moments they spent together, Casto learned to appreciate Renaldo's sense of humor and his intelligence. And even if he did not like it, he found it harder and harder to view the Barbarian as a cold-hearted killing machine who would do anything for the right amount of gold.

CURIOUS, THE demon watched the world the goddesses had created out of chaos and magic. He was a child of the same chaos, born on the other side of reality, a place where time held no power. Nothing alive could endure here or even take solid form. The demon himself was nothing more than an idea, a possibility that could never become real—*at least not* inside the chaos. But there in the orderly world of the goddesses, where time reigned, things were different. Suddenly everything inside him was longing for a solid form, but without knowing what it was that he was craving.

The demon did not know what had brought him here. Something—a strange, powerful call—had guided him to this place, and he could still feel the echoes of it inside. Something was luring him in, but without a suitable body, he was not able to follow the call into that world so full of strange rules.

The demon gave in. Without knowing what would happen, he submitted to the laws of the new, unknown place. Everything he could be flowed into the form closest to what he truly was. His perception changed again, and suddenly he felt an insuppressible urge to run.

Before he had even learned the true extent of his powers, the new Emperor of the Storms defeated his first thunderstorm.

CASTO SPENT quite a lot of time with Lady Noemi, a woman he admired deeply for her gift and knowledge.

Since they had come back to the Valley, Lady Hulda had started to join them on a regular basis. The sensual woman was married to Lord Wolfstan, the armorer. She was a trained killer, the mother superior of an order of assassins, and Casto had already decided to never provoke her wrath. Neither the beautiful face, with the noble features and long golden-blonde hair that made her look like a court lady, nor the motherly charisma could hide the fact that this woman was merciless when it came to dealing with her enemies. Luckily for Casto, she wasn't able to withstand his perfect manners and well-trained charm that made all their meetings enjoyable and worthwhile.

Following his well-honed instincts, Casto started to deepen his relationship with the two women, not only because he liked spending time with them, but because he knew they were among the most powerful allies he could choose in the Valley. It had been easy for him to see through the power structures within the Pack, although his observations did not make sense sometimes.

Canubis and Renaldo were absolute rulers whose will was indisputable. Casto could not understand why those two powerful men would bend to the laws of the Pack, but they did. Where Casto came from, laws were more like guidelines, always negotiable, especially when enough money was involved. The strict code of honor among the mercenaries was as immovable as the mountains surrounding the Valley. Those rules, carved in stone, made any gamble for power almost completely futile and contributed to stability within the ranks of the warriors.

There was a close circle of counselors around Renaldo and Canubis, consisting of the Ladies Noemi, Hulda, and Cornelia—who was some kind of caretaker for the whole Valley. Wolfstan, the armorer; Noran, the master smith; Bantu, Cornelia's brother and head of the library; as well as Aegid and Kalad, completed this illustrious circle. Among them, Hulda was the most influential, closely followed by Cornelia. Noemi did command great power, but she was always willing to bow to her husband's will without hesitation. Sometimes it seemed as if her influence filled her with horror. Hulda, on the other hand, carried her authority with the natural countenance of those who had been born and raised to be leaders.

Casto's relationship with the other slaves was bad. Those who were not jealous of his privileged status were disgusted by his high-handed nature. Sic was the only one who talked to him freely, but the young smith was always busy running errands for his intimidating master and had no free time on his hands to deepen their relationship. Casto was not really sad about it. He had learned the hard way not to trust people easily. He was able to deal with the animosity and hatred of the slaves— they were emotions he could understand, that he had grown up with, and that he could handle easily. Affection and loyalty could change, but hatred usually persevered. Most of the slaves avoided him anyway, and the ones he had to deal with because of the horses only talked about the necessary things with him. Because of that, he was surprised when one day a female slave approached him on her own.

Casto was busy preparing Ghost for training when her voice engulfed him coldly. Her tone caused the hair on his neck to rise. Something about her was deeply suspicious, but he could not exactly say what it was.

"You think you're special because the god has chosen you, but believe me, you're as ordinary as dirt."

Already deeply annoyed, Casto turned around to face the woman. He did not want to have a conversation like this. "I haven't been chosen by anybody. Leave me alone."

The woman laughed. She was beautiful in a rough way, with long, thick lashes shadowing her golden eyes, a broad mouth, and a wild mass of brown curls. "You don't even know who he really is, and yet you're allowed to share his rooms."

Slowly, it dawned on Casto that she was talking about Renaldo.

"He's not a god, but a damn barbarian who's keeping me against my will. And now leave me alone, I've got work to do."

"You dispraise the god! You abuse his name! Why is he keeping you when no one else can satisfy him?"

Before Casto could answer, Renaldo's voice rang out behind the woman.

The Angel of Death was obviously angry. "Because unlike you, he's not completely insane, Amelia." Renaldo's gray eyes turned to Casto. "Go and start your training. I'm taking care of this."

For a change, Casto obeyed without giving any back talk. He was grateful to escape from the crazy female's presence. The last thing he saw before he left the stables with Ghost trailing behind him was Amelia, who knelt in front of the Angel of Death. Among the slaves, Renaldo was renowned for being a merciless, relentless master, whose name alone commanded fear and horror. Casto could not verify the rumors—to him the Barbarian always showed lenience—but he could easily imagine from where the fear stemmed. When Renaldo got angry, the air around him seemed to boil.

THAT EVENING, Renaldo apologized for the incident.

"I'm sorry that she caused you trouble. She had strict orders not to come close to you, but she lives in her own world."

"I've noticed as much. In that world, you seem to be a god." Casto did not even try to keep the derision from his voice.

"Oh, that's the truth. I'm your god as well, if you must know." Renaldo sounded casual, but his gaze was glued to his slave.

Casto snorted. "You are neither my lord and master nor anybody's god. You're a barbarian, a mercenary who conquers cities for money and slaughters people on the command of the highest bidder."

Renaldo got up abruptly. He had simply intended to provoke Casto a little bit and was surprised at his angry response. It wasn't the first time he'd had to face disbelief regarding his origin, but for some reason, he wanted Casto to acknowledge him.

He sounded strained. "You can believe me, slave. Canubis and I are gods. Or rather demigods, at the moment, but that is sure to change. We've been living for a long time on this world and yes, we conquer, maraud, and kill. We're gods of war."

Casto rolled his eyes derisively. "Please stop before this becomes even more ridiculous than it already is. Gods don't exist. They're merely stories to lead the dumb ones on."

"I take it you don't believe in the Mothers?"

Casto pretended to suppress laughter. "Two women creating the universe from nothing? No, not really. What kind of mothers would allow so much injustice in this world?"

"Be careful, Casto, you're walking on thin ice."

Renaldo's tone told Casto that the Barbarian was only a few heartbeats away from snapping. But Casto was irritated as well, which was why he kept on bickering. He tried to sound as challenging as possible with his next words. "Don't tell me you truly believe in such nonsense? And if you do, what makes you think you're a god as well?"

Roaring with fury, Renaldo grabbed Casto's upper arms, lifted him up, and pressed him against the wall. His slave's derogative attitude made him angrier than he had ever thought possible. "You're talking about my mothers!"

"Let go of me, Barbarian!"

"Apologize this minute!"

"Never."

Breathing heavily, they stared at each other. Gray eyes bored into blue ones, trying to find a way in, to discover a weakness. The two men were so close that each could practically smell the other's fury. Time seemed to stutter, a singeing heat started spreading between them, and then their lips began to move.

When the Barbarian's tongue entered his mouth, Casto could not suppress a sigh of satisfaction. It was his first kiss, the first time he had ever allowed somebody to come close enough to affect him. His heart beat loud from excitement and fear, and made Casto worry it could reveal his conflicting emotions. Although he had not been raised in prudery—quite the contrary, in fact—Casto had no experience with intimacy. It was against his suspicious nature to give in to a partner in the way one had to when entering the bed, but the moment their lips touched, he realized how much he had longed for this. The sensations swamping his body all of a sudden were so overwhelming, he did not know how to react to them. A blazing fire seemed to burn his nerves; everything inside him longed for something he could not grasp with his mind. Insecure and desperate, he looked for guidance and help in the only person who could give him both—the Barbarian who had made him his property.

Renaldo could not believe it. Just one simple kiss, but it was more intense than anything he had experienced so far. He could barely remember a night that had not been made interesting by at least one warm, willing body in his bed and he prided himself in being so skillful they all had fallen for him. Only since he had won Casto had the endless stream of sex partners ceased. Instinctively, the Angel of Death had realized that the blond man was special, a treasure he had to carefully keep. The ecstasy now overwhelming his entire body confirmed this assumption and was the reward for his abstinence.

Casto's lips were soft, and he offered his mouth like a sacrifice. His hands caressed Renaldo's back helplessly, arousing him even more. Renaldo could feel a fog of red-hot lust obscuring his senses. All he wanted was to finally possess this beautiful young man—to deepen the wonderful feeling he got from completely subjugating him. Without thinking, he ripped Casto's clothes off, lifted him up, and carried him to the bed, not once losing contact with his lips. It was the sweetest obsession, and he was afraid it would wither should he stop kissing him for even a second.

Like a man about to drown, Casto clung to his master. The Barbarian's lust overwhelmed his senses, made him helpless, and at the same time prepared him for something he could not control, which he should have been afraid of. A part of him wanted to escape, wanted to prevent this loss of himself, but Renaldo's hands were everywhere and caressed and inflamed him to the point where all thoughts dissipated in ecstasy. Renaldo took Casto in his hands while he came, panting heavily.

Made greedy by this promising reaction to his ministrations, Renaldo turned Casto around, searching with his index finger for the hole. It was tighter than he had anticipated and a tiny voice in the back of his mind tried to focus his attention on this fact, but it was winked out by the feral lust burning inside him. Barely able to restrain his need, he tried to insert a second finger in order to prepare Casto. A pained whimper pierced through the red fog obscuring Renaldo's senses. With the last vestiges of control he possessed, he reached for a small vial of oil kept beside his bed for exactly this reason. The scented oil trickled down Casto's butt crack and Renaldo used it to loosen the young man. The sounds of pain quickly turned into groans, inviting Renaldo to finally claim his property. His vision hazy from lust, he opened Casto's buttocks; his penis, big and hard, started sliding into him. Heaving and blinded by lust, Casto arched his back upward, welcoming his master's weapon. Although he still felt a last shred of resentment, Casto knew he had no chance to deny the Barbarian's will, not when his whole body longed to be touched by him.

To his surprise, there was no pain, only the uncomfortable feeling of being stretched in a place where he had never been touched before. Renaldo was huge and Casto felt as if he had been completely stuffed. When the Barbarian started to lunge into him with long, powerful thrusts, it took some time before his discomfort was replaced by lust. Once the fire started to blaze again, Casto felt as if his entire being drowned in the heat. There was no room for anguish or hatred, all that counted was this hungry beast inside, demanding to be sated. He had to receive the Barbarian, his hands, lips and tongue, as well as his heat, otherwise he would die right then.

Renaldo's hands were fastened to Casto's hips in an unrelenting grip; he took Casto with increasing speed, trying desperately to feed the beast, to soothe his urges. And then it was like a wave crashing down on both of them, lifting them to the greatest heights and releasing them happy, yet still longing for more. The most primitive and feral part of them had taken over, forcing them on.

Two more times, Renaldo led Casto to the utmost pleasure, finding relief deep inside Casto's body. Panting, they lay on the bed, still connected most intimately—the demigod on top of his slave, his lips buried in Casto's hair.

Renaldo inhaled the young man's scent deeply while his senses slowly returned to him. Never in his whole long life had he experienced something like this, had a simple act inflamed him so thoroughly and burned him to ashes so completely. He felt as if he had understood for the first time what it meant to be one with somebody else. He hoisted himself up carefully and retreated slowly from Casto's body. Casto moaned, whether in protest or for other reasons, Renaldo could not tell. He turned Casto around as if he were made of glass. The blue eyes connected, reluctant yet sated, with his own.

"Is everything all right, Casto? Did I hurt you?"

The young man furrowed his brows. "I don't know." He hesitated. "Doesn't seem bad."

"Wait here."

Renaldo kissed him on the forehead, then went to the bath. He returned with a bowl of water and a sponge. "Turn sideways."

Without protest, Casto obeyed. He was too tired and confused by what had just happened to resist. He flinched slightly when the Barbarian started washing him with the warm water.

Renaldo's voice was soft. "You're still twitching, Casto. Did I overdo it?"

There was a moment of heavy silence, interrupted by Renaldo's now-horrified voice. "Don't tell me this was your first time?"

Casto's silence was answer enough.

Renaldo felt guilt overwhelming him. He knew he had not forced Casto, but in his greed to finally possess him, he had been too brutal, too demanding. He, who had always been so proud of his skills as a lover, hadn't even noticed that it had been Casto's first time. No, he had noticed but decided to ignore it because of his own uncontrollable urges.

The unusual obedience from his slave only enhanced his shame. "Holy mothers, Casto! I'm so sorry. I didn't know. I thought you....

You're always so self-confident. I didn't even think of the possibility that you could be a virgin. Please, forgive me."

Casto turned around. It was hard to read his expression—obviously he didn't know what to make of the situation. "What is there to forgive, Barbarian? I wanted it as much as you did and you can be sure, I enjoyed it—at least halfway through. A little discomfort is a small price to pay for the ecstasy I experienced, and only to be expected. You were a little rough, though. For somebody who claims to be more than a thousand years old, your technique surely sucks." Casto's voice was firm when he lodged these insults, so at least he did not seem to regret what had happened. Renaldo was grateful for it.

"You're very generous, Casto. And I do apologize for my poor performance. It was shameful indeed. The first time should be special. Not a fast, brutal pairing without any ceremony. I took that from you."

Casto smiled. Seeing Renaldo so humble tickled his fancy. Sensing that he had the upper hand at the moment, he decided to take things a little further. "I'm willing to forgive you, Barbarian. Perhaps it was better that I didn't have time to think. Otherwise I might have refused." The smile turned into a challenging grin when he saw hope and relief blossoming in Renaldo's features. Time to find out what the Barbarian was made of. "And about the ceremony—you can show me now. Needless to say, I do expect something that blows my mind." Renaldo's gray eyes displayed his hunger openly, and Casto averted his gaze. He could feel the heat rushing back into his body, and for a heartbeat, he regretted his foolish challenge.

"Are you sure?"

The fire was already blazing again, burning every coherent thought to ashes. "Yes." It was no more than a whisper, and all Casto could muster when confronted with Renaldo's pure lust.

With a satisfied smile, Renaldo drank in the details of the naked, trembling body that had just been offered to him. "I promise I'm going to give you some real love now."

Renaldo bent forward; gently his lips engulfed Casto's own. He took his time savoring the young man's mouth, although every fiber in his body screamed to possess and subjugate him again. Because he had messed up before, it was his duty to make it better this time. He caressed

Casto's soft skin, followed the supple lines of the muscles, and made him moan with lust.

Touching Casto was like playing a rare, exquisite instrument. Casto reacted to his master's attentions with more sensitivity than Renaldo would have expected, given his usual stubborn attitude. Now Casto lifted his hips in silent invitation, his fingers clinging to the fur bedcover. Renaldo intensified his assault; his tongue penetrated Casto's mouth deeply, toying with him. With a shrill cry, Casto climaxed again. Then he turned around, offered himself in all his naked glory. His trembling buttocks were almost more than Renaldo could take. He grabbed Casto's hips, and his penis started to caress the twitching circle.

The young man made a sound deep in his throat, whimpering as if he could not believe what he was doing. Then he started to beg, his voice hoarse. "Please. Please take me. I want it."

Renaldo clenched his teeth. He started to kiss Casto's nape while teasing him first with one, then two fingers. Moaning, Casto matched his rhythm and gave in to the sensations his master was inducing. He climaxed again, trembling all over, his fists helplessly digging into soft fur. Seeing Casto so intoxicated and lost in his lust excited Renaldo to the point where he started to lose control again. He withdrew his fingers, ready to take what was exclusively his.

"I'm begging you, Barbarian. Please don't stop!" Casto had almost screamed those words, his back arched and his inner muscles clamped down tightly, as if he intended to never let go of Renaldo again.

Renaldo growled. He knew he was losing it again. A last vestige of the hard-won control, which never left him entirely these days, prohibited killing a lover with his lust, but he took Casto hard—harder than he normally would have—and he didn't stop. As a demigod, his stamina was inexhaustible—a fact he always had to keep in mind when pairing with humans, but Casto was more determined than he thought possible.

Until long after midnight, Casto sated his master's hunger and still begged for more. Given the young man's normal detachment, Renaldo could only guess at what hidden desires he had unleashed.

Renaldo only stopped when Casto lay motionless between the furs, unable to even turn around on his own. He picked him up, carried him to the bath, and carefully placed him in the water. Then he followed Casto into the bath, washed him thoroughly, and took him back to bed.

Too tired to resist, Casto allowed Renaldo to draw him close and engulf him protectively with his muscular arms.

"Go to sleep now, Casto. It's been a long night."

Casto wanted to answer, but at that moment fatigue overwhelmed him and his eyes closed of their own accord. He was completely relaxed. With a sigh, he snuggled closer to Renaldo, a satisfied smile played around his lips for a moment, and then he fell asleep.

Renaldo took some time to watch Casto's surprisingly peaceful expression while sleeping. Then he, too, lay back to rest.

It was to be the first night since his escape from Ummana that Casto was not woken by a nightmare.

2. ANTAGONISM

"SO YOU finally did it." Canubis watched his brother from the side. They were sitting in the sauna, sweat pouring down their naked bodies in little streams.

"Yes."

Such a short answer was atypical for Renaldo, which made his brother suspicious. "It wasn't good?"

Renaldo's unreadable eyes were clouded. "It was better than anything I've ever experienced."

"That's not how it sounds."

Renaldo's gaze was unsteady. He still felt guilt for having been so brutal, and Canubis was close enough to him to pick up on it. "Brother, he was a virgin. I took him pretty hard. We were both angry and agitated. I didn't know and he was so—willing and demanding."

"Is he angry?"

As always, Canubis cut to the chase. Renaldo shook his head.

"No. He even allowed me to take him again. We had our fun. But still—I have problems keeping my cool around him. All I can think about is ripping off his clothes and taking him to bed. I can hardly recognize myself."

"Could it be that you're a little bit in love?"

"Perhaps, but I doubt it. I think it's more carnal, some abnormal infatuation."

Canubis grinned. "Whatever it is, enjoy it, and try not to anger him too much when you end it. I want him in our army, no matter the cost."

"What makes you think I'll end this relationship?"

Canubis's eyebrow went up in mockery. "Please, brother. You always do this. You aren't cut out for being close to anybody for any length of time. Which is also the reason why nobody can bear to stay with you for long. Admittedly, Casto has broken all the records by now, but nobody doubts it'll end soon. Especially now that you've managed to have him in your bed. The bet pool is almost bursting at the seams."

Renaldo's gaze darkened. He knew that the other members of the Pack often bet on his behavior, simply because he was so unpredictable, but he was a little miffed that even his brother took part in it. "You too, traitor?"

"Of course!" Canubis feigned indignation. "By now the pot is worth more than two hundred pieces of gold. But that's no surprise, since it's already the third round."

Now Renaldo was curious. "What have you bet on?"

"First, when you'd sell Casto. That didn't happen, so the next one was about when you'd get him into your bed. That bone, too, was lost. It never took you so long before! The next will be, I guess, when he's had enough of you."

"I don't know if I should be irritated or amused."

"Relax. Should we lose this time as well, the money belongs to you."

Renaldo started grinning, suddenly reconciled. "I almost forgot about that! Go on, bet, and use all your money. All the better for me."

FASCINATED, THE slave watched as her blood trickled into the golden cup the priest had set up in the middle of the crude magical circle. The hissing sound when the droplets hit the metal indicated that the magic was working. Every full moon the two met here, in this far-off shed, to fuel the shrouding spell with new energy. The location was not what she would have called perfect. Although the shed was not in close proximity to the other buildings in the Valley, it was probably only one storm away from destruction, the old, battered wood groaning like an old man when the slightest breeze hit it. But protecting their secret was the most important thing, and so they kept on meeting here, in this potential death trap. They were not the only followers of the Good Mother who had managed to sneak into the Valley, but it was a question of safety not to let anyone know about what they were doing.

Assani met Damon's fanatical gaze. "I'm always surprised how well the spell works, here, in the heart of the Valley."

The priest smiled coldly. "Blood is a powerful fixative. But the main reason is the simplicity of its purpose. It concentrates on the essence. And as long as nobody mentions my name and the spell in one sentence, it's indestructible."

"What would happen if somebody did?"

"The veil would tear immediately and the bastards would know. As much as I resent it, they are the sons of goddesses and therefore they react very sensitively to such things. The spell is like the fog: it clouds the senses but doesn't affect them otherwise. Which is one of the reasons it doesn't require a lot of energy to keep it going. And that's why only the two of us know about it. Makes it less risky."

Assani hesitated. She was not as good with magic as Damon was but knew enough to see the drawback. "The spell clouds your sight."

"Yes, it does. But I know it's there, which makes it easier to work around it. According to the prophecies, she's already here—Renaldo's heart. We only have to find her before him, then we will triumph."

"Do you have any idea who it could be?"

"There are a few females I'm watching closely, but the heart is well protected. It could take years until we find her." Assani sighed. Damon's look grew stern. "It doesn't matter how long it takes. Always remember that the Good Mother will reward us for our hardships."

Assani's features brightened up again. A cruel smile flashed over her lips. "It would be reward enough to see the bastards going down."

"I'm sure the Good Mother appreciates your attitude."

CASTO RACED through the forest on Lys's back, his thoughts in turmoil. He still did not know what to make of the things that had happened the night before. Never before had he felt so good, so sated and in harmony with himself. Sharing Renaldo's bed had given him a feeling of finality and peace, as if lying in the Barbarian's arms were his natural place. Which couldn't be. He hated the Angel of Death! The man had captured him, taken away his precious, hard-earned freedom. He was a barbarian: uncivilized, crude, and common.

While he was still clinging to this litany, another, annoyingly persistent voice kept reminding him that Renaldo was none of those things—quite the contrary. He was intelligent, polite, even caring. Casto regretted that he and Lys could not leave the Valley before spring. Even though the first snow hadn't come yet, it was already promised in the air as a sharp, foreboding smell, warning him not to do anything rash. Escaping now would be a dumb move. He simply had to stay away from the Barbarian. The laws of the Pack stated clearly that Renaldo was not allowed to force him, so all Casto had to do was announce his disinterest. If he didn't want to get into real trouble, he had to keep his distance.

Lys listened to his brother's whirlwind of thoughts but refrained from commenting. He was curious as to when his stubborn rider would admit to himself that he had fallen in love with his captor.

In the evening, Casto entered the Barbarian's rooms, determined not to get lured in again. But Renaldo had only to look at him, and they both were as lost as they had been the night before. Their lust ignited time and again just by feeling each other's hunger, and their longing grew with every time they tried to sate it.

Very soon they established a rhythm that scarcely changed throughout the winter. Every morning Casto woke up, determined to finally get away from Renaldo, to end their relationship. Then the Barbarian would kiss him, which inevitably led to more carnal things. After that, Casto was so angry with himself that he either fled into work or tried his hardest to provoke a fight. The more intense the fight, the more brutal was their reconciliation in the evening. They both liked it hard, and sometimes they would push their quarrels on purpose to fan the flames of their lust.

Their relationship would have been perfunctory if it were not for the moments of tranquility: when Renaldo asked Casto to recite a poem or read a story and they discussed it for hours, or when they started talking about the military techniques described in some of Renaldo's books. In those moments they both were aware of an unspoken harmony between them, an inexplicable bond that connected them but could not be explained.

It was not only Casto who shied away from that bond on a regular basis. Both men fought it unconsciously by provoking the other, fighting over petty things, and drowning it all in their fiery passion.

Thus the winter passed, and Casto rarely thought about escape anymore.

"HELLO CASTO!" Smiling as usual, Sic approached. He carried a linen bag, which gave an occasional clanking sound.

Casto returned the smile. It was impossible not to like Sic, and during the winter he had started to enjoy their brief encounters. Today, too, the young apprentice was in a hurry, so Casto only detained him briefly. "Can you explain to me why everybody is so excited? I feel like I'm trapped in a beehive."

Sic grinned. "It's because of the Spring Ceremony. It'll be held in two days, and everybody is looking forward to it."

"There's a feast?"

"The most important one here in the Valley. Lord Renaldo and Lord Canubis assemble the Emeris and all the warriors to get the blessing of the Mothers for the coming year. Rumor has it they've been doing this ever since they came to the Valley. It's a celebration of life and marks the end of winter. For a slave, it's an honor to be invited."

The odd way Sic phrased the last sentence made Casto suspicious.

"What exactly happens during this feast?"

Sic looked at Casto thoughtfully. Like everybody else in the Valley, he knew Casto shared Renaldo's bed, but Casto showed a reservation bordering on prudery and was eyed with grave suspicion by the extremely laid-back members of the Pack. Being chosen by the powerful Angel of Death was a rare honor that had propelled Casto's status within the strict hierarchy of the slaves.

According to the rules, every slave chosen as a personal servant by the Emeris or one of the two leaders occupied a high position. Casto did not seem to be aware of this—perhaps he was ignoring his standing on purpose. With him, it was always hard to tell, but it was no secret how much he resented being a slave. Casto not knowing anything about the Spring Ceremony only showed how little he cared about the customs in the Valley.

Sic could not suppress a certain glee when he explained matters to the blond man. "It's an orgy! The Mothers love every form of bodily affection, and during the Spring Ceremony their followers express how much they share this notion."

A shade of crimson crept into Casto's cheeks. He had already found out on various occasions how open-minded the inhabitants of the Valley were when it came to bodily contact. The only thing setting them apart from animals in heat was the set of strict rules limiting excesses. Nobody was to be forced, and partners had to be at least sixteen. Otherwise anything went, although it was considered bad style to fool around if you had a fixed partner.

Casto did not know if Sic had a lover, which was why he was interested in whether the young man was going to the feast. "Are you going?"

"No. I'm still a virgin. That's why I'm not allowed there."

Sic looked down, and Casto knew he had touched a sore subject. He regretted his question from the bottom of his heart. "I'm sorry. I didn't mean to pressure you."

"It's okay. You couldn't know. I assume Lord Renaldo hasn't asked you yet?"

"No. And it would be better for him if he didn't."

Casto's menacing tone made Sic shudder. Casto had a very strong personality, and Sic could not help but be fascinated by him. He slung his bag over his shoulder again. "You'd better be nice to your master or else you won't get a present."

"And what is that?"

Sic was already leaving, but he paused by the door. "When a master is satisfied with his slave, then he'll give him a present on the morning after the Spring Ceremony. It's an old tradition. I've heard Lord Renaldo is very generous with his servants."

"Then I might as well give up. The Barbarian and I are always arguing." Casto thought for a moment. Again Sic's tone of voice had alerted him. "What have you gotten so far?"

Sic lowered his gaze again. Obviously, Casto had managed to hit the mark once more. "I haven't gotten anything yet. I'm a bad slave. I'm lazy, clumsy, and tardy. Although Lord Noran saved my life, I'm unable to serve him well. I'm not worthy to receive anything." A sheepish silence grew between them, but when Sic looked up, the laughter was back in his eyes again. "But I'm working hard, and perhaps one day I'll be worthy enough to get a present from my master."

With that, he parted from Casto, who thought about Sic's words for a long time. Sic was definitely neither clumsy nor lazy—on the contrary, he served his master with such devotion it seemed eerie to Casto at times. Especially when he thought how grumpy and short-tempered Lord Noran could be.

He just wanted to know which sin Sic was really paying for.

ON THE eve of the Spring Ceremony, Casto watched the Barbarian getting dressed for the feast. He did not like to admit it, but in his dark blue silk tunic with the gold embroidery, Renaldo looked even better than usual, although that seemed hardly possible. Renaldo had not asked Casto to accompany him, which slightly annoyed Casto. Not that he would have agreed—there was no way that would ever happen—but they did share the same bed every night, so it would have been polite to at least ask, or so Casto thought.

Now Renaldo pecked him on the cheek. "Have a nice evening. Food will be brought later. Only the best, of course. You don't have to wait for me." A suggestive smile crossed his lips.

Casto made a face. "Don't get too full of yourself. I won't get bored. Have fun."

Renaldo completely ignored the ironic tone in Casto's voice. He was looking forward to the feast so much, and he had no intention of letting a petty fight with Casto spoil it. Because of that, his answer was unusually tame. "I will, don't worry."

With that, he left his chambers.

The Spring Ceremony was his favorite feast of the year. He simply loved getting physical together with his brothers-in-arms. Not that he lacked amusement throughout the year—his bed was seldom empty— but on this night, things were different. During the Spring Ceremony, Renaldo didn't feel like the outsider he was, superior to his brothers-in-arms in ability and ancestry, and even cut off from his brother, Canubis, because of his looks and the fire deep within.

Renaldo had gotten used to being recognized for his perfect beauty alone. Only Canubis truly knew him, and even he was sometimes distracted by Renaldo's perfection. Most people would not believe it, but looks like Renaldo's could be a burden as much as they were a blessing. In his case, quite a heavy one, since nobody matched him. Of course, it made things easier as well. Renaldo never lacked for bed partners, but the downside was they only saw his face, never him. Blinded by his perfect facade, they retreated hastily, very often terrified to the bone, when they caught a glimpse of the man behind the mask.

That was one of the reasons Renaldo found Casto so irresistible. His slave was a rare beauty himself and did not let his master's looks fool him. It almost seemed as if Casto might despise him for it.

Once, Renaldo had asked him about it, and Casto's answer had been: "Nobody can be blamed for how they're made. I've seen true monsters hiding behind a glittering exterior, fooling everyone around them, even themselves. The only thing that counts for me is how people act. That's why you can't impress me. You might be pleasing to the eye, but you behave like a barbarian."

A heated argument had followed, which they had finally resolved in bed. Although he had reprimanded Casto for his boldness, Renaldo had been secretly thrilled that his slave did not bother to gape in awe at his master's beauty. A little more respect would have been nice sometimes, but given the choice, Renaldo preferred Casto's brazen attitude.

IN FRONT of the great hall, Renaldo was waiting for his brother and sister-in-law. Canubis was wearing a black tunic with exactly the same embroidery as Renaldo's. Noemi followed her husband and master naked, her body covered in gold dust. Her fiery red hair was intricately braided, and she wore a heavy gold collar with several black diamonds set into it. A thin chain of pure gold ran from the jewelry to her husband's hand. The whole getup was meant to visualize and enhance her status as the heart of the Wolf of War, and she was strong and powerful enough to carry it off with dignity and grace. Renaldo bowed elegantly to his sister-in-law.

"Noemi, you look stunning, as always."

A soft laugh like water bubbles in a brook was his reward. "And as always, you're overdoing it, Renaldo. I think I'm quite acceptable, but I also know that Hulda's going to outdo me just like every year. Not to mention you, my good-looking brother-in-law."

Canubis caressed his heart's cheeks endearingly, his amber eyes so full of love that Renaldo felt a twinge of envy. It was surely an unbelievable feeling to finally regain one's heart. Not for the first time did he ask himself why Ana-Isara had taken this essential part from them. Degrading them to demigods had been only the outcome, definitely not the reason.

His brother's voice was a soft whisper when he spoke to his wife. "For me, you're always the most beautiful, my precious jewel."

Noemi's face reddened slightly. Although she had by now gotten used to being exhibited like a rare and expensive flower at every Spring Ceremony due to her status as Canubis's heart, he still managed to embarrass her. "Stop it with the sweet talk, O husband mine. You don't have to catch me with sugared phrases anymore. I already belong to you."

Renaldo started to laugh. Words like these reminded him that his sister-in-law was far more than just a beautiful face submitting so eagerly to his brother's will. Noemi Amerasu was a powerful witch and the wife of a future god, and even though she hated to show it, a woman with a will of iron. She was capable of influencing her husband's decisions any time she wanted.

Now she took her position three steps behind the brothers, her gaze downcast, a silent signal that she thought it was time to start the feast. Together they entered the decorated hall where their brothers-in-arms, as well as the chosen slaves, were waiting for them.

Like every year, Renaldo was overcome by the mood. On the day of the Spring Ceremony, even the rather loose chains keeping the passions of the warriors in check were forgotten. This night was solely to please the Mothers, a task they all loved to accomplish.

With measured steps, they started their journey toward the high table where the Emeris were already waiting for them. Kalad and Aegid looked positively regal in their dark green tunics, cinched at the waist by belts so white they were almost blinding. Next to them was Noran, dressed in a scarlet gown embellished with the black fur of mountain rabbits. The dark aura that usually surrounded him like a wicked spell was somewhat softened tonight, and the smith, too, was already caught up in the atmosphere of the feast. Between the two high wooden chairs that were Renaldo's and Canubis's seats, Bantu stood with a faint smile on his lips. He was alone, as every year. His sister, Cornelia, never attended the feast, and Renaldo felt anger rise inside him whenever he remembered why. The pain she'd endured had been enough to thoroughly disgust her about the Mothers' gift.

To keep his mind off these dark thoughts, Renaldo let his gaze wander toward Wolfstan and Hulda.

The armorer wore his usual simple clothing, consisting of a woolen tunic dyed in a rich, vibrant brown and leather boots that almost reached his knees. Given the queen who was standing next to him, he did not need any trumpery.

Hulda was simply breathtaking. She was a beautiful woman to begin with: her long, golden hair flowing down her back like silk, her body curved at exactly the right places, her movements as graceful and languid as those of a contented cat. Those obvious blessings were heightened by the arrogant, merciless look in her eyes, which only softened when she turned to her husband, and her body language that screamed louder than words how powerful and ruthless she was—and how much aware she was of her status. She was indeed a queen—a queen of death—and it was always a wise idea to be on her good side.

Renaldo smiled happily. Although their lineup was still missing one Emeris and one heart, it was already mighty impressive. The Good Mother would be nothing but a distasteful memory once they were complete.

When they reached their seats, the excited chatter died down. All activity stopped, and the eyes of everybody fixed on the two demigods. Renaldo and Canubis shared a long look. The admiration, love, and power they received from their followers, as well as the awe and fear coming from the slaves, were heady like a very old wine. And just like every year, the brothers wondered what it would feel like when the energy all those people were emanating would be directed toward them as well. At the moment, that energy still went to their mothers, Ana-Isara and Ana-Aruna, but a time would come when the goddesses left this world, and then the power would be theirs.

With some effort, they regained their focus.

Canubis let his gaze trail over the assembled Pack. "Brothers and sisters, welcome to this year's Spring Ceremony. It has been yet another successful year, although taking Arana was not what I would call a challenging task." He waited a moment until the laughter died away. "But the booty was satisfying, we had only a few, regrettable casualties, and all in all, it was a refreshing exercise. So let us beg the Mothers to bestow their blessings on us for the coming year as well. May all our enterprises bear fruit and our lives prosper!"

The mercenaries roared their approval. The deafening sound echoed through the Valley, accompanied by the howling of the wolves who honored the Mothers in their own way. Now Canubis held up a golden cup Kalad had handed him. He slowly tipped it, and the bloodred wine trickled from the rim to the ground.

"*Blod an Ana-Darasa!*"

"Blood for Ana-Darasa!" The warriors repeated the chant in the dialect of the North, since there was hardly anybody besides Renaldo and Canubis who could still speak the language of the Ancients.

Renaldo took another golden cup from Bantu's hands and stepped next to his brother. "*Muaro an Ana-Isara!*"

"Death for Ana-Isara!"

Together they spoke the next lines. "*Anoro an Ana-Aruna!*"

"Life for Ana-Aruna!"

"*Blod, muaro, anoro!*"

"Blood, death, and life!"

"Ana-Isara, Ana-Aruna, *reana na orono an sem!*"

"Ana-Isara, Ana-Aruna, bestow your blessings on us!"

They repeated the last sentence four times, and every warrior nicked the skin on their hands with a dagger when they reached the end of the chant. Canubis and Renaldo did so as well—nothing deep, just enough to draw a drop of blood that would follow the wine.

Then Canubis smiled broadly. "Let the feast begin!"

With another roar, the warriors started to feast on the splendid food, the delicious wine, the well-groomed slaves, and of course, each other. Renaldo, too, grabbed a female who had just been passing by with an empty plate in her hands. He bent her upper body over the table and exposed the white, soft flesh of her asscheeks. But when he entered her, he immediately felt something was wrong. He missed the usual glamour, the intoxicating lust that normally swept him away the moment he made his first move. To make things worse, he was not able to establish the mental connection to his brothers-in-arms that was the hallmark of the Spring Ceremony. It did not happen on a conscious level and was something none of them could control. Enjoying the orgy together cemented the bonds between the warriors of the Pack and their leaders. It was the annual renewal of the vows they had taken. But now, Renaldo could not even feel Canubis, his own brother. It was as if he had been cut off from the rest of them.

Renaldo looked down on the slave: her eyes were of a boring blue-gray color and her breasts slightly drooping. She was not ugly—during the feast, nobody was—but she was not charming either.

Casto's sparkling blue gaze appeared in his mind, and Renaldo heard Casto's derisive laughter. Enraged that Casto was ruining this special night, Renaldo started taking the woman harder. She whimpered, clinging to him, her ordinary eyes burning with desire. Like everybody else in the hall, she had already fallen prey to the numbing rush that was the trademark of the Spring Ceremony. Slightly annoyed with himself, Renaldo sent her away.

He took another female slave, then two males, then again a female. It was always the same. He was giving his partners pleasure but did not feel any himself. He looked around. Others were enjoying themselves; nobody noticed his discomfort. Only Canubis shot him a questioning look before he returned his attention to the moaning Noemi in his arms.

With a shrug, Renaldo beckoned another slave. It was still two hours till midnight; then he could officially leave the feast. It was the first time he had ever considered this, and it really riled him up.

In Renaldo's chambers, Casto paced up and down. About an hour ago, a slave had brought the promised food, a whole plate of specialties: a refined roast of lamb, a haunch of wild boar, and three generous slices of honey cake. As tempting as the food looked, Casto could not stomach even one bite. The whole time he thought about the Barbarian, picturing him having sex with dozens of slaves and enjoying himself.

For that, he hated Renaldo. Hated him because he could not stand the thought of him pleasuring others; hated him because he was keeping such a tight leash on Casto, forcing him to wander around unable to get the least bit of peace. Casto couldn't believe it, but he was actually jealous! Of the Barbarian.

How low would he have to stoop to finally end this affair? Was Renaldo sleeping with other men? Or did he keep to women? The thoughts circled in his mind until he was desperate enough to try some of the awful wine the Barbarian preferred, but all he got from that was a horrible headache, which did not improve his mood.

He was on the verge of going outside to have a ride with Lys when Renaldo returned. By then, Casto was so angry he no longer cared about manners. "Already back, Barbarian? You must have broken every record, fucking the members of your Pack."

"Shut up."

Renaldo said no more. He took two fast steps. Then hungrily his lips engulfed Casto's.

They honored the Holy Mothers until the sun came up.

DARAN

1. DARAN

FROM HIS hiding place between two stalls, Daran watched the hurly-burly of the marketplace.

On days like this, merchants from cities as far as Medelina and Da'Kara clustered in Kwarl to do business. Among them were also mountain people, who came to get everything they needed and perhaps to sell cattle or other goods. Even for a pickpocket as bad as Daran was, the masses were an invitation to get into the pouches of strangers.

Daran loathed taking other people's money, but if he did not bring home any booty today, his stepfather, Egand, would surely punish him. Unfortunately that man didn't settle for harsh words, he always got physical. Unconsciously, Daran rubbed the almost-faded remnants of the bruises he had gotten the last time Egand had been displeased.

Daran had stopped working as a beggar two years ago, after puberty had hit him hard. Now, at the age of seventeen, he had lost everything remotely childlike, and people did not tend to give money for free to healthy-looking young men. Daran had tried to work in an honest trade, but without any training or recommendations, no master had felt an inclination to take him on.

The one time Egand had tried to work him as a prostitute, Daran had thrown up all over his customer.

Daran had been deeply appalled by the fat old man, who reeked of some terribly sweet perfume and was renowned for paying big money to have the pleasure of robbing young women and men of their virginity. Since he paid very large sums, nobody cared how violently and brutally he acted. Daran's honest reaction had really ruined the customer's day, and Egand had brutally punished Daran for that. The only good thing in the whole incident had been that his career as a whore had ended on that very night.

Egand never stopped nagging about his stepson's uselessness, but even he had to accept that constant complaining did not get him anywhere. After Daran had failed in every other shady profession, he ended up becoming a thief.

He was, under normal circumstances, a nimble young man who showed surprising control of his body, but when he had to take honest people's money, his hands turned to clay. He simply could not do it. Daran had no idea where his debilitating morals came from—he did not know his real father but was pretty sure he was no better than Egand or his mother—but hardly a day went by when he did not curse his scruples from the bottom of his heart.

His wandering gaze stopped at two men inspecting some jewelry on one of the stalls.

These men had caught his eye because their skin color was darker than that of the people living around Kwarl. Their apparel was rich and they were heavily armed with two swords and at least six daggers between them. Warriors, without a doubt. The smaller man wore his hair in dozens of braids that fell to his shoulders. His eyes seemed to sparkle and his mouth moved constantly. His companion was almost two heads taller—one of the biggest men Daran had ever seen. His short hair was white as if he were an old man, and his eyes were a milky blue in stark contrast to his dark skin.

For a moment, Daran thought the man might be blind. His face and hands were covered in tattoos, which seemed to spread like a disease over his skin. The men were not what Daran considered perfect victims—they had way too many weapons on their persons for that—but they fulfilled most of the requirements he had for his "customers." They were not citizens of Kwarl, their body language was relaxed—which made it easier for him to steal from them—and most importantly, they looked rich enough to deal with the loss of some money.

Unobtrusively, he moved in their general direction, even allowing the masses of people to carry him away from his prey before he came back in a semicircle. Around the stall with the jewelry, the crowd was very dense, which made it easy for Daran to press himself against the giant's back and take his wallet. Just when he went to retreat with his booty, an iron grip closed around his wrist.

A deep, not unfriendly voice resounded in his ear. "I think this is mine, little thief."

The warrior had not raised his voice, but Daran tensed involuntarily. If anyone had heard him, Daran's fate was sealed. Luckily, nobody called for the guards, and Daran relaxed a little before facing his next problem. The fist of steel was still holding him, and the two warriors moved toward a narrow side street away from the protection the crowd offered.

Daran pretended to give up. Although every fiber in his body screamed at him to fight against the tight grip, he forced himself to relax. His plan worked. The pressure on his wrist loosened a bit, and Daran did not hesitate. With a quick yank, he freed himself and started to run.

A surprised yell followed him while Daran disappeared into the crowd. As soon as he felt safe, he slowed down. Nothing was more suspicious than somebody moving faster than everybody else. He let the crowd move him to the other end of the market before he sauntered into another side street. With a last, reassuring glance toward the crowd, he vanished into the safety of the twilight.

Again a hand landed on his shoulder.

The same voice as before carried a hint of malice now. "That wasn't too bad, little thief. But try it again, and I'm gonna break your arm, do you hear me?"

Full of panic, Daran stared into the tattooed face in front of him. He wondered how the man had managed to follow him. As if he had read Daran's thoughts, the second warrior enlightened him.

"It wasn't as difficult as you might think. Admittedly, you're fast, but it was pretty obvious that you wanted to get away from us as far as possible. We only had to come around and wait for you here."

Daran gulped. He didn't know what the men wanted from him, but it could not be good. In his panic, he started to plead with them. "Please, let me go. I promise I won't do it again."

The faces of the warriors turned serious. The one with the braids brushed Daran's cheeks with his fingertips. It was only a light touch, like a butterfly's wings, but it sent shivers down his body. He couldn't keep himself from thinking that he wouldn't mind sharing their bed. The image was so disturbing that he felt himself blush like a virgin.

The braided warrior smiled; his gaze was unfathomable. "Of course you won't steal again. My brother and I are going to see to that."

Daran's pulse started to race.

"Please, don't kill me. I'll do anything you ask, anything. But please, let me live!"

"Oh, you will do as we ask, no doubt about that. And you'll even enjoy it." Again the fingers brushed over his face. "Are you hungry?"

The sudden change of topic surprised Daran so much that he answered truthfully. "Yes. I'm starving."

"Then come."

This time, without loosening his grip, the tall warrior led Daran around the market to the best tavern in town.

It was crowded inside, but the waitress seemed to know Daran's captors, because without them saying anything, she opened the door to a small room at the back where they were alone. As soon as they were seated, two big plates of roast meat, a bowl of sauce, a loaf of bread, and two jugs—one of wine and the other water—were placed in front of them. The waitress left again, and Daran was alone with the two intimidating men.

Before his insecurity could rise again, the tall one nodded at him, his voice soft as though he wanted to tame a wild animal. "You can start eating, you know."

Since Daran's last meal had been two days ago, he ate hungrily. Whatever was going to happen next, he would not have to face it on an empty stomach. After he had eaten his fill, the smaller warrior started to talk.

"My name is Kalad. This is my desert brother, Aegid."

"I'm Daran."

A satisfied smile crossed Kalad's lips, as if Daran had just passed a test. "Very well, Daran. Why did you try to steal from us?"

Daran felt his cheeks darken in shame. He could not bring himself to look up from his now-empty plate. There was no lie that could explain his despicable behavior satisfactorily, which was why he settled for the truth.

"It's been some time since I was last able to please my stepfather. I'm not what you might call a gifted thief."

Kalad laughed. "We've noticed that. What else?"

"You seemed as if it wouldn't bother you too much—losing some money, I mean—which is why I chose you." Daran saw the men exchanging a meaningful glance and it made him shiver. "I'm really sorry, you must believe me. But when I get home without any booty today, Egand is going to punish me."

Aegid placed a finger under Daran's chin and forced him to look him in the eyes. "I hope you're not lying to us. We hate lies."

Vigorously, Daran shook his head. He did not want the intimidating men to get any angrier at him than they already were. He made a desperate attempt to soothe them. "No, Master. I would never lie to you. Why should I? I'm at your mercy."

Upon hearing those words, the warriors' eyes lit up. Again, an excitement that terrified him to the bone washed over Daran. What was it about these men that he felt so drawn to them? If anything, he should have been anxious about being held captive by two complete strangers, but that was not the case. It was as if nothing bad could happen to him as long as he was with them. Not that he was not scared, but he was more afraid of Egand than of these two.

"You can relax. This Egand guy isn't going to do anything to you, because you'll be coming with us."

This shocked Daran. He wanted to get up, but Aegid held him down. Aegid's hands were warm, and he did not squeeze harder than necessary, but Daran realized that Aegid could easily increase the pressure and break Daran's arm if he chose to do so. Frightened, Daran stared into those milky blue eyes that seemed to draw him in.

"What do you mean?"

Kalad smiled, but it was not a friendly gesture. Daran felt like a mouse in the paws of a playful cat. "You tried to steal from us. For that, you'll pay dearly. Until we decide that you have repented enough, you'll be our slave."

The blood drained from Daran's face. The feeling of security dissolved like fog in the morning sun. "You can't do that! I'm a free man!"

Aegid shrugged. "You either become our slave or we hand you over to the guards. As far as I know, the punishment for thieving is still the loss of a hand. The decision is yours."

Like an animal driven into a corner, Daran looked for a way out, but his heart told him that he would comply with the warriors' will. Proudly, he lifted his chin. "Where will you take me?"

"We're from the Valley."

Daran bumped his knees on the table in utter shock. "You're living with the gods?"

A thousand terrifying pictures flashed before his eyes. Every story he had ever heard about the Valley and its fearsome inhabitants flitted through his mind, which was already overtaxed by everything that had happened to him today. He felt cold sweat break out on his skin.

Aegid touched his arm in an attempt to soothe him. "Shh. It's okay, little thief. There's no need to be afraid. Whatever you've heard about us is probably exaggerated. We won't hurt you, at least not as long as you are compliant."

Daran looked down; the words had not put him at ease. No wonder those men had been able to capture him so easily. Dumb as he was, he had made the most dangerous of all the people in the market his target. Now it was too late to ponder the mistakes of the past. He had to try to make the best out of the current situation, which, above all, meant staying alive. Obediently he lowered his gaze. "I'll do whatever you ask of me."

"That's good to hear." Kalad patted Daran's upper arm with ill-concealed satisfaction. "We'll ride home tomorrow, but first you need some better clothes. I hope you know how to ride a horse?"

"Not very well, I'm afraid. Why do you ask?"

Kalad raised an eyebrow in amusement. It was obvious that Daran had just made a mistake. "Not that it would be of any interest to you— slave." He accentuated the word in a way that made his new servant blush. "But it's a two-day ride back to the Valley. If you have to walk, it'll take a lot longer."

Daran stayed silent, his gaze still cast downward.

Aegid started to laugh. "What did you think? That we would drag you behind our horses, clad in those ugly rags?"

"The thought had crossed my mind, yes."

Again Kalad touched Daran's arm with his fingertips. His voice was very soft; he wanted to put the young man at ease. "We might be barbarians, but I assure you, we do *not* take pleasure from unnecessary cruelty. You're our slave, and we expect your obedience, but in return we owe you shelter and care. As long as you're ours, you can be sure that we'll look after you."

Still somewhat insecure, Daran looked up. His new master's words had not failed to calm him. The feeling of safety was slowly coming back, and with it, Daran's sense of irony. Before he could stop himself, he had answered. "That doesn't sound very barbarian to me. Are you sure you live in the Valley?"

For a moment the room fell completely silent, and Daran had plenty of time to curse his loose mouth, but then the two warriors started to laugh. After another shocked second, Daran joined in. He had been afraid of their reaction, and now he was relieved that they seemed to share his sense of humor, which was not a bad sign at all.

Aegid placed a hand on his nape; his voice was strange, almost tender, and made Daran nervous again. "You're a good match for us, little thief. I like the way your mind works."

THREE EXHAUSTING hours of shopping later, Daran lay on Aegid's bed, sleeping soundly.

The desert brothers watched him, full of interest. The young man had caught their eye even before he had decided to steal from them, which was why they had stayed at the stall for so long. They had watched Daran like he had eyed them.

It was rare for them to feel drawn to somebody like they did to Daran, but something about him, which they could not yet grasp, had woken their attention. When he had tried to steal Aegid's purse, they had stopped wondering how to get him to follow them to the Valley.

"He'll be a real asset to our bedroom." Aegid was very satisfied. "I'm looking forward to teaching him. He really is remarkable. Wait till he's wearing our colors and has gained some more weight."

Kalad, too, was happy about their acquisition. "He's indeed pleasing to the eye. And not only that. Have you seen how he reacts to our touches? It shouldn't be too difficult to seduce him."

At the mere thought of what they planned to do with their prisoner, both men felt a throbbing in their loins.

"But we should take our time. He's gone through a lot." As always, Aegid was the more sensitive of the two.

Kalad only shrugged. "He's strong and brave. He'll pull through."

Again they were lost in watching the young man. Daran was one of those people who did not know their own allure, which was part of his charm. Daran was only slightly smaller than Kalad; his long black hair hung down to his waist in a thick braid. The bronze-toned skin was like velvet, spanning muscles which, with some training, would turn into a body that looked like chiseled marble. The brown eyes were lively, full of intelligence and a hint of malice. His face possessed neither the exquisite perfection of Renaldo nor the majestic predominance that made Casto irresistible. For that, Daran's features were too flat, the chin too pronounced compared to the rest of his face. Every part of his body taken alone made Daran attractive but not breathtaking. What made him so alluring to Kalad and Aegid was the combination of his features, highlighted by an inner fire that was pure magnetism.

Despite his young age, Daran was already too weary, a sure sign that he had not had it easy in his life. Still he radiated an optimism bordering on naïveté that made him all the more attractive. Aegid and Kalad were fascinated by this contradictory man—something that had not happened in more than two hundred years.

THE NEXT morning, they left early. Kalad helped Daran get into the saddle of the sturdy brown gelding they had bought for him the day before. The beast let it happen with an air of patience, even though the play of his ears showed clearly how unhappy he was.

Carefully, Daran stroked the horse's neck. "I'm sorry. I'd prefer walking on my own two feet as well, but the way things are, we'll have to make the best of it."

Aegid tied a lead rope to the gelding's bridle and smiled at Daran.

"Don't worry. Riding is all about routine. I promise, before we reach the Valley you'll be a lot better. Once we get home, we'll ask Casto to teach you. He's an arrogant bastard but a very good teacher."

"Don't frighten Daran. Listening to you, one could get the impression that Casto is a monster." Kalad sounded slightly amused, as always.

Daran wondered if there was anything that could darken the quirky man's mood. Aegid shot Kalad a look that spoke volumes. "He's definitely not what I'd call a worthy slave. If he was ours, I would have beaten him into submission a long time ago." There was acid in his words. Casto was obviously a sore topic.

Kalad sighed.

"But he's not ours, and I begin to think that this is for the better. He's too strong and stubborn—which, admittedly, is part of his charm. I doubt he can be disciplined by being beaten. That's just bound to make him stronger. Renaldo seems to understand that, although I don't know how he manages to stay so patient."

Daran kept out of this conversation but wondered secretly who this Casto person was and why his behavior gave reason for discussion.

The journey to the Valley soon turned out to be a never-ending martyrdom for Daran. On the second day, he was barely able to walk because the muscles in his thighs were constantly on fire. The tiniest movement made pain explode in his sore body, and he could feel the impact of his time in the saddle even in his sleep. His masters mocked him good-naturedly until he could not take it any longer.

"Please, stop it already. I'm feeling horrible enough as it is! Thinking about it, you really ought to let me go right now, for I've repented the sins of a lifetime."

Aegid smiled at him as he bantered. "Nice try, slave. But the decision about when you've paid sufficiently for your mistake is up to us. This is just the start. Wait until Casto has started teaching you and we've shown you how to train your body properly."

"Even more sore muscles? That's not fair."

Kalad shrugged Daran's complaint off. "Life rarely is. You'll deal with it."

Since the mood was so relaxed, Daran dared to ask the question that had been burning on the tip of his tongue for a while now.

"Who is this Casto? You're talking about him as if he were some kind of nuisance, but at the same time you seem to admire him. I don't understand."

The warriors exchanged a glance, and then they seemed to reach a conclusion.

Kalad puffed out his breath. "Since you're going to meet him anyway... Casto belongs to Lord Renaldo."

"The Angel of Death?" Daran was awed.

"Yes, exactly," Kalad said. "And now stop interrupting me. You really lack manners." Sheepishly, Daran shut up. "Where was I? Oh, yes, Casto. Renaldo made him his property last spring. He's stunningly handsome, very intelligent, and as hard to tame as a sack full of fleas. He's also the first person ever to capture the Angel of Death's interest for more than a few days. He's special in more ways than one and absolutely annoying. We still regret that he's not ours."

This admission disturbed Daran more than he was willing to admit. To distract himself from his insecurity, he made a joke. "I'm not your first choice? That's kind of harsh."

"Idiot."

Aegid's massive fist gripped Daran's shoulder. "You're now our first choice. That should be enough."

"Whatever my masters wish." The young thief bowed in mockery. When he righted himself, his face had turned serious again. "What are you expecting of me? To be frank, so far I don't feel like your slave, more like a guest. You've given me new clothes, you're feeding me exceedingly well, and I even got a horse from you. You don't behave like barbarians at all."

Kalad shook his head in outrage. "I knew it! We should've beaten him first thing. Not like barbarians! What an insult!"

"I feel deeply wounded in my pride as a barbarian warrior." Aegid was laughing, his pale eyes trained on their acquisition. "So, it's valid to conclude you're no longer afraid of us?"

Daran returned the look openly. He really was not afraid anymore, much to his surprise. He was still wary, but that was a trained reaction he could not simply shake off. Although these two had forcefully pried him away from his freedom, they had been a lot friendlier than his own family. In addition, he felt drawn to them despite his attempts to ignore that feeling for the time being.

"Not anymore. When you captured me, I was very afraid, but you've been so nice, I can't help but feel safe. If anything, I'm very grateful, and I want to do everything according to your wishes."

Kalad brought his horse next to Daran and caressed his cheek. Again Daran felt heat coursing through his body.

"You've been doing well so far," Kalad said. "We haven't found a reason to be disappointed. There's a certain set of rules established in the Valley that you have to know and follow so as to not get into trouble, but we'll explain those clearly to you." A lewd grin spread on his lips. "Concerning us personally, we'll accustom you to our preferences bit by bit.

"As I said earlier, slaves do not only have obligations, they also have some rights. For example, nobody, not even Canubis himself, is allowed to force himself—or herself—on you. It's one of the biggest taboos in the Valley, stated by the Mothers themselves. Intercourse must be consensual because it's our way of celebrating life and honoring the Mothers. Anybody going against that rule faces serious consequences. Rape is the worst punishment we know of and only executed in the most severe cases, such as for traitors. All the time we've been with the Pack, that has only happened twice."

Lost in thought, Kalad followed the patterns of a thin cloud in the otherwise clear blue sky.

"You've the right to choose your partner freely, male, female, slave, free man. The only thing you should be wary of is whether your partner is in a relationship, because that is dangerous. When you're seeing someone, fidelity is expected."

Daran listened with his eyes wide. Never would he have expected that such strict rules applied to life in the Valley to which so many bloody stories were attached. He was dimly aware why Kalad had been so explicit about the rules regarding sexuality and fidelity, but he was not yet ready to ponder that thought.

Instead, he went for another small joke. "That doesn't sound barbaric at all. I've been thinking about whips and chains."

Aegid nodded. "We do have those as well, but as long as you're obedient, you needn't be afraid. But should you try to flee, you're in deep trouble. The punishment for that is a public flogging with the glass whip. After that, your legs will be broken and then your master decides whether you are to live or to die. If the slave is pardoned, he usually stays crippled as a warning for others."

Daran felt his hands shake. This kind of punishment fitted his image of the Valley and its inhabitants way better than the laws Kalad had told him.

Kalad picked up from Aegid. "Concerning us, there's only one thing we find unforgivable, which is lying. We really loathe that, and the punishment is severe. When you make a mistake, tell us truthfully, even though it might be hard on you. Because should we find out that you lied to us, the consequences will be a lot worse."

Despite the warmth of the fall day, Daran felt cold shivers running down his spine. He did not want to imagine what it would be like to incur the wrath of the two warriors. "*Now* I'm afraid."

Aegid patted Daran's shoulder. "And that's okay, little thief. We don't want you to panic every time we raise our hands, but a good measure of respect will come in handy."

"I'll keep that in mind."

ABOUT THREE hours after their conversation, they finally arrived at the Valley. Daran was completely wrapped up in gaping at the unique landscape and marveling at all the new impressions that came with it. Like everybody growing up and living so close to the Pack, he had heard a bunch of wild stories during his childhood, each bloodier and more appalling than the last. And although he had already revised some of his prejudices due to his new masters' gentleness, he was still surprised at how peaceful the place was where the most powerful army in the world resided. The only thing matching the childhood stories perfectly were the wolves that appeared time and again between the trees like deadly shadows. Daran's horse kept close to the two warriors' stallions, nervous of the predators whose presence left the other horses completely unfazed.

It took two more hours until they finally reached the center of the Valley where Aegid and Kalad stopped in front of the stables. The giant Aegid was just helping Daran off his horse when a tall warrior approached them. Daran did not need to look twice to know it was Lord Renaldo, the Angel of Death. The stories about his unearthly beauty had not been exaggerations, then, because never before had Daran seen such perfection in a face or body. The Angel of Death was heading directly toward them, a welcoming grin on his face.

"Aegid, Kalad. Good to see you back! You brought a visitor?"

Kalad grabbed his leader's forearm in traditional greeting. "This is Daran. He tried to steal from us at the market. He's going to make up for that mistake in the months to come."

Renaldo's face contorted into a titillating grimace. The Angel of Death did not seem to mind that his brothers-in-arms had brought home a thief. "I'm sure you'll find befitting methods to make him repent."

Aegid, too, shared an arm clasp with his leader. "You can bet on it. But since you're already here, do you think Casto could give him some riding lessons?"

A shadow flitted over Renaldo's face. "You can ask him anytime. I'm on my way to meet him, so why don't you come with me? I've got to warn you, though. He's in a terrible mood today."

Kalad cocked an eyebrow. "What did you fight about this time?"

"The usual and a bit more. It was pretty nasty."

"I still think it would be best to beat him up for good. That should change his attitude. I really don't understand why you're putting up with his brazen behavior."

Aegid directed his words at Renaldo openly. He had been with him long enough to know that his leader was not immune to criticism as long as it was voiced with respect.

Now Renaldo was smiling, knowing full well that Aegid was articulating what everybody in the Pack secretly thought. He gave his silent, composed fighter credit for not holding back his opinion. "First of all, it amuses me. It's been a long time since anybody has dared to oppose me like that. And second, the sex is unbelievable. I've more fun between the sheets than ever before."

Aegid rolled his eyes at this blunt statement but refrained from commenting any further.

While they talked, they passed the stables and were then in front of a huge space bordered by a low fence. A young man was riding there on top of a pitch-black stallion. Even Daran, who did not know the least thing about horses, could instantly tell that this steed was special, and that its rider was exceptional.

The stallion did not wear a saddle or bridle, which made his jump over a hurdle of more than one pace in height all the more impressive. When they landed, the rider went down on one side, touching the ground with his feet for a moment, and then leaped again onto the back of his still-galloping steed. The black horse made a detour and advanced on the onlookers at full speed.

Without thinking, Daran hid behind Aegid's broad back when the stallion came to a sliding halt less than a pace in front of them. Up close, the beast was even more intimidating. The rock-hard hooves drummed a threatening beat on the ground, and Daran was sure he was facing a man-eater. The stallion's big eyes looked down on the helpless humans before him with way too much intelligence for a mere animal; the long, silken mane could not hide the muscular neck the horse carried so proudly. He seemed to eye the group in front of him with contempt.

The man on his back struck Daran immediately as unappealing. He had a gorgeous, regal face, but his blue eyes were full of arrogance. Under that gaze, Daran felt like a piece of rubbish even though the rider had not uttered a single word yet. His mere presence was enough to intimidate Daran even more than he had been before.

Now those piercing blue eyes turned to the Angel of Death. "What is it?" Even though the tone was sharp, the voice was pleasant—a melodic tenor that caressed the ears.

Before Renaldo could answer, the stallion snorted imperiously. Casto—for surely this was he—rolled his eyes skyward and murmured something in a language Daran did not recognize. Then he dismounted and showed Renaldo something that vaguely resembled a bow, but without any respect in his attitude.

The Angel of Death only smiled mildly. He did not seem to mind his servant's ridiculous behavior. "Thank you, Lys. You know way better than your rider what's appropriate."

There was another snort, and Daran could have sworn it was full of mockery. "Aegid and Kalad wanted to ask you if you could train their new slave."

Casto's sharp gaze homed in on Daran, who wished with all his heart to be someplace else. The blue eyes seemed to turn him inside out, staring directly into the core of his soul, only to drop in disgust what they found.

In honeyed tones Casto answered his master. "Of course. No problem there. Thanks to you and your brother, I spend my days in leisure. It's an honor to be responsible for the training of a newbie as well."

"Casto."

A warning note had crept into Renaldo's voice. Daran could feel the hair on his back standing up. Challenging this warrior's anger was surely a bad idea, but Casto seemed to be thoroughly unfazed.

Casto went on in a more respectful tone, but there was still a hint of defiance underneath. "Calm down. I'm serious, though. I simply don't have the time. All I can offer is one hour a week, and perhaps some random lessons whenever I've the time. But this will have to be very spontaneous since I can't plan for it."

Kalad placed a hand on Daran's shoulder, sounding amused. "That's not too bad. And he doesn't have to become an expert. It's enough if he can manage a few days in the saddle without getting crippled from the strain."

"That I can guarantee."

"Then we're grateful, Casto."

Kalad bowed generously, as if Casto were some kind of prince.

The gesture was so full of sarcasm that it did not escape the blond, as Daran could clearly deduce from the sour face he made, and he gave an unfriendly nod in response. "Don't overdo it."

The desert brothers took Daran and walked off. The last thing Daran heard was Casto addressing the demigod.

"So, what do you want, Barbarian?"

Aegid, too, had heard Casto. He hissed at Daran through tight lips. "Should you ever dare talk to your masters like this, you'll wish you'd never been born, understood?"

Aegid's face was so furious that Daran felt the pressing urge to placate him. "I'd never dream of talking to you like that, Master. I'm not that brave."

As he had hoped, this demure answer made the warrior smile. Aegid grazed the naked skin on Daran's upper arm with his fingertips. "I think you're braver than you give yourself credit for, little thief."

That touch felt like an electric current driving through Daran's body. To distract from his growing unease, he returned to the sore topic of becoming Casto's pupil. "Can't I do my riding lessons with somebody else? I don't think Casto is very nice."

Kalad laughed. "Casto isn't nice to anybody except Lysistratos. Nevertheless, he's the best rider I've ever seen, and believe it or not, he's also a very good teacher. I'm sure you'll get used to his special ways in no time."

Daran doubted this but kept his mouth shut. His masters led him away from the stables to a massive building that seemed to be the main house. He could see that one wing housed a kitchen while the others contained living space. The whole construction was rather flat, very solid, and without ornament. It had obviously been standing there for some time yet was not the least bit shabby or run-down, but very orderly and clean. The thick stone walls gave a feeling of security, and Daran realized instinctively that within those walls nothing bad could ever happen. Aegid and Kalad followed a long, scarcely lit corridor to the southern part of the building. They stopped in front of an oaken door studded with blue steel.

"This is going to be your home from now on." Kalad opened the door pompously and, with a grand gesture, invited Daran to enter.

A little shy, Daran inspected the rooms that would become the center of his world for the foreseeable future. He did not really know what he had expected, but surely not the overflowing luxury that was taxing his sight and was in stark contrast to the practicality of the rest of the house. The main chamber was home to several lounges made of black, glossy wood and were covered with cream silk. Huge brocade down-filled pillows dyed in a vivid shade of dark green were piled on the lounges. A large open chimney tiled with marble dominated the whole room, accentuated by tapestries on each side. When Kalad became aware of Daran's interest in them, he led him closer.

"This is where we come from, the Hot Heart. It's the biggest desert on Ana-Darasa, and the most deadly one." Pride and a certain longing tinged his voice. Aegid moved closer as well, staring at the scenes displayed.

"It's our original home." He sighed deeply. "We didn't know what snow was until we met Renaldo and Canubis."

Daran could not help but grin. "Is that why you're wearing all these additional clothes although it's really warm for the season? I've been wondering."

The two warriors shuddered. Kalad covered his eyes in a mock gesture of despair. "Our definition of warm is different from yours. Makes me doubt our compatibility."

Before Daran could decide whether this was meant in earnest, Aegid took his hand to show him further around. Again Daran was caught up in the sheer splendor of the room. Wherever he looked, he saw expensive cloth, intricately woven rugs, beautiful jewelry, and elaborate weapons. Daran was so overwhelmed by all the riches that he could only stand there and gape with his mouth open like the poor commoner that he was.

"Do you like it?" Aegid's voice was right next to his ear and made him flinch.

Daran felt as if the warrior had caught him fantasizing. "It's awesome!" was all he could whisper.

Aegid seemed satisfied with this answer. Casually he slung his arm around Daran's hips. "That's not all. Come, we'll show you where you're going to sleep—for the time being."

Daran blushed but did not take the bait. He was so dazed by everything that had happened over the past few days that he was grateful to be able to remember his own name. Reacting to his masters' advances in a fitting manner just was not possible at the moment.

Kalad opened another door, which led into a room big enough to contain a spacious bed, a wardrobe, and a small washbasin. The place was not as splendid as the main room but still elegant enough to awe Daran.

"You want me to sleep here?" He spilled the words without thinking.

"You don't like it?" Kalad sounded worried.

Daran shook his head vigorously. He was so bewildered he had trouble speaking. "*Like* it? It's perfect. I thank you." Instinctively he knelt down, bowing his head low to show his gratitude.

Carefully, Aegid lifted him up again. "It's just a bed, Daran, nothing special. To be frank, we did not expect to bring somebody here, that's why it's rather unsightly, but you're free to decorate it in the way you prefer. As we said, we'll take care of you."

Daran could feel tears welling up in his eyes. He had to concentrate not to start crying openly. "You don't understand. This"—he waved around the room with a vague gesture—"is more than I've ever had before. I spent all my previous nights on the floor, sometimes with a little straw for a mattress. I'm so awed, I don't know what to say."

The desert warriors remained silent for a moment, digesting the impact of what Daran had just revealed to them.

Then Kalad answered him firmly. "From now on you have a bed." His grin became salacious. "And if you behave yourself, we'll even allow you to sleep in our bed."

Before Daran had time to think too much about this last comment, Aegid took his arm and led him to the front of the main chamber. There were two more intricately ornamented doors, one of which Kalad opened while gesturing toward the other. "That is our sleeping room, and this—" He stepped aside so Daran could get a clear view. "—is the bath."

Speechless, the young man took in the world of wonder revealed to him. The whole room was tiled in white marble; the expensive stone even covered the ceiling. At the center of the room were two pools, a round one about one and a half paces in diameter, and a square one a little over one pace broad and almost two paces long. They both were filled to the rim with water that seemed almost black because of the dark green marble that covered the bottom and sides.

On a pedestal at the far end of the square pool, a basin made of green marble stood under a mirror about half an ell in diameter. Two massage benches made from polished blackwood perfected the setting. Daran had thought that after the wonders displayed in the main room, nothing could shock him anymore, but now he was standing here, enchanted by the wonders before his eyes. He doubted that any king, no matter how powerful, could call such a splendid bath his own.

"What are you waiting for? Undress and get into the water. The warmth will be good for your sore muscles." Aegid was clearly amused; Daran's amazement had not evaded him.

Daran looked at his masters disbelievingly. "Are you serious?"

With shooing motions, Kalad moved him along. "We seldom joke about hygiene or your well-being. The last three days have been trying for you, so you deserve this. Take your time. It's your first day in the Valley, so we'll cut you some slack. Starting tomorrow, we'll introduce you to your tasks, and then you'd better be refreshed, because we won't go easy on you."

Still not entirely convinced, and slightly unsure, Daran bowed to the two warriors who had entered—and changed—his life so abruptly. "I thank you, Masters."

Both men touched his cheeks lightly, and then they left him alone.

2. TWO MASTERS

"YOU'VE BEEN really impolite today, Casto. One might think the young thief had offended you personally." With a slightly amused expression, Renaldo watched his stubborn slave taking off his dirty boots.

Irritated by Renaldo's comment, Casto flung the offending footwear into a corner. "You know all too well why I was so impolite, Barbarian. That poor sod had nothing to do with it." His voice was tense.

"Please, don't tell me you're still angry about this morning. That fight wasn't so terrible. We've had worse."

The sky-blue eyes darkened. Casto had not forgotten about the fight, and he was not inclined to forgive even one word. "That may be the case, but you've never insulted me like this before. You've doubted my whole upbringing!"

Remembering what Renaldo had said, Casto felt his rage starting to seethe again. Under different circumstances, he would probably have said the same things about his made-up family, but Renaldo had no right to do so. That most of Renaldo's comments had hit the mark made things even worse.

Sensing how distressed Casto was, Renaldo tried to placate him. "Would it help if I told you that I'm sorry? I surely didn't mean it the way it might have sounded."

Casto shot his master a scathing look. "My ancestry might be common compared to your barbarian standards, but be assured, my family was highly valued on the plains before fate destroyed us so cruelly. And I do realize that you didn't mean it like you phrased it, but the fact remains that you said it." He hesitated for a moment and then chose his next words as carefully as a hunter selecting arrows for his bow. "On the other hand, what did I expect from a mere barbarian who clings to the delusion of being a god?"

The challenge worked. Renaldo's eyes sparked into furious life as well. "Watch your mouth, Casto! Even though I put up with quite a lot of back talk from your side, I won't hesitate to punish you when you go too far."

"Why so tetchy all of a sudden, Barbarian? This morning you confronted me with things far worse than this."

"Casto…."

The warning growl grew in intensity. Casto knew his master was only seconds away from losing his composure. He glared at Renaldo, deliberately challenging him, hoping to make him snap. "What? I'm just stating some facts."

Growling like an enraged mother bear, Renaldo shot forward, grabbed the young man who had just aggravated him so carelessly by the scruff of his neck, and kissed him brutally. With a contented groan, Casto nestled against him, inhaling his anger and fury and giving it back to him.

In no time at all, they both were naked. Like hungry wild beasts they attacked each other without reserve or consideration. This was the one way they could both channel their seething emotions, the one thing that drove them equally.

The irrational, unfathomable lust they felt for each other erased all other feelings and allowed them some temporary peace.

LATER, THEY lay silent and sated in bed, but both of them knew from painful experience how one wrong word could ignite the next fight.

Renaldo was musing about how aggravated his beautiful slave had become in the last few weeks and what he could do to soothe him. During the winter, Casto seemed to slowly get accustomed to being the Angel of Death's possession, but ever since summer had started to change into fall, Renaldo felt himself reminded of their first, steamy weeks when Casto had been all snippy words and denying behavior. If there had not been the regular, brutal pairings, he would have doubted whether Casto felt anything but contempt for him.

To make matters worse, Renaldo was starting to question his own judgment. Had any other slave shown such blatant disregard toward him, Renaldo would have severely punished them and then sold them to the most unpleasant bidder, but for some reason Renaldo could not stand the thought of having to spend a single day without Casto. This insight made him irritable, and he had to admit, it was unfair.

Casto's thoughts ran on similar paths, but unlike his master, he knew the exact reason for his own bad temper. During the summer, Renaldo had managed to gain his reluctant respect, which then, much to Casto's horror and dismay, had started to turn into love. When he looked at Renaldo, his heart started to race as if he were some stupid farm maid. The mere idea made him furious. He longed to hate his captor because it would have been just and equitable, but Renaldo had some undeniable assets, and he managed time and again to impress Casto. Torn between his growing affection for Renaldo, his resentment of it, and his anger because Renaldo was keeping him against his will, Casto clung to the all-consuming lust they shared in bed. If he concentrated on sating his hunger, he did not have to think about what his feelings really meant.

Casto had learned early in life that he could trust nobody, and that love was nothing but an ephemeral idea in the face of cold reality. He was all the more terrified to be dependent on another person—especially if that person was Renaldo.

Renaldo seemed to follow a similar logic, because he was always willing to let Casto provoke him to the point where he saw red and then bedded the impudent young man hard and without mercy.

Deep inside, both men knew that a relationship like this was unhealthy to the point of destruction, and that they had to find a way to get along outside the bed as well, but neither of them was willing to take the first step.

This confession of weakness was something neither the powerful demigod nor his slave, who had been steeled by a terrible childhood, wanted to show. So they lay next to each other in the dark until Casto fell asleep.

DURING THE first weeks after his arrival in the Valley, Daran was introduced to the tasks his masters wanted him to fulfill, and he learned more about his new home. He thanked the holy Mothers every night for having brought him to a place that seemed like paradise to him.

Aegid and Kalad were very caring; they had given him a complete wardrobe of new clothes and he was regularly fed with the most splendid food and allowed to use the luxuries offered by the desert brothers' chambers whenever he wanted. Every morning he served his masters their breakfast, an exercise that could take some time since neither of them was a morning person. They preferred absolute silence at the table until they were awake enough not to react grumpily to every little thing. Daran had quickly learned what to do at which exact time to not offend the warriors, and he performed his duties diligently.

After breakfast, Daran went to one of the smaller training rooms and worked his body the way his masters had instructed him. Nobody disturbed him; he always had the room exclusively to himself. In the beginning, he was surprised by this, until he dared to ask Aegid about it.

The warrior just smiled, looking rather satisfied. "You're our personal slave. You outrank most of the other slaves, and our brothers-in-arms respect us enough to give you some room. It's only natural that you can move around more freely than others."

Because his master's voice had been so completely unruffled and casual, Daran suddenly realized how powerful and influential his owners were. He was also dimly aware that they were forming him the way they wanted to, but he did not really care so long as he was provided for so completely.

After the training he had time to get changed. Then it was either a lesson with Casto or self-study with the chestnut horse the warriors had bought for him back in Kwarl. Daran had befriended the gelding and called him Rajan, which meant something along the lines of "cuddly" in the language of the Eastern Kingdoms. The name fitted perfectly for a horse that could never get enough attention from its rider.

The lessons with Casto were not as bad as Daran had feared. Not only was the stunning young man an outstanding teacher who was able to explain things clearly, but he was also very patient, something Daran would have never guessed after their first encounter. Before they had started the training, Casto had even apologized for his arrogant behavior. Besides his commands during their lessons, Casto did not talk much to him, something Daran resented him for at first. He thought Casto was too arrogant to get involved with common people like himself, but very soon he realized that Casto behaved like this toward all members of the Pack. What Daran had dismissed as arrogance was nothing but a mechanism with which Casto protected himself. Daran could not imagine what somebody like Casto could be afraid of, but Daran had tasted bitter despair often enough to recognize it in other people's faces. After realizing this, he was more lenient in his attitude and no longer able to hate his trainer.

Like Casto, Daran did not have any contact with the other slaves. Sometimes there were short encounters in the chambers of the desert brothers, but Aegid's words resounded in his mind: he was a personal slave and nobody dared to contact him on their own. Daran did not mind. He was used to being alone, and his new life was still too exciting and confusing to make him open to new friendships.

After riding, Daran returned to his masters' chambers to do some intensive stretching. He had always been very flexible and had even earned some money as a street acrobat back in Kwarl. It was a talent he did not want to neglect, especially since it seemed to please the warriors. When he was done with his exercises, he had time to enjoy the pleasures of the pompous bathroom, and he did so fervently. Daran loved lazing on one of the marble lounges, feeling the warm water caress his body and dreaming, with his eyes closed, about the sea. Stories about beautiful sea creatures and deadly monsters had been stirring his fantasy for many years. Daran had never been able to conceive a place where an ocean existed so wide that you could not see the shores on the horizon from where you were standing. But here, in this wonderful bath, he could imagine he was really there, in a place where the waves crashed down on the beach with brute force, only to retreat, seemingly tamed, into the ocean.

When he was done with bathing, Daran put on the clothes Aegid and Kalad had given him and relaxed until they returned. He did not know for sure what they were doing the whole day, but some of their time was reserved for training the mercenaries. Although he was curious to find out, Daran was still too shy to ask them directly. So he waited patiently for their return every day to express his gratitude with his obedience.

Dinner was the most confusing part of Daran's day, and he always anticipated it with a mixture of agitation and joy. He served his masters the same way he did breakfast, but the mood was a lot more intimate than in the morning, when the warriors did hardly more than grunt a short greeting. In the evening they were lively and open. So open, indeed, that Daran felt disturbed. Both Kalad and Aegid kept touching him and acted as if it were coincidence at the same time. They fed him the best morsels of their meals and treated him to innuendos that made his cheeks burn. Unable to cope with this game, Daran was nothing but a ball the desert brothers tossed each other. Daran could only surrender to the seduction played out so skillfully by the two experienced men, and he was more than willing to give in, but whenever he thought they would finally act, they retreated as if nothing had happened.

This constant change between tension and rejection grated on Daran's nerves. In these moments, he felt utterly helpless, unable to influence things or change the pace so that it suited him more. His own reactions made it even harder for him to assess the situation. He had grown up on the streets, so he was no stranger to sexual intercourse. He'd had his first experiences in that area some three years ago with the hookers working for his stepfather, who liked to forget about their hard work in the arms of a pleasing young man. Daran had learned quickly that the women especially, who had to deal with many dominant suitors, liked to have the upper hand now and then. He had always enjoyed the attention of the prostitutes but had not been interested enough to look actively for partners himself.

He had always neglected the invitations of men, not for lack of interest, but because he knew that a man would take what he wanted with force whereas a woman would use other, subtler means. Daran was afraid to be forced, which was why he had always kept a distance from men.

Aegid and Kalad did not give him that chance. On top of that, they were so skilled that after no time at all, Daran was willing to submit to their constant coaxing.

That evening, the warriors teased him so much that Daran felt he was at the limit of what he could bear. When Kalad tried to feed him some sweet cake, Daran turned away with crimson cheeks. "Don't, Master. I'm not hungry anymore."

Kalad was not convinced at all. "You've hardly eaten anything today."

A slight reproof was in those words, as if it were Daran's fault for not having an appetite. Still, he had been conditioned so well that he immediately went for damage control. "I'm sorry."

Daran retreated a few steps, his gaze cast down.

Aegid looked at him sharply. Most of the time the big warrior was very composed and let his brother do the talking, which made it all the more terrifying when he raised his voice. Now the pale blue eyes drilled into his shivering property. "What is it, Daran?"

"I.... It's nothing. I'm just not hungry anymore. It was a tiring day, so please forgive me."

"We'd do so if you had told us the truth. You're a terrible liar, Daran, so refrain from doing it in the future. You know how much we resent it."

Sheepishly, and also a little frightened, Daran looked up. He had not anticipated being found out so quickly, and now he was afraid of their wrath. Although he had not been living with them for long, he had already witnessed what happened when somebody tried to lie to them. "Am I going to be punished?"

He hated how his voice was shaking, but he was truly terrified. What he feared most was not the physical pain—he knew he could endure that somehow—what made him freeze in terror was the thought of his masters abandoning him. Even though they could be strict, they had still saved him from a pointless existence under Egand's thumb. The thought of insulting or displeasing his benefactors made him drown in darkest despair.

What Kalad said next did not help to ease Daran's mind. "Yes, you're going to be punished, but not immediately. Before that, we want you to tell us what the problem is."

Kalad's voice was still soft but with a steely undertone that made Daran tremble with fear. He did not want to think about all the things those two could do to him. In his misery, he spoke the naked truth this time.

Stammering, with his gaze lowered again, he tried to voice his inner turmoil. "It's.... I don't know how to say it. All the attention I'm getting from you—it confuses me. I don't know how to react, and I'm always asking myself what you want from me. And I'm afraid to tell you this, because I feel I'm not living up to your expectations. I just want to know what to do."

He was still looking down, so Aegid used his forefinger to lift his chin up.

Aegid's voice was soft and soothing, as if calming a frightened child. "I think it's obvious what we want. We're wooing you, and we're taking our time because you're insecure and don't know what you should do—or what you want. We want you to burn for us; we want to be the only thing you can think of. To put it bluntly, our goal is to get you into our bed, to possess you. And so far, we're pleased with your progress. But you've also told us that you're inexperienced when it comes to relationships with other men. We want to give you time to get accustomed to us. After all, you'll have to handle both of us, which doesn't make it easier for you to decide. We certainly don't want you to do anything you might regret later."

Emboldened by these words, Daran looked into Aegid's milky eyes. It took all his courage to speak, but he did not want to disappoint the incredibly generous men. "I like it when you touch me. I feel safe in your presence. What else I want, I can't tell, but I'm more than willing to try. I trust you, Master."

The hunger that blazed in Aegid's features then was like a bonfire, a lust that both terrified and attracted Daran. His heart beat like a war drum, and his hands shook so hard he had to press them against his thighs. Kalad approached from behind; he touched Daran's shoulders gently.

"When you get frightened, when you don't like what we're doing, then tell us. We'll stop immediately."

With his gaze locked on Aegid's massive form, Daran nodded. He knew what they said was true. If it was his wish, they would stop. Still his thoughts were in turmoil. He could not believe it would really happen now. He wondered what his masters expected and hoped not to disappoint them.

As if reading his thoughts, Kalad whispered in his ear. "Relax, little thief. Leave everything to us."

With a sigh, Daran obeyed. All his fearful tension dissipated from his body in the sure knowledge that this was the point of no return.

Aegid took his face in both hands; his lips engulfed Daran's softly. Automatically, Daran opened his mouth, offering it willingly, agitated and full of anticipation. His well-built master was an experienced kisser who took his time to inflame him. When Daran snuggled up to Aegid on pure instinct, Kalad started caressing him from behind. Kalad's strong hands seemed to be everywhere at the same time, skillfully taking off Daran's clothing while Aegid was still distracting him with his lips and tongue.

Both warriors worked together like a well-oiled machine. For them, the seduction of the young man was like a dance they had performed countless times with perfect choreography. During their more than eight hundred years of life, they had played this game so often that it had become a little boring recently, but something about Daran—perhaps the open, willing way in which he reacted to them, perhaps the limitless trust he showed—woke a hunger they had not known for some time. They had to restrain themselves not to ravish him instantly.

Kalad then entered Daran with one finger, and Daran reacted with a whimper from someplace deep inside him. The fire his masters had stoked already enthralled Daran, and without thinking he arched his back and started moving against Kalad. Pleased by this reaction, Kalad placed a hand on Daran's erection and started to pump.

With a scream that was swallowed by Aegid's lips, Daran found his relief, his hips bucking wildly. He did not even notice when Kalad continued opening him with practiced ease.

Then Kalad retreated, using Daran's fluids to make him slick and to prepare him for what was still to come. Aegid sat down on one of the lounges, taking Daran with him, without losing contact with his lips, and caressing him with his callused hands. The stark contrast between Aegid's almost pitch-black skin and the much lighter tone of their slave pleased both men and intensified their hunger. Obediently, Daran went down on his knees, presenting his backside so invitingly it made Kalad's breath falter. With lustful eyes, he knelt between Daran's spread legs, applied some oil on the tight ring, and positioned himself, ready to take Daran for the first time.

Aegid soothingly stroked the panting young man's back. "Relax, little thief, don't be afraid."

Despite the calming words, Daran clung desperately to Aegid when he felt Kalad enter him. He had not expected it to be so good, that his lust would consume him so completely. Moaning loudly, he pressed his back against Kalad's abdomen, enjoyed the sweet pain that was dealt to him.

Because there was pain, but it was not bad—a small price to pay for the warmth spreading through his body.

Now his master entered him to the hilt. Daran could feel Kalad's balls pressing against the backs of his thighs. For a moment, Kalad did not do anything, and Daran was getting ready to beg when his master finally started to move. In one long, measured stroke, Kalad slid back, only to penetrate again. Daran panted; the feeling was so exquisite he could not find words to describe it. Again and again Kalad rammed into him, his movements accelerating, becoming harder. Then Kalad released inside him, and the knowledge that he had just pleased Kalad drowned Daran in sexual bliss, sending him over the top again in the sweet certainty of having satisfied his partner.

Panting heavily, he lay in Aegid's arms. A warmth he had never felt before engulfed him while Kalad slowly and carefully retreated. Kalad touched him lightly, a sensation that made him sigh in pure, unabashed happiness.

"That was really good, little thief," Kalad said softly. "Rest a little. Then we're going to wash."

Confused, Daran looked up. Kalad's words had pried him from his lustful trance. With a hint of concern, he addressed his other master. "What about you, Lord Aegid? You haven't—" He was still too embarrassed to talk openly, although they had just been so intimate.

As if reading his thoughts, Aegid touched his cheeks. "I won't today. I can wait."

"You don't have to. I'm not that tired."

Kalad's hands were heavy on Daran's shoulders; he was clearly amused. "That might be the case, but you're wonderfully tight. Aegid is bigger than any man I know. It'll take some time before you'll be able to receive him without pain."

Insecure, Daran stared at the mighty erection in front of him. Kalad was surely right—Aegid was more than he could deal with. He shuddered at the mere thought of what it must feel like to be taken by such a big man. He hesitated for one more moment, and then he looked up, completely determined.

"I don't want you to go to bed like this. You've just shown me pleasure I never thought possible. I wouldn't be able to forgive myself if you had to pay for it with discomfort."

"You really are sweet." Aegid kissed him lovingly. Then a mocking smile challenged Daran. "I'm not going to take you, but since you're that determined to give me some relief, then there is a possibility."

Silenced by his excitement and grateful for this opportunity, Daran nodded.

Aegid leaned back and let his legs fall apart. "Lick me."

The order was brusque but that did not offend Daran. He had other things to worry about and moistened his lips with his tongue while leaning in. "Will you tell me what to do?"

"If necessary. But I've got a feeling you're going to perform well."

Not wanting to disappoint his master, Daran drew closer. His tongue glided slowly over Aegid's massive erection. Like everything about Aegid, this part was exceptionally big as well. Daran was not sure if what he was doing met his master's expectations, but a low moan told him that he was at least on the right path. He closed his lips around the crown and slipped his tongue into the slit, licking up the first drops that were proof of Aegid's pleasure. Then he started sucking harder while the massive cock went deeper into his throat. Aegid's moans grew in intensity, and he closed his hand around Daran's head, not to force him but to assure him that he was doing well.

Daran understood and sucked even harder, determined to give his master the utmost pleasure. A pulsing warned of Aegid's oncoming orgasm; his essence spilled into Daran's eager mouth. The taste was unlike anything Daran had known before, but it was not unpleasant. He sucked in rhythm with the pulsing, making Aegid cry out in rapture. Aegid moved his hips violently, ramming his penis deep into Daran's throat. Daran did not stop milking him until Aegid retreated with a satisfied groan.

Kalad's voice was soft at Daran's back. "I think I'm jealous."

Instinctively, Daran turned. He got up from his crouch, his lips level with Kalad's pelvis.

Kalad smiled happily, then helped him up. "It's okay, little thief. There's time for this later. You've been so good today. We don't want to overdo it."

Aegid had gotten up as well, and together the three of them went to the bath.

After cleaning up, the warriors returned to the roomy bed in which they spent their nights. They took Daran along, and he was now lying naturally between them, tired and happy but a little uneasy because he had just remembered he had a punishment waiting for him.

Daran gazed intently at his hands and asked about it. "May I inquire when I'll be punished?"

The desert brothers shared a long look. Then Aegid stroked the naked, soft skin they had just possessed. He felt rather playful and it showed in his tone. "That's a good question. But an even better one would be *how* we're going to punish you."

Kalad grinned with a hint of malice in his lively brown eyes. "Usually it would be the whip. You lied to us, and we did tell you what we think about that."

Daran blanched. He knew it was only just, that it was his own fault, but he could not help but be terrified.

Sensing their slave's distress, the warriors kept on teasing him. Aegid stroked Daran's black silky braid.

"Don't be mean, Kalad. He has just served us pretty well. Don't you think we can cut him some slack?"

"The cane, then. Less blood, but still quite painful."

Daran's eyes filled with tears. The warm glow from their earlier exertions was gone, and he felt utterly miserable. "Please. Just tell me when and how. I'm begging you!"

He sounded so desperate that Aegid took pity on him. "We'll do it now. I think you'd prefer that, or am I wrong? Turn around."

With ice crystallizing in his stomach, Daran obeyed.

"What do you think, Kalad? Twenty strokes with bare hands?"

Since Daran was lying on his stomach, he was not able to see the amusement sparking in Kalad's eyes as he tried his hardest to remain serious. "No cane? I've been looking forward to that. Well, never mind, twenty strokes sounds fair to me." Kalad's fingertips traced Daran's naked buttock. "What about you, slave?"

"I'm yours. It's your decision."

"Good boy."

The first slap reddened the twitching cheeks. The brothers were not going easy on Daran, but they weren't brutal either. They dealt the stinging blows in quick succession, then turned their slave around and kissed him tenderly.

Daran swallowed hard. He had gotten away easily. Other slaves had suffered far more brutal punishment for less. "Thank you for showing mercy."

Kalad smiled warmly. He had enjoyed their pairing and the teasing immensely and was now in a sated state of mind. "Let this be a lesson to you. You can trust us, Daran, and we expect you to do so, understood?"

"Yes, Master. I won't forget it."

"Then it's all right. And now go to sleep, you look worn out."

Only minutes later, Daran was sleeping soundly.

His masters watched him fondly. Aegid was the first to break the silence.

"That was incredible. Did you see how deeply he took me? And the way he used his lips—I'm more than pleased."

"You look like a cat with a bowl of whipped cream. But you're right, he's indeed special. And gloriously tight. It felt as if I was held by a velvet fist."

"Are we falling in love?"

Kalad thought about it for a moment. Love was not an easy topic for those whose life knew no end. Every human they had ever approached had to leave them sooner or later, a victim to time, always walking with death by their side. It had taken them a while to truly understand this dilemma, but from then on they had restricted themselves to sexual relationships only—which had earned them the reputation of being promiscuous. As things were, short, steamy affairs were the healthiest option for both the brothers and their partners.

Compared to that, their feelings for each other were more complex than any love relationship could ever be. They were brothers in more than one respect; their lives so interwoven they seemed like one. Letting somebody else in on this complex, mature partnership that had grown over so many years was difficult and dangerous. Aegid's question was loaded in more than one respect, for the answer could bring both of them, as well as Daran, great suffering.

Kalad was quick to give things a happier outlook. "No. We're definitely too old for that. We're simply enjoying a delectable slave."

Relieved, Aegid closed his eyes. He was always glad when Kalad took matters in hand. "Then I'm at ease. I'm looking forward to what we can teach him."

Wolfish smiles crept onto their features. They were highly satisfied with the situation. During the winter, Daran would help them kill the spare time they had on their hands in a satisfying manner, and once the initial ardor cooled, they could still decide to let him go. Should he prove talented, they would keep him a little longer. Theft was a serious crime for which a man could be sentenced to slavery for at least two years.

The following weeks passed like a trance for Daran, who did not suspect anything about his masters' plans. They bedded him several times a day, showing him lust he had never dared dream about. He quickly forgot his punishment, but from then on was hell-bent not to lie to them again. There was no way he wanted to incur their wrath a second time.

Even his riding lessons showed progress. He did not feel as tired afterward and was finally gaining some control over Rajan. Daran was so content, so happy, he did not notice the storm brewing over the Valley.

BATTLE OF WILLS

1. ESCAPE

RENALDO WAS cantankerous. He knew this word was an understatement, but it sounded so much more elegant than petulant or pissed and was therefore better suited to describe his current mood. With narrowed eyes, he watched Casto pulling his clothes off with impatient movements.

Casto was irritable as well, but Renaldo found that he did not feel attracted by this mood as usual. On the contrary, it made him angry. For the last few days, Casto's temper had gradually turned from edgy to completely insufferable; not even the most violent sex had sufficed to reel him in. They had reached a point where Renaldo was willing to give his capricious property a well-deserved hiding. His resolution was only strengthened by the demeaning look on Casto's face.

"What are you staring at, Barbarian? Whatever you want, I'm not in the mood today."

Renaldo felt those words sink into his brain like lead, fueling a chain reaction that was long overdue. With an angry growl, he snatched his provocative slave, struck him twice so hard that his head lolled back and forth, and then pressed him against the wall so that his feet lost contact with the floor. Renaldo could feel his inner fire awakening and roaring for blood. He was close to killing this insolent worm who always defied him so carelessly, and he would do it with one mighty blow.

At the last possible moment, Renaldo held himself back, fought down the anger boiling inside him, and instead hissed at Casto like a snake shortly before it attacks. "Shut up, slave! I'm fed up with your games and your impertinence." Renaldo's voice was strained and full of anger. "You're going to show better manners from now on, or I swear I'll have your hide in bloody scraps. If you don't change your attitude, I'll seriously consider one of the offers from my brothers-in-arms and sell you for the highest bid. Do you think Aegid or Kalad or Noran would tolerate what you're pulling with me? It's high time you show me the respect I deserve. I'm your god and master, and you're a slave, a mere possession. You had better start accepting it, or there's no telling what I might do to you!"

Casto's eyes widened in shock. It was obvious he was surprised by the violent outburst, and for a moment he seemed completely helpless. Helpless enough to strike a chord in Renaldo. Seeing the confusion in the young man's eyes, Renaldo was almost willing to forgive him then and there.

Casto reached for his master's arms with both hands, but then he let them slide down as if all the power had been drained from him. His whole body relaxed, the angry tension leaving the slender limbs as if it had never been there. His lips trembled. "You hit me."

Casto's voice was more surprised than accusing, as if he could not believe that his master had really hurt him.

Renaldo's gaze was cold. He had no intention of letting the young man off the hook this time. "Yes. And it was high time. Your attitude is unacceptable. I won't stand for it any longer."

Casto swallowed hard. Renaldo could almost see his complicated mind starting to buzz. He was curious about Casto's next reaction, but what followed still came as a surprise.

Casto lowered his gaze, the stubbornness vanished from his eyes, and his voice sounded demure. "You're right, Master. My behavior was unacceptable. I'm sorry."

Renaldo was so baffled he let go of Casto immediately. He simply had not expected the apology. For a moment he did not know what to do, and he felt his anger dissipate like fog in bright sunshine.

To gain some time, he cleared his throat. "It's okay, Casto. We're both agitated. Go to bed. We'll talk tomorrow."

His gaze still cast downward, Casto obeyed.

When Casto was gone, Renaldo sank down on one of the lounges, trying to make sense of what had just happened. His logic fought against the surrealism of the situation. A compliant Casto was as exceptional as snow in the summer or sunshine at midnight.

IN THE bath, Casto washed himself with fast, angry strokes. How could that damn barbarian dare to raise his hand against him? He could not believe Renaldo had really hit him.

And he could not believe how good it had felt to get a demonstration of the Barbarian's strength. Only once before had Renaldo held him like that, shown him how utterly helpless and vulnerable he was when confronted with his power. Like that first time, Casto had been strangely turned on by being so defenseless. If Renaldo had expressed the wish to bed him at that very moment, Casto would have complied even if it meant more blows. But before those dangerous thoughts could reach the surface, Casto had interrupted things and submitted. Years of training had helped him to play the role of subdued slave convincingly, while at the same time, his resolve to leave the Valley strengthened. He did not know why it had taken him so long to make that decision. It was not as if Renaldo or any of his servants—human or wolf—could stop him. The plan to escape had been made the day he first came to the Valley and could be put into action at any time.

By tomorrow night he would be free again.

Comforted by that thought, Casto slept deeply and well.

PROUDLY, THE black demon overlooked the plains before him. He was deeply satisfied with the form this world had given him. Ever since he had come to flesh, the call had grown louder. Instinctively, he followed the summons, feeling deep in his bones that this was the true reason for his existence. On his way to his destination, he tested his power, learned its limits and countless possibilities.

He was fast. Without tiring, he could run away from the day, and because he had been born from the shadows, he was closer to darkness than light. During the night he was even faster, running through the gloom without effort like a passing thought in somebody's mind.

Best of all were the storms.

The first one had been an accidental meeting. He had enjoyed defeating this force of nature while running. It had not taken him long to learn not only how to challenge the storm but also how to control it. He could call the winds whenever he liked, and obediently, they followed his will.

He was Lysistratos, Emperor of the Storm.

THE NEXT morning, Casto was so compliant and demure that it caught Renaldo off guard. Without further punishment, he let the young man leave his chambers.

In the stables, Casto went directly to Lys, who greeted him with a happy snort.

Casto stroked his brother's neck. "Get ready. Today we're leaving this place."

The powerful stallion rested his heavy head on the young man's shoulder and showed his consent.

Casto smiled. "Finally we'll be free again!" he whispered into Lys's ear, and it sounded like a prayer. Then he did his work as if nothing had happened.

While the morning dragged on, the storm started to gather, and every time Casto looked up at the darkening sky, his heart skipped a beat in happy anticipation. Lys was really outdoing himself, but they needed something spectacular to cover their escape and wipe out all traces the wolves might be able to follow.

After the training with Daran, Casto went to Lys and saddled him. He had felt a strange throbbing in his heart while he was giving Daran his last instructions. Daran was a good pupil, and as far as Casto could tell, a decent man. As was his habit, he had not let Daran get close to him, but their teacher-student relationship had, of course, created more affinity than Casto usually felt comfortable with.

Although Daran had always been polite and open, Casto had remained suspicious. He could not understand why the charming thief would give in to his fate as a slave so easily and even less why he seemed so eager and pleased about it. Daran was a devoted slave to his masters and obeyed them so completely that it made Casto want to throw up whenever he saw the three of them together. Thanks to his finely honed instincts, Casto knew there was more to Daran than just the pleasant surface. For somebody as young as him, Daran was too cynical, and in unguarded moments an overwhelming sadness would surface in the deep brown eyes that was able to move even Casto. For this reason, he could not bring himself to dislike Daran, which was why he had given him some praise as a kind of parting gift. Daran had been so happy, he reminded Casto of a puppy that had just been acknowledged by its owner. Apart from Sic, and perhaps Noemi, Daran was probably the only person Casto was going to miss.

He led Lys out of the stables and mounted him. Some of the stablemen looked at them in disdain but did not try to stop them from going out in this weather. Their relationship was so bad, they would gladly watch him get into trouble. Casto did not care at all. He had learned long ago to deal with the loneliness without getting consumed by it.

Once they left the houses behind, Lys started to move faster but without showing his real abilities yet. They could still be discovered, so it was better to be careful. This was a crucial part of the plan: they had to move quickly enough to be close to the main buildings when the storm went into full gear, but they had to be inconspicuous enough not to be detected.

In their hideout at the lake, Casto filled the saddlebags with supplies and armed himself with the sword and daggers he had worn when Renaldo had caught him. He was very specific about not having any debts and left some of the coins he had gotten for his time as a mercenary to pay for the food he had taken and the clothes he was wearing. After everything was in place, they went back into the open. The storm was close to its peak now, whirling debris and branches through the air. Not a soul was outside anymore; everybody had fled into the security of their homes.

Casto patted the stallion's neck. "Let's go, brother."

Lys whinnied excitedly, and then the storm broke with all its might. Hungrily, the blasts reached for Casto's coat, gripping the cowl, trying to pry him from Lys's back, but Casto was not afraid. It had been some time since he and Lys had last run with a gale strong enough to kill a person, but he knew there was nothing to fear. He was sitting on the back of the master of all storms. They were two kings, united by destiny as brothers.

Around them all hell broke loose. Trees were uprooted, tiles and planks whirled through the air as if they had no weight at all, and dust and debris darkened the day. Lys screamed triumphantly and started to run. At the entrance of the Valley, nobody tried to stop them; the guards had retreated to the safety of the watch house and closed all windows against the commotion outside.

Casto and Lys passed the ravine and reached the road leading to the plains.

Lys went at full speed. The landscape flew by while the storm followed them, erasing all traces they might have left behind them.

WHEN THE storm started, Daran had been really nervous. It was the first time he had ever witnessed nature's untamed forces so directly, but his masters had soothed him. They assured him that the main building had seen worse and was absolutely safe, but when he still flinched at every blast, they took him to the bath. The warm water helped him relax, and his masters' loving attention put his mind at ease. Soon Daran was so caught up in his lust that he did not notice anything besides their strong, massive bodies.

The warriors kept him entertained all through the night, and when they finally released him, he was so tired he slept for most of the day.

Daran woke in late afternoon, when the storm had lost most of its power. Since neither Kalad nor Aegid were present, he went to the bathroom, still exhausted and sleepy. When he remembered what they had done during the last night, a smile crept onto his lips. He had never been so happy before.

Daran had just left the pool when the door opened with such force that the hinges squeaked in protest. Daran's masters entered, fully clothed and armored and more furious than he had ever seen them before. While Daran was still trying to make sense of the situation, Aegid grabbed his upper arm and dragged him into the main room.

"Where is he? Tell us! Where did he go?"

Daran whimpered. Any feeling of happiness was gone in an instant. Instead, he felt naked panic rising inside him. "Please, Master. You're hurting me."

The merciless grip grew stronger, Daran felt as if Aegid's big hands were squashing his muscles to a pulp.

"Where is he, slave? Where did Casto go?"

Caught off guard, Daran looked up. He wondered why the warriors would inquire about Casto's whereabouts when they were angry with Daran himself. "Casto? How would I know?"

From nowhere, Kalad's hand snaked out and hit Daran brutally. "Wrong answer, slave. You were the last to see him, so where did he go?"

Desperate, Daran looked from Kalad to Aegid, hardly recognizing their faces anymore. "I really don't know. I swear!"

Without another word, Aegid pulled him up. He and Kalad took Daran before Lord Renaldo.

The Angel of Death was out of his mind with rage; his gray eyes sparked deadly embers and his beautiful face was contorted into a mask that was all the more terrifying because it added to the powerful lord's appeal.

Ruthlessly, Aegid pushed Daran to the floor from where Renaldo seized him.

"Where is he? You're the last one who talked to him. You're bound to know something." Renaldo's voice was flat.

Where the demigod's hands touched him, Daran felt an unpleasant heat. It was as if his skin was on fire. He still was not sure what this was about, only that he wanted it to stop. As demurely as possible, he answered. "My lord, I don't know anything. He just trained me as usual, nothing else."

The gray eyes bore into him. "Was there anything unusual? Did Casto behave strangely? Anything!"

Daran answered carefully, knowing full well it could cost him his life, given how agitated the Angel of Death was. "Everything was normal, Master. The only novel thing was that he praised me after training. He's never done that before, but I didn't think anything of it, I was just happy. Then he sent me away because he wanted to work with Lys. That's all I know, I swear."

The Angel of Death was just about to question him further, when his brother, the Wolf of War, interrupted him.

"The wolves have found something. We should get going."

For the last time, Renaldo addressed Daran. His voice was a cold hiss, his eyes two narrow slits that barely contained the deadly fire within. "Should I find out that you've lied to me, people will cower in fear at the mere thought of your punishment, do you understand?"

"Yes, Master" was all Daran was able to say. He was so afraid, his voice croaked.

The Angel of Death let go of him abruptly. Daran crouched on the ground, too afraid to move even a finger. Canubis, Renaldo, Aegid, and Kalad left the room.

Kalad turned to his slave one last time. He looked tense. "Go back to our chambers and wait there."

Daran got up awkwardly. Pain exploded in his arms, so badly that, for a moment, he thought he would faint. Still overwhelmed, he stared blindly at the door through which his masters had just left. Tears pricked at the corners of his eyes. He did not understand what had happened, he only knew that the picture-perfect world he had built had been smashed to pieces.

It was painful to choke back the sobs welling in his throat, but he somehow managed to do so and returned to his masters' chambers.

IN FRONT of the stables, a group of warriors—among them Aegid, Kalad, Wolfstan, and Hulda—had assembled.

Renaldo addressed his brothers-in-arms angrily. "Whoever brings him back to me gets his weight in gold and a blue diamond on top. I want him unharmed and alive, since I'm planning to deal with him personally."

With a greedy glint in their eyes, the men rode out. Canubis galloped next to his brother.

"How long had he been planning this? What do you think?"

"Knowing Casto, since the day he first set foot here in the Valley. He just had to wait for the right conditions, which would also explain his horrible temper during the last weeks—he'd been waiting to escape."

Canubis looked at his brother sharply. "There's more, isn't there?"

Renaldo did not meet his leader's gaze. "I beat him. For the first time. I was really furious because of his stubborn behavior, and then I castigated him."

"He's your slave, and he was more than disrespectful. It was your right."

"This may be as you say, but I doubt Casto saw it that way."

"How did he see it?"

"I don't know. First, I thought he would fight me immediately, but then he suddenly complied. He even apologized, and Casto is surely not the type of man who gets all docile because of a few blows. I should have known that something was wrong."

"What are you going to do once you have him back?"

Renaldo was silent for a long time. His gray eyes were trained on the horizon. "To be honest, I have no clue."

"Then you should get one. Because one thing is for sure, once he is caught, things will get emotional. You could do something that you'll regret later on."

"Would it be all right with you if I let him live?"

"Of course. I do insist on proper punishment, though. This is about our credibility as well."

Relief flooded Renaldo. If Canubis had asked it of him, he would have killed Casto for his reckless deed. For Renaldo, the person of his brother was sacrosanct. Nevertheless, he was pleased that Canubis was willing to let him keep his slave.

"I thank you, brother. That means a lot to me."

The Wolf of War smiled hungrily, his amber eyes lit up golden in the last rays of the evening sun. He loved making his little brother happy. "It's my pleasure, as always. But first let's get your slave back."

DARAN WOKE because he had turned in his sleep. The pain needling through his arm was not as bad as three days before, right after his masters had hurt him so carelessly, but it was still hard to bear. Groaning, he got up to dress himself.

The warriors had returned the previous night, which meant the hunt for Casto was finally over. Daran had pretended to be asleep because he hadn't felt any desire to face them, but now there was no more escaping it.

In front of the mirror, he carefully arranged a strand of hair to hide the nasty bruise that marred his cheek in shades of blue and green. A long-sleeved tunic concealed the ugly marks on his upper arms as well as the burns on his skin where Renaldo had gripped him. When he lived with Egand, he had always made sure that nobody could see how badly he'd been hurt. That was a triumph he did not want the barbarians to have either. He might be their property from now on, in more ways than he could have imagined possible, but he would be damned if he let them see his weakness.

The violence he had experienced at their hands was all the more frightening because he'd felt safe before. Stupid as he was, he had believed them when they said they respected him. Now he knew it had all been a lie, sweet words to get him into bed more easily. Daran was deeply ashamed of his credulity, of how fast and cheaply they had been able to buy him. It was too late now, and he doubted it was possible to withdraw from their bed. He would bear whatever might come and just cling to the hope that they would let him go one day as they had promised, although there wasn't much chance for that to happen. And why should they? He was cheap labor, bought for the price of a hot meal and dumb enough to get seduced by two men at the same time. He was unique in the truest sense of the word, if only uniquely stupid. After one last glance in the mirror, Daran left his room to go face his masters.

Breakfast was accompanied by oppressive, aggravating silence. Daran tried hard to serve his owners without getting too close to them. He held his gaze down at all times, hoping they would leave him alone. For some time it looked as if the two warriors would comply, but then Kalad placed his hand on Daran's arm.

His voice was soft. "Daran, we're truly sorry."

When Daran withdrew from the touch with an awkward gesture, he did not look up. "You don't have to be sorry about anything, Master. I'm your property. You can do with me as you please."

Kalad got up so abruptly that Daran stumbled backward, only to bump into Aegid's massive form. Frightened, he froze in place. Kalad lifted his hand and carefully pushed the strand of hair away from Daran's face.

Daran averted his gaze; he couldn't bear the thought of letting his master see the impact of what he had done. Kalad stopped him with a truly worried expression.

"We're so sorry, little thief. We didn't want things to turn out like this."

Daran felt anger welling up inside. He tossed Kalad's hand aside. "Yes, you wanted it! You hurt me although I did everything you asked of me. Despite my being obedient, you left me to the Angel of Death. You want me to trust you, but you can't do the same for me? Do you have any idea how frightened I've been?"

Shocked, Kalad withdrew his hand while Aegid took the now crying Daran in his arms.

"Shh, little thief, it's okay. Everything's fine. Please, calm down. We're so sorry."

Daran had collapsed in Aegid's arms, his body shaken by violent sobs. He desperately clung to him while the tension of the last few days finally found its release. Both desert brothers comforted him until he calmed down. Then they pulled him up and sat him on one of the lounges. Kalad tugged the loose strand behind Daran's ear and undid the fasteners on his tunic.

"Allow us to look after you, little thief. I promise we'll be careful."

With a sigh, Daran gave in to the hypnotic voice of his lord. He knew all too well that it didn't make a difference if he hesitated or not, because his masters would get their way no matter what. So he allowed Kalad to cleanse and cool the bruise on his cheek while Aegid started massaging his wounded arms. Daran couldn't suppress a whimper, which made Aegid freeze for a moment.

Aegid's voice was so contrite that a part of Daran's defense collapsed immediately. "I'm sorry, little thief. The bruises will disappear faster if they are treated. I'm going to be more careful."

Shyly, Daran looked up at his masters. There could be no doubt about their sincerity, and he suddenly felt cheap because he had been so angry with them.

"I thank you, Master."

"It's fine. We owe you."

After they took care of his wounds, they fed him. Kalad chopped some cold chicken and two slices of bread into bite-size pieces, and Aegid offered Daran a cup of fruity red wine, the kind he really loved. While he was eating, they kept on talking as if they were afraid that he would get angry again.

"We really didn't want to frighten you, little thief. It was a shock when we suddenly realized that Casto had fled from the Valley. This has never happened before. Until now, nobody has ever managed to escape from here. Renaldo is out of his mind with fury. We haven't seen him like that very often, which is why it always makes us nervous. You were obviously the last one Casto spoke to, and given his massive head start, you were the only promising lead."

Daran lowered his wine. Slowly he began to understand his masters' behavior. The Valley's security was legendary, even outside the impenetrable stone walls. If anybody managed to flee, and word got around, it would be like a chink in the intimidating image of the Pack. The apparent ease with which Casto had accomplished the impossible must have been a grave shock for the lords.

"I really don't know anything. He was normal, except for the praise at the end. Perhaps it was his farewell to me, but he didn't say anything else."

"We do believe you, little thief. But we're still upset."

This surprised Daran, since his masters appeared very calm on the outside, almost as if nothing had happened. "I don't understand. You must have caught him, otherwise you wouldn't be here."

Aegid took Daran's face in his hands; his expression was serious.

"We haven't caught Casto. He managed to escape. The storm erased all traces he might have left behind. The wolves are still searching around the Valley, but there's little hope they will find anything. Apparently, Casto had planned his flight in all detail. Renaldo is seething."

Daran swallowed hard when he realized what the brothers had just told him. "What's he gonna do to me?"

Kalad shot him a quizzical look. "What do you mean?"

"Lord Renaldo said he would punish me severely. Am I going to die?"

"Holy Mothers, little thief! Of course not!" Kalad sounded truly mortified. "You've told us that you don't know anything, and as long as you aren't proven wrong, you're safe. We already told you, the laws of the Valley protect you."

Automatically, Daran gazed at his bruised and burned arms. The laws had not protected him from that.

Aegid touched him lightly on the knee. "We have hurt you without cause. We, as well as Renaldo, owe you satisfaction."

"Are you serious?"

"Of course."

Daran stared his masters fully in the face. There could be no doubt about their sincerity. "What does that mean?"

Kalad smiled. "That we have to apologize—profoundly. You can expect some serious groveling in the coming days. And you will be compensated by us. Your injuries aren't serious enough for you to hope for your freedom, but you're entitled to some privileges."

Daran could only stare with his eyes wide. Since he had no idea what to say next, he blurted out the first thing that came to his mind. "What kind of privileges?"

Kalad shrugged, a wistful smile on his lips. Whether it was Casto's escape that still shook him or the fight with Daran was hard to tell. "Whatever you want. Clothes, jewelry, a license to have sex with others besides us. It's your choice."

Daran didn't have to think long. Everything his masters were offering, he already had—except for the license, which he had no use for—and he really didn't need more trumpery. What he wanted was security. "I don't want jewels or sleeping with others. All I want is for something like this not to happen again."

Aegid caressed Daran's back with long, soft strokes. "We can't promise that, but we know now that we can trust you. Next time something like this happens, we'll ask you first."

Daran had recovered from his shock and was willing to forgive the desert brothers. As was his wont, he showed it with a joke. "And then beat me up? That doesn't really sound like an improvement." The words were snippy, but Daran smiled at his masters while saying them. His brown eyes were full of mockery.

The warriors smiled happily, relieved that their unusual slave forgave them so easily.

Aegid's grin was challenging. "If you're lucky, this won't happen again. You just have to keep away from trouble in the future."

Daran gladly picked up on the easygoing tone, which told him, more than anything else, that things were back to normal. "How should I do that? Trouble tends to find me, no matter how hard I try to avoid it. Otherwise I wouldn't be here now."

"You're right. Seems like all you can do to protect your precious self is lead a life above reproach."

Kalad leaned forward to kiss Daran, who dodged him, laughing hard. "'A life above reproach' usually includes chastity. I'm going to avoid your bed from now on."

Aegid's hands landed on Daran's hips, his voice was an almost inaudible growl. "Who in the world told you that you need a bed to have fun? If you promise to be good and compliant, we'll show you what tables and lounges are *really* for."

Daran felt the blood rushing to his loins. His breath hitched and his hips thrust forward of their own accord.

Pleased with this obvious and inviting reaction, the warriors smiled. Aegid trailed his hands down to Daran's linen trousers while Kalad bent the thief's head back and started kissing him. There was a hot whisper in Daran's ear.

"Relax, little thief. This is all for you."

Groaning, Daran obeyed.

2. DREAMS

"DID YOU really think you could escape us? You're even dumber than I thought."

The voice ringing out from the shadows was deep, mocking, and way too familiar. Casto squirmed desperately in his chains, but there was no chance of escape, they had been set too tight.

"We've always been close, waiting for the perfect moment. It was foolish of you to run from the barbarian, because now you're ours again."

Voltara entered the light; his sadistic smile distorted the ratlike features to an unpleasant grimace. He held a leather whip with three knots at the end.

"May I introduce you to my little friend? She can hardly wait to get a taste of your blood. Since you made us look for you so long, I got permission to play with you as I see fit. I'm curious how long it will take to make you beg for mercy."

Casto struggled against the iron binding him. He would have loved to tell the torturer where he could stick his threats, but he had been gagged quite effectively. The sadist now took up position behind him, rolling his shoulders to loosen them. Then he raised his arm, whip in hand. Casto tensed, ready to receive the first blow and determined not to let his tormentor have the satisfaction of hearing him scream.

Around Voltara, the shadows started to shift. Casto concentrated on this strange dance, happy to have found something to distract him from the pain, but when he looked closer, he flinched. From the darkness, Renaldo emerged like a demon of the night, his eyes filled with red-hot rage. His sword flickered through the air in an elegant arc, resembling a deadly strike of lightning. The air turned solid. Casto's heartbeat slowed to a lazy thumping. Time itself seemed to solidify. Voltara's head fell with a stomach-turning *thud*, the face now a lifeless mask that no longer wore any threats.

The body remained upright for another moment, as if it could not understand that it was only dead flesh now, and then it sagged like a rag doll. Renaldo, the Angel of Death, turned to Casto, his gray eyes filled with hunger, consuming him with their intensity, dragging him down into a void he had hoped to escape.

A single drop of blood gathered at the sword's tip like a perverted tear and slowly extended downward. When it hit the floor, shattering into tiny shards, the sound was so loud that Casto closed his eyes.

Renaldo disappeared into the shadows like fog on a sunny morning. The following silence buried Casto under an irresistible wave from which there was no escape.

Gasping, Casto woke up. With greedy gulps he inhaled the stifling air in the small, cramped room while he darted glances into every corner, trying to fathom the shadows. He almost expected the Angel of Death to loom over his shabby bed like a monster from a fairy tale, but he was as alone as he had been every night since his escape.

Cursing under his breath, Casto got up, knowing full well that sleep was out of the question. For ten days the dream had marked the end of his nights. He wondered furiously how far he had to run in order to forget the damn Barbarian.

He and Lys had already reached the border of the Eastern Kingdoms. They had made the journey that would have taken a normal horse more than a month in about two weeks. There was no possibility the Barbarian could catch up with them. Apparently he didn't have to—to his dismay, Casto had taken him along.

Still cursing, Casto got dressed and left the run-down tavern for the stables. It was still dark outside, but that didn't present Lys with any problem at all. Lys was a child of the gloom; the night was his natural habitat. He shot his rider a sidelong glance when Casto started saddling him, but Casto shook his head.

"Don't ask, and don't say anything. I only hope this damn nightmare vanishes soon. It's starting to get on my nerves."

Lys only snorted. This was something his rider had to find out for himself. Given how stubborn Casto was, it could take some time until he finally realized where he truly belonged, but Lys would never push his brother. He enjoyed being free again, wandering through the world and sleeping at a different place every night; it befitted his mercurial nature. He already knew in his bones that this would soon come to an end.

BEFORE DAWN, Renaldo woke from the same dream that had tortured him every night since Casto had left.

Tired and annoyed, he went to the bath to splash himself with some cold water from the washbasin. He couldn't believe how much he missed the young man. His anger about Casto's escape had finally vanished and been replaced by sorrow, mixed with fear for Casto's safety. During the few good moments he had, he even felt pride growing inside him.

His clever slave had fooled them all—even the wolves. It took a great deal of intelligence and guts to go out in a storm like that and just ride away as if it were nothing but a relaxed stroll. Casto was indeed worthy of being Renaldo's personal slave.

With a sigh, he went back to bed, although experience had taught him that sleep would not bestow its peace on him now that he had woken. He tossed around in restless agitation for some time, but the absence of his beautiful slave was too much to bear.

When the sun sent her first reluctant rays into the Valley, Hulda stopped by for a visit. The beautiful killer was worried. She had known Renaldo long enough to see how bad his condition was. "You look awful, Renaldo. Still damn good, but awful."

He cast a quick smile that couldn't fool her. "I'll take it as a compliment, although I don't know why."

Hulda placed one of her hands on his arm. Her soft tone betrayed her worries even more than her gaze.

"You have to sleep, my god. It's not a good idea to lie awake the whole night and ponder the past."

"But I am sleeping, Hulda. It's my dreams that torture me. Or, to be more precise, one dream."

"What kind of dream?"

Suddenly, Hulda tensed up, although the Angel of Death couldn't see why. He shrugged. "I've been having it since Casto's escape.... I'm in a palace, everything is sumptuous, the luxury is really blinding. The kind of place I'd definitely want to raid should the opportunity present itself. There seems to be some kind of feast going on somewhere, I can hear music and laughter, but I'm moving away from it, down into the cellars. Once I reach the bottom, I start following a voice. It's unpleasant, and I don't understand the language. It sounds a little like Ummanian, but I'm not sure—you know how I loathe dealing with the merchants. Anyway, I reach a cellar. The door is closed, it has a small window at the top, and I smell decay and mold.

"I see Casto, he's chained to a wall. For some reason, he's naked and gagged. A man is standing in front of him, with a whip in his hand, and I know he's going to flog Casto. I'm overcome by anger and burn the door with my fire. It disintegrates without a sound, as if it had never been there in the first place. I draw my sword and decapitate the disgusting bully. It makes me really happy to watch that pig bleed out at my feet, and I'd like to savor the moment, but I'm drawn in by Casto. I make a first step toward him, to tell him that I want him to come home, but at that moment a drop of blood falls from my sword and I wake up."

Hulda stared at him, shaking her head. She couldn't believe what the man she had sworn fealty to was telling her. Pure acid dripped from every syllable when she said, "And you mention this 'little something' only now? You really are a fool, Renaldo. Sometimes I don't understand how you've managed to survive until now."

Renaldo pinned the beautiful woman with an angry glare. He wasn't in the mood for being lectured. "Watch your mouth, Hulda. It's a dream, nothing more."

Again she gave a vigorous shake of her head. "Just a dream? Just a dream! When was the last time you had the same dream twice? Or even thrice? This is far from normal. You're a god, Renaldo. Nothing that happens to you is coincidence."

Hulda's ferocity took him by surprise. "What is it you're telling me?"

Hulda sighed. She looked at him as if he were a child having trouble comprehending. "It's so obvious, I don't know how you could miss it. I'll bet you any amount of money that Casto is having the exact same dream. His subconscious is reaching out for you, and because you're his master and god, you can hear him."

Renaldo shook his head. He had a nagging feeling that she could be right. Her intuition was usually dead-on, but right now, he didn't like it. "I doubt that. You know how much he resented being my slave."

Hulda didn't give up. She knew when she was right and had no intention of letting her suffering lord off the hook.

"His mind, yes, but the mind is not necessarily trustworthy. To me, it looks as if your slave is more infatuated with you than he might want to admit."

"And what good does that do me? I don't know where he is, and in the dream I cannot speak."

Again a glare that shamed him. "You're his master! Take control and tell him to get the hell back home. I'm fed up with watching you pity yourself. Admit that you like him and act accordingly!"

Speechless, Renaldo watched as she got up gracefully. It had been a while since he'd last been subject to a scolding as ferocious as that. Now the mother superior bent down, placed a kiss on his forehead as if he were still a child who had yet to learn the ways of the world, and then left his chambers.

THE NEXT morning Hulda visited her god again, curious whether her chiding had made any impact. One glance at Renaldo's face and she knew things had not progressed as expected.

The Angel of Death was almost contrite when he summed up the events of the night.

"He threw me out. As if it were nothing. He's unbelievably strong."

Hulda couldn't suppress a sigh. "Of course he is. He's been living with you. If he didn't possess a will of iron, you'd have broken him long ago, like all the others before him."

With a voice so tired it stirred her pity, one of the most powerful men in the world turned to her for guidance. "Hulda, what should I do?"

Thrown a little off-balance by Renaldo's helplessness, Hulda decided to give him another piece of her mind.

"Damn it, Renaldo. Get a grip on yourself! You're a god of war, not a damsel in distress! Use your will against him and subdue him. No matter how strong Casto may be, not even he can resist a god's will."

Renaldo started to smile broadly. He truly loved that woman. "Sometimes you frighten even me, Mother Superior. You can be absolutely merciless, can't you?"

"You only realize this now? For those I love, I would drench the whole world in blood and even throw over the laws of order."

Renaldo hugged the beautiful female. "I'm grateful you're one of us, and proud to call you my friend. Tonight I'm going to get Casto back."

"That's the right attitude! Finally you behave like a man again!"

With this dubious compliment, she left her god alone.

VOLTARA'S VOICE washed over Casto like waves on the beach. Since he already knew the text by heart, he didn't bother listening anymore. Instead he concentrated on the shadows where his master would appear at any moment. He despised himself for it, but he missed the Barbarian, missed the Valley. A part of him got excited every night when the dream started, because there he could see Renaldo, even if it was only for a moment. Last night the dream had felt different, as if Renaldo had really been there and not just a product of his longing. But after a moment he had disintegrated as always, and he'd been alone again.

Now the time had come. The shadows grew deeper, and then the Angel of Death emerged from the darkness. His sword cut through the thickening air; the torturer's head fell. Renaldo rammed his weapon into the ground, watching his enemy's dead body without a hint of regret. Casto drank in his master's appearance; he would be gone again all too soon.

Only this time it did not happen. Instead Casto got the same disturbing impression as the night before, as if something were slipping through his fingers like quicksand. Renaldo started to talk to the room in general, stating a fact that felt as if it would hold true for the rest of eternity. His voice was as smooth and superior as always and the conviction in it made Casto shiver.

"Nobody threatens Casto and goes unpunished. He's mine, under my protection." He looked up, his gaze homing in on Casto. Now his voice softened, but in his eyes burned a hunger that betrayed his tone. "You've been running away long enough. It's time to come home."

The Angel of Death came to him, ungagged him, and kissed him hard. Casto wanted to withdraw, but Renaldo held him in an unwavering grip.

"Shh, this is my dream now. You'll do as I say."

Renaldo's lips engulfed Casto's mouth again; his hands stroked Casto's naked skin hungrily. Moaning, Casto twitched in the Barbarian's arms, rubbed himself against his muscular body, and groaned in protest when Renaldo retreated a step to turn him around. The chains restraining Casto tensed, but Renaldo pressed him against the stone wall nonetheless, and his bare hand landed heavily on Casto's buttocks.

The pain needled through Casto's body, racing along his nerves like wildfire and stoking a lust he had not known before. As brutal as their pairings had been, Renaldo had never hit him before. Casto was surprised at how good it felt.

Surprised and outraged. The anger that had been building for the last ten days started to seethe and then overflowed, giving Casto the strength to shatter his restraints and stumble out of Renaldo's reach. The Angel of Death was so surprised that he could only stare at his slave, who was hissing at him like a furious alley cat.

"That's definitely not what I had planned."

"I don't care what you've planned, Barbarian! Get out of my mind! Stop invading my dreams! Just leave me alone, you brute!"

Renaldo sighed. This could have been so nice, but then again, it was Casto he was dealing with. He reached out for the young man, but that only made Casto retreat farther.

"I did not invade your dreams. Honestly, I've better things to do than chase after you in this manner. It's you who keeps sucking me in every night, and I'm getting tired of it. If you really want to be free of me, then stop calling me."

"You liar! As if I had any reason to call you!"

Renaldo's gaze hardened. "Have I ever lied to you, Casto? *Ever*?"

Casto's beautiful face displayed utter confusion. Now Renaldo felt pity for the young man. He knew how downright detestable it was when a fact you had been denying with all your heart came back to bite you. His eyes suddenly widened. When he had taken control of the dream, Casto had been bound and naked. The moment Casto had managed to break free from his grasp, he had been fully clothed in the leather breeches and long-sleeved tunic he usually wore in the Valley. That he was able to bend a dream controlled by a demigod was more proof of the young man's immense willpower.

Now Casto's clothes were shimmering and twisting and coiling along and around the outline of his body, changing shape so quickly it made the mind reel. There were hints of all kinds of fashion and styles, but one in particular started to outshine all the others. It was a foreign and exotic—but now very real—outfit that reminded Renaldo of the long-gone glory of the kings of Ata-Umman and Ata-Eltam in the South. There were hints of silk and golden threads, of precious jewels, intricately crafted shoes, and even, for the blink of an eye, some sort of crown. But before Renaldo could really understand or be sure of what he was seeing, the image faded and Casto was back in his normal clothes. His features had calmed again and only the nervous flickering of his clear blue eyes betrayed his despair.

His voice was hoarse, as if he had been screaming for too long. "No, you've never lied to me. But how can I be calling you when all I want is to get as far away from you as possible?"

Renaldo was pretty sure that the young man was not talking to him directly, and that he wasn't really expecting an answer, but he gave it nevertheless.

"Perhaps there's a part of you that wants to stay by my side?"

He had expected outright refusal, but instead the stunning blue eyes looked confused and lost. Renaldo sensed his chance and kept on talking.

"I think you don't resent living in the Valley as much as you want to make yourself believe. I know you like riding the horses, and how much you enjoy roaming the forests with Lys. Even if you don't want to admit it, the Valley has become your home, hasn't it?"

The silence following these words lasted so long that Renaldo was afraid he had lost his prey. When Casto finally spoke, he did it slowly and uncertainly.

"I don't know. I think you might be right, but I don't know."

Renaldo smiled reassuringly. He dared to take a step toward Casto, and then, when he did not rear back, Renaldo closed the distance between them as quickly as possible. He closed his arms around Casto's body and placed a soft kiss on the wheat-blond hair. He bent down, unable to resist the sensuous lips of the exquisite morsel in front of him. When he didn't meet any resistance, he basked in the knowledge that he had finally won.

"Come home, Casto. I'm waiting for you."

After that, Renaldo vanished, disintegrated into the darkness like all the days before as if nothing had happened, as if he had not just turned Casto's whole life upside down.

Casto woke up, shuddering all over. His gaze wandered around without finding a trace of his master. Shaking fingers touched the lips still trembling from the Barbarian's kiss. His backside hurt as if he had really been spanked and not just dreamed about it.

Casto started to cry. Raw sobs fought their way from his throat to the surface. He cried because he knew he had lost. The Barbarian had defeated him once again, and he would go back to his side, even if it meant death. Casto had no more strength to run away, although the realization, like a dark flower that had started to bloom deep inside him, made him scream in defiance—he preferred death over living without Renaldo.

DEEPLY FOCUSED, Daran lifted his legs slowly. His abdominal and back muscles tensed, and then he was in a handstand. He stayed absolutely still for a moment, listening to his body, before he started shifting his weight onto his left arm, while at the same time extending his right arm sideways. He almost lost his balance then and there but managed to adjust his right leg just in time to regain his equilibrium. After a few measured breaths, he let both of his legs move to his left side, so all of his weight was concentrated on his left arm. In the end, it was all a question of body tension. When your middle was firm—

A sharp knock at the door sent Daran tumbling to the floor. The knocking came again, more persistent this time, and Daran hurried to see who it was. These days it was never a good idea to annoy a free member of the Pack, no matter whom. Casto's escape was like an evil curse lingering in every corner of the Valley.

The Angel of Death spent most of his time in his chambers, talking only to his brother or occasionally one of the Emeris. The closest counselors, as well as the other mercenaries, were as nervous as hell, and their attitude toward their slaves had hardened. Now even the smallest mistake was punished without mercy, for fear other slaves would take Casto's example and try to flee.

That fear was not completely irrational, for the slaves in the Valley had been caught by a strange, fast-spreading fever: a mixture of anxiety toward the masters, excitement that another slave had managed to escape—even though that slave was Casto, of all people—and a lingering hope that what he had accomplished could be repeated by others as well. Because although life in the Valley was less strenuous than outside, there were still many who wished to be masters of their own destiny. Daran couldn't understand it. He had tasted the worst of what life could offer and was more than willing to give up his unfulfilled, sad existence in freedom for the shelter and comfort his masters offered him. He thought it absurd to even consider doing the same as Casto, when it was more than obvious he had only been able to escape because of his strong, unwavering character, his intelligence, and above all, his exceptional stallion. Daran hadn't met any slave, not even many mercenaries, in the Valley who could hope to even come close to the capricious blond.

Concerning the overall tension, Daran, too, was eager not to displease his owners, although Kalad and Aegid were among the most relaxed of the lords. After they had enjoyed some very intense make-up sex, they had treated him with the same gentleness as before. He did feel their lingering unease, though, and since he knew it calmed them when he was absolutely obedient and submissive, he did them that favor, even though he got even less sleep than usual.

Daran opened the door and froze in panic when he caught sight of the Angel of Death. He quickly dropped to his knees in front of the demigod who frightened him to the core.

"Lord Renaldo! I greet you. My masters aren't here. They'll return at night."

"That I know, Daran."

The lord's voice was smooth and not unpleasant to Daran's ears now that the seething rage was gone from it. Nevertheless, Daran felt his heart skip an anxious beat. The memory of the burning, merciless grip; the cold, unrelenting stare; and the menacing aura of this man—whom even Daran's masters respected deeply—was etched into his very being.

When he addressed this intimidating personality, he couldn't stop his voice from quivering with fear. "What can I do for you, lord?"

"First of all you could invite me in. If you're not busy."

Daran wasn't sure, but the powerful warrior sounded almost amused. He hurried to get up and make room for this man who had inspired so many legends. After closing the door, he remained on his spot, gaze cast down, not knowing what to do. Nobody had prepared him for a situation like this. He knew that the Angel of Death had the right to give him orders, and that he had to obey if those instructions did not collide with his masters' will, but he had no clue how to behave in front of him.

The Angel of Death seemed to sense his confusion and took over again. "I'm here because I owe you an apology. It was wrong of me to force you like I did based only on suspicion. I'm sorry."

Daran was so taken aback, he answered without thinking. "It was a difficult situation. You needed answers quickly. I can understand that."

"No matter how difficult a situation, I don't have the right to violate the laws. I have done you wrong, and I apologize for that."

Shyly, Daran looked up. He still had problems with the fact that a man as powerful as Lord Renaldo would apologize to a mere slave like him, but his masters, who were second only to the Angel of Death in the hierarchy of the Pack, had asked his forgiveness too. This was one of the reasons why the Valley was so special. Daran gave the Angel of Death the same answer he had given his masters.

"It's very friendly of you to ask my forgiveness, and I give it wholeheartedly." He hesitated for a moment, then added, "I thank you that you did it although I'm just a slave."

A smile broke out on the face of Lord Renaldo, lighting it up like the mountains around the Valley kissed by the first rays of the morning sun. "The law is the law. I can understand why your masters are so happy with you. This is a token of my gratitude."

With a flourish, the Angel of Death presented a box about a hand broad and a span long to Daran. The surface of the wood was polished, and it gleamed in the sunlight coming in through the windows.

Not really knowing what to do, Daran looked at it. After a moment's hesitation, he took the surprisingly heavy box, his gaze still demurely downcast. "You're very friendly, Lord Renaldo. Is there anything else I can do for you?"

"No, that's all. I'm going to leave now."

The Angel of Death turned around. Daran could feel a thick coat of sadness returning, which Casto's escape had wrought around this mighty lord. He felt the need to say something, to soothe the pain that was radiating from Renaldo like heat from a bonfire.

"Please forgive me, my lord, since I know it's not my place to speak, but I don't think that Casto has run away from you. He's in love with you—I'm sure of that. To me, it looks as if he's running away from himself, not you."

The Angel of Death let go of the door and returned his gaze to Daran, one of his brows raised in mocking question. "How do you know? You're a mere child."

Daran gulped, already regretting his impulse. A man like the Angel of Death surely didn't need comforting from somebody like him. It was too late now, though, and so he kept on talking. "That might be the case, but I've seen the way he looks at you. Believe me, he loves you."

Renaldo sighed. "Nevertheless, he's gone now. But thanks for trying to comfort me. You weren't that bad at all."

The Angel of Death finally left the chambers, and Daran realized that he had to change his opinion of him once more. There was a lot more to Lord Renaldo than just a blinding exterior for a merciless, deadly inside. He had also sensed a friendliness he wouldn't have expected from a man like him.

Daran could understand better why Casto was not afraid of the lord. He was sure Casto had seen something in the terrifying warrior that had escaped everybody else.

THOROUGHLY BORED, Joran looked out onto the snow-covered road leading to the Valley. The thick white stuff was piled high on both sides and would not disappear for at least another month. He knew that nothing interesting was likely to happen in the coming days, not even in weeks. Winter had put this part of the world effectively to rest. Nobody in their right mind would go out in this cold longer than was absolutely necessary.

In the distance, Joran could hear the wolves howl. A rider was coming. The pack sounded pretty agitated, but Joran put that down to their still-lingering rage over Casto's escape. The predators had taken it almost more personally than Canubis and Renaldo.

Thinking about the last few weeks, Joran had to suppress a shudder. The wrath of the demigods and their Emeris was still so pressing that everybody tried to avoid them whenever possible.

The slaves, too, were in uproar. There were a lot more violations of the rules than normal, and even his own favorite behaved differently. He had tried talking to her—they were lovers, after all—but she hadn't been able, or willing, to give him a reasonable explanation. All he could hope for was that this dark mood wouldn't last much longer.

Now a rider rounded the bend almost three hundred paces before the guardhouse. Even at that distance, Joran could see it was an exceptional steed stomping through the snow. He was still musing who the rider might be when Ibo, his guard partner, let out a low whistle.

"Holy Mothers! It's Lysistratos!"

Joran reared up, his hand on the hilt of his sword. Now that the horse was closer, he also recognized it, as well as the rider. "It's Casto!"

Joran wanted to rush outside to retrieve the slave who had caused so much trouble for all of them, but Ibo stopped him.

"Put your sword away, idiot."

Joran listened, his head slightly bent. In the distance, the wolves howled again.

"Lord Renaldo already knows. He'll be here in no time."

"Ibo, what will he say if we don't do our duty?"

"And what will he say if we do? You know how hard it was for him to lose Casto. Do you really want to be the one to give him back his favorite possession, damaged? Not to mention the pain the black demon is going to cause you if you dare lay a hand on his master."

Joran hesitated. Ibo was right; it was definitely not a bright idea to touch Casto. He wasn't as sure about Renaldo's reaction as Ibo was, but one glance at the powerful stallion was enough to cool his heels. The steed was more intelligent than any other horse, and Joran knew all the stories they told about him. He had no inclination to lose his arm, or even his life, in one act of stupidity.

With a mocking bow, he let Ibo pass. "I heed the wisdom of your words, my friend. After you."

Ibo grinned. "Good boy. There's still hope for you."

In front of the door to the guardhouse, Casto had stopped. Full of distrust, he eyed the two guards. It was easy to see how uncomfortable he felt.

Ibo greeted him as if nothing were amiss. "Casto, it's nice that you're back."

Lysistratos snorted and danced a few steps away.

Joran held his breath. If Casto decided to turn around now and run for it—Joran didn't want to think about what Renaldo would have to say about it. There surely wasn't a quick, easy death in store for them, more the contrary.

No doubt harboring similar thoughts, Ibo held up his hands in a soothing gesture. "It's okay. We won't do anything to you. Renaldo already knows you're here. He's on his way."

Strangely enough this news seemed to calm Casto down. With his usual grace, he pulled back the hood from over his head. His wheat-blond hair blazed like a crown of light under the weak winter sun. His disturbing blue eyes gazed into the distance as if looking for something that could never be found in this world. Then he dismounted Lys with an air of determination.

Ibo flashed him a careful smile. Just because Casto had left the saddle didn't mean he couldn't still escape. "You look cold. Do you want some tea?"

Again a glare full of distrust; then Casto nodded.

"That would be nice. I've been traveling for some time." He sounded truly grateful.

Ibo shot Joran an imperious look that made him dash to get the beverage. He gave the cup to his guard partner, who handed it to Casto. While the young man drank, Joran thought about this stranger who had entered their lives so suddenly some two years ago.

Everybody in the Valley knew the stories about the Angel of Death—that he broke hearts on a daily basis and that nobody could cope with him because he was too demanding, too exhausting. His fire burned everybody who came too close. No personal slave had endured more than a few days with the demigod, whose moods could change as abruptly as the weather in the mountains. His presence terrified even his normal slaves, who didn't see their master on a regular basis, so they sometimes dropped out of his service before they had gotten accustomed to all their chores.

Then Casto had been captured. Casto, who was neither intimidated by Renaldo's rage nor driven away by his burning desire. Casto, who was not afraid of a man who had obliterated entire cities without batting an eyelash. The Angel of Death seemed to have finally found somebody who meant more to him than just the satisfaction one night could offer. Whatever you thought about Casto, he was special in more ways than one. Despite that, Joran wondered why the young man had come back. He surely knew he was facing a gruesome death—if Renaldo felt merciful.

But whatever power had bound the Angel of Death to the blond youth, it obviously worked both ways.

In the distance, they could hear the steady thumping of a horse in full gallop. Lysistratos's ears played nervously back and forth, and then he snorted. Without minding the two guards, Casto dropped the tea, turned in the direction Renaldo would come from, and sank to his knees.

This gesture, which would have been submissive if done by anybody else, wasn't the least bit servile in Casto's case. Casto generated a calmness Joran had never witnessed before. His gaze was steady, his breathing regular. He did not look like a man afraid of his impending death. If anything, Joran thought, there was excitement in the bright blue eyes.

Then Ghost rounded the corner, his rider's hair flying in the wind. The Angel of Death hadn't taken the time to put on a coat or even saddle his horse.

Ghost stopped right in front of Casto, his hooves digging deep into the snow. Renaldo jumped down hurriedly, radiating excitement and a hunger that made Joran flinch. If emotions as intense as these were to be directed at him, he would surely flee, but all Casto did was emanate the same insane longing that was almost unbearable to witness.

Time seemed to hold her breath, together with the world.

Both men stared as if they wanted to penetrate the other's soul, as if they wanted to drown in each other. All of a sudden, the Angel of Death yanked his slave from the ground, crushing him to his chest so hard his ribs creaked. Casto gave as much as he took, almost crawling into his master's grip, as if he wanted to merge into him.

They stood like that for a long time, displaying an intimacy that made Joran ache with jealousy despite his fear of its intensity. Deep inside, he felt himself wishing for the same bliss in his own life, even though he knew the price for it was probably more than he could afford. Abruptly, Renaldo stepped back. His gaze drilled into Casto.

"Come." Renaldo's voice was raw with emotion.

Both men got onto their horses and raced into the heart of the Valley.

Joran swept the sweat off his face. The heat between them had come off in waves. Being right next to the Angel of Death must have been unbearably hot. The demigod's power was more than just slightly frightening, but Casto didn't seem to have noticed.

"Are you glad that you followed my advice?" Ibo grinned broadly at his partner.

"What do you think the lord would have done to me should I have laid a hand on Casto?"

His friend's expression turned serious. "With luck, you would have died fast, although I doubt it. Whatever force is driving these two, I'm glad I don't have to endure it."

Wiser words, Joran thought, had never been spoken before.

AT THE stables, Renaldo left the horses in the care of a rather surprised boy, and then he grabbed Casto's wrist and dragged him to his chambers.

He shut the door with a loud *bang* before turning around to Casto.

Casto looked somehow lost, standing in the middle of the room, gazing hungrily at Renaldo. The chambers seemed to overflow with different emotions: some of them open, some restrained. Anger, relief, hunger, despair. There were too many to make a decision as to which one Casto should give in to. Renaldo took that from him.

With a growl, he extended his hand. His slave's blue eyes homed in on him, and they both charged. Renaldo could not wait to see Casto naked, and he ripped off his clothes without thinking twice about the damage he did to the fabric.

Casto yanked off his master's belt with the same unbridled impatience. He got rid of the troublesome trousers and gave a satisfied whimper when Renaldo bent him over one of the lounges to enter him.

For the next few hours, they ravished each other like demons from the other world, desperate to eliminate the hunger and loneliness that had accumulated during the last few weeks. All fights were off; they simply wanted to erase the emptiness that had tortured them both so mercilessly.

It was after midnight when Renaldo spoke for the first time. He had pressed Casto against the wall. His right hand balanced him, and his left pressed around Casto's waist so relentlessly that Casto would carry the marks for days to come.

Renaldo's voice was barely audible, a growl coming from deep within. "Don't ever do that again, do you get me? Ever!"

Instead of an answer, Casto raised his backside in an attempt to invite his master in again and, gladly, Renaldo complied.

Later, when their hunger was finally sated, they lay in Renaldo's bed.

Renaldo looked down on his slave in a thoroughly satisfied manner. "I've missed you."

Casto closed his eyes for a moment. When he opened them again, the blue seemed to have intensified. "I've missed you too." He hesitated for a moment. "Master."

Renaldo smiled, deeply pleased. "That's the first time you've called me that."

Casto met his gaze. "Apparently, I don't have much of a choice."

With his index finger, Renaldo traced Casto's cheek. "I'm glad that you're back."

"You called me. There was nothing I could do but to obey."

"And if you could have defied me?"

A shadow clouded the beautiful eyes. "Then I wouldn't be here now. You slapped me, Barbarian. Slapped me and spanked me!"

Renaldo sighed. The peaceful atmosphere had evaporated faster than he'd thought possible, and although he was more than glad to have Casto back in his arms, he did not plan on giving in to him. "You deserved it for being so unruly."

"I do admit that I wasn't a prime example of courtesy, but that's your fault alone, not mine."

Surprised, Renaldo lifted an eyebrow. "How can your undue behavior be my fault?"

An angry growl was the prize for his teasing, but then Casto continued, and he sounded unusually serious. "If you were the primitive barbarian I so want to see in you, then it would be easy for me to defy you, but unfortunately, you're more than you seem. You're devious. You've occupied my heart and thoughts, and now you even take my dreams from me. That's beyond unfair."

Strangely touched by his slave's sudden honesty, Renaldo caressed the back of his hand, a gesture Casto allowed for once. "I've already told you that life is never fair. I'm a god. It's my right to sneak into your life—although I wouldn't use such a rude term to describe the honor of having me by your side."

Those words managed to rile Casto up and he tried to back away from Renaldo, but the warrior stopped him.

"I called you because I wanted you back, because I missed you so much. Life seemed to have lost its shine. I can banish you from my thoughts no more than you can banish me from yours. When I look at you, all I can think about is how wonderful it is to own you in every sense of the word. It makes me happy, knowing you're back here in my bed, my chambers, my power."

Casto's features contorted into an angry grimace. "I'm not some ox you bought in the market!"

"No. You're my slave, my precious possession! You're valuable to me. And don't tell me you didn't like what we did for the last few hours. You reveled in being mine, in submitting to my will. Don't try to deny it!"

Casto roared in anger. Every word the Barbarian said was true, and he didn't know whom he loathed more for it—himself, or the cause of all his grief. "I hate you! Why can't you just leave me alone? Yes, I do enjoy the sex, but that's it. I don't know what else we have in common. I'm certainly not a possession, and I'll never be, never!"

Spurred on by Casto's violent outburst, Renaldo felt his anger rise. The young man's denial of the obvious made him furious.

"*What we have in common*? You want to know what binds us?"

He grabbed Casto's shoulder, yanked him forward brutally, and kissed him hard. He could feel his fire waking, could sense how it made the air around him boil, but Casto didn't seem to be troubled at all, if he even realized what was happening.

Casto was too busy fighting the kiss, as well as the touch, and what both stirred inside him. With all his willpower, he held back his own lewd responses even as he tried to inspire them in Renaldo. Now they were back to the old fights for dominance, although there was a lingering feeling of loneliness. They both drowned in a stream of emotions that neither of them understood or was able to control.

It was impossible to tell who had won this battle. A cynical bystander might have said there was no way either of them could prevail.

Panting, Renaldo engulfed Casto in his powerful arms.

"Give it up! You've come back. Now you have to play by my rules."

Casto fought the embrace. "Never! Leave me alone!"

Renaldo gave up. This was leading nowhere. He let go of Casto and changed the topic, as he always did when they had reached a dead end in a fight.

"Go and wash yourself, grab something to eat, and then go to sleep. I'll punish you tomorrow."

For a moment, fear flashed in the blue eyes, but it was immediately taken away by a defiant wave. Casto would never admit that he was afraid of Renaldo's retaliation.

"As you wish, *Master*."

Renaldo did entertain the idea of letting his unruly slave spend the night in uncertainty, but as much as he had wanted to strangle him just a few moments ago, he could not bring himself to torture him like that.

"I'm not going to kill you, and you won't be crippled. You're simply too valuable, Casto. My brother wants your blood, though, and I agree with him. The other slaves mustn't think that we tolerate behavior like you've shown. You'll be whipped in public."

Casto nodded, his face an icy mask. He tried to hide his relief, for he had anticipated far worse. "I understand." Then he turned around and vanished into the bathroom.

Renaldo was surprised by the youth's calm demeanor, but when he thought about it, Casto didn't really have a choice, and he could be surprisingly fatalistic for somebody with such a hot temper.

"YOU REALLY have to learn obedience, Prince. Your father is displeased by your behavior." The torturer's voice was full of sadistic glee; he enjoyed being able to aggrieve his highborn victim like that.

The prince tried in vain to get rid of the chains around his wrists, looking for an escape that did not exist.

The helpless struggles of the still-childish body woke feelings of a different kind in the torturer, but he held himself back. The joy of punishing the prince on a daily basis was tied to rather strict constraints, which he never violated. Not to sexually abuse his victim was one of them. Another, that there shouldn't be any permanent marks on the royal skin. For somebody as skilled in inflicting pain as he was, it wasn't a great problem. The torturer grabbed the broad leather thong he had chosen for today and set it *whoosh*ing through the air.

Upon hearing the high-pitched noise, the prince shivered, but then his azure gaze hardened. He would not cry out, no matter how hard the man whipped him. This was the final line he would never cross, the triumph he would never permit.

3. TRAINING

DARAN WAS standing between Kalad and Aegid in front of the main hall. They waited together with all the other inhabitants of the Valley to see Lord Renaldo appear with his slave.

The news that Casto had returned to the Angel of Death of his own free will had spread like wildfire, as well as the fact that he would be punished today. The reactions to that news varied greatly.

Most of the mercenaries were glad that their leader had gotten his highly valued possession back and would therefore be in a better mood from now on. They were willing to go along with any punishment Renaldo would administer even if it was not the ultimate one. Many of the slaves, especially those who had to deal with the demigods and the Emeris directly, were glad as well. Casto's return meant an easing of the tension that had made their lives difficult since he had fled. There were also many who would have gladly given Casto a more severe punishment; they were forced to witness the spectacle of his sentence, which was nothing less than a cruel statement about their own low status. Nobody thought Casto should be spared, but being shown the consequences for wrongdoing in such a brutal, blatant manner was not something they enjoyed. It deepened their animosity toward the reason for this demonstration of power.

Daran was one of the few who thought it a blessing that his masters were with him. Although they had to keep up appearances, the two desert warriors stood close enough to him to ease his mind and help him bear what was to come.

Now the Angel of Death approached from the main hall with Casto in tow. The young man walked a few steps behind his master, his long blond hair flowing freely down his back. Despite the chill, he wore only blue linen trousers that hung so low on his hips they seemed likely to glide down at any moment. He was so good-looking that it took Daran's breath away. The muscles on Casto's torso were perfectly sculpted without being vulgar, and his skin gleamed like polished bronze in the sun. The outline of Casto's regal face, partly obscured by wayward strands of hair, reminded Daran of an expensive painting he had once seen. Casto looked like an elegant racehorse, or a dancer, completely in charge of every fiber of his well-trained body. He emanated that special, ingrained arrogance that never left him, not even in a situation like this.

Daran understood better now why the other slaves hated Casto so much and why everybody wanted to own him. Possessing him meant an immediate upgrade in prestige, no matter how badly he behaved sometimes. He was a sparkling accessory that heightened Renaldo's status like nothing else could. Being able to acquire, and keep, a rare gem like the hot-tempered Casto demonstrated the power and prowess of his owner. Seen in that light, even the mood swings Casto displayed so openly were desirable.

In the middle of the space, where a pole was rammed into the frozen earth, the two men stopped. Casto knelt in front of his master, his head bowed low. Daran had never seen his teacher so submissive, and he did not like the idea that this proud man should be humiliated in front of so many witnesses.

Renaldo's gray eyes scanned the crowd, stopping for a moment at his brother's face, then returned to the kneeling slave. When he spoke, his voice was loud and clear. Neither his tone nor his expression gave the slightest hint of the emotions boiling behind the mask.

"You're all here to witness the punishment of an unruly slave. Casto has dared to flee. You all know the consequences of doing that."

Trembling, Daran reached for Aegid's hand, not caring about the dirty looks he got for that from all sides. He couldn't believe that Lord Renaldo would really do that to his slave: the glass whip and crippling—it was beyond cruel. While Daran saw the worst possible scenarios running in front of his inner eye, Lord Renaldo kept on talking.

"But Casto did not only escape, he also came back of his own free will, which alleviates his punishment. Fifty strokes with the leather whip, and may this be a warning to you all not to question or challenge our authority again!"

Daran couldn't suppress a relieved sigh. Fifty strokes was not child's play, but regarding the alternative, it was the better choice.

Aegid caressed his arm, his voice barely audible. "We told you it wouldn't be that bad."

Daran squeezed Aegid's hand. "I'm sorry, but I simply couldn't believe you. And when Lord Renaldo started talking like that—I really thought he would break Casto's legs."

"You sweet little idiot. Now that he's finally back?"

Kalad teased him as always, and Daran flashed him a grateful smile. With a lift of his chin, Aegid indicated that business was about to start. Obediently, Daran turned back to witness his teacher's punishment.

On Renaldo's command, Casto got up. Two overseers chained him to the pole with his arms extended sideways. The silence was palpable when Renaldo received a leather whip with knotted ends from his brother's hand. Such an instrument could cause terrible wounds and was almost as feared among the slaves as the glass whip. Renaldo took position behind his slave and started flogging him without hesitation.

As the first blows were dealt, Daran cringed; he thought he could feel the pain himself.

Casto stood motionless, silent. He didn't make a single sound, no whimper, no panting. His gaze was fixed on something Daran could not see. Daran admired his courage. He himself would have started begging for mercy at the first blow. It was fitting how Casto bore the pain and did not do anything degrading. Daran would have thought it inappropriate if the proud young man had been reduced to humiliating pleading.

Blood trickled in thin streams from the wounds the Angel of Death caused with such cold precision. The sound when the leather tore the skin made Daran choke. He had seen merciless brutality before, but this scene was strangely surreal and he didn't know what was worse— Casto's silence, the distance in Renaldo's gaze, or the shocked hush of the spectators.

As if he could read his mind, Aegid placed his hand on Daran's neck, trying to comfort him, but Daran still had difficulty witnessing the cruel scene any longer. To distract himself, he looked around. The faces of the Emeris and mercenaries were frozen and did not betray any emotion at all. Only Lady Noemi showed something akin to compassion on her face, but Daran was not sure if this was because of her being a healer or because she really felt for Casto. The witch was almost as hard to read as Lord Canubis who instilled nothing but utter fear in Daran.

In the eyes of the slaves, Daran read pure terror. The scent of Casto's blood was like a poisonous perfume in the air, reminding them all how much they were at the mercy of their masters. A few faces were twisted in hatred for their owners, but fear of their lords was all too prominent.

Only one other set of eyes was full of pity and sympathy. Sic, the smithy apprentice, was standing close to Daran. Behind him, the massive bulk of his master was like a looming shadow. Noran's face was cold. His hand rested on his slave's neck, but not to soothe. To Daran, it lay there to heighten the threat. The master smith was the Emeris Daran feared the most. He was so bad tempered, coarse and brutal, that Daran couldn't understand how Sic managed to deal with him. Sic even seemed to admire him, which was beyond comprehension. The friendly young man never had much time on his hands—his master kept him constantly occupied—but on the few occasions when they had exchanged words, Daran had learned that Sic not only admired but also idolized the gruff man. He wondered what Sic had had to endure to think a man like Noran was worthy of respect, but so far he hadn't dared to ask.

The whip kept on tearing Casto's skin without mercy. The only good thing was that it was over fast. Renaldo did not extend the punishment unnecessarily. Right after Daran had counted the last stroke under his breath, Lord Renaldo released his slave personally. With a defiant glare, and biting his lips in anger and pain, Casto went down on his knees again. This was the sign for everybody else that the spectacle was over. They all left in grave silence. Daran was led away by his masters. Before he walked off, he caught a last glimpse of owner and slave in the middle of the arena, and he wondered if anybody else had noticed that not only Renaldo, but Casto as well, stood in a puddle of molten snow.

After the last slave departed, Canubis approached the two silent figures. He patted Renaldo's shoulder in silent recognition of what he had just done. He knew how hard it had been for his brother to humiliate and wound his slave the way he had done. He turned to the still-kneeling Casto. Canubis was more than a little impressed by the young man's bravery. It wasn't easy to bear the pain inflicted by a leather whip so stoically, especially when Renaldo was the one wielding it. Casto was indeed a worthy servant to his brother, albeit a stubborn one.

"Did you learn your lesson, slave?"

The young man's voice was a little ragged. A slight trembling betrayed the pain he was enduring. "Yes, lord."

"Get up and look at me." Graceful as always, Casto rose to his feet. His gaze met the Wolf of War's without fear or submission. Canubis sighed. A worthy servant, indeed. "Will you be more obedient in the future?"

"I won't try to escape again, if that's what you mean. It turns out I'm not able to do it."

Canubis knew he had to be content with that. Renaldo had already warned him, and it wasn't as if he needed more. Casto couldn't leave the Valley anymore; he was bound to his master. Even though Canubis would be damned if he did not voice his thoughts clearly. He had felt Renaldo's pain like his own, and it made him furious that Casto did not seem to understand the damage he had caused. He grabbed Casto's shoulders, letting him feel that he could increase the pressure anytime to make him suffer, and addressed him in a cold, threatening voice. He wanted the capricious young man to understand once and for all the position he was in.

"If you ever grieve my brother like this again, if you ever cause such chaos in my Valley for a second time, I swear you'll wish you'd never been born. Do you understand?"

It was hard to tell whether the harsh words and the inflicted pain had gotten through to Casto or not. Canubis felt irritable. He wasn't used to this kind of defiance, and he felt the sudden urge to throttle this insignificant little worm to get his message across. Somehow he managed to hold back, shocked that a mere slave could make him lose his cool. He began to understand his brother a little better. There was something about Casto that stirred up emotions Canubis had long thought tamed. It was not unpleasant, this feeling, but it caught him off guard.

With a shrug, Canubis freed himself from Casto's strange allure. "I leave him to you, brother."

The demigods shared a short hug, and then Canubis turned toward the training halls.

Renaldo took Casto's hand. "Come. You better get out of the cold."

Casto shot him a nasty look that spoke louder than words of how displeased he was with the whole situation, but he followed him into the chambers nevertheless. There, Renaldo cleaned the wounds on Casto's back while Casto tried not to cry out in pain.

The Barbarian was a skilled torturer who had almost managed to break him.

"I'm very proud of you, Casto. You were unbelievably brave."

"I'm always happy when I manage to please you, Barbarian." Pure acid dripped from every syllable.

Renaldo grinned, knowing that Casto couldn't see his expression. "It's always good for a slave when his master is satisfied with his performance. In your case, it means your wounds will be healed. Noemi is stopping by later."

Casto turned his head in surprise. "I'll be healed?"

"Of course. But don't get any ideas—it's mainly because I don't wish to mar your beautiful skin permanently. That would lower your value considerably. Plus you have some work to do. After you left, the stables turned into chaos."

Casto rolled his eyes, then scrutinized his master suspiciously. "Why is Lady Noemi not here yet?"

"She'll come this evening. The pain you'll endure till then is part of your punishment. I won't let you off easily."

"I hate you."

"I know. Now come, I want to kiss you."

For a moment Casto thought about neglecting Renaldo's wish, but then he shrugged. The punishment had taken its toll, and he had no energy left for further discussion.

"If you insist."

"I insist. And now shut up."

LOST IN thought, Damon passed the stables on his way back to the sleeping quarters. He was still busy processing the events of the day and of the last few weeks. It wasn't really surprising that Casto had managed to escape from the Valley; the arrogant little bastard had the backbone it took to pull off such a stunt. His voluntary return, on the other hand, was unexpected, as was the fact that he was still alive and not crippled.

Rumor even had it that the Angel of Death had called his slave back with the power of his thoughts.

There was no doubt about the steadily increasing power of the brothers. Ever since Lord Canubis had found his heart, their potency had been growing, but Damon couldn't, and wouldn't, believe that they were already that strong. Even a magically talented man like himself had considerable difficulties when tapping into the tamed powers of the stream of magic. Without help from the Good Mother, it would be impossible for humans to use magic on Ana-Darasa. The rules introduced by Ana-Isara and Ana-Aruna were gradually taking over this world, and should Renaldo and Canubis win against the Good Mother, only they and the Emeris would be able to go against those laws.

Although the price Damon had to pay for using magic was steadily increasing, he could not imagine a life without it. His family had its roots at the beginning of the second era and had always been magically blessed. For him, magic was as natural as breathing. The mere thought of one day losing those abilities made him as dangerous as a cornered wildcat.

Without checking, Damon knew that Casto's escape was a first in the Valley's history. The question was how he could make use of that. Obviously, the Angel of Death was infatuated with the arrogant bastard, which made him the perfect material for blackmail.

Deep inside, Damon already suspected who Casto really was, but at the moment, his mind still thought the idea absurd. He decided to wait, observe, and perhaps, when an opportunity presented itself, make contact. Should Casto stay at his difficult master's side through this second winter, though, there was still time to take action. It would be even easier if the bond between them became stronger.

Casto was the perfect target for any kind of scheme, since he wasn't exactly popular with the other slaves. Now he was back, they hated him wholeheartedly for throwing away the freedom they longed for so desperately. Isolating him shouldn't pose a problem, especially not for somebody as experienced in these matters as Damon. Only Sic, the stupid little boy serving Lord Noran, and Daran, the brat Lord Aegid and Lord Kalad had taken on as their latest plaything, were truly friendly toward Casto. Getting rid of Sic wouldn't be too difficult, since his master was so strict and merciless, and Daran was so wrapped up in pleasing his masters he hardly noticed anything beside. Not that a man as proud and conceited as Casto would ever stoop so low as to ask for help. Regarding this, he was the perfect target.

Damon was satisfied. Things were going according to plan, and the defeat of the bastard brothers was only a question of time.

TWO DAYS after Casto's public punishment, Daran waited for him at the training area, with Rajan saddled and ready for action. Daran had been more than surprised when his masters had told him that he was to resume his training with Casto, but they had ignored his questioning looks and sent him on his way.

Now Casto was coming from the stables, his face as dismissive as always, his blue eyes glinting in annoyance.

"Why aren't you on your horse already? You should be warmed up by now!"

Against his better judgment, Daran had to smile. Somehow he had expected Casto to be different after his punishment—perhaps softer— but it seemed that the whipping had made him even worse tempered than before.

"Why are you grinning like a madman?"

"I'm sorry, Casto. I'm just glad and surprised that you're up and about again. The way Lord Renaldo treated you, I thought you wouldn't be coming here for the next few weeks."

If Daran had hoped to placate his teacher, he learned differently. Casto's eyes narrowed to small slits when he was reminded of his public humiliation.

"I'm fine. And now get up. I want to see if you've trained diligently while I was gone."

Daran gave up. He followed Casto's orders and submitted to his bullying for an entire hour. At the end, his foul-tempered teacher beckoned him closer.

"That wasn't too bad. You practiced quite well, which means we can start with something new soon." Casto sounded somewhat reluctant, though, as if he couldn't believe he was actually praising his pupil.

Daran got down from Rajan's back and smiled at him, knowing full well that this annoyed Casto even more. "Thank you. I can hardly wait."

"You're done already? That's good."

The two young men turned to the person who had addressed them, and Daran went immediately to his knees.

Casto only shot his master a dirty look. "What do you want, Barbarian?"

Daran felt cold chills running down his spine when he heard Casto talking to the Angel of Death in such a disrespectful manner, but Lord Renaldo seemed to be more amused than angry.

"You'll find out soon enough. Daran, you can get up. I don't bite."

Reluctantly, Daran got up, his gaze still lowered.

"Nice collar."

Lord Renaldo's voice was suggestive, yet that was not what made Daran's cheeks go crimson but the memory of how he'd gotten the slave mark around his neck. The day the Angel of Death had apologized to him, Aegid and Kalad had returned shortly after. Together they had opened Lord Renaldo's present, and Daran had been rendered speechless. Lord Renaldo had given him two bracelets made of pure gold and formed like snakes with eyes made of emeralds. His masters made him wear only those when he served them dinner, and he had been side dish, main course, and dessert before they took him to the bedroom. There, Kalad had given him a second box containing the collar he wore now. It was made of the finest leather from mountain deer and dyed dark green with a golden clasp.

Daran had looked at his masters imploringly. "Why only now?"

Kalad had caressed him with his usual reverence and love. "We didn't want to overburden you. We thought it would be easier for you if you had time to get accustomed to living in the Valley first, before marking you in such a distinct way."

Daran had been speechless. The two barbarian warriors showed him more consideration than his own mother had done. Full of gratitude, respect, and love, he had kissed his masters' hands before they fastened the leather around his neck and then bedded him again.

Daran focused on his hands. "Thank you, Lord Renaldo. I owe this present to you. The bracelets are very beautiful. My masters were pleased."

"I thought so. You may go now, Daran."

"Lord Renaldo, Casto."

Daran bowed again, and then he led Rajan to the stables. As he left, he could hear the Angel of Death talking to Casto.

"Did you see how obedient and subservient Daran is? That's what I call well trained. You should follow his shining example."

Casto's answer was snippy as always.

"If he's that wonderful, why don't you go ahead and buy him? You could leave me alone then."

The warm laughter from the Angel of Death followed Daran to the stables. Again he wondered, as so many times before, what kind of relationship those two had. And just like everybody else who had pondered that question, he had to give up. The interplay between them was too complicated, too willful, and definitely way too dangerous. Given the powers the demigod controlled, it was a wonder that Casto had been able to survive till now. Any outsider who thought about intruding in their convoluted game could only find death when caught in the crossfire.

Daran shook his head to banish those disturbing thoughts. He had to be grateful for Kalad and Aegid—two relaxed, laid-back masters who couldn't burn him to cinders in a violent fit of temper.

MEANWHILE, RENALDO led Casto to the training hall. This house was almost as big as the main building and made from the same sturdy material. It was the second-oldest structure in the Valley and the main reason for the deadly power of the Pack. On both sides, the mercenaries' weapons, all of them of the highest quality, made from the finest blue steel and ground to razor sharpness, were stored in various chambers. Like the buildings, the weapons fitted their purpose without any ornamentation or useless gadgets. They were tools for war and treated as such. Even Canubis and Renaldo, who loved finely made and decorated swords, wore simple weapons in battle, whose only beauty lay in the way they could bring death to their enemies.

The remaining parts of the hall were divided into rooms of different sizes, which could house five to fifty warriors. Each chamber had the same layout, with room for free exercise and a special area where a variety of practice activities could be conducted. On the walls hung training weapons made of wood. Some of them were even heavier than their brothers made from steel, to heighten the effects of training.

In one of the smaller rooms, Renaldo had taken off his coat and tunic. He shot Casto a demanding look. "If I were you, I'd take off my tunic as well. You'll get pretty sweaty in a moment's time."

Casto was cautious. He thought he knew what the Barbarian was up to, but he had problems believing it. "You want to teach me? Why?"

Renaldo made a vague gesture. "I've been thinking. One of the reasons you were able to escape is because you're not busy enough. This is a simple means to make you so tired that you're unable to think straight at the end of the day, let alone plan an escape. Despite that, you're a talented fighter. It would be a waste to let that go. With the right kind of training, you can become a dangerous warrior."

Casto's eyes showed a range of emotions before his expression settled down to his usual detached calm. Casto didn't react to the challenge in Renaldo's last words but did something that the Angel of Death would have never anticipated. He stepped forward, bent his knee, bowed his head low, and took his master's hands and pressed his forehead against them in a gesture of respect.

"I thank you, my lord. I'm truly honored."

Renaldo closed his eyes and allowed himself to enjoy Casto's unusual obedience for a moment. Yet again Casto had managed to surprise him, and his suspicion that the young man was more than a mere merchant's son grew. Reading a situation like this correctly and reacting to it in a befitting manner was something most of his mercenaries would not have been able to do.

He took his hands away reluctantly while giving Casto an encouraging smile. "You phrased that quite well. Now get up, I want to start with the training."

Gracefully, Casto rose, stripped, and took the sword Renaldo gave to him.

It had been more than a year since Casto had last fought with a blade, but his training during childhood had been thorough, if harsh. It did not take him long to get into the rhythm again, forcing the first reluctant words of praise out of Renaldo.

"I see you haven't forgotten your basics. Let's see if you're still as good as before, shall we?"

Casto grinned; he enjoyed this more than he was willing to admit. "Be my guest, Barbarian."

Lessons with Renaldo soon proved to be a lot more demanding and challenging than with Master Dwor, Casto's teacher in Ummana, but they lacked the cruelty the old man had exercised on a daily basis. Renaldo was strict but not brutal. He was good at explaining things and showed an amount of patience Casto wouldn't have thought him capable of.

At the end of the lesson, Casto was covered in sweat, exhausted, and strangely happy. He had enjoyed the hard workout, testing his body's limits and then going beyond them. It had felt good to go through the basic patterns of offense and defense again, and he marveled at how easily his body remembered all the moves.

Renaldo raised his sword with a broad smile. He, too, was highly satisfied with this first lesson. He had pondered for a long time how to get Casto accustomed to living in the Valley. Since Casto couldn't be bribed with presents, Renaldo had decided to lure him in other ways. Another advantage to this method was that he could supervise Casto's training personally.

It had been a long time since Renaldo had last seen a fighter as intuitive and gifted as Casto, and he felt excitement rising inside when he thought about all the things he was going to teach the exceptional young man. "One last fight. Then we're done for today."

With snakelike movements, Renaldo attacked and Casto hurried to block his sword.

It was crystal clear that Casto was able to do it only because Renaldo was holding back, but Casto didn't plan to make it easy for him. With willpower alone, he forced his exhausted body back into fighting mode. He fenced with all his might and even managed to break through Renaldo's defenses once, which was a small miracle since the Barbarian did not make mistakes. As if to punish him for this small triumph, Renaldo spun around, his sword weaving a complicated pattern in the air, and just like that, Casto's weapon was gone.

The tip of Renaldo's blade rested on Casto's throat; the gray eyes sparked in triumph.

Casto didn't like that at all, but there was nothing he could do.

"You've lost."

Casto swallowed hard. He was slightly annoyed but also strangely turned on. Something about the way Renaldo was looking at him reached places deep inside his body and made them boil. He wet his dry lips with his tongue. "I know."

"The loser must do what the winner wants."

"I know."

His sword still on Casto's throat, Renaldo forced him against the wall. "Open your trousers and pull them down."

Trembling with lust, Casto obeyed. Under normal circumstances he would have resented his master's bossy tone, but Renaldo's ferocity had inflamed him as well.

As soon as Casto's sex was bare and hard in front of him, Renaldo let go of his blade. He took Casto's face in his hands and kissed him hard. "Open my trousers."

Casto whimpered when he felt Renaldo's hardness against his hands. Although only their lips had touched so far, he was as ready as he could be. He could not wait to feel Renaldo.

Again Renaldo kissed him deeply. After what felt like eternity, he turned Casto around and pressed him against the wall, using his entire body as leverage. Renaldo bit Casto's ear in a playful manner. On the hot breath engulfing Casto's left side, Renaldo huffed a taunting question. "Tell me slave, how does it feel to be defeated twice? Do you like being subdued by me?"

Anger flared inside Casto. The question reminded him why he hated Renaldo so much, and he could feel the flames of lust that had been driving him crazy just moments ago being doused, as if by a bucket of cold water. He was not some kind of toy the Barbarian could use as a dummy and then bed whenever he felt like it!

Casto tensed, willing to fight back, and Renaldo suddenly realized that he had lost the upper hand. Before he could do anything to turn the tables in his favor again, Casto had already slipped from his embrace.

Casto's breath was ragged and his eyes shot furious sparks despite his exhaustion. "Keep your hands to yourself, you brute! I'm not here to be your toy, and you better remember that in the future. I truly hate being played with like that, loser or not."

There was a moment of shocked silence, during which Casto closed his trousers again. Still half-naked and flushed, he looked at Renaldo, who was staring at him like he had just grown a second head, and Casto couldn't help but laugh. He bowed, half-mocking, half-serious, and bent down to pick up the training swords.

"I thank you for the lesson, Master. It was truly delectable. But I think you should get dressed again. You look a little—indisposed."

Renaldo snapped out of his trance. His gray eyes shot daggers. "You little tease! Cutting me off like that! And just when things were about to get interesting!"

Casto's grin broadened. "Then you shouldn't have started talking nonsense. I was with you until you thought that one of your little games for dominance was in order. It's your own fault that you're high and dry now."

Still angry about the sudden interruption of what could have been a very worthwhile afternoon, but also amused by Casto's quick repartee, Renaldo put his trousers back on. "I admit defeat on that one. You really got me there. But the duel was my win."

"How childish can you be? But yes, you won the duel. So let's call it an impasse, O Master."

"Just this once, O my impertinent slave. Just this once."

IN THE evening Casto fell down on one of the lounges with a whimper. He was too exhausted to take off his boots. All he wanted was to close his eyes and sleep.

Renaldo observed him with a broad grin. "Looks like my plan has worked out. Are you very tired?"

Casto shot his master a look that said it all, but he didn't bother to answer.

Renaldo laughed. He was immensely pleased with himself despite the sour outcome of their first training session. "I thought so. That's why

I've called for Frankus." He picked up Casto and carried him to the bath, where the servant was waiting.

He, too, was grinning gleefully. "Let's see if we can't revive his spirits. You can leave him to me, Master. I'll take good care of him."

Renaldo kissed Casto's forehead before leaving him in the care of Frankus.

Casto was too tired to do more than let himself be commanded by Frankus. The man washed him skillfully before massaging herbal oil into Casto's aching muscles. For Frankus it was sheer bliss to treat a body as exquisite as that one, and in addition he got the chance to view Casto up close.

Frankus had been in the Valley since his birth. Both his parents had been slaves, which technically made him one as well, but his mistress had always treated him more like a son than a slave, and the other free folk had followed her example. After he became a man, he had even been offered a place in the Pack by Canubis, but Frankus had always preferred the peaceful life in the Valley over the hardships of the battlefield, although he was a skilled fighter.

Frankus had become master of the sauna and had kept on developing it ever since. With his magical hands, which could find any tension in the human body, he took care of the mercenaries' well-being.

Treating Casto was an honor that accentuated his standing and reputation with the demigods. Renaldo had made clear what would happen to those who dared to lay a hand on his slave without his permission.

While he was massaging Casto's tense muscles, Frankus thought about the beautiful young man. Like everybody else in the Valley, he was fascinated by the loud, turbulent relationship Casto shared with Renaldo. It was obvious that he did not fear his short-tempered master and that his own temperament was an equal match. What exactly they saw in each other, Frankus could not guess. The connection was so layered that not even Casto and Renaldo seemed to know what drove them.

Frankus smiled. One thing was for sure, as long as this moody young man resided in the Valley, things wouldn't get boring anytime soon.

Almost two hours later, Frankus took his leave while Casto stood next to his master, deeply relaxed and wearing only a loincloth.

After Frankus had gone, Renaldo turned to his wayward slave. "Are you feeling better?"

"Yes, I am." Casto hesitated for a moment. "Why are you doing this, Barbarian? Why are you being so friendly?"

Renaldo smiled a little wistfully. He chose his next words carefully, as he did not wish to fight this evening.

"Because I'm very glad that you're back with me. Because I know how much you resent having to serve me, and above all, because I want you to feel at home in the Valley."

For a long time, Casto remained silent. He, too, did not want to fight. When he finally spoke, he turned away from his master so that Renaldo wasn't able to see his expression.

"I do feel at home in the Valley, Barbarian. There are even days when I'm truly happy. But there are also those moments when I hate the mere fact that I'm waking in your bed. Those are the days when I don't care about anything, when it doesn't faze me to insult you."

Casto concentrated on his hands. It was the first time he had been so open toward Renaldo, but the Barbarian's sincerity had deserved an equal answer. Casto just hoped it wouldn't blow up in his face.

Renaldo touched his shoulder. "What kind of day is today?" His voice was inquisitive.

"A happy one. And one for which I'm grateful."

Renaldo's fingertips caressed his back. "And obviously relaxed."

Something in Renaldo's voice made Casto look up. He hadn't been mistaken. Renaldo was as aroused as he was, and they still had some unfinished business between them. With a sinful smile, he took a step backward. He wet his lips and touched his collar lightly, then lowered his hand to his loincloth. His voice came from deep within—a hoarse, inviting whisper. "Oh yes, I'm completely relaxed. I'm thinking about retiring early tonight."

Renaldo pulled him close. "If that's your wish. I think I'm coming with you, my sweet one."

Arm in arm they sauntered toward Renaldo's bed, already drunk with lust that was languid and lascivious this time. When Renaldo laid him down, Casto seemed confused.

Renaldo gave him a soft kiss. "What's the matter?"

"In my dream, you hit me."

The memory made Renaldo's eyes light up in hunger. "Yes, I did."

"Why?"

"Because you deserved it. And because I wanted to."

Suddenly uneasy, Casto undulated on the furs, averting his eyes from Renaldo's steady gray gaze. "Do you want to do it now?"

Renaldo reared back. The question had come out of the blue and made him suspicious. "Are you suggesting I should give you a hiding?"

Casto's tongue darted nervously at the corners of his mouth, something Renaldo couldn't fail to notice. It was obvious he didn't know what he wanted. That Casto trusted his master enough to even think about it made Renaldo giddy with joy.

"If I don't like it, will you stop?"

Renaldo's gaze softened. Inside he was wound tight like a bowstring, but as an experienced hunter, he knew how to lure in his prey. "But of course. You really give me permission to spank you?"

The longing in his master's eyes was now overwhelming; it burned so brightly and inflamed him so much that Casto had to look away. His own voice sounded strange in his ears when he answered. "Yes, I do."

A growl emanated from Renaldo's throat. Unable to restrain himself any longer, he grabbed Casto, yanked him up, and placed him over his knees. He could feel Casto tensing, but he didn't try to free himself. With his fingertips, Renaldo drew circles on Casto's trembling skin. He deeply enjoyed the feeling of having him so completely under his control.

Then he started hitting the firm, naked flesh. He dished out ten blows in rapid succession, then paused, caressing the reddened cheeks. "Shall I continue?"

Renaldo was sure he would die if Casto declined now. Instead of answering, Casto lifted his hips slightly. Relieved and turned on to the point where he found it hard to think straight, Renaldo kept on spanking him. Owning and subduing Casto like this was an urge that had its origin in the darkest part of his personality. It was the god inside him, the monster that had been born to rule without regard for anybody or anything. That creature was not only used to getting what it wanted, but saw it as a natural right. And it had set its eyes on Casto—a promising prey that kept refusing and teasing and daring it. Sometimes the stimulus was almost too much.

Normally, Renaldo kept this animalistic part of himself under tight restriction, for he knew what would happen if he let it free. Ever since he'd met Casto, he had found it hard to restrain himself. Casto stirred feelings inside him that went far beyond what was normal or acceptable, even in the Valley. Renaldo was more than aware of the illogic of the situation. He hated to hurt Casto and felt the urge to protect him from everything bad. Whipping him in public had taken all the discipline Renaldo possessed, and only his brother's strict gaze had stopped him from asking Noemi to heal Casto while he was still tied to the pole.

Renaldo also enjoyed—and craved—tormenting Casto until he was helpless with lust. Hurting him was the ultimate proof that Casto was his, and Renaldo had the right to do so, a right he would never grant to anybody else. That it did not go beyond those well-administered slaps was due only to Renaldo's phenomenal self-control. If the monster were given free range, it would probably tear Casto apart just to demonstrate its right to do so.

Renaldo carefully balanced the pain he dished out in bed, to give his precious slave pleasure. A pleasure that would bind him even tighter to his master, who loved giving in to his dominant streak. It was a dangerous, thrilling game, where just a bit too much or too little could ruin everything. Still surprised by Casto's sudden obedience, the Angel of Death kept on playing; concentrating to give Casto pleasures he had never known before. The prize of this game was more than worth the wager.

LATER, WHEN they were both lying in bed, satisfied by the things they had done, Renaldo kissed Casto tenderly. Now that his darkest urges were doused—for they could never be truly sated—he was able to touch Casto with the reverence he deserved.

"That was really good today. I hope you liked it too?"

A shade of crimson crept into Casto's cheeks, but this time he didn't avert his gaze.

"It was not displeasing."

"Do you want to abstain in the future?"

Casto thought about it for a moment. If he was honest with himself, he really liked this kind of sex. It gave him the opportunity to let himself go in a way he had not thought possible until now. The memory alone made him crave more, as well as the knowledge that Renaldo couldn't, and wouldn't, do anything without his express permission. But he could also sense the beast his owner was desperately trying to control, and he was aware of how much Renaldo enjoyed this game. Casto had no intention of trusting him and submitting to him any more than he had already done. If things progressed like this, there truly was no hope for him to ever escape Renaldo's grasp again. He would simply drown in the darkness, be consumed by the fire that always lurked there, ready to claim him forever.

Renaldo had sensed Casto's reluctance and intuitively said what he needed to hear. "You know that you can stop me anytime, don't you? You simply have to say the word. I'd never take you against your will."

Casto narrowed his eyes at Renaldo. At times like these, he was unable to hate his captor. On the contrary, he felt a reluctant respect for the Barbarian, knowing full well that this deadly, overbearing man was telling the truth. To relax the tense mood a little, Casto chose his next words with care.

"I know, Barbarian. I'm grateful, and it would be nice to try it a few more times so that I can make a well-informed decision."

The smile he got for an answer warmed his heart.

4. KALAD AND AEGID

THE NEXT day Casto made haste to train the horses because he was planning a visit to the library in the afternoon. As always he took Lys out last, so they could enjoy their time together without any pressing chores biting their heels. They were both in a playful mood, and so they decided to stay at the training area and work on their fighting instead of prowling through the Valley. After a particularly spectacular move, where Casto went under Lys's belly to emerge on the other side and throw a dagger at a wooden target, he heard the sound of somebody clapping. Slightly annoyed, Casto looked around. A slave he had not seen before stood at the fence and watched him with interest. He was handsome in a haggard sort of way, with a slim build, sharp nose, chiseled jaw, and high cheekbones that highlighted dark, slanted eyes. His hair was short and of an unobtrusive brown that reminded Casto of a mud puddle. The man did not wear a colored collar, and his clothes were clean but nothing fancy, a sign that he belonged to the great, faceless mass of ordinary slaves who saw to it that the masters of the Valley could spend their days unburdened by mediocre worries such as when to harvest the crops or where to get something to eat.

"Nice riding. You truly are amazing."

The words were meant to sound friendly, but Casto could practically taste the hatred they were sugarcoating. He knew most of the slaves loathed him, but even without that knowledge, he would have been able to sense the animosity and danger coming from the man. Where Casto had grown up, a certain empathy was necessary to survive, and he had honed that skill to perfection. Looking at the slave, Casto could almost see his eagerness to harm him.

Slowly, without dismounting Lys, he approached the man. "What do you want?"

He kept his tone brisk to discourage further flattery. For a moment the dark eyes showed open hostility, but the look was gone so fast Casto would have missed it had he not been watching for it.

"I don't want anything in particular. It's just that I've been watching you for some time now and I really think your riding skills are extraordinary. Before I was enslaved, I was a fairly good rider myself, so I know talent when I see it."

Again Casto could taste rancor and other, even more unpleasant things, behind that all-too-clean, all-too-friendly facade. He decided to end this charade before this disgusting presence sullied him.

"Since you don't need anything, I would appreciate it if you left me alone. I still have some training to do."

Casto's clipped tone didn't fail to annoy the slave. His facial features twisted, and when he spoke now, his voice mirrored his true feelings.

"So the rumors are true. You're arrogant and conceited. Do you really think you are so high above us normal slaves? In the end you have to bow to your master's will, just like us."

Casto tensed. Ever since his return to the Valley and his public punishment, this was a topic so sore he tried not to think about it at all, and he surely wouldn't allow this sneaky weasel of a man to touch it either. "I may be arrogant and even conceited, but that is none of your business. As for you, no matter how friendly you're trying to look, there's something ugly hiding inside, and it gives me the creeps. I wouldn't let somebody like you come close to me if my life depended on it. And now get out of my sight before Lys decides you're a threat."

As if on cue, the stallion's ears went flat on his head. He bared his teeth and made some threatening steps toward the slave.

With his hands held up in a soothing manner, the man retreated as fast as he dared, his hostility barely concealed anymore. "I'm telling you, it's not a good idea to make so many enemies among the slaves. There'll come a day when you regret this, mark my words."

With that parting shot, he hurried off, leaving Casto with an acid retort stuck in his throat. He buried his face in Lys's mane and tried to calm down. This was the second time another slave had approached him on their own, and he doubted this episode would have a better outcome than the meeting with Amelia, the slave who had basically been the reason for his first sexual encounter with Renaldo.

Sighing, Casto turned Lys away from the fence.

Lys was even more agitated than his rider. The black one had a very sensitive antenna for impending danger, and that slave was bad news.

But there was nothing they could do at the moment, and so they resumed their training.

STILL PONDERING the events of the afternoon and the possible consequences of angering the slave, Casto looked around the antechambers of the library that was Bantu's domain. In the distance he heard rhythmic hammering. The building was getting another add-on to house the flood of books Bantu was hoarding.

Casto didn't know that Emeris well. The small spry man spent most of his time with his beloved books, seemingly without caring much for what went on in the Valley. He shared his rooms in the main hall with his sister, Cornelia, who was responsible for the administration of the Valley's daily affairs. Cornelia, an Emeris with rough features and a perfect singing voice, was always busy ensuring the smooth and effective running of the Pack. The siblings were the least dominant of the counselors, but Casto had learned the hard way to never underestimate the silent ones. He was good at looking behind masks. Bantu and his sister might appear meek, but they possessed wills of steel and in their own ways, were quite powerful.

While Casto was still assessing his surroundings, slaves passed by without taking notice of him.

At a table laden with books and scrolls, an elderly woman eyed him with deep suspicion out of small, beady eyes. "What do you want?" Her voice was cool; it was obvious she resented Casto's presence.

He took a deep breath, counted to ten, and then flashed his most charming smile. If Renaldo had seen him, he would have been surprised how diplomatic his slave could be. "Please excuse the intrusion. I'm looking for Lord Bantu."

"Many do so. The lord is very busy." She sounded dismissive and had fixed her gaze back on her work as if to demonstrate just how insignificant Casto was to her.

"I do have some urgent business with him. So please, if it's possible."

The small eyes showed open disdain. "Why should I do you a favor I wouldn't grant anybody else?"

"Because he's the personal favorite of your god, as you well know, Ewandra."

Bantu's voice was soft, as always. The slight rebuke in his words could hardly be taken for a threat, but his next sentence clearly was.

"You know how displeased the Angel of Death is when his authority is questioned. Almost as much as I."

The slave lowered her gaze. "Please forgive me, Lord Bantu."

Without changing his mild manner or his tone of voice, Bantu rejected the apology. "It's not me whose forgiveness you should ask."

Casto could see the woman's nape turning crimson with anger. He hated being used as a vehicle to bring someone's point across, because it usually meant he was the one getting the blame. Ewandra, too, held him responsible for her humiliation. Her eyes shot daggers while she apologized. With a small nod, Casto showed his consent and ended the display as fast as he could. Completely unfazed by the small drama he had just caused, Bantu led him into his rooms.

Naturally the private chamber of an Emeris would have been spacious, but an oversized desk and three areas of shelving that went up to the ceiling and were crammed with books of all sizes gave a crowded air. Even the meticulously scrubbed floor was littered with piles of books, crates full of writing utensils, and baskets full of scrolls, looking like bizarre flowers that would never bloom.

Casto felt immediately at home. The tranquil atmosphere reminded him of the few good times he'd had during his childhood. With his eyes closed, he stood in the middle of the room, inhaling the soothing fragrance of aging paper, tooled leather, ink, and dust that seemed to belong to such accumulations of books like the cold to the winter.

"I'd have never thought you were a man of books, Casto. It seems I've to redeem my opinion of you."

The amused words startled Casto out of his daydream. He could feel the crimson creeping into his cheeks and fought against it with all his willpower. Nobody could ever find out who he really was—he had to avoid that at all costs. If Renaldo got even the slightest idea of who he was keeping in his chambers, he would remove Casto from the Valley before springtime. This Casto could not allow.

Backed by the self-control he had honed over the years, he smiled at Bantu apologetically. "Please forgive me, Lord Bantu. This room reminds me of my father's study. I always enjoyed staying there and watching him work."

As intended, Casto had distracted Bantu. He looked truly affected.

"It's me who has to apologize. I didn't intend to remind you of sad memories."

For a moment Casto felt a slight pang of guilt for leading the friendly man so astray, but his survival depended on it. "Don't worry about it, Lord Bantu. The memory isn't unpleasant, just sad."

Bantu flashed him a relieved smile. It was obvious that he was nervous to be unable to read the situation correctly. "Then I'm composed. What can I do for you?"

Casto rearranged his features into a contrite expression to reassure Bantu further. Although Bantu appeared to be less dangerous than the other Emeris, Casto did not make the mistake of underestimating him.

"Since I'm going to stay in the Valley longer than I had intended to, I'd like to find out more about the place."

The intelligent blue-gray eyes sparked with interest. "You don't believe that Canubis and Renaldo are gods."

Bantu's words confirmed Casto's suspicion that there was far more to this man than met the eye. "No, I don't."

Bantu nodded understandingly. "It's rather hard to believe, even when you're confronted with the evidence on a daily basis. It might help if you read the chronicles I've written about the Valley. Please follow me. I'll take you to a place where you can concentrate better."

Casto followed him through shelves piled with the wisdom of the world. He still thought it strange that the barbarians, of all people, should have such a splendid library, but on the other hand, it was only logical. On their countless raids, they were sure to get their hands on the most valuable books. Letting all that knowledge go to waste was a sin not even the warriors were prepared to commit.

Bantu opened a small chamber with a desk, a safety lamp, and a lonely shelf. "Make yourself at home. I'll go get the books."

Casto sat down and let his gaze wander over the bare walls, which offered nothing to distract the mind of the person sitting at the desk.

Sooner than expected, Bantu returned with two thick tomes bound in dark blue leather.

"Everything that might be of interest to you is written down in these books. You can leave them here and return whenever you want. If you wish to mark a page, please do so with a piece of straw. Don't use other scraps of paper. I don't want the ink to rub off. If you need anything, I'm in my rooms."

Casto took the two heavy books and bowed respectfully. "I thank you, lord. You're very helpful."

Bantu smiled happily.

"I'm always glad when people are interested in expanding their knowledge. You're truly welcome."

With that, Bantu left his god's favorite alone.

It didn't take a genius to deduce why Casto was suddenly so interested in the Valley's history, and he was willing to give the young man all the support he needed. Everything that helped Casto get used to being Renaldo's possession was for the benefit of them all. Together with his sister, Bantu had lived in the Valley for more than five hundred years, and in all that time, he had never seen Renaldo as happy and content as in the almost two years since the arrogant blond had entered their lives.

During the weeks following Casto's escape, it had become obvious how much Renaldo valued the capricious stranger. Because of that, Bantu had not been surprised when Casto wasn't sentenced to death for his recklessness but instead raised in rank. It wasn't easy to bear Renaldo—the flame deep inside him burned too hot, always a danger for anybody who got too close to it. Casto managed the feat of stoking that flame to a blaze without getting burned. It was a talent he didn't seem to be aware of.

Like the other Emeris and most of the mercenaries, Bantu was glad that his master had finally found a mate after decades of restless searching.

MEANWHILE, CASTO stroked the tome's fine leather wrapping with reverence, admiring the gold letters on the spine. He had always had a soft spot for books, especially when they were so obviously loved. Carefully, he opened the first page and started to read the introduction.

Bantu used the third person to talk about himself, a style that had gone out of fashion some two hundred years ago but was fitting for the friendly Emeris.

In the following, the author will describe the history of the divine brothers and their familiars, the Emeris. The lore about how the Mothers created Ana-Darasa and gave their sons to the humans will be omitted.

The chronicles start with the brothers entering the Valley. The author emphasizes that the information regarding the first third of the Fourth Age stems from the divine brothers themselves as well as from the Emeris Lord Aegid, Lord Kalad, and Lady Hulda. The author himself only started living in the Valley during the second third of the Fourth Age, but warrants the veracity of his witnesses.

Distressed, Casto shook his head. It appeared that even levelheaded members of the Pack, like Bantu, had been taken in by their leaders' delusions. He seriously questioned the use of reading on, since the author of this book backed up Renaldo and Canubis's ideas. The problem was, if he wanted to understand Renaldo, he had no choice but to read the chronicles.

The fact that he wasn't able to leave the Valley against Renaldo's will had struck Casto hard. He had never been at someone's mercy like this before, and it made him both uncomfortable and furious at the same time. Determined, he went back to the slightly crumpled pages.

Bantu's style was a pleasant mixture of facts and stories, which made it easier for Casto to filter the important information. In the beginning it was all about how Canubis and Renaldo had found the Valley and made it their home, as well as listing their countless campaigns. This tiring recitation of facts suddenly got interesting at the chapter about Aegid and Kalad.

The desert warriors had been the first to join the ranks of the Emeris. Their story started in the West, deep inside the endless vastness of the Hot Heart....

DUMBFOUNDED, KALAD stared at the traces in the sand. He was about a three-day ride from his tribe, in an area that wasn't called Valley of the

Damned for nothing. The Hot Heart itself was not the most hospitable of places to begin with, but here, in the Valley of the Damned, circumstances were truly malicious even compared to the scale of the most barren desert in the world. There was no water here, no oasis, not the smallest underground well. The sand was more finely granulated than anywhere else, and ground that had been solid a moment ago could turn into lethal quicksand in the blink of an eye.

There was always a steady wind blowing over the dunes but without being cooling. Instead, it only picked up the fine sand and rearranged it constantly, so that the surface of the valley was never the same. Nobody who came here ever returned to tell the story.

Kalad loved the valley because he was the only one here. As the future leader, it was technically his duty to stay with the tribe and look after the well-being of its almost one hundred members. Kalad hated that responsibility. He was still young—only twenty—and his father was already pressuring him to take a wife and start a family. Kalad could feel his future life like a noose around his neck, steadily tightening to take the last breath from him, and so he used every excuse to get away from the tribe and the boring routine of camp life. Apparently this day was about to get interesting. The track was fresh; whoever made it had been here not an hour ago. The way the footprints wavered around, as if laid by a drunk, told Kalad that the person was teetering on the brink of death and using up their last strength to move, which meant that Kalad had to hurry. He urged his camel on before the wind could eradicate the tracks.

Kalad didn't have to search for long. At the foot of the next dune, he spotted a slumped figure. He approached the huddled form slowly, his urge to help restricted by the need to tread carefully. When he knelt next to the stranger, the man gave a tortured groan. Kalad turned him around as gently as possible, which wasn't an easy feat since he was a giant of a man who must weigh roughly two hundredweight. Why the stranger was barefoot, with his torso exposed and only a small loincloth around his hips, Kalad failed to understand. The dark skin was covered in sand, but Kalad could still see a pattern of fine lines that spread over the body like a spider's web. Most noticeable about the man was his hair. It was pure white, very short, and stood in stark contrast to his skin.

Kalad helped the dazed man to get up, and then he offered him his water bottle.

The man started to drink greedily but stopped after a few gulps, a sure sign that he had grown up in the desert and knew precisely how easily you started throwing up when drinking too much water too fast. He opened his eyes and Kalad retreated in shock—the man was blind. A milky layer covered the light blue eyes that now gazed at him in frightening intensity. "Thank you."

His voice was no more than a hoarse croak, but Kalad recognized the dialect as one used at the eastern border of the Hot Heart. He smiled reassuringly. "Don't mention it. Can you get up?"

With a groan, the stranger managed to lift himself. Kalad helped him to climb onto the crouching camel's back. Then he grabbed the reins and led the camel out of the Valley of the Damned.

The journey took the better part of the day. Night was descending when they reached a small oasis Kalad had used on previous occasions. He lit a fire, assisted the stranger when he cleaned himself, and shared his own supplies with him. For some time they sat in silence, and then the man started to talk, his voice still hoarse from the hardships he had endured.

"Again, thank you for your help. My name is Aegid, by the way."

"I'm Kalad. And you're welcome." He grinned. "You didn't give the impression that you would be able to go on much farther."

Aegid returned the grin. "I wouldn't. You managed to show up at literally the last moment."

Now that he was cleaned up, Kalad could see that his whole body was indeed covered in tattoos, which made it difficult to guess his age.

"And you aren't angry that I've thwarted your plans?"

"Which plans?"

"Killing yourself! Seriously, to march into the desert without supplies and water is stupid enough, but to go into the Valley of the Damned practically naked looks like a deliberate act."

Aegid's face darkened. "Believe me, if I'd had a choice, I wouldn't have gone like that. Unfortunately, the shamans of my tribe thought I'd be an even better sacrifice for the spirits this way—since it wouldn't take me so long to get to them."

"Which tribe are you from? I don't know of any that dabble in human sacrifice."

"I'm a T'ki'an. And no, my people are very peaceful, normally. But because of my looks and growing influence in the tribe, the shamans decided to get rid of me. They said my hair and eyes are proof that I'm really a ghost and only here to return my tribe's prayers to the ancestors." With his fingertips he caressed his left arm. "My people's wishes, all here, under my skin."

Kalad stared at him. "You didn't do this voluntarily?"

He had been in the hands of a tattooist before and knew the pain it involved. What Aegid had endured went far beyond the norm.

"It took them six days, but when they were finished, the tattooists were worshipped like heroes. I was just grateful when the pain finally subsided."

"I'm truly sorry. To be treated like this by your own people…."

Aegid shrugged. "It can't be helped. But I can't go back."

"What are you going to do?"

"I don't know yet. First, I'll have a good night's sleep. Then I need equipment. After that, who knows."

"If you'd like, you can come with me to my people. I'm the leader's son, so I can voice an invitation."

Aegid stared at him with disbelief in his milky eyes. Hospitality wasn't a matter of course in the Hot Heart. "You'd do that?"

"After the pains I took to rescue you? Of course. Despite that, my conscience wouldn't let me sleep if I left a blind man alone in the wilderness—although I have to admit that you did very well."

The giant started to laugh. "Thanks for the sympathy, but I'm not blind. My eyesight is probably even better than yours, leader."

"But—your eyes!"

"Messenger for the spirits, you remember?"

"Has there ever been somebody who looked like you in your tribe?"

"No. I'm the first. Much to my dismay."

After this, their dialogue faded out. Although Kalad was almost bursting with curiosity and had about a hundred questions he wanted to ask, he could sense how tired his new acquaintance was. If their calculations had been right, then the big man had survived in the desert for five days. He was surely exhausted, and Kalad, too, could feel the last hours taking their toll. Kalad reined his curiosity in. If the stranger took his offer, then he would have more than enough time to ask all the questions burning at the tip of his tongue.

"THAT WAS unwise, my son."

The scorn in his father's voice made Kalad seethe. If he was honest, everything about the old man irritated the sheer hell out of him, and at the moment he had to hold back, otherwise he would strangle him to death.

"This stranger isn't good for the tribe. You should never have brought him here."

"With all due respect, Father, are you even listening to a single word I've said? His own people chose him as a sacrifice. A human sacrifice! He survived for five days in the desert. How could I have left him alone?"

A thunderous expression appeared on his father's face. The older he got, the more superstitious the once-powerful leader grew.

"You said he was dying when you found him. That means you've taken away the sacrifice from the spirits. They won't be pleased about this."

"I don't give a damn about that! If the spirits wanted him that badly, why did he survive for so long? I did what I thought was right. Isn't that exactly what you're always asking of me?"

The withered hands flew up in indignation when the tribe's leader shot up, his eyes narrowed in his fury. He did not like being opposed, especially by his own son.

"I want you to behave like a man, not like a spoiled child! You should take responsibility and not sneak away like a thief in the night whenever you feel like it. Don't you dare think I didn't notice! You're evading your responsibilities whenever it is convenient for you, and now you're trying to use what I've been preaching against me? You've sure got some nerve. Until you learn to act as befits a leader, you won't succeed me."

Kalad opened his mouth for a sharp retort, but his father held up his hand, a sure sign that he had made up his mind, and any further discussion would be fruitless.

"I don't want to hear any more. You'll listen to me and do as you're told, am I understood? You're going to take the stranger back to where you found him, and then you'll leave him. Should he survive, good for him. If not, then it's the spirits' will. After you come back, you'll take one of the women I've introduced to you as a wife and start a family.

"And Kalad, don't you dare go against my will. Son or not, I'll punish you accordingly."

Frozen by rage, Kalad bowed to the man he had called Father his entire life but who was nothing more than a stranger to him now. They had never been especially close. Kalad was the firstborn, a fact that chained them eternally to each other. He would have preferred to leave the honor of succession to one of his many brothers, of whom two were a lot better suited for the demands of a leader, but his father didn't want to know anything about it. Their forced relationship had caused Kalad to have feelings toward his sire no child should harbor, but it also made his decision easier now.

"As my leader wishes."

He hurried to leave the tent before he did something to the old man he would surely regret later. Back in the fresh air, he took some deep breaths while trying to figure out what to do next.

"Things didn't go as planned?"

Kalad turned to face Aegid, who greeted him with a sheepish grin. He didn't know why, but the presence of this man who had just entered his life two days ago calmed him down. He knew exactly what he had to do now, and he was no longer afraid of the path that lay ahead.

Aegid spoke. "It's okay, really. I don't want to trouble you."

"I'm pretty good at troubling myself, Aegid. And rest assured that I won't leave you alone."

"I'm a grown man. I'll manage."

Kalad shook his head. "Not here, believe me. The Hot Heart is even crueler than the desert as you know it. Without knowledge about the waterholes around here, you're as good as dead."

"Which means?"

A crooked smile mixed with pure lust for adventure was the answer. Kalad felt completely free all of a sudden. "It means the two of us are going to do something really stupid."

Kalad went to start getting everything ready for their departure, but Aegid held him back.

"Why are you doing this? You have a future here, a family. I'm just a stranger to you, and an unlucky one at that."

With a serious expression, Kalad laid a hand on Aegid's arm. The calm he was feeling now told him that he had finally found his destiny. "My so-called future here is a prison I've been trying to escape ever since I found out what was expected of me. You might be a stranger to me, but I've never felt as comfortable around anybody as I do with you. I feel like I've always known you. The way I see it, you really are a messenger, but not from the world of spirits."

For an eternity hidden between heartbeats, the two men gazed at each other. The bond between them, formed long before they were even born, was now visible for the first time. They didn't have to explain anything, didn't have to apologize, justify, or express gratitude. In the other, each had found the family he couldn't obtain by blood. Finally they knew where their home was.

Together, they loaded the camels in silent contentment.

Kalad's father did not show up to bid his son farewell, but his mother took him in her arms, a sad smile on her wrinkled features.

"I wish you all the best, my son. I'm really proud of you." Seeing his confused expression, she made a sound between a laugh and a sob. "I know you well, fruit of my womb. You won't return. I can feel it in my bones. I'm just glad that you've finally found your path. Follow it, and always be true to yourself."

"Mother."

Kalad wasn't able to say anything else. He had always known that his mother was a unique woman, and he truly regretted leaving her behind, but he had to find his own destiny, and it wasn't with the tribe. Her smile told him that she not only understood, but that it was fine too. She was the most generous, loving woman he had ever met.

A last kiss that was also a blessing, and then Kalad and Aegid rode into the desert.

"Where are we going?" Aegid looked at his friend with a weary expression. He had thought about their options for a long time and didn't like the conclusion he had come to.

"Unfortunately, we can't circle the camp. As soon as my father realizes that I won't come back, he'll start looking for us. That makes it too risky to stay in the tribe's territory. We'll ride through the Valley of the Damned."

"I understand. That way, we spare your father the trouble of killing us himself."

Kalad gave a weak smile. He could understand his companion's nervousness, since Aegid had barely made it out of the valley alive. But after long, careful thought, Kalad decided this was their only real chance. To soothe Aegid, he deliberately chose a light tone, although he was fully aware of how grave the situation was.

"Please, a little less sarcasm and more trust in my abilities would be nice. I know the area very well. We'll make it."

Aegid breathed a theatrical sigh. "I guess I don't really have a choice but to trust you." He grinned broadly, wanting to lighten up the dark mood. "Since you've already saved my life once, it isn't too much to ask."

"Finally we're getting somewhere. You're smarter than you look."

"Be careful. Just because I need you doesn't mean I'm going to put up with everything you say or do."

All of a sudden, Kalad was serious again. "To tell you the truth, I really don't know who needs whom more. You're all the family I've left now."

Aegid rested a hand reassuringly on Kalad's shoulder. "I'm also the only family you're gonna need in the future, I swear."

With a satisfied smile, Kalad urged his camel on. "A promise I'm only too happy to give back to you, brother."

"It's nice that we've talked this through. Now all we have to do is survive the Valley of the Damned, and nothing will stand in the way of our bright future."

"To be honest, I think the valley will be the least of our problems."

And thus one of the most dangerous places in the world ironed out the bond between two strangers whose destinies were so closely interwoven that they couldn't tell them apart anymore.

"OKAY, EXPLAIN it to me again. What exactly are we doing here?" Although Aegid was whispering, he managed to sound stern.

Kalad sighed. Since they had left the Hot Heart, three months had passed. Months in which they had roamed around aimlessly, not knowing what they really wanted or where their life's path should lead them. They enjoyed each other's company, their bond now as deep as if they had grown up together, but they still lacked direction. This gave rise to the idea to become swords for hire.

By chance, quite a big army of mercenaries was camped at the farthest borders of the desert—there to conquer a city, the name of which they had never heard before. It was risky to just walk into the lion's den, but on the other hand, the leaders of this army could surely use two more swords.

A guard stopped them, and after they pleaded their case, disarmed them. They were on their way into the heart of the camp where they were supposed to meet the commanders of this vast army. Their names were enough to strike fear in the hearts of even the bravest men, but Kalad was determined to try his—and Aegid's—luck with them.

Lord Canubis and Lord Renaldo must have been informed about their arrival, because they were awaiting them in front of two plain tents overlooking a vacant area in the otherwise crowded place.

Kalad involuntarily hesitated when he first laid eyes on the two men whose decisions influenced the well-being of entire countries.

Lord Renaldo was simply the most beautiful man he had ever seen. It was a beauty combined with danger that fascinated everybody when they first met him. To the two desert warriors, it almost seemed as if a god had descended from the heavens to walk among humankind.

How close this first impression was to the truth, Kalad would only find out later. The breathtaking beauty of the Angel of Death was only surpassed by the cold dominance emanating from his brother.

Lord Canubis commanded the whole situation, as well as all the people present, without moving a muscle. His body language alone stated clearly who the master of this army was. His piercing, predatory gaze turned without showing any emotion toward the two applicants. "So you wish to fight at my side?"

Kalad held the glaring gaze, seemingly unfazed by the threat in it, although his stomach did some turns in revolt.

"Yes. That's our wish."

"Are you aware that we take only the best? We've no use for amateurs or cowards."

"We do know. We both have been trained more than thoroughly—and regarding our courage, we're children of the desert. It's in our blood."

For a moment it almost seemed as if the warlord was suppressing a smile. His amber eyes sparkled with mischief.

"Prove it," Canubis said. "Renaldo."

Lord Renaldo had come forward, a broad grin on his face. He, too, seemed amused by a joke only the two leaders understood. A mercenary brought three heavy wooden swords. Kalad and Aegid did a few test strokes with them. For the purpose of the exercise, they weren't too bad. These swords were heavier than their own sharp blades, but not so much that it would be a hindrance.

Renaldo gave them a nod. "Attack me."

Aegid retreated to let Kalad have the first go, but Canubis stopped him with a small gesture.

"No. You *both* will fight at the same time."

"That doesn't strike me as honorable."

Again the predatory eyes couldn't conceal their merriment. "Your sense of honor suits you well, but be assured that it's out of place here. My brother is the best swordsman in the world."

The desert warriors exchanged a glance without commenting on the arrogance of this statement. Then they took their positions.

The Angel of Death awaited them in a relaxed pose, but Kalad did not let that fool him. He could practically feel the tension in his opponent's body. The man resembled a poisonous snake waiting for its prey to come close.

Carefully they started to circle each other, and then Aegid made a first attack that was mainly to determine how good Renaldo's reactions were.

The outcome was devastating. The man was fast—very fast. Aegid increased his efforts, and Kalad helped him to corner the Angel of Death. Renaldo escaped their attack loftily and then countered. He gracefully danced out of Aegid's reach and went straight for Kalad with venomous speed. At the last possible moment, Kalad managed to evade the blade so that it only grazed him lightly. Still, the strike was done with so much force, he felt the breath whooshing out of his lungs. This would have been Renaldo's chance to get rid of him, had it not been for Aegid, who attacked with an angry scream. Renaldo let go of Kalad to fend off Aegid.

Despite his mass, Aegid moved with deadly grace that had cost many a fighter his life. It was a lethal mistake to underestimate his speed. Unfortunately, Renaldo didn't do them that favor. He seemed to know exactly what his opponents were capable of and acted accordingly.

While Renaldo and Aegid exchanged a series of blows, Kalad got back on his feet. Without thinking, he tried to strike their seemingly invincible opponent from the side, something Renaldo shouldn't have been able to evade. But somehow, he did and hit Aegid hard enough to make him stagger backward. With the same motion, he turned aside, blocked Kalad's sword, and sent him right after Aegid. Both of them hastily regained their balance and got ready for the next round, but Canubis raised his hand.

"That's enough. You aren't too bad. Welcome to the Pack."

Aegid and Kalad stared at the warlord in disbelief.

"You let us join just like this?"

Renaldo approached them, his hands outstretched in welcome. "But of course. You're good, and we can always use talented fighters. Besides, there's still your probation time." His smile broadened. "But I'm sure you'll pass that with flying colors."

AEGID GLARED at his brother. "I'm holding you responsible for this mess." He didn't bother to conceal the threat in his voice.

Kalad tried to calm his outraged companion. "It won't be that bad, just wait and see. And it's not that cold, is it?"

"Not that cold? Kalad, fall has just begun and I'm already feeling as if my toes are freezing off. What do you think will happen when it's winter? Renaldo told me they get snow in the Valley! Do you have any idea how cold it has to be in order to snow?"

"But we agreed that it would be a good idea to stay with the Pack for some time. We've only done one campaign and already we're rich."

"And frozen."

"Come on! We'll get used to it! If you want, I can snatch us another brazier."

Aegid didn't bother to answer but concentrated on the comforting warmth spreading from the chimney instead.

They had fought alongside the Wolf of War the entire summer and then accepted his invitation to stay with the Pack for the winter. They hadn't taken the oaths that would bind them to the warlords for the rest of their lives, but they considered it an option, and to get a better picture of what awaited them, they had decided to take part in the life of the Valley.

It was a decision Aegid was deeply regretting. He and Kalad were children of the desert. Heat of any kind did not faze them in the least, but the damp cold in the Valley did them in. He simply couldn't understand how those born in this region could still run around half-naked while he was freezing to death despite his thick winter clothes. With his endless enthusiasm, Kalad viewed it all as one big adventure, but Aegid already doubted the wisdom of their decision.

The men and women of the Pack were far better than their reputation. Their life was shaped by a series of strict laws that required great discipline but also made them a very tight-knit family. It was the kind of lifestyle both Aegid and Kalad were used to, so they had had no problems adjusting to it.

Canubis and Renaldo were capable, albeit ice-cold, leaders. They seemed to believe themselves to be some kind of gods, and after Aegid had witnessed their skills in battle, he was prone to do the same. Renaldo was the best swordfighter he had ever seen, killing his enemies with such grace and elegance it was awe inspiring. And Canubis was the most dominant leader you could imagine. The brothers did not tolerate any back talk and asked for absolute obedience from their underlings. In exchange, they were willing to risk their own lives for their people's sake.

Aegid sighed. He knew he liked living in the Valley, running with the Pack, and not just because Kalad loved it. But the damn cold was a serious drawback.

ONLY TWO months later, the snow had piled up to more than a pace high and buried the world underneath as no sandstorm ever could. Aegid left their cottage only when it was absolutely necessary; the remaining time he spent in front of the fire, covered in countless furs.

Even Kalad's excitement about this new adventure had literally cooled down. When the winter storms had first set in, he had bravely tried to cope with the unfamiliar weather, but now he was cooped up with his brother. "You were absolutely right and I've been an idiot. Can you forgive me?"

Aegid put some more wood on the fire. "Of course. I mean, you did save my life. But next time I tell you something isn't a good idea, you're gonna listen to me, agreed?"

"Agreed. Let's get to bed. I doubt that anything interesting is going to happen today."

After feeding the fire one last time, they snuggled under the heap of furs and blankets they had hoarded in their bedroom. It hadn't taken them long to find out that the cold wasn't as biting when they were naked and huddled together under the covers. Although the situation was practically an open invitation, nothing had happened so far. They loved each other honestly as brothers of the desert and each was willing to give his life for the other, but in this deep and highly complex relationship that was still growing and evolving as they went along, there was no room for sex. It almost seemed to Aegid it would be a sacrilege to sully their bond with something as mundane as lust.

At the beginning of their restless wandering, they had chosen their bed partners individually, and Kalad had been the one with the greater appetite. After Canubis had accepted them into the Pack, more and more often the same person served them both. Aegid would never have thought that he could find it arousing to watch another man having sex, but with Kalad it was different. Witnessing how his brother prepared and took the partner of their choice was sometimes more than Aegid could bear. They were never jealous of each other. This was a sacrament they shared, another proof of their deep bond. The female or male they used to express this bond was nothing but a tool, a body through which they shared something sacred.

That night they hadn't been sleeping for long when a strange flickering light woke them. Both of them were immediately wide-awake.

The strange light could only mean that their home was on fire, which wouldn't be surprising given how many sources of heat they had.

They searched methodically, but neither the chimney nor the braziers were alight.

Aegid furrowed his brows, he had the distinct feeling that something was off. Once he realized what it was, he touched Kalad's shoulder and gestured him to look down. They were no longer standing on the carefully scrubbed planks of their cottage; instead, their toes were gouging into the fine sand of the Hot Heart. When they turned around, their sleeping chamber, the cottage, even the whole Valley, were gone, and they stared into the endless depths of their desert home.

"What's this?" Kalad's hand automatically jerked to his side, but of course he wasn't wearing his sword. They both were still stark naked. Aegid shrugged, but before he could answer, a melodic voice rang out behind them.

"You don't have to fear anything, brave warriors. I've created this scenario to make you feel at ease. But it seems my efforts were in vain."

A woman stood in front of them. She was rangy, nearly as tall as Aegid, and her long hair flowed white around her lean, almost bony frame. The red lips were like an open wound in the pale face dominated by two expressive dark eyes that made it appear like an elaborate death mask.

"Who are you?" As always, Kalad took over.

The stranger kept on smiling in a friendly way, as if she had not heard the threat in his voice.

"My name is Ana-Isara. I'm the mother of Canubis and Renaldo. Some people call me the Empress of the Dead."

Kalad hesitated. As a child of the desert, he didn't believe in the goddesses, instead honoring his ancestors, but he had heard legends about how the world was created by two goddesses. And the last few months with Canubis and Renaldo had made his earlier conviction waver.

"So it's true? They really are gods?"

Ana-Isara bowed her snow-white head in silent confirmation.

"Yes, they are. But they've been robbed of their true powers. You two are part of those powers, and I'm very glad you've found your way into the Valley."

Kalad remembered blurrily that the sons of the goddesses had lost a great deal of their powers due to the unfaithfulness of humankind. Deep down he started to suspect what the goddess was talking about, and he didn't like it in the least. "What do you mean by that?"

As if she sensed his obstinacy, the goddess spoke in soothing tones. "You two are Emeris. The first who will serve my sons."

Kalad raised his hands in defense. He didn't want to take part in this game anymore. "Slow down! We're nothing like that. Especially not some… Emeris. We've just decided to leave the Valley come next spring. It's simply too cold for us up here."

The goddess smiled kindly, but her tone did not allow any opposition. "The Valley is your home. You can't just leave here. It's your destiny to stay with my sons and fight for them."

"Shouldn't that be our decision?" Kalad's voice had become hostile. He didn't like being cornered.

Aegid placed a placating hand on his arm. He, too, had started to suspect that there was no escape for them, but unlike his mercurial brother, he looked at the situation from a practical point of view. "What does that mean for us?"

The eyes of the goddess started to shine with a disturbing dark light. It was difficult to read her masklike features, but Aegid was sure she felt triumphant right then.

"My kiss will grant you immortality. Like my sons, you'll no longer be susceptible to aging and death. Additionally you will be blessed by my sister and, of course, me. But from then on you're bound to the Gods of War. Irrevocably."

"Can we get out of this?" Aegid was asking that question for form's sake, not because he was interested. He already knew what the answer would be.

"What do you think?"

After this affirmation, given in a slightly gleeful tone, Aegid's shoulders slumped. "I suspected as much. Let's get this over with."

"Have you gone crazy? I don't want this!" Kalad hissed like a snake. His whole body had tensed as if he were waiting for a reason to attack.

Aegid didn't doubt that this was an exceptionally bad idea, which was why he laid a restraining hand on Kalad's chest. "Calm down, brother. We've already talked about how we don't have a goal in life. Now one is offered to us, and it seems like we're going to have a hell of a lot of time to achieve it. This is surely better than roaming the world for a lifetime, never finding what we're looking for."

"I can assure you, if you follow my sons and serve them loyally, you'll be generously rewarded for your services. And not just in a material way."

Something about the lady's tone made Kalad perk up. He stared into her eyes for a long time, as if reading something in the dark depths of her inhuman gaze. Then he took Aegid's hand. His voice was firm. A sarcastic smile masked his true feelings. "I'll go wherever you go. Without you, it would be boring anyway."

Aegid returned his brother's grip as well as his smile. He was relieved but also nervous where their path was going to lead them from now on. "That's good. You'd just get into trouble otherwise."

Together they turned toward the goddess.

Ana-Isara bowed to them, a gesture so oddly formal it only heightened the severity of the situation. "It's my honor and my pleasure to welcome you into the family, *ana mearo La'id* and *ana rieto La'id*. I promise you'll never regret your decision."

She approached them. Her cold lips touched first Kalad's and then Aegid's forehead. Her white hair fluttered as if disturbed by a breeze and her dark eyes glittered with satisfaction. "You will now feel the pain of being marked. Don't be afraid. Once it's over, you'll be part of the future. My sister and I will protect you."

With these last, cryptic words, the goddess parted from them, and the brothers were back in their cottage in the Valley. They looked into each other's eyes, knowing deep in their bones that their bond was now for eternity.

"Well, that was something, wasn't it?" Kalad tried to sound sarcastic, but his voice shook.

What they had just experienced was more than any mere human should have to bear. Aegid still held his brother's hand, already feeling the pain coming on. He started to answer, but his features twisted, and he let out a groan.

The agony of the runes, proof of their new kinship with Renaldo and Canubis, burning into their flesh was indeed almost unbearable, but somehow they managed to pull through. And when the pain finally subsided, they knew for certain where they belonged.

5. HULDA

TIRED, CASTO rubbed his eyes. The desert brothers' story had captivated him so completely that he hadn't realized how late it had gotten. The busy atmosphere in the library had abated—only here and there could he still spot the flickering light of a safety lamp. As instructed by Bantu, he used a straw to carefully mark the page where he had stopped reading. Then he doused the lamp and left Bantu's realm.

Casto's thoughts were in turmoil, his reason fighting an epic battle with his heart. The story had been so real that he was tempted to believe it, but his levelheaded brain listed numerous explanations for what he had just read and rejected the idea that the inhabitants of the Valley—and particularly Renaldo—could be more than met the eye.

"You're late today."

The reproachful greeting ended Casto's musings. Suddenly annoyed, he shrugged. "There was a lot to do."

Renaldo furrowed his brow but didn't react to the barely concealed challenge. Instead, he carried on in measured tones. "You've been very good today. I'm satisfied with your performance."

"That's very nice of you, Barbarian, but I'm quite capable of assessing my performance myself," Casto snapped angrily. "It was okay, but not that good." He hated nothing more than condescending behavior toward him.

"And since when are you the trainer?"

"Since you started to deny the truth."

Renaldo's gray eyes seemed to glow with his inner fire. He had kept back for quite some time, but now it seemed as if he would explode at any moment.

Casto prepared himself in happy anticipation. Now he would get what he wanted: a heated argument to distract him from his unsettling thoughts.

"You're pretty bold, considering the fact that I just disciplined you a short while ago."

The memory made Casto shudder with lust. Nobody was more surprised than he at how much he enjoyed being dominated with force between the sheets. It was his excuse to let himself go completely. He trusted the Angel of Death enough to know that he would never force him beyond his limits. No matter how much Renaldo got lost in his own lust or how much he desired to subjugate Casto, he never lost control. He made Casto feel safe—another reason why he kept on challenging him.

"Perhaps I need to be reminded."

With his usual speed, Renaldo got up from his lounge, grabbed Casto's arms with a steely grip, and pressed him against the wall. "As you wish."

Casto did not resist when his master dragged him to the bed to follow his words with deeds.

A GOOD deal later they were lying in the warm water of the pool, Casto snuggled against Renaldo's chest. Both were exhausted and sated from all the sex they'd just had. Softly, Renaldo's hands—the same hands that had just spanked his slave to their mutual satisfaction—caressed Casto.

"Why do you enjoy irritating me so much?"

Casto turned his head slightly. "It's the only scrap of control I have. Besides, I like it when you lose it in bed." He sounded lazy as he answered with unusual openness.

"That didn't escape me. But I must warn you, Casto—don't overdo it. If you push me too far… I couldn't stand losing you."

"Don't tell me you're getting sentimental over me, Barbarian."

At Casto's mocking tone, Renaldo couldn't suppress a broad grin. He loved it when Casto challenged him so openly.

"What do you take me for? It's just that I've gotten used to having you around. It would be troublesome to start teaching your replacement."

Casto snorted derisively. "Teaching for only a few nights is a waste of time and effort." Seeing Renaldo's surprised face, he reacted with a faint, condescending smile. It felt good to have the upper hand once in a while. "I know very well that I'm the first to ever stay with you for longer than a week. Should I leave you, you'd soon start having partners for one night only, like before me."

Renaldo wrinkled his forehead in annoyance. He didn't like the direction their dialogue was taking. "And how, pray, do you know this?"

Casto sprawled leisurely against his lover before giving his answer. "You mean despite the fact that I'm constantly asked about my phenomenal endurance? You do know I meet the ladies Noemi and Hulda on a regular basis, don't you? I honestly doubt that anything in the Valley could happen without the mother superior knowing about it."

"Those vixens! Gossiping hags, both of them. I guess I have to scold them seriously."

"That, I want to see!"

Casto grinned boldly. Nobody in the Valley, not even Canubis, would go against the mother superior of the Sisters of the Night without good reason.

Renaldo gave him a playful slap on the shoulder. "You really are badly behaved." He sighed theatrically. "If only all those wishing to buy you for enormous amounts of riches knew about it."

"You're getting offers for me?"

Casto sounded so shocked, it was now Renaldo's turn to smile smugly. "But of course, my beautiful, unmanageable slave. Since the day I won you, people who wish to have a piece of you have approached me on a regular basis. You might be flattered to learn that you're worth three times your weight in gold at the moment."

Casto's breath hitched.

It took Renaldo a moment to realize that Casto was truly worried. He pulled him close. "Don't worry. If those potential buyers knew how unbearable you are, they'd immediately back out. There's no danger of me selling you since I don't want to be accused of fraud."

As planned, those words kindled Casto's anger again and distracted him from his fears.

"When do I behave unreasonably? Haven't I just given you some pleasurable hours in bed?"

"You have. But let's not forget that I did most of the work."

"Work you enjoyed immensely, if I recall correctly, Barbarian."

Renaldo turned Casto in his arms and hungrily touched his lips with his own. His hands caressed Casto's muscular back, then wove into Casto's wet hair, forcing his neck and head into an arc.

"Oh yes, I did enjoy it a great deal. And right now, I feel like starting all over again."

Casto tensed in unspoken agreement. "You're one lucky barbarian. Right now, I can't imagine anything better than serving you again."

"How many times do I have to tell you that I don't appreciate your sarcasm in bed? But you're doing this on purpose, aren't you?" While saying this, Renaldo lifted Casto onto the tiles at the side of the pool, held him at the hips, and bit into the curve of his lower ribs.

Casto made a whimpering sound when the pain swamped his body and then turned to lust. He managed a breathless answer. "And it works nicely—"

Before he could go on, he was cut short. Suddenly, Renaldo spanked the naked buttocks in front of him, without mercy, until they turned crimson. For the rest of the night, Renaldo made his shrewd slave pay for his impertinence.

THAT SAME night a blizzard broke out that forced all life in the Valley to a standstill for three days.

Renaldo used the time to drill Casto in the art of close combat, which led to steamy scenes in bed on a regular basis. The unaccustomed strain exhausted him to such an extent that he did not argue with his master as usual. Instead, he was grateful for every moment of rest he could get. Their relationship became so harmonious that Casto regretted it when the storm finally ceased. Those three days away from the tedious routine of their daily affairs had almost made him forget the situation he was in.

Renaldo harbored similar feelings. He had enjoyed having his slave exclusively to himself—without the constant fighting and bitching.

Normality forced its way back into their lives without mercy, and all they could do was grit their teeth and bear it.

Due to the three days' break, work in the stables was overflowing. It took Casto a week before he found the time to return to the library. The place Bantu had given him was unchanged, which pleased Casto. Although he would have never admitted it, he was curious about how the chronicles went on.

Approximately a hundred years after Aegid and Kalad arrived, Hulda joined the divine brothers.

FROM THE shadows, Hulda watched the movements in the camp of the Barbarians. Against her will she was impressed. According to the description of Count Urman, she had expected a bunch of bloodthirsty, undisciplined savages who either killed or bedded everything that moved. But instead of the savage, brutal chaos she had anticipated, she had an almost anticlimactic view.

The tents stood in perfect lines. She couldn't spot any drunk warriors, the slaves worked swiftly on their chores, and the fighters trained or relaxed under the banners that had been set up against the sun. Everybody was clean and properly dressed. Even the slaves looked well fed and healthy.

Hulda had some trouble harmonizing what she was seeing with what the count had told her. Of course she had heard about Canubis and Renaldo before. The brothers were possibly the most powerful mercenaries on the continent; their names induced fear in the hearts of even the bravest warriors. But Hulda hadn't become the mother superior of the most dangerous order of assassins in the history of mankind for nothing. For three hundred years, the ruling classes had turned to the Sisters of the Night when they wanted an enemy gone for good in a clean, discreet manner.

Hulda had joined the Order at the age of four. The mother superior of that time had chosen her because of her unique talent—she was able to step behind time. For Hulda, this talent had been so natural she was surprised when she learned that not everybody was able to do it. The trainers at the Order taught her to perfect her skills and combine them with her natural inclination for killing. The outcome was a young woman who spread the Order's credibility on the whole continent, and she was elected the youngest mother superior ever.

As leader, it was no longer her duty to take on missions, but Count Urman had insisted that she should personally kill the Wolf of War. Considering the sum the count offered, Hulda had been more than willing to comply. Contributing to the Order's ever-growing wealth was one of the foremost duties of its members, and Hulda always loved to fulfill this special responsibility.

While watching the camp, she started to suspect that Urman hadn't paid her enough. The man was deeply afraid of the brothers and their military strength. It was a legitimate fear. Like greedy locusts, the two warlords descended on the plains year after year, and their client from the previous year could be the victim in the next. Despite that, the ruling classes relied on the services of the Pack—as the barbarians called themselves—even more regularly than they did on the Order.

One reason, undeniably, was the costs. It was a lot cheaper to pay for an army of mercenaries for a summer than to maintain your own standing army. And the brothers never lost. They fulfilled their contracts with unrivalled precision and to the letter. The main reason for their dominance was the sheer force they wielded. By now, it had become impossible to defeat them. The only bright spot was that they weren't interested in politics. They came, besieged and depredated, and then retreated come fall. Sometimes they even missed a summer, only to strike even more brutally in the following year.

The fighting abilities of the brothers were legendary. Rumor had it that nobody could defeat Canubis and Renaldo in combat man-to-man.

Hulda got a grip on herself. The more difficult the mission, the greater the fame. Of course, she could always infiltrate the camp at night and kill Canubis in his sleep. If she stepped behind time to do so, not even the big gray wolves that patrolled the camp like deadly shadows would be able to stop her.

Hulda had no intention to slaughter a brave warrior like the Wolf of War as if he were an ox. The members of the Order who raised her did have a soft spot for honor and bravery despite their fearsome credentials. It always added to their fame when an assassin was able to kill a worthy opponent openly. Brainless butchering was something any idiot could do, but making a strong enemy yield due to one's own abilities was something entirely different. For that, you needed a killer with style. The Wolf of War could claim such an honor anytime, and he deserved an open confrontation.

Hulda retreated to assess her plan once more, and then she went on her way.

THE GUARD at the entrance of the camp was more suspicious than she had anticipated. The dress she had chosen to approach him could only be called so because there was *some* cloth to cover her naked skin. Normally, her good looks opened even the best-barred doors for her, but this particular guard didn't seem to notice her stunning beauty.

The men employed by the brothers were definitely well trained. After some agonizing minutes, Hulda finally managed to talk him into granting her an audience with the warlords. She expected him to take her there, but he sent a messenger instead, who returned with two armed warriors who then escorted her to her prey without uttering so much as a greeting to her.

Upon coming closer, Hulda had to use all her discipline not to stare openly. She had heard countless reports about the brothers, especially from Urman, but had always thought them exaggerated. Now she saw that the truth was far more outrageous than any story could be.

Canubis's charisma alone would have been enough to impress her, but as if to heighten it, his brother, who was standing next to him, was so perfect it took Hulda's breath away. She was a beautiful woman herself; there were even men who'd kill for a kind word from her. But she knew how ephemeral and often useless unusual beauty could be. It was as if the Angel of Death mocked that insight.

Raising a sword against him was a sacrilege, and Hulda couldn't imagine many people would dare to oppose a man who embodied everything humankind could ever hope to achieve.

Next to the leaders stood two dark-skinned men. They were both impressively built and gave off a feeling of danger. The taller one caught her eye because of all the tattoos covering his skin. Hulda felt a shudder run down her spine. There was something about him that made the hair on her neck stand up.

To distract herself from this disturbing warrior, she concentrated on her prey again. Canubis's amber gaze looked at her with only a faint trace of interest. He, too, was unperturbed by her beauty. She could feel the other mercenaries, men as well as women, eying her with lust, but nobody made a comment. Before the situation could become even odder, she bowed gracefully to the warlords.

"What do you want, woman?"

The voice was harsh and impatient; Canubis already regretted granting her an audience. She straightened, a cold smile on her lascivious lips. Very soon the Wolf of War would regret his whim even more.

"I'm here to give you Count Urman's best regards."

While Canubis mulled over her words, Hulda attacked. She sidestepped the guard standing next to her, rammed her elbow into his stomach, and knocked him out with a well-placed hit on his temple. Before the second guard could react, her left foot connected with his throat and sent him down as well. Quickly, she regained the knives they had taken from her. She loved her daggers like nothing else, and it had been hard to hand them over. After a short, loving glance at the knives, she turned round, ready to deal death.

Again the barbarians surprised her. She had moved really fast, and no ordinary man would have been able to react that quickly, but Canubis and his brother were already prepared for the fight. They had drawn their swords in an instant, waiting for her to make the first move. This forced Hulda to change her plans. Honor be damned, she was realistic enough to know that she didn't stand a chance against both of them. She stared into the brothers' eyes, saw that they had come to the same conclusion, and then stepped behind time.

Surprised screams reached her hears, muffled by this strange nonplace where everything was dull and gray, untouched by time. It was like a distorted picture of reality, a mirror showing the moment obscured by thick layers of fog. Hulda was approaching Canubis slowly when his bright eyes suddenly homed in on her. She hesitated. She was absolutely sure that the Wolf of War couldn't see her, yet it felt like he knew where she was.

"Don't be ridiculous, stupid cow." Her own voice jolted her back into reality. She was the infamous Mother Superior Hulda; it was shameful to behave like a shivering novice. Without further delay she stepped forward, her arm snaking out toward the warlord's chest. He went down with a groan, the dagger in his heart twisted to cause as much damage as possible.

Instantly, the warriors formed a circle around their fallen master. The wolves came running, their angry howls piercing the air. With his expressive gray eyes, the Angel of Death scanned the place.

A satisfied smile curling her lips, Hulda retreated. Nobody was able to see her or follow her. Once she left the camp, she stepped back into time, took off the offensive clothes, found her horse where she had left it, and went on her way back to the Order.

That night she hid in a small, well-concealed cave where she enjoyed a simple meal of bread and dried meat while basking in her triumph. Entirely at peace with the world, she lay down to sleep.

UNLIKE AEGID and Kalad, Hulda knew immediately that she was dreaming. You didn't become mother superior of the Sisters of the Night if you weren't able to distinguish illusion from reality. Slightly annoyed, she spun around in her own chambers in the heart of the Order's stronghold. Her attempts to shatter the dream were in vain, however, which didn't improve her mood. Drawing her dagger, she stared into the darkness beyond her rooms, sensing that somebody was watching her.

"Whoever you may be, show yourself! I'm not in the mood to play games."

"Who says I'm playing?"

A beautiful woman with snow-white hair, night-dark eyes, and lips as red as a fresh wound appeared. She fixed her amused gaze on the dagger. "I'm impressed. I surely didn't plan to give you a weapon."

"But I do have one. And now end this, before I decide to make use of it."

"Aren't you interested in what I want from you?"

"Not really. I don't appreciate it when people enter my thoughts and start controlling my dreams. I want you gone!"

"Unfortunately I can't. Not yet, anyway. You've hurt my son today. About that, we need to talk."

"Son?" It took a moment until Hulda realized what the stranger was talking about. "In case you're talking about the barbarian, he's not only hurt, he has left this world."

Her satisfaction in a job well done resonated in her words, but the other woman wasn't impressed. A faint smile played on the voluptuous lips.

"You're wrong, Hulda. My son is alive, and he will still wander this world when all his enemies are long gone."

Dazed, Hulda stared at the woman. She couldn't believe what she'd just heard, but her instincts assured her it was the truth. "That's impossible! I rammed the dagger right into his heart. I saw him fall!"

"You, of all people, should know that our eyes can deceive us."

Again the smile returned, driving Hulda crazy. She tensed, ready to end the situation. No way would a stranger play her like a child. But her attempts to step behind time proved fruitless. For the first time in her life, Hulda's talent failed her. She stared at the strange woman in helpless rage.

"What have you done? Stop it!"

"Don't worry, Hulda. I can't take your talent from you. It's a part of you. We're at a place that doesn't know time, which is why you can't step behind it, that's all."

Enraged, Hulda decided to switch tactics. "Who are you?"

"Finally you're starting to ask the right questions. My name is Ana-Isara. I'm the Empress of the Dead and mother to Canubis and Renaldo."

"And what do you want from me?"

Hulda was speaking with more respect now. She hadn't been raised in the religion of the Mothers, but she knew the legends about how Ana-Darasa had been created. Although she had never believed them, she was willing to trust the evidence in front of her eyes. The pale woman had been strong enough to invade her dream, and she was definitely telling the truth—though Hulda did not care for her attitude. Nevertheless, she behaved more politely now, since it never paid to anger creatures that powerful.

The goddess raised an eyebrow in mockery. She, too, had noticed the sudden change of tone but was wise enough not to comment on it. "You showed great bravery when you attacked my sons all on your own. You're not only blessed with a unique talent, you also have the heart of a lioness. Your courage, foresight, and leadership abilities will be valuable assets in my sons' service. You have been aptly named, *ana regena anoso*."

Slowly it dawned on Hulda what Ana-Isara was trying to tell her. She shook her head. "That's not going to happen. Even if Canubis doesn't kill me the moment he lays eyes on me, I already have responsibilities. The Order needs me."

"Your Order's days are already running out. It won't exist three hundred years from now. You, on the other hand, will see eternity at my sons' sides. You're an intelligent woman, Hulda. Listen to your heart. It'll tell you the answer."

Hulda closed her eyes, although it wasn't really necessary. The call of her inner voice was too loud, too clear. Some part of her had recognized Ana-Isara the moment she appeared. It was the same part Canubis had been able to see, although she'd stepped behind time. There was no denying it—she was linked to the brothers, no matter how much she resented it. "They're gonna be pretty mad at me."

Ana-Isara smiled, this time with real humor. "You're underestimating your brothers. They're very impressed by you."

The goddess held out her arms. Without hesitation, Hulda stepped forward and let those arms embrace her as if she were a child. The bloodred lips sealed her own; the kiss was a strange mixture of cold and warm, life and death.

"Welcome to the family, my daughter. The pain of being marked will come upon you now, but rejoice. Once you've gone through it, you'll be purified and under my protection."

THE AFTERNOON of the following day, Hulda stood in front of the guard again. Her night had been plain horrible, and her mood was according. What made her even crankier were the two black symbols now carved into the soft skin above her heart. She didn't make the effort to dismount her horse.

"Your masters are waiting for me."

The man was torn between fear and determination. He pointed his sword in Hulda's direction for a moment, then lowered it again. She sighed.

"If I wanted, I could simply march past you without you even noticing it. Now be a good boy and take me to your leaders."

After a short internal struggle, the man gave up. "Please follow me, my lady."

This time a lot more distrust and alarm met her walk through the camp, but nobody dared to raise a hand against her, although quite a few escorted her, walking beside her horse with their hands on their weapons.

At the center Canubis and Renaldo were waiting for her, both of them as relaxed as if nothing had happened. How Canubis had managed to recover from his deadly wound so quickly was a mystery to Hulda, but she was determined to solve it once she'd dealt with this situation. Canubis smiled in greeting, a gesture that reminded her of Ana-Isara and therefore rubbed her the wrong way.

"I hope you're satisfied!" she hissed at them while dismounting her horse. "It seems as if we're going to spend a lot of time together."

Canubis cocked an eyebrow. "How long that's going to be isn't decided yet. What made you come back?"

"Don't play dumb! That only makes me more furious!"

The Wolf of War retreated a few steps. Even though his authority was absolute, he wasn't immune to the power Hulda was emanating. Right then she felt no inclination to hide her true, dominant self in any way.

"I'm not playing. Why have you come back?"

"Because I got a visit from your mother last night. If I'd known what she was going to do to me, I'd have rammed that dagger between her ribs."

Renaldo's eyes went wide and all color drained from his face when he realized what Hulda was telling them. "You are Emeris?"

"That's what she said. A part of the family."

"Show me." Canubis's features had hardened.

In one fluid motion, Hulda opened her vest and exposed the two black runes carved into her skin.

Canubis's predatory eyes started to glow. "It's true. The sign of the Mothers and the rune for death. How absolutely fitting." He offered Hulda his hand. "Welcome to the Pack—?" He looked at her imploringly.

"Hulda. My name is Hulda."

"The Mother Superior? *The* Hulda?"

"So you've heard of me. How flattering."

"Yes, we have. What an honor, I've been killed by a master!" Canubis said wryly.

"About that…."

"Don't mention it. You're forgiven."

"That's not what I was going to say. How did you manage to survive?"

Hulda didn't know what was better, the stunned expression on the face of the powerful warlord or the good-humored laughter from his brother and the other warriors. She could feel her anger subside. A group that could laugh about its leader in such a careless way surely had room for a professional killer like herself.

ELAM

1. POLITICS

ATTENTIVELY, COUNT Markon followed the snow-covered path through the Valley. Winter had already passed its peak, and down on the plains, most of the snow was gone by now. But here in the Valley, high up in the mountains, the cold still reigned with a fist of ice. Here and there a dark, threatening shadow could be glimpsed through the trees. Their invisible wolf guard hadn't left them ever since they'd entered through the stronghold. The huge predators were a reminder of how dangerous a place they had come to.

Markon was fully aware that in coming to the Valley and asking the brothers for help he was playing with fire, but he didn't have a choice. The Eastern Kings were insatiable in their lust for new territories, and if he wanted to survive, he needed gold to ransom his small kingdom. Gold the mercenaries had already fetched him once. Of course, the kings in the East wouldn't be pleased when their personal piggy bank was plundered by the barbarians, but as long as they couldn't trace the contract back to him, Markon could play the role of innocent rich sponsor, which would protect his kingdom from the grip of the Eastern armies.

The Barbarians were agreeable negotiators—if it weren't for the fact that one look from Canubis was enough to make Markon lose control of his bladder. Still, as frightening as the warriors were, they were also dependable. When you offered them a reasonable price— in this case a generous percentage of the booty plus a handsome fee in advance—as well as a good fight, they were willing to do almost anything. They had no interest in politics and never asked unnecessary questions. Markon was never entirely sure if this was due to ignorance or calculation, but it suited him and all the other "customers" of the brothers.

Their arrival at the stables disturbed Markon's train of thought. After he and his escort had dismounted, the count started looking around for somebody to take their steeds. A blond slave was wandering toward the main hall, with a bridle in one hand and a half-eaten apple in the other.

"Hey, you!"

The count's voice was as sharp as always; he was used to giving orders. The young man ignored him, although he'd surely heard him. Markon raised his voice in indignation. He couldn't believe that a simple stable worker dared to ignore an obviously important guest like him.

"I'm talking to you, slave! Come here and take our horses."

Then the slave finally stopped. His shoulders tensed and the hand holding the apple was trembling slightly—whether with fear or with rage was hard to tell. Slowly he turned round to face Markon who involuntarily made a step backward.

The young man was breathtaking. His piercing blue eyes glared as if he had just encountered a rabid dog barking at him. A strand of wheat-blond hair caressed his cheeks as a lover would do, and his entire body radiated an animosity that was definitely uncalled-for. Markon could see him preparing for a sharp answer—

"Count Markon! You're already here?"

With those words, the Angel of Death moved between Markon and the beautiful slave as swiftly as a shadow. Instead of apologizing to his guest for the rude behavior of a mere slave, the powerful warrior placed his hand gently on the blond's shoulder. His voice had a soothing tone as if he wanted to placate a whimsical princess.

"It's okay, Casto. We're going to talk later."

For a moment it seemed to Markon as if the slave was contemplating throwing a tantrum, but then he tossed the wayward strand of hair out of his face with barely concealed irritation.

"As you wish, Barbarian."

Markon felt his blood freeze. The Angel of Death would surely kill the impertinent slave then and there, but all that happened was a friendly slap on the young man's rear.

Meanwhile, two stable workers had appeared to take care of the horses. Markon shot his personal servant and closest counselor, Jar, a look that ordered him to stay at the stables. Jar was an excellent spy who had a talent to make other people confide in him. Something about his aura made even the hardest people approach him to tell him their life stories. It was a talent that had often proved valuable in the past. If there was information worth knowing in the Valley, Jar would find out about it.

Markon followed the Angel of Death to the main hall.

JAR HELPED the two stable workers take care of the horses. After they had worked some minutes in silence, he threw out the first bait without expecting too much from it. It was a harmless comment to deduce the mood.

"The blond one sure is in trouble, isn't he?"

The reaction to this random sentence was overwhelming. The two men exchanged a look full of hatred and outright rage. Then the older one spat on the ground.

"Casto never gets into trouble. Lord Renaldo will probably reward him for his rude behavior."

Jar was seriously surprised. His well-tuned senses had told him from the beginning that the young man was special, but he would never have expected to meet a favorite of the Angel of Death here in the stables. According to rumors, Renaldo was so insatiable that he changed his bed partners like others did their underwear. Additionally, he was a strict, often merciless lord who did not suffer recalcitrant servants lightly.

"Are you serious? After everything I've heard about the Angel of Death, it seems to be a miracle that the boy is still alive."

Again the men exchanged a glance that told Jar more about Casto than the menials wanted to tell.

"The lord is strict. Very strict. Only Casto has free rein with him."

"It's probably because of his talents between the sheets." The younger servant's voice dripped venom.

Jar relaxed. The way those two were wired, he would only have to listen. As if to confirm his thoughts, they kept egging each other on.

"It's so unfair. He can do whatever he wants. No matter what, the Angel of Death is thrilled."

"For the things he says to the lord, every other slave would lose his life."

"For what he's done just now, each and every one of us would be flogged."

"Is he really that special?" Jar's voice was soft; he did not want to disturb his informants in their tirades and stop the intel, but he had to make sure that listening to them proved useful. Their animosity already told him that Casto enjoyed privileges that the other servants begrudged him. Knowing the reasons for this hatred could prove valuable.

His voice grumpy, the older servant spat out, "Depends on your point of view. He's quite a good rider, you have to give him that."

"And that's his task? Riding the horses?" It wasn't hard for Jar to sound surprised. He hadn't anticipated this.

"Yes. And to serve the Angel of Death. Something he's been doing for quite a long time now."

Jar pinned the menials with an imploring look. He hated it when people spoke in riddles that were not accessible for bystanders. The two men shrugged and went on.

"We've both been in the Valley for more than fifteen years. In all that time, Renaldo has never kept a personal slave longer than a few days. He's too volatile, too trying, and too strict. It's impossible to satisfy him. But Casto has been serving him for almost two years now, and that's truly remarkable."

"Not half as remarkable as the fact that he escaped last fall."

Jar listened up. An escaped slave? The stories about the brutal punishment for those who dared to flee the Valley were legendary on the whole continent. Casto had to be a lot more than a mere toy if he dared to oppose his master like that. "He was captured?"

"No. He really managed to get away. The lords were furious. But then he returned—of his own free will. Just like that. And Renaldo didn't exercise the death sentence—he didn't even cripple the little bastard. He whipped him in public and then asked Lady Noemi to heal his wounds."

"Don't forget that only a few days later, they started to train in swordplay together."

"A slave with a weapon?" Jar was truly awed. This was getting better and better.

"Yes. As we said, when it's about Casto, Renaldo's ability to judge goes down the drain."

"You don't seem to like Casto."

It was more a statement than a question, but Jar received a venomous answer nevertheless.

"Why should we? That arrogant little prick is simply obnoxious."

"Does he use his standing against you? I know how bad that can make a person feel."

"If only he would! No, he'd never stoop so low. He's way too exalted for that. He acts as if the lord's grace is a nuisance. Renaldo fulfills his every wish, and he brushes it off like it's nothing. One of the two most powerful warriors in the Pack has chosen him, and he behaves as if he'd been sold like a cheap courtesan!"

The picture of the hated young man became clearer with every word the menials spoke. Jar thought he knew why the Angel of Death was so infatuated with the blond, but that was beyond the grasp of those two dim-witted creatures. It was something those whose lives were completely controlled by others could never understand. Jar couldn't even hold it against them. It was only natural that they instinctively fought against an intruder like Casto, who called into question their whole concept of living. To confirm his suspicions about Casto being extraordinary, Jar tackled the topic of dependency. The bonds between a master and his slaves were manifold: some obvious, like the collars, others more subtle, like the tone when they spoke or the living conditions the master provided. How a slave reacted to those things could tell an experienced man a lot about his character—and the character of those around him.

"Does he accept presents?"

"No!" Anger and disbelief mixed in the menial's voice. He obviously couldn't understand why Casto would repudiate the riches he was offered. "That, too, is beyond his dignity. He could have anything he wanted, and he settles for nothing!"

Jar was listening only halfheartedly while the men kept on ranting. He already had what he wanted. The information that the invincible Angel of Death might have a weakness was indeed precious. Markon was going to be pleased about this news. Of course, he still had to confirm how deep the warrior's infatuation ran, but evidence suggested it was quite strong.

This could be useful one day.

"HAVE YOU calmed down yet?" Still amused by what had happened earlier, Renaldo watched Casto take off his boots with his usual energetic movements. "I can assure you Count Markon was deeply impressed by your rude behavior."

Instead of reacting to the teasing, or even provoking an argument, Casto tilted his head.

Renaldo furrowed his brow. "What is it, Casto? Has something happened? Don't tell me you're sorry for what you said to Markon!"

Casto shook his head. "No. He deserved that. But... I'm sorry for questioning your authority in the presence of strangers. That was stupid of me."

"You question my authority on a daily basis, and you're never sorry about it!"

"That's different. Markon's a stranger, perhaps an enemy. My behavior weakened your credibility and perhaps even created an opening for this weasel. I'm sorry."

The unusually serious tone had Renaldo worried. It was untypical for Casto to show his underbelly like this. Renaldo took Casto in his arms, his voice soothing.

"Don't fret it. Markon is too afraid of us to make a big deal out of your little performance. Plus, he has to depend on us. He's not so stupid as to challenge our wrath."

"You should've punished me. That would've prevented any further problems."

Renaldo was speechless. He would have never thought that Casto would hand himself over even more than he already had. "Ha! And then I would spend the next few weeks trying to placate you! In case you haven't noticed, you can hold a grudge for ages. Besides"—Renaldo took Casto's face in his hands, eyes sparkling adventurously—"I thought it was very erotic when you showed that greedy rat his place."

"Erotic? You're a strange one, Barbarian."

"Yes, I probably am. But still, I had to restrain myself from taking you on the spot."

Upon hearing these words, Casto's breath sped up, a soft crimson conquered his cheeks, and his hands caressed his master's back in a demanding way. Whether it was due to Renaldo's words or his proximity, Casto did not know. He only knew that the fire he was trying to keep under control had just broken free again and burned every sense of reason. "Do you still think it's erotic?"

Renaldo's lips sealed Casto's mouth. He, too, felt the flames rising. He loved that moment when their tongues mingled for the first time, when he could sense the tension in Casto's muscular body, this longing that was so similar to his own. After a sweet eternity, he finally let him go. "Does that answer your question?"

A mocking smile flitted across Casto's features. "Partly."

"You really are impertinent. Perhaps you're right and I should've punished you."

"Don't restrain yourself, Barbarian."

"Did I mention how much I value your temperament?"

Casto grinned against his master's lips. "No. If I recall correctly, you're usually disturbed by my wayward behavior."

"Not always, my slave. Not always."

Renaldo lifted Casto and carried him to the bath without breaking contact with his mouth.

MUCH LATER, when Casto was fast asleep in his master's arms, Renaldo mused about his words. He already knew that Casto was not only educated but also highly intelligent. That he owned a very sharp tactical mind had managed to evade Renaldo until now. Casto had been truly disturbed, and not because he was sorry about the action itself. He had done and said worse things without giving a damn about his master's reaction. What had worried him were the political consequences.

Until that incident Renaldo had assumed Casto was led by his emotions alone—which wasn't a fault, given his youth. Now it turned out that he could think further ahead than others of his age, which hinted at a more thorough education than Renaldo had anticipated. He asked himself what plans Casto's father might have had for him. Surely he had seen his son's talents and promoted them accordingly, but a simple merchant didn't invest so much time, effort, and money if he hadn't a certain outcome in mind.

Sighing, Renaldo pulled his mysterious slave closer. He knew he would find out one day, but the waiting was driving him crazy. That didn't change the fact that he had truly enjoyed the sight of Casto confronting the count in such an arrogant manner. He was proud of Casto's iron backbone, although there were times when he wanted to strangle him because of it.

With a whimper, Casto snuggled closer. He fumbled around for a few moments and then rested his hand on Renaldo's chest. This caused a satisfied smile on Renaldo's lips. At least when asleep, the young man was honest with his feelings.

Renaldo grabbed the furs so that his lover wouldn't feel cold, and then he, too, closed his eyes.

"WHAT DID the count want?" Over the rim of his tea mug, Casto shot his master a questioning look.

Renaldo leaned back. He was in a playful mood and decided to test the limits of Casto's patience a bit. "And why would you care, my beautiful slave? That is about business, and I doubt you know anything about it."

Before Casto could give a sharp answer, Renaldo went on. "But you were such a good boy last night that I'll grant your selfish request, although it doesn't concern you."

With remarkable discipline Casto controlled himself, since he really wanted to know what the stranger had wanted.

"Count Markon has requested that we conquer Elam for him."

"The miners' city?"

"Why am I not surprised that you know this?"

Casto ignored the Barbarian. He stared into his mug, contemplating what he'd just learned. "Elam is the treasure chest of the Eastern Kings. They won't be happy when the city is attacked. What does Markon want?"

"I don't know, and to be honest, I don't really care. We get one third of the gold, everything of value, and the captives. That's quite the prize for a pitiful place like Elam."

"And you aren't the least bit suspicious? Elam may not be big or grand, but it's important. The gold price is going to skyrocket everywhere on the continent. It will induce unforeseeable power shifts. The count must know that, so what does he want?"

Renaldo shrugged. "Quit brooding about it. If you don't stop thinking so hard, you'll get wrinkles, which would be a pity at your age."

With a guilty expression, Casto lowered his gaze as if his master had caught him having an indecent thought. He tried desperately to hide his terror—he had been a hair's breadth from blowing his cover in an outburst of anger.

"I always knew you were fixated on appearances. That's truly pathetic, Barbarian."

As expected, Renaldo reacted to this impertinence with fury. "I'm *pathetic*?"

"What else would you call your concern for my looks?"

"As if your inner values were that overwhelming! You should be grateful for being easy on the eyes."

"You're offending me, Barbarian!"

"And what is it you're doing?"

Made careless by panic, Casto threw his half-full tea mug against the wall. The brown liquid dripped slowly down the white paint and onto the scattered remains of the cup.

Casto's breathing was labored; he was getting furious now.

Renaldo, too, had given in to his anger. As always, they had egged each other on. He got up so abruptly that his chair fell back; his voice was a hoarse hiss. "I've already made it clear on several occasions that I don't appreciate it when you throw things. Pick up the mug, now!"

"No."

"Casto. I'm dead serious!"

"No."

When Renaldo tried to grab him, Casto dived out of his reach, but his small triumph did not last for long. Growling, Renaldo forced him into a corner and his hands closed around Casto's arms. He lifted him up, giving Casto a taste of a demigod's superior strength. He ignored the deliberate kicks against his legs and increased his grip until the bones in Casto's arms creaked. Casto whimpered, a mixture of pain and lust that inflamed Renaldo immediately. For a moment he mused if they would make it to the bed, but then gave up. He needed Casto right now.

Renaldo set him back on his feet, turned Casto's face to the wall, ripped his trousers off—not giving a damn that he had just destroyed the finest silk—and then entered his slave without hesitation.

While Casto and his master were showing their feelings in the only way possible for them, the tea in the kettle turned to steam. The weapons on the wall gleamed cherry red and the fire in the chimney roared, burning the logs to the finest cinder.

The men drowning their anger and unspoken love in their all-consuming lust were not aware of any of it. For them only the presence of the other mattered. It was an intoxication they sought unconsciously, fought against with all their might, and yet could not free themselves of, no matter how much they might wish for it.

2. FUTURE

DURING THE weeks that followed Count Markon's departure, Casto found it impossible to steal any time to read the chronicles.

Renaldo had intensified his training, saying they wouldn't have enough time once the campaign started. In addition, Aegid and Kalad had asked him to teach their thief as often as possible, using the same argument.

Daran and his sometimes-lethargic horse were well matched and had progressed impressively since training had begun. The desert brothers were so thrilled that they had given Casto a new winter coat as a token of their gratitude. It was made of the finest leather and dyed a vibrant light blue that matched the color of Casto's eyes. The inside was lined with the fur of a certain variety of stag that only lived in the mountains surrounding the Valley. These animals stayed in the high mountains throughout the year, and for protection against the biting cold, they grew a coat that could reach a span in length. The thick underwool stored body heat and kept its wearer comfortably warm no matter how cold it got.

It was a gift fit for a king that Casto had declined at first. He was well aware that Daran's quick learning wasn't solely due to Casto's abilities as a teacher, but because Daran possessed phenomenal body control and an almost fanatical desire to please his masters.

Only after Kalad had insisted strongly had Casto accepted the exceptional gift. He hadn't regretted it for a single second. For the first time since he entered the Valley, he did not feel as if he would freeze to death at any moment.

Renaldo had only raised his brows in mockery when he saw the coat. A few days later, he gave Casto matching boots to make up for the fight they'd had because of it.

Only two days before the Spring Ceremony, Casto managed to go back to the library.

The chronicles were still in place, but Bantu had left an additional book on top of the others. It was a lot thinner and bound in red leather. There was a piece of paper attached to it.

These are the prophecies of Dweian and Dria. They regard our leaders and those following them. You might find this interesting.

Puzzled, Casto took the small book. He had been looking forward to reading the story of Bantu and Cornelia, but when the mild-mannered Lord of the Books recommended the prophecies, he would follow his advice.

Casto got comfortable, opened the first page, and started to read.

DWEIAN AND Dria were siblings who had lived during the second era and seemed to have known the Holy Mothers personally. It was thanks to them that Ana-Isara had not killed her sons after the humans' treachery but had taken their hearts instead.

Dweian and Dria had been powerful seers who had written down the destiny of the brothers in this book....

Or something similar, because this was obviously a translated version. The seers had portended the names of all the Emeris, although one was still missing. He was called *"ana ligtos wanda,"* the "one walking in the light."

Casto shook his head in disbelief. But then a line caught his eye and he kept on reading. This part was about the hearts of the divine brothers.

The hearts will find their way back to their masters. Under the protection of the Holy Mothers, they shall return home. Ana dragda slan, the daughter of the snake, will serve the Wolf of War and increase his power. Ana blod brester stratatos, the sister of the wind, will serve the Angel of Death and turn his fire into a gale.

Casto stopped. The book fell from his lifeless hands. His heart beat violently in his chest and his breath came in labored fits and starts. All his innermost fears had taken solid form. To the Angel of Death, he was really nothing more than a toy, a pleasurable pastime until he found his heart.

Casto's hands tightened into fists. How stupid of him to think he could be more to Renaldo than just a pretty body that was easy to fuck! The pain made him angry and reminded him why he had forbidden himself to develop feelings for other people. But the Barbarian had been very cunning—he had snuck into Casto's heart like a thief in the night, bound him with invisible, unbreakable chains to have his fun with him, and would toss him aside like a pair of old boots. And Casto couldn't leave him, couldn't break up with this cruel tyrant, because he was irrevocably his.

In his anger about the injustice, Casto forgot that he didn't believe in things like prophecies and other superstitious nonsense. All his fury and hurt were concentrated on the fact that he had fallen in love with somebody who didn't return his feelings.

Unable to read on, he stumbled out of the library. For a brief moment, he contemplated going to Lys for a quick ride, but it was already dark and he couldn't risk blowing their cover if anybody found out how effortlessly the stallion could move through the night. Dazed, as if he'd been hit on the head, he returned to Renaldo's chambers, so caught up in his feelings that he didn't even sense his master's presence.

Only when Renaldo took him in his arms with an enticing smile on his lips did Casto react. He pushed him away angrily, baring his teeth like an attacking beast. The last thing he wanted right now was to fall even deeper into Renaldo's trap. "Leave me alone!"

Confused, Renaldo retreated a few steps. By now he had gotten used to Casto's sudden mood swings, and he could tell Casto was serious this time.

"What is it, Casto? What has happened?"

The azure gaze clouded over like a clear sky just before a thunderstorm hit. At the same time, Casto furrowed his brows in confusion, insecure about what he should do.

The mixture of anger and despair touched Renaldo. He could see Casto was agitated and hadn't decided yet how to react. Renaldo extended his hand to touch Casto again, but Casto backed off, his eyes wide in terror. Casto's breath came in pained gasps; it was obvious something was troubling him. He looked like a wild animal in a trap, but it excited Renaldo. He waited, his gaze glued on Casto, unsure what to do. Experience had taught Renaldo that one wrong word could lead to catastrophe.

Casto's gaze darted around the room like he was a madman, but it finally stopped at his master. The darkened blue cleared up, became bright once more, but his voice was hoarse, full of self-loathing. "Hurt me, please. Whip me. I want to hate you."

Renaldo growled deep in his throat. He knew it was wrong, that he should be aiding the young man whose helplessness had touched him, but this explicit invitation stirred the beast that slumbered deep inside him.

Hungrily, the most primitive and feral part of the demigod awakened and set its eyes eagerly on the trembling prey in front of it.

Renaldo didn't know why he wanted Casto so absolutely. It was a longing he had never experienced before, and he didn't like facing it. Most of the time, he managed to keep his urges under control, but when his slave was helpless like this, he felt his inner restraints crumble. Again the plea fell from those sensual lips. Casto looked vulnerable, and it challenged the beast to take over.

Renaldo grabbed Casto's arm mercilessly and struck him so hard that the last vestiges of self-control vanished. He dragged him to the bed. When he pushed him down with his weight, his face less than a hand away from Casto, something rose in those unfathomable blue eyes— something Renaldo was all too familiar with.

A fire, as wild and untamed as his own, flared to life in Casto and turned the prey Renaldo had just wanted to devour into a worthy opponent, something the beast inside liked even better. Casto fought back now; he kicked and scratched and bit his master, even tried to get away from him. Due to their regular training, Casto's stamina had increased considerably. He was able to defy him for quite some time.

It was a game Renaldo loved; he enjoyed it as a cat might enjoy playing with a mouse. He deliberately held back, increasing his strength gradually until he had exhausted his slave and was able to control him completely.

Over the next few hours, they hurt each other deliciously, and Renaldo enjoyed the rush, reveled in letting the beast off its leash like never before. He had always had to consider the fragile nature of his partners. Not even with Noran had he been able to let himself go as he did with this wonderful young man.

He took Casto one last time. His teeth penetrated the soft skin on Casto's nape and he hungrily inhaled the unique scent of sweat, a hint of blood, and both their emissions. This odor brought him to the brink of insanity time and again, and contained an ecstasy he'd never known before. Casto emanated this wonderful scent and captivated him with his smooth skin and the hard muscles beneath. Casto… always, always Casto. Renaldo shivered at this insight.

Then it was over. His slave lay under him, his elegant limbs trembling from exhaustion. Now he was more prey than opponent again.

Renaldo got up; he turned Casto around with his free hand. When he saw the damage he had caused, he cursed himself. Casto's right cheek was swollen, his lips thick and bloodied. He was covered in blue marks and a long red streak across his chest where Renaldo had scratched him.

The worst thing was Casto's gaze, empty of the fire that had burned within. Now he was only desperate and sad. Shivering, Renaldo picked up this young man he would probably never come to understand, carried him to the bathroom, and entered the hot water with him. Casto snuggled up to him in an unusually obedient manner, still shaking, his whole body tense.

Gently, Renaldo caressed the young man's upper arms with his fingertips, his voice a whisper. "I'm sorry, my own. I didn't want to hurt you." He hesitated for a moment. "Not like this, anyway."

A shiver ran through Casto's tightly strung body, subsiding gradually. "Don't say that, Barbarian. Don't say you're sorry."

"But it's the truth, Casto. I shouldn't have done this."

"It was me who asked for it."

"You did, but I doubt you knew what you were doing. I gave in and that was a mistake. We both know I'm stronger than you. It's my duty to protect you from myself."

Casto made a whimpering sound. "Stop it! Shut up! I just want to be able to hate you. If you apologize, I can't."

Slowly it dawned on Renaldo what it was that Casto wanted. He still didn't know the cause for his slave's self-destructive behavior, but he understood the intent. "I don't want you to hate me. I can't bear it. I would like to atone for my mistake. Please."

Casto remained in silence for so long that Renaldo suspected he hadn't heard his plea at all. Then Casto sighed and a last shiver ran through his body, followed by relaxation. He rested his head on Renaldo's shoulder, thus expressing his consent.

Full of gratitude, Renaldo turned his slave around and touched the swollen cheek gently with his lips. "Thank you, my own. You won't regret this."

While Renaldo was taking care of his slave, his mind was in control and the beast was safely chained again. He concentrated on giving Casto pleasure to make up for the pain he had inflicted and to bind him even more. Renaldo took his time; he caressed Casto's body until he was soft and compliant in his arms. The warrior loved the young man gently, without their usual fights for dominance. It was a completely different way of owning, one that did not need visible signs of subservience. Renaldo offered Casto lust, and in exchange, Casto submitted to him and gave his body freely. Renaldo allowed their mutual lust to inflame them both without using anger as a catalyst.

The moment Casto reached his climax, Renaldo realized that this was the first time they'd had sex without their usual ferocity. And it felt good, better than he had imagined. They both were too short-tempered to have a lot of those epiphanies, as this night had shown clearly, but it was nice to know they were capable of such tenderness.

After their needs had been taken care of, Renaldo tended to Casto's wounds before carrying him to bed.

Casto was so tired he fell asleep in an instant. While Renaldo watched him breathing, a pastime he never got tired of, he asked himself what had happened this time to throw Casto so off-balance. Whenever he thought he had finally managed to understand this complicated man, something happened that taught him otherwise, like today. The past few weeks, their relationship had been quite peaceful, which, in hindsight, was highly suspicious. Renaldo didn't have to worry about Casto escaping from the Valley anymore. Even if he should flee again, it was child's play for the demigod to get him back. And Casto wasn't so dumb as to make another futile attempt when he knew how it would end.

But that didn't mean Casto had come to terms with his destiny. On the contrary, he was still waiting for a chance to free himself of Renaldo's grasp. Renaldo knew how pathetic he was, but by now he was prepared even to buy the young man's affection. He wanted his capricious slave to be happy, no matter the cost, because then he would be more inclined to stay at Renaldo's side. Renaldo knew very well that he was granting Casto more freedom than was good for him, but whenever he thought about treating him more strictly, Casto provoked a fight and reminded him how refreshing it was not to be surrounded by complete subservience.

It wasn't just that, though. Renaldo also loved his slave's inquisitive mind, his sharp tongue, intelligence, and allure. If he wanted to, Casto could be the very picture of sexual desire.

Lost in thought, Renaldo traced the naked skin of his slave. He couldn't remember ever being so sexually sated as when he was with Casto. He regretted that the youth was mortal and he couldn't keep him for eternity.

Eternity.... Renaldo furrowed his brow. There was something about that thought—

At that moment, Casto stirred in his sleep, interrupting Renaldo's rumination with a whimper. He leaned in to soothe him, only to see he was awake.

Casto's features were still softened from sleep, his voice came from someplace deep within. "You're still awake?"

"It seems so." Renaldo offered his lover a lazy, tempting smile that was reciprocated as if there had never been a moment's insecurity.

"Then it's a good thing I'm awake as well."

Lust kindled again in Renaldo, burning every thought, every feeling, and leaving pure desire, equally returned by Casto, as he well knew. He placed his lips on the young man's mouth… and everything started again.

"ARE YOU going to tell me what got into you yesterday?" Over the rim of his mug, Renaldo looked at his now-relaxed lover.

Casto was staring into his tea. Delicate crimson tinged his neck and cheeks. "I'd rather not."

"Are you going to get angry should I insist?"

"I was stupid. Can we leave it at that?"

Casto's voice was pleading, which was why Renaldo decided not to pursue the matter any further. The night had ended on a surprisingly peaceful note, and he had no desire to start a new argument. They ate in silence for some time, and then Renaldo brought up the other festering topic between them.

"Tomorrow is the Spring Ceremony."

"I know." Casto's voice was prim. He did not try to hide his disdain.

"I assume you don't want to accompany me?"

"How did you know that, *Master*?"

"Don't be so forward. It's not as bad as you think."

"Not as bad? Correct me if I'm wrong, but the Ceremony's deeper meaning is to have lots of sex with as many partners as possible. I've no inclination whatsoever to play your whore."

The words were meant as a challenge, but for once Renaldo kept his cool. "Do you really think I see you like that?"

"You're asking me to give my consent to you fucking me in front of everybody in the Valley. So yes, I do think you see me like that, Barbarian."

Renaldo's eyes narrowed. He had planned not to let himself get dragged into another pointless fight, but Casto managed to rub him the wrong way without effort. Even ignorance should have its limits. "Everybody in the Valley knows you're sharing my bed—and my bed alone. So what difference does it make?"

"For you, there might be no difference, but for me it's simply too much. Can't you understand that?"

Casto was almost screaming now, his face contorted in open disdain, and he was trembling with rage.

Renaldo raised his hands in a soothing gesture. "No, I can't, although I'm trying real hard. And you don't have to come. I just wanted to ask so that you don't feel left out."

"That's so considerate of you, Barbarian. The answer's no."

"Okay, okay. I understand." A mocking glint appeared in his eyes. "So you're free tomorrow evening. Enjoy it!"

Casto shot him a venomous look but kept his mouth shut. He was glad Renaldo hadn't dug any deeper regarding his strange behavior the previous night, and he wasn't so dumb as to push his luck. He couldn't imagine what had gotten into him. As if he would really believe such superstitious nonsense! The Barbarian might be exceptional, but he definitely was not a *demigod*. How stupid of him to fall for the ramblings in a shady book. Besides, it was downright ridiculous to be jealous of Renaldo. He was a Barbarian and a station on Casto's way, nothing more. As soon as Casto found a way to rid himself of Renaldo, he and Lys would leave the Valley without shedding a tear for a single one of its occupants.

Right then his biggest problem was to get through the following night, but he had already planned how to burn through the empty hours while he was forced to wait for Renaldo.

He finished his breakfast without provoking his master any further and even allowed Renaldo to take him again. It was a quick pairing that sent them both completely relaxed into the day. Then Casto went to the stables to do his work.

CASTO WAS pacing back and forth in the chambers, unable to calm down. It was already dark, and Renaldo had left him about two hours ago for the orgy with the other warriors.

His meticulous plan about how he would spend the evening without his master had gone to shreds the moment Renaldo was out the door. As it had happened the year before, a slave had brought Casto the finest food, which stood untouched on the table. Every time he thought about taking a bite, he could feel bile rising in his throat. His thoughts were constantly circling around Renaldo: unwanted pictures of Renaldo with other men came to mind. He was torn between his anger about Renaldo, desperation because the Barbarian found relief in somebody else's arms, and outright rage that he cared about what Renaldo did.

Casto's restless pacing took him to the bath, and he decided to look for some relaxation in the hot water. It even worked for a short time, but then he became antsy again.

He left the pool in a cantankerous state of mind, dried himself, and applied scented oil to his skin without enjoying the procedure as usual.

For a moment he contemplated getting dressed, but then he remembered that Renaldo preferred him naked. Irate that he would even consider this, he grabbed a tunic, only to throw it aside again.

He positively hated the Spring Ceremony and was glad it was celebrated only once a year. Although he had grown up in more than liberal surroundings, where almost anything went, he couldn't understand why an orgy should be satisfying. The thought of being watched by strangers during the act killed even the strong desire he felt for Renaldo. Casto was sure that the ceremony was nothing more than an excuse for the mercenaries and their leaders to show their sexual prowess and virility. Why being chosen for the feast was deemed a top prize among the slaves, he would never understand.

Still caught up in his dark thoughts, he heard the door open. He couldn't keep himself from hurrying into the main room, his heart pounding. Renaldo was back! He was standing there, his beautiful face full of longing, his gray eyes so imperious that Casto had to fight the urge to kneel. At moments like these, he could almost believe that Renaldo was indeed a god.

Casto approached his master, and restlessness and anger fell off him like an old skin. Everything he wanted, all he could think about, was how desperately he longed to be with him. He stopped in front of the powerful warrior, tilted his head back and parted his lips in happy anticipation.

Renaldo took Casto's face in both hands, allowing his lust to build up until the tension was unbearable. "You haven't eaten anything."

"I wasn't hungry."

"I, on the other hand, am very hungry. For you." Casto's knees gave out, but his master held him in a tight embrace. "It's nice that you're already naked. Otherwise I'd have to wait for my feast longer than would please me."

With this, Renaldo picked him up and carried him to bed.

CASTO WOKE up late the next day. The sun had already passed its zenith, but he was simply too worn out to seriously contemplate getting up. Renaldo had taken him the whole night and far into the next morning, testing Casto's stamina, bringing him to his limit and then dragging him beyond. A smile lit up his features when he thought about the things they had done. Renaldo might have many flaws—a lack of ingenuity wasn't one of them.

"You're up already? I knew it. I should've spanked you that last time."

Renaldo sounded amused and relaxed. He, too, had enjoyed the night.

Casto turned around, his gaze full of greed. "Do it now."

Renaldo sat down on the bed, pulled him close, and kissed him deeply. "I must say, you're a wellspring of brilliant ideas, my gorgeous darling. Keep this one in mind. I'll sure get back to it, but now it's time for your presents."

"So, you did it again?"

Renaldo's attempts to give Casto presents were a constant source for good-natured banter between them.

"Well, since it didn't go that badly last year, I thought I'd give it another try. Come and see."

Casto feigned a groan but allowed Renaldo to pull him off the bed and lead him to the main room. There stood a trunk made of blackwood, with a heavy lock at the lid.

Renaldo offered him a key. "This is for you."

Casto took the key and kissed his master's hand. Out of principle, he usually neglected all presents from him, but not accepting a Spring Ceremony gift was an insult he would never commit. "You're very generous, Barbarian."

"Don't thank me before you know what I got you. I don't want to start fighting right away."

Casto blushed. The memory of Renaldo's first attempt to give him a present still embarrassed him. "I've already told you that I'm sorry about my harsh reaction!"

Renaldo kissed him fondly. "I know that. But I love teasing you now and then."

"You truly are a strange one, Barbarian."

Then Casto knelt down in front of the trunk and opened the lock. After lifting the lid, he went silent for some time. "Are you serious?"

"You don't like it?"

XENIA MELZER

"I do. More than I can say. You've already been so generous during the last year, giving me a complete new outfit and everything. This is—a lot."

"Well, what can I say? I'm pleased with you."

Abruptly, Casto turned around with a wild expression. "I escaped. I oppose you whenever and wherever I can, I'm stubborn and arrogant, and I question your authority on a daily basis. And you're *pleased*?"

Renaldo grinned. "It's nice that you at least realize your behavior isn't normal. But yes, I am pleased. Since I met you, I haven't felt bored for a second. I like it when you oppose me, because nobody else dares to do so, and your arrogance is refreshing. Plus, I like throwing you off-balance from time to time."

"If that's the case, then I thank you for your generosity, Barbarian. And now leave me alone, I want to inspect my new stuff."

Renaldo's hand fell hard on Casto's shoulder. "That's not going to happen, my own. I owe you a spanking."

With a feverish look in his eyes, Casto opened his lips in invitation. "For once, Barbarian."

Laughing like a wicked little boy, Renaldo dragged his lover back into the bedroom. Their games weren't as intensive as he had planned, since he could feel that the night hadn't left his slave unaffected, so Renaldo settled for taking him once and then delighted in drawing lazy circles with his fingertips on Casto's naked skin.

Casto rested his head against Renaldo's chest and wallowed in the feeling of relaxed exhaustion.

On the day after the Spring Ceremony, there was never a lot to do. Almost all the inhabitants of the Valley were busy sleeping off their intoxication and recovering from the strain. It was nice to enjoy the quiet for a change. After almost an hour of blissful silence, Casto asked a question he had been pondering for some time now.

"How come you never force me?"

The lazy circling of Renaldo's fingers stopped for a moment. "Force you to do what?"

"You know full well what I mean, Barbarian. You never hesitate to take what you want, but regarding the bed, you bow to rules almost as strict as those in a monastery. I don't understand why you would relinquish the one thing about a slave that's interesting besides his ability to work."

Renaldo started his fingers circling again. Casto's tone suggested that he was serious about his question, and Renaldo was willing to give him a thorough answer, although he had to digress in order to do so.

"First and foremost, it's a question of respect. Not toward the slaves but toward the Holy Mothers. Although we're gods of war, or perhaps because of it, we do know the value of life. And sexual intercourse is the symbol of life. Always was, always will be. It's a holy act, though it might look different at times. Gender isn't important because it's about the act itself, not if it actually creates anything. Ana-Isara and Ana-Aruna are Death and Life, the two sides to everything that is. They represent the basic rhythm to which the universe dances. Becoming and passing on are the two constants that govern everything, no matter the timespan. Sometimes this span is very short, as for you humans. Sometimes it's so long that it doesn't seem to have an ending at all, as it is for Canubis, me, and the Emeris. But at the bottom of it all, Life and Death are always there. And the lust we find in each other is the symbol for this cycle and the two principles.

"Not everybody shares this view, but here in the Pack we do. That's why forcing your partner is prohibited under any circumstances. It would be a perversion of this unique gift."

"Except for punishment." Casto sounded a little defiant; he didn't want to admit that Renaldo's words had impressed him.

"Yes. For punishment, it is allowed. But only when the crime justifies it. Basically, there are only two cases in which we do it: treason and rape."

"Rapists get raped?"

"Something like that. But perhaps you can understand better now why the Spring Ceremony is so important to us. Admittedly the Pack isn't a place where prudery is common, but during the Ceremony things are slightly different. You could say the unrestrained sex is kind of official. A prayer to the Mothers." A happy smile flashed over Renaldo's features. He was extremely pleased that Casto was listening to him so intently. Then Casto looked up with a puzzled expression.

"You said that is the main reason. What else could make you hold back, though it's against your very nature?"

Renaldo laughed heartily.

"Convenience. It's far more satisfying to interact with a willing partner than to search for fulfillment on your own. I like it when my partner's lust inflames my own."

"And because nobody can deny you, it's not really a problem, is it?"

Again Renaldo roared with laughter. "Of course it's easier that way. But as you've already realized, it's not unconditional bliss for me either. So far, I was never able to bind a partner for any period of time. You're the first, and you made me wait so long, I was starting to get worried."

"Did that hurt your ego?"

"A little. I mean, I'm the man with the face of an angel. Under normal circumstances I only have to make my choice and the rest is taken care of. But you didn't even realize that I had chosen you. That threw me off-balance, but it was also what piqued my interest. I mean, somebody who doesn't give a damn about my looks or my status? That was an absolute novelty. You don't have intercourse with me because you want something out of it or because you've fallen for my beauty, but solely because it's fun. That pleases me more than I can tell you."

Casto didn't react to this praise; the rare candor had rendered him speechless. Instead of an answer, he snuggled closer to Renaldo, inhaled the scented warmth he was emanating, and thought about his words.

Casto really could understand the mercenaries better now, although many things still didn't make sense. But he was trained to use his mind to analyze any given situation, and the more he did so, the clearer it became that he had been swept away by his prejudices.

It was time to cut the Pack some slack.

3. CAMPAIGN

"WHAT DO you mean, I'm not ready yet?"

"Exactly what I said. You're not deaf, are you?"

Casto and Renaldo were glaring at each other across the table.

Casto had clenched his fists, and was trembling with righteous indignation. "What's the meaning of training me so mercilessly and then forbidding me to fight?"

"You will fight. When I decide that you're ready."

"And when will that be? Do I have to remind you that I defeated three Emeris on our first encounter?"

"No. You *and Lys* defeated three Emeris. That's an entirely different thing."

Casto's eyes glinted. He prepared for an acid retort, but Renaldo stopped him with a gesture. Renaldo's voice was strained; he had problems reining in his anger. "I don't doubt that together with Lys you're an impressive opponent. You could probably even go against me. But during a battle the strangest things happen. You could get separated from Lys, and without him, your chances decrease rapidly. You're good, but not good enough."

"I thought I had progressed so incredibly well?"

Casto's voice was ripe with sarcasm and irritated Renaldo until his blood started to boil.

"You've become quite apt, but it's not enough for battle. You may not like it, but I'm responsible for you as your teacher and master. I sure as hell won't let you walk into danger unaware."

"I'm perfectly capable of looking after myself!"

"No, you aren't! Yes, you defeated three Emeris, and yet you're here with me. That's all there is to say."

The effect those words had on Casto was overwhelming. He froze as if he had just been hit on the head, and the fury on his face turned into something else. All his angry tension disappeared, and at that moment he reminded Renaldo of a wounded animal that had no hope of escaping the hunter.

"You're right. I'm here. Against my will."

With his eyes cast downward, Casto got up. His hands shook.

"Where're you going?"

"To Lys. If you allow it."

Spooked, Renaldo got up as well. Under normal circumstances, Casto would have said those words with so much sarcasm that his meaning would have been crystal clear. But now it seemed as if he were serious in his subjugation. Renaldo realized that he had hurt him deeply.

He hurried to take Casto in his arms. "I'm sorry, Casto. I shouldn't have said that."

"But it's the truth. When you captured me, you were superior to me. You still are."

"That's nothing you should worry about. I've been doing this my whole life. You're young. I promise your time will come."

"When?"

"Sooner than I feel comfortable about. I can't stand the thought of you getting hurt. I'm asking you to be patient with me for this summer, and I promise you'll fight next year."

Gently, Casto pried himself free. "Really?"

"Have I ever broken a promise I've given to you?"

Casto blushed slightly. "No, you haven't. Please forgive my insolence."

Imploringly, Renaldo looked at Casto. "Does this mean we're good again?"

"It depends, Barbarian."

"Depends on what?"

"What you plan to do with the remaining evening."

The challenge in Casto's body language and words met happy acceptance with Renaldo. "I think you'll be satisfied. Come here."

He pulled Casto closer and started kissing him. Since the Spring Ceremony, Casto had been oddly compliant. Renaldo used this time of peace to spoil him as much as he could in order to bind him all the more. The fight just now had been the first bigger one for some time, and that Casto gave in so readily was a small wonder that Renaldo accepted without hesitation.

RENALDO GLARED at the walls of Elam with open disdain. A siege was not his favorite variant of warfare to begin with, and this cursed city was one of the most obnoxious he had ever seen.

Elam was a rat's nest in the truest meaning of the words, populated by the scum of society, people so low and degenerate they barely resembled humans anymore. They had been driven to this forsaken place by the never-ending greed for wealth that seemed to be ingrained in the soul of every mortal. There was no law in Elam, nobody to prevent the worst excesses. In this city, everybody was on their own. As long as the gold kept coming, the Eastern Kings did not care how the place was run. Because of this, the Pack was facing an army of marauders—men and women who had never received any tactical training but were used to fighting dirty in order to survive. And dirty their fighting was.

To dig up and cleanse the gold needed a lot of chemicals, none of which could be labeled as safe or healthy. And above all, most were highly flammable. Elam's defenders filled the liquids into bottles and spheres made of clay, ignited them, and then threw them over the walls. That way, they had managed to fend off no fewer than three attempts to storm the city.

Under normal circumstances, Elam would have been under the Pack's command by now. It was not built to withstand an army, but the determination of the defenders, the poisonous surroundings, and the ignoble tactics had kept the mercenaries out until now. Renaldo hated to admit it, but he was as irritated as hell about this. Those puny mortals dared to defy him and his brother! They would pay for this insolence very soon. No matter how violently they protected their walls, their numbers were dwindling, and Renaldo could sense where the breach would open.

"To me!" Upon this command, Elua, Xi'an, and about thirty of the mercenaries gathered. Like a real pack of wolves, they followed Renaldo to the weak spot where only a few desperate defenders were left. They had no more clay spheres and had to rely on battered old weapons to fend off the mercenaries.

Elua was among the first to enter the wall, together with Renaldo. While her leader killed his opponents by simply swinging his sword in a deadly arc, making use of the reach of his arms, the smaller female relied on her speed. She quickly ducked under the spear a worn-out-looking man was aiming at her, closing the distance between them in less than a heartbeat. Her first dagger pierced the man's heart, while the second one slit his throat open. With an expression of surprise and a hint of relief, the corpse dropped down the wall. Elua spun around to block the sword of the woman who had tried to creep up behind her. A brutal kick with her left foot swept the attacker off her feet, and before she could get up again, Elua ended her life with a swift move of the daggers.

Xi'an had arrived on top of the wall right after Elua. He stayed back while she took care of the man with the spear, waiting for the next opponent to appear. A bear of a man with a chest like a beer barrel and an impressive, double-headed axe in his hands jumped forward, trying to use his sheer body mass to force Xi'an down the wall again. The man rained a series of uncontrolled blows on Xi'an, who parried them with his sword. Although the blade was crafted from blue steel, like all the weapons the mercenaries used, it trembled under the attack like a young tree in a storm. It was only a question of time until it would break under the strain. Xi'an evaded another wide swing by retreating a few steps. Determined to end this encounter, he then rushed forward, diving gracefully under the axe while his sword came around in a half circle. It cut the man's legs off neatly, making him scream in pain. The axe dropped and was immediately followed by its bearer's head when Xi'an finished the job.

Out of the corner of his eye, Renaldo saw how his men killed off the few defenders who were left on this part of the wall. In front of him, only two remained, gripping their swords with hopeless expressions on their faces. Despite all the stories about his cruelty, Renaldo didn't take pleasure from killing the weak. He preferred strong, cunning opponents over cowering sheep who could do nothing but wait for the butcher's knife to strike. The two men in front of him could have been nonexistent as far as he was concerned. Weakened by hunger and frozen by terror, they weren't even able to lift their swords to block the blows that severed their heads. Disappointed by this unsatisfying slaughter, Renaldo glared at the corpses as if they had offended him. He felt the fire rising when the beast inside him stirred. The Angel of Death shook his head vigorously. This was not the time and place to give in to the urges of his most primal part. Even though they had killed all the defenders on this part of the wall, he was still on a battlefield and couldn't afford losing his focus. The fire subsided, the beast retreated.

Renaldo stepped forward to the edge of the wall to get a better overview of the situation. Down on the city side, the streets were empty; the people had fled from the death coming to claim them. Renaldo was satisfied. Finally this stubborn place would yield to their command.

Out of the corner of his eye, he glimpsed movement. He spun around quickly. A surely mortally wounded female crawled toward a heap of empty barrels stashed at the wall, leaving a broad trail of blood behind her. Renaldo did not see her as a threat.

It was too late when he realized how wrong he had been. From somewhere under her ripped and bloodied clothes she produced a tinderbox, struck one of the matches with difficulty, and with a groan dropped it into one of the barrels.

Then she rolled over. Her dying gaze met Renaldo's and her eyes lit up triumphantly.

"Get back! *Retreat!*" Renaldo screamed at the top of his lungs, and his roar startled the warriors, but absolute obedience toward the demigods had been drilled into them from the day they joined the Pack. They rushed to follow their leader's commands.

The barrels exploded with a thunderous blast, emitting blue and green flames and eradicating a good part of the wall, but thanks to the warning, most of the mercenaries escaped unscathed.

Stunned and helpless, they watched as the Angel of Death was engulfed in flames and then buried under scattering debris.

IN A foul mood, Casto scrubbed his dirty boots. In order to wash the gold from out of the argillaceous earth, the citizens of Elam used a poisonous cocktail made of various chemicals that now, after years of diffusion, could be found in the soil as well. In a radius of thirty leagues around the city, the water and earth were poisoned; nothing that grew there could be consumed without risk. Everything needed for survival had to be bought from outside this lethal circle, and if he didn't clean his boots twice a day, the venomous dust destroyed the leather.

The districts surrounding Elam were so dull that it got on everybody's nerves. Of course, the unusually rich gold seams justified the sacrifice that turned the landscape into a region of death where nothing could prosper. The gold from this cursed city was a trusted currency throughout the continent, yet when confronted with the annihilation of the land, Casto wondered if the price for all that wealth wasn't too high.

Casto was glad the city was about to fall. It meant they could leave these barren lands, that seemed to absorb all hope, and return home.

He mused about how naturally he viewed the Valley as his home now. When he thought about his place of birth, he felt dirty and sullied. He had only known pain and hardship there. But in the Valley, where the most feared army in the world lived, he had found security and happiness. He did realize that he had Renaldo to thank for that, and although he still hated the Barbarian for taking him hostage, he was also grateful. Renaldo might be many things, and the fear his enemies felt toward him was justified, but he was also a man with unwavering principles and admirable intuition. Although he would never admit it, Casto was aware that Renaldo treated him specially. He made Casto feel more like a guest than a slave, even if he didn't have the freedom to leave. That he wasn't allowed to fight at Renaldo's side still vexed him, but he had accepted his decision. Renaldo was his honorable trainer, and of course he had the right to forbid him to fight. In this respect Casto trusted Renaldo's judgment, even if he didn't like the outcome.

He had decided he would train so hard during the coming winter that Renaldo would have no choice but to let him fight next spring.

Casto wasn't exactly furious that he didn't have to run against the slimy walls of Elam. The whole city was like a festering wound on the face of Ana-Darasa—a fat, abhorrent toad, sitting in the center of the devastated landscape, sucking the gold from the guts of the earth like a greedy parasite.

The sovereigns of the Eastern Kingdoms used the city as their personal treasure chest from which they took the riches without a second thought, pumping the gold into the trade of the continent, not caring what it meant for the stability of entire kingdoms. If ever a city deserved complete destruction, then it was Elam. Even though Casto didn't fall for the illusion that all problems would be solved then. The kings would revive their main source of gold soon enough, and there were always enough soldiers of fortune and poor souls who were willing to spend their lives at a sorry place like Elam in exchange for wealth.

Elam wasn't the problem, not really. The real problem was the lack of stable alliances in the East. The rulers there were so busy fighting each other that it was impossible to get firm commercial agreements. Contracts didn't last long enough to allow their ink to dry. Not to mention the less than satisfying security on the trade routes—

"Casto!"

Sic's voice tore him from his tactical musings. The smith was panting and his cheeks were red because he had run so fast. Casto greeted him with a genuine smile. Although they couldn't talk very often, Sic was still one of the few slaves in the Valley whom he got along with. Casto felt some sympathy for him, a sentiment that was entirely new to him. It was a dangerous emotion he had always tried to suppress, but Sic was so open and friendly, Casto found it hard not to return the feeling.

"What is it, Sic? You really shouldn't run so fast in a heat like this."

Sic's blue-gray eyes were serious. "I came as soon as I heard. I didn't want you to be alone."

Casto furrowed his brows in confusion. "What's happened?"

Sic's hand flew to his mouth. "You don't know yet?"

"I don't know what?"

"Oh Casto! I'm so sorry! Lord Renaldo is missing."

Casto's knees gave way. His voice was a hoarse croak and he heard himself as though through several layers of cloth. "Missing?"

"He was leading the attack, as always. When he was on top of the city wall, they blew it up. Lord Renaldo was right at the center of the explosion. They say he was buried under the debris. Of course they're looking for him, but they have to secure Elam first."

Sic kept on talking, but Casto didn't listen any longer. All the blood had drained from his face; he felt empty, as if somebody had sucked all the energy from his body in one go. If Sic hadn't helped him, Casto would have fallen.

Sic led him into the tent, sat him down gently, and gave him some water. His voice still echoed in Casto's ears.

"Don't worry. I'm sure he's fine. He's a god. He can't die, you know that."

Furious, Casto pushed him away. "Stop it! He's not a god! He's a Barbarian, a mercenary! Nobody survives an explosion. He's dead, and I've lost him!"

Taken aback by Casto's wild reaction, Sic retreated a few steps. "It's okay, Casto. Really. He'll come back, I know that."

Hot tears pricked Casto's eyes, but he blinked them back. Even though Sic was friendly, Casto wouldn't show weakness in his presence.

Sic had his arm around Casto's shoulders again. "I'm going to wait with you. If that's your wish."

Casto's first reaction was to send him away, but then he thought twice. It wasn't a bright idea to be alone right now. Even though the young man was talking nonsense, he was another human being, and Casto was in dire need of sympathy. His normally impenetrable shield of arrogance had shattered due to the shock, and he felt lonely and vulnerable.

In silence, they sat next to each other, stared at the ground, and waited for a miracle.

THE MIRACLE happened shortly before the sun descended on the horizon, and it came in the shape of Lord Noran.

The bulky master smith opened the tent flap and scanned the room. When he saw Sic, his brow furrowed. "Sic! What are you doing here?"

The young man knelt hastily. Again Casto was reminded that Sic had only the greatest respect for his owner.

"I've kept Casto company, Master."

"And dodged your work. You truly are an incorrigible sluggard. Go back to the smithy; we'll talk there."

The threatening tone made it clear that Sic was facing punishment, but he did not try to defend himself. With his gaze cast to the ground, he quickly left for the smithy.

Casto was about to say something in Sic's defense when a noise at the entrance disturbed him.

Canubis entered the tent. In his arms he carried Renaldo's lifeless body. Casto couldn't suppress a scream. Renaldo looked terrible—all that was left of his clothes were rags, his hair was burned, his once-beautiful face a bloody mask, and his nose looked like it had been smashed by an iron bar. On some parts of his body, the skin was in shreds. Blood dripped to the ground from various wounds, and those parts that weren't bloodied or torn were covered in dirt and soot.

When Canubis placed his brother on one of the lounges with a strangely detached expression, Casto saw that the bones on Renaldo's right thigh had broken through the flesh. The gruesome sight made him heave. It was obvious Canubis had carried a corpse to the tent, but Casto still had to ask, "Why didn't you take him to Lady Noemi?"

"Because it would be useless." Canubis looked at him, unfazed. His brother's death didn't seem to touch him at all. "He's already started to heal."

Stunned, Casto gazed at the ruin that had been the Barbarian's body. It seemed impossible that among this mass of bloody tissue should be a spark of life, but even while he looked, a deep cut across Renaldo's chest closed as if by magic. When Casto concentrated, he thought he could see Renaldo's chest moving in the rhythm of breathing.

Canubis's voice penetrated the veil of shock and desperation around Casto.

"It'll take some time, but he should be fine by tomorrow. I hope you won't bother him with your usual games tonight."

Casto glared at his master's brother with hatred. He didn't like his implication. His reply was full of venom. "Who do you take me for?"

Noran's hand shot forward to punish the insolent slave, but Canubis stopped him with a look. The predator eyes bore into Casto's sorrow-stricken face and his voice was suddenly gentle. "I apologize, Casto. That was cruel of me. But it doesn't happen every day that I have to watch when my beloved brother gets buried under an entire city wall. I know you're a man of honor and will behave accordingly."

With that, he turned and left Casto alone with his master.

When Casto was sure the two men had left, he collapsed next to the lounge with a whimper. Deeply shocked, he took in all the damage Renaldo had endured. Although the wounds were already starting to look better than a few minutes ago, the sight was still gruesome. In some places Casto could see bones shining ghastly white between all the blood and gore.

A strange sound, like a breaking twig, resounded. Casto's gaze shot downward, and before his amazed eyes, the bones at the thigh healed themselves and the wound closed without leaving a trace. His mind still fought against what he was seeing, especially against the deeper implications of this wondrous occurrence. By now he had gotten used to the fact that Lady Noemi was able to heal wounds and cure illnesses due to her gift, but if Renaldo didn't need her gift to return from the dead, it could only mean one thing.

That he himself isn't truly of this world.

Casto's rational mind couldn't accept that, although the proof was right in front of him. To evade the uncomfortable topic, he concentrated on the fact that his master had survived. He got up to fetch a bowl of water. Carefully he started to cleanse the spots where the wounds had already healed and only dried blood and dirt remained to stain the perfect body of the Angel of Death.

He was about to turn to his master's torso when Renaldo's right hand shot up and closed around Casto's wrist like a claw.

"What're you doing?" Renaldo's voice was hoarse, but audible.

Casto was so thrilled, he smiled broadly. "I'm washing you, Barbarian. You reek."

The ghost of a smile flashed across Renaldo's strained features, which were once again beautiful. "I'm kind of thirsty."

Casto got up immediately to get him a glass of water.

Renaldo drank, and then he grinned at his slave. "That's the first time you did my bidding so promptly. Don't tell me you were worried about me?"

"Don't get all high and mighty. I just feel no inclination to get used to a new master."

"So you admit you're mine?"

Casto's eyes narrowed to slits. For somebody who had just returned from the dead, Renaldo's mind worked surprisingly well. "I'm just admitting that, at the moment, you have a certain claim over me that I do not wish to bestow on anybody else. But it doesn't mean I'm your property, not in the least."

"Quirky as ever. It's nice to know some things never change."

Instead of an answer, Casto fetched fresh water and continued cleaning his master.

While he was swiping the blood and dirt from Renaldo's skin, Renaldo delighted in the sight of the young man. Even for a demigod, it wasn't pleasurable to be at the center of an explosion and afterward buried under a collapsing city wall. Luckily he had been unconscious most of the time, but he remembered very well that his last thought before the darkness had consumed him had been about his beautiful slave—and that it had been a soothing one. Now the blond looked up at him, his voice shaking, betraying his feelings.

"How on earth could this happen?"

Renaldo shrugged. It hadn't been the first time he had been injured so badly, and it wasn't that big a deal. Bothersome and aggravating, but not really worth mentioning. Still he could sense that Casto was really worked up, and he tried to calm him down.

"It was unfortunate. The defenders were so desperate that they were willing to sacrifice their city walls just to kill me. Nobody could have foreseen that. These things happen."

"How many times? How many times have you died?" Casto was almost hysterical.

"I'm a god of war, Casto. What do you think?"

Renaldo's voice was soft. He could see how uncomfortable the topic was for his slave. It wasn't just his grave injuries; Casto didn't believe in gods, and the last hours must have come as a shock to him. Gently, Renaldo caressed Casto's cheek in an attempt to get through to him.

"Stop worrying about it. I'm here, fine and healthy. If it'll help you, I can annoy you, and then we can have a fight."

A smile appeared on Casto's lips. He understood that Renaldo wanted to distract him and was grateful for it. "Unfortunately, I have to decline. I promised your brother I would behave."

"So far you're doing really well, my beautiful slave. If you truly want to please me, you could get me something to eat. And some wine."

A delicate shudder made clear what Casto thought about this request. "You've just narrowly escaped death and still want to drink that abhorrent swill?"

"I'm a barbarian. That's how we are."

Barely concealed disgust showed in Casto's noble features. Nevertheless, he got up to do his master's bidding.

4. SIC

IN THE smithy, Sic crouched next to his master's forge, crying with raw, desperate sobs. After he had expressed his displeasure about his personal slave in an extremely physical way, Noran had returned to the battlefield without sparing his victim a second glance.

No matter how hard he tried, Sic never managed to please his owner and benefactor. He was seriously wondering why Noran kept him around if Sic was a source of constant disappointment to him. Sic knew that nobody in the Pack understood why he was so drawn to the grumpy, strict, merciless master smith, but he had only to close his eyes and think of the day when Noran had bought him, and his heart overflowed with love and gratitude. Even though he had been his master's property for almost eight years now, he could clearly remember the autumn that had changed his whole life.

The trees had already started to shed their leaves. Everywhere the farmers were busy bringing the harvest in, and the nights saw the first frost. At that time, Sic was living at the edge of a tiny village in a run-down smithy operated by a brutal drunkard named Dalwon. Since his master was either drunk or sleeping off his drink, it was up to Sic to attend to the few orders they got. Although nothing more than a malnourished boy of eleven years, Sic was already able to shoe a horse, as well as make horseshoes and repair and produce tools for farmwork. He'd had the choice to either learn fast or starve to death. In one of his few sober moments, Dalwon had showed him some of the knack, the rest Sic had taught himself, to satisfy the last customers they still had.

Sic's days followed a never-changing rhythm in sync with his master's sleep pattern. Dalwon started drinking early in the morning and got more and more aggressive during forenoon. If Sic wasn't careful, he got his first beating then, mostly without cause. Around noon, Dalwon fell asleep, which was the time when the customers came, knowing well that they would meet the gifted apprentice and not the drunken master.

After a few hours, during which Sic tried to get as much work done as possible, Dalwon woke again with a terrible hangover that he tried to cure with more alcohol. When he had already beaten his apprentice in the morning, he sometimes refrained from doing it in the afternoon as well, as long as the boy didn't provoke him. For Dalwon, it could be a provocation when Sic moved too noisily or dared address him.

On that special day, the drunkard had already whipped his slave cruelly in the morning and was now, in the afternoon, ready to do it again. Why his master was so ill-tempered, Sic couldn't tell, but he wasn't really interested either. He just wanted to avoid another beating. He tried to break free from Dalwon's grasp.

Sometimes it helped when Sic walked in the woods before he returned to the smithy. Then, over two or three bottles of cheap wine, the smith often forgot why he wanted to punish his slave. But when Sic tried to run from his torturer this time, he collided with a giant of a man.

He fell down, and before he could duck out of reach, Dalwon had dealt him two brutal kicks in the ribs.

"That should teach you to accept your just punishment." Mercilessly, Dalwon watched his slave writhe in pain before turning to his visitor. "How may I help you, lord?"

Disdainfully, the stranger took in his surroundings. His brown eyes showed their contempt openly. The forge's fire shone on his shaven head, his lips were a thin, derogative line, and in that light the tattoos on his cheek were barely visible on the coffee-colored skin. He was big and unbelievably bulky, and he towered over Dalwon like a mountain over a hill. He looked like a bear, perhaps a little clumsy at first sight, but nevertheless dangerous. An intimidatingly long and heavy sword with a delicately crafted grip bearing a ruby the size of a child's fist dangled at his side. It was obvious the warrior wasn't happy to be there.

When he spoke, his voice was gruff. "My horse has lost a shoe."

Dalwon bowed low. He instinctively knew that it was better to show this man only the best of manners. "We'll see to it. Please, take a seat. May I offer you some wine?"

While attending to the frightening stranger, Dalwon still managed to kick Sic one more time. "Get going, you lazy bastard. You heard the lord. Go and shoe his horse!"

Sic hurried to his feet. Out of the corner of his eye, he shot the stranger one more glance, then hastened to obey his master. At least punishment was off for now, and if the warrior paid well, there was a possibility that Dalwon would completely forget about it.

Inside the smithy, Dalwon and the stranger shared a table. Dalwon was drinking carelessly from the jar, which his guest had declined with a disgusted frown.

"Are you sure the boy will be fine on his own? I'm riding a warhorse that can be quirky sometimes."

Dalwon shrugged. He simply did not care if anything happened to Sic. "The little bastard isn't too useful, but he knows how to shoe a horse. If he'd been too stupid to do even that, I would've given him the sack a long time ago."

"Where did you get him? He is quite young."

"From the orphanage in Kwar. Old Mother Mali is a friend of mine and has left him to me for two pieces of copper. He's not the sharpest knife in the drawer, mind you, but when he gets beaten on a regular basis, it's fine."

The stranger nodded, his face an impenetrable mask. After a few moments of loaded silence, he got up abruptly. His voice was even more aloof than before.

"Please excuse me for a moment. I just want to make sure my horse behaves."

Dalwon took another gulp. "Whatever you want. I won't run away."

The warrior stepped outside, only to find his horse already shod.

The skinny boy was just returning from the well with a bucket of water. He respectfully cast down his gaze as he addressed the stranger. "I made a new shoe for your horse. I also fixed the others. They're still good, although the nails at the left hind foot were badly hammered in. It's probably the next one you'll have to change."

"That was very considerate of you. Thank you."

The voice was still gruff, but all Sic heard was the praise. Dalwon never praised him, so he was all the more excited that this stranger was satisfied with his work. "You're very friendly, lord. Is it all right to water your horse?"

"But of course. I'm going to pay your master now."

The stranger returned into the smithy and looked at Dalwon with so much scorn it would have made a normal person uncomfortable. But the drunkard was oblivious, all his concentration focused on his booze.

"Your apprentice is done. How much?"

"A new shoe is two copper pieces, shoeing the same."

A furrowed brow was the answer to this exorbitant price, but the voice remained calm. "I will give you two more copper pieces and you will let me have your slave."

The bloodshot eyes regarded him with greed. Dalwon might have been a drunkard who had sacrificed most of his mind to alcohol, but his instincts for trade still functioned. He thought it strange that this expensively clad man would be interested in a starveling like Sic, but who was he to question the whims of a lord? "Three and he's yours."

The warrior's hand went to his sword and drew it. "Insolence! I'm already paying more than enough for the shoeing, so take the offer!"

Dalwon eyed the one and a half ells of cold steel in silent terror. The shock over the stranger's angry reaction had almost sobered him up. His instincts for impending danger still worked properly despite the years of heavy drinking. At that moment, they were shrilling like crazy, telling him to comply with the dark warrior's will.

"Of course. Just take him."

The rage vanished from the face; the features turned back to unreadable. "Does he have some decent clothing?"

Dalwon looked surprised first, as if he couldn't believe that the stranger was really interested in how a slave was dressed. When he realized how serious the stranger was, he cowered even more. "I'm sorry, my lord, but what he's wearing is all he has. I'm not rich, you see, and can hardly afford to feed him, let alone buy him fancy clothes."

The stranger only glared at the groveling Dalwon, knowing there was no changing some people. After a few heartbeats, during which Dalwon wished from the bottom of his heart for another bottle of wine, the stranger simply shook his head. Without sparing him a second glance, he left the smithy. Sic waited next to the horse, the empty bucket dangling from his left hand.

"My name is Noran. From now on, I'm your master."

The expressive green-blue eyes widened in fear. The boy let go of the reins and the bucket and knelt, his gaze on the ground. He was obviously used to being treated as if he were nothing but chattel and not a human being. He showed no signs of protest against his destiny.

"My name is Sic, Master."

The stranger nodded. "Well, Sic, get up. I want to leave now."

The boy obeyed and waited until Noran had mounted the horse. He didn't know where they were headed, he only hoped it wouldn't be too far so that he wouldn't tear his bare feet. It was an experience he'd already had several times and he found he could quite happily abstain from it.

His new master waved a hand irritably. "What're you waiting for? Come here."

With his head bowed demurely, Sic moved to step in front of the horse, thinking his new master wanted him to walk there, but Noran grabbed his shoulder.

"Just give me your hand, idiot."

Stunned, Sic obeyed. The warrior lifted him up without apparent effort, as if he didn't weigh more than a newborn. The strong arms closed around Sic's body, a bulky cage made of muscle, and then the horse started to move.

Sic was silent during the ride because he was afraid to anger his new master. At the same time, he was so happy he wanted to scream. This strange, distant man allowed him to ride! He did not force Sic to run next to the horse as was the custom. At that time, what Sic felt for his master was the pure, innocent admiration of a child toward the first person who was kind to him. As he grew older, that admiration slowly turned into a love still rooted in the idealized picture of the past.

When the sun started to go down, they reached a small town. Sic, who hadn't seen anything other than the smithy and the forest since his days in the orphanage, looked around with open curiosity. Noran headed toward a store that sold clothes. Sic was glad when he helped him off the horse. He wasn't used to riding, and despite the slow pace Noran had chosen, he still felt exhausted. His master ushered him into the store where an obliging merchant was waiting.

"I wish you a good evening, lord. What can I do for you?"

"My slave needs clothes. And shoes. See to it."

If the man was annoyed by his customer's rude behavior, he didn't show it. With the unfailing instincts of a seasoned merchant, he realized that the stranger had enough financial prowess to be as unfriendly as he pleased. So he took the stick-thin boy, measured him, and selected warm underwear, trousers, socks, two woolen shirts, and a doublet made of leather, all under the burning gaze of the customer.

"He's going to need a coat. Something warm."

The merchant showed the customer a felted coat lined with rabbit fur. "Watertight and warm."

After a condescending nod from Noran, the coat went onto the growing pile, followed by a pair of warm boots. When Noran had paid, the merchant helped the boy to get dressed.

Sic was speechless. For the first time in his life, he wore shoes—even fur-lined ones, the likes of which he'd seen only on rich farmers. With shaking fingers, he felt the soft leather of his doublet and marveled at the silky feel of his new shirt.

Noran dragged him along. "Come on. You can finger the cloth later. I'm hungry."

Sic hurried to follow his master. When they entered the street, he dared to address the bad-tempered man. "I thank you, Master. You're very generous."

Noran dismissed his slave's thanks with an angry gesture. "First and foremost, I'm hungry. Now come."

They found an inn with a vacancy, and Noran ordered an opulent meal. Shyly, Sic watched his master sit down at the table in the middle of the room to eat.

Noran shot the boy an impatient look. "Sit down. Do you need a special invitation for everything?"

Sic hurried to obey as Noran filled his own plate with roast meat, gravy, and bread and started to eat hungrily. Sic could feel his stomach constrict as he eyed the food. He couldn't remember when he'd last seen anything so delicious. But experience had taught him never to expect anything from his master, especially enough food. With his head bowed, he waited while Noran enjoyed his meal.

After some time, Noran looked up with furrowed brows. He was about to scold his new slave again when he realized that the boy did not dare take the food. With a sigh, and already doubting his decision to buy him, Noran filled a plate for Sic and placed it in front of him.

"Eat. You're way too thin. It's still a four-day ride back to where I live, and if you don't fatten up a little, you've nothing against the cold."

Gratefully, Sic obeyed his master.

Later, when he was safely tucked into soft furs and listening to his owner's regular breathing, he let his tears flow. He thanked the Holy Mothers for sending this benefactor his way, and he swore to serve Lord Noran to the end of his days.

Sic sighed. Again he had failed to show his master the respect he deserved. When he had heard about Lord Renaldo's accident, his first thought had been to help Casto. From the bottom of his heart, Sic liked the young man who had managed to capture the Angel of Death. He would like to be his friend, but Noran didn't approve, and Casto himself, while always nice, retreated whenever Sic got too close to him. Earlier that day had been the first time Sic had been able to see behind the arrogant mask Casto usually wore.

It was pointless to muse about this. Noran had made it pretty clear what would happen to Sic should he fail to keep his distance from the capricious slave. Filled with newfound determination, Sic wiped away the tears that had been streaming down his face. He still had to complete a lot of tasks today, and his master would be less than pleased if he forgot even one of them.

5. DEPENDENT

TREMBLING ALL over, Casto knelt next to the bier on which his master was resting. Somebody had washed away the blood and clad the Angel of Death in a silken tunic. He was lying pale and cold, his beautiful face forever empty of life. Hot tears stained Casto's cheeks. With a desperate whimper, he buried his face on his master's chest that was as cold as marble.

He was caught in blackest despair, and it was not because he would soon belong to a new master, and his freedom was forever out of reach. Casto had lost the love of his life, his reason to live. He hadn't wanted to admit it, was angry even now about how much he needed the Barbarian, how impossible it had become for him to go on without the warrior. But the naked, ugly truth was that he had fallen in love with Lord Renaldo, that he was unable, and unwilling, to go on without the arrogant, complacent Barbarian. Casto had already dreaded it after his forced return to the Valley, and his suspicion had turned into fact after he read the prophecy. But a part of him was still fighting against it.

It simply couldn't be that his master was a god—it was impossible that Renaldo was waiting for his heart, and it was unthinkable that he, Casto, should fall in love with a barbarian from the North. Yet here he was, kneeling at his master's deathbed, crying like a little child, the only thought in his empty head the terrible loss he had just endured.

"What's so surprising about this?"

Voltara's voice was like a winter chill. Casto froze, not daring to turn around. The torturer went on in his usual mocking, cold tone, clearly enjoying the pain he inflicted on his prey.

"You've lost the only protection you ever had. And why? Because, as always, you've been too arrogant to face the truth. I win the game, my prince. Now there's no escaping me anymore."

A cold hand landed heavily on Casto's shoulder. Despite his struggles, the torturer pulled him upright, away from Renaldo's lifeless body. The young man fought back desperately, he even started to plead, something that never came easily to him.

"Please, let me stay with him a little longer. I'm begging you! Then I'll do whatever you want, whatever you please."

Mocking laughter was the answer. "Why should I be merciful, Prince? You've evaded me. You dared to flee. This is only the beginning of your punishment. And he's not going to help you anymore."

He spat on the bier and then started to drag the desperate Casto with him. Darkness descended on the Barbarian's corpse.

The last thing Casto saw was the perfect face that was now devoid of all emotion and would soon decay and fade away like an abandoned dream.

RENALDO WOKE up because Casto was screaming his lungs out. Even during their first weeks together, when the young man had still slept alone and had been woken by bad dreams every night, he had not screamed like that. It reminded Renaldo of a wild animal that had stepped into a deadly trap. Anger, mixed with fear and desperation, as well as a last, defiant protest already tinged with defeat.

Renaldo pulled his slave closer and held him tight when he started to cry. The experience he'd gained during the last years had taught him that this was all he could do for Casto. As long as Casto didn't confide in him, didn't tell him what was torturing him so ruthlessly, Renaldo was damned to watch while he fought this futile battle alone.

After some time the young man's body relaxed and the sobs became deeper, a sure sign that he had finally woken up.

Renaldo caressed his back gently. "It's okay, my darling. Everything's fine. You just had a nightmare. Everything's fine."

Still clumsy from sleep, Casto untangled himself from the Barbarian's grasp. His blue eyes glinted in the darkness like those of a hunting cat. Renaldo tensed; he knew how much his complicated lover hated to show weakness.

Casto reached out and his trembling fingers glided over Renaldo's naked chest. "I thought you were dead."

He started crying again. Still shivering all over, he bent forward and began to kiss Renaldo hungrily.

Surprised but happy, Renaldo slung his arms around Casto's hips and reciprocated the kiss with all the passion his beautiful slave always stirred in him. Casto trailed his hands farther down. Impatiently he grabbed his master's linen trousers. "Please, take me. And take me hard. I need to feel you, your power. Show me that you're still alive, that I haven't lost you." Casto's voice was still raw from crying.

Renaldo growled. Never before had Casto offered himself so explicitly. This obedience, which Renaldo hadn't had to fight for as usual, made his fire explode. Greedily he took what his slave was offering so freely, and celebrated his triumph over death and destiny.

After the first rush had cooled a bit, he placed a loving kiss on his exceptional slave's mouth.

Despair dampened the light in Casto's clear blue eyes. "I thought you had left me."

His voice was like that of a lost child; his lower lip trembled as if he'd start crying again at any moment.

Gently, Renaldo touched Casto's cheek. "I'll never leave you, darling. You're mine forever." He raised an eyebrow. "Something you're not too happy about, if I recall correctly."

A weak smile flashed across Casto's face. "Tonight I'm very happy about it."

With a triumphant grin, Renaldo towered over his property.

"ARE YOU free around noon?"

Renaldo was standing behind Casto, his arms snaked around his slave's torso, his chin resting comfortably on the soft locks.

Casto rested his hands on Renaldo's forearm. "I am. Why?"

"You're terribly nosy."

"Do you dislike it?"

"No. Just a statement. To answer your question, I want to give you a present. Most of the booty is already in the camp, so you can take your time."

"You're very generous, Barbarian."

"After everything you had to go through because of me, it's only fair."

"In case you're referring to last night, that was only nerves. Don't get too full of yourself."

Renaldo suppressed a grin. He thought it a pity, but Casto's obedience from the previous night had already evaporated like water on a hot stone. "I'd never think something like that. Nevertheless, I want to give you something."

"Then I'm grateful, my lord."

Renaldo sighed. "That would sound a lot more convincing if there were more respect in your voice. Like yesterday."

"Don't push it."

"How could I?" Renaldo turned Casto around in his arms, kissed him long and passionately, and started to leave when he was sure his beautiful lover was steady on his feet again. "See you at noon!"

Slightly out of breath, Casto's gaze followed Renaldo. He would never admit it, but he was immensely relieved that the Barbarian was doing well again. The possibility of losing him had hit Casto hard, especially since it had been so sudden. His anger about being left at the mercy of somebody else fought heavily with the insight that he really loved Renaldo. And if that wasn't enough already, he also had the nagging feeling that Renaldo could really be who he claimed. Which meant that the prophecy was real as well—and Casto was nothing more than a distraction for Renaldo while he was waiting for his heart.

It hurt Casto's pride that he didn't mean as much to the Barbarian as he did to him. But as painful as this understanding was, it was overshadowed by the fact that he would stay with Renaldo regardless, simply because he was no longer able to leave the powerful warrior. He shook his head with grim determination. It was useless to torture himself with these thoughts. Things were the way they were, and only time would show if he could hope for redemption. It was a hard lesson, one he had learned thoroughly in Ummana. As long as Renaldo never found out who he really was—what Lys was—they were safe. Because one thing was for sure, not even his persecutors would dare to pry him from the arms of the Angel of Death.

Casto went to the smithy. He wanted to thank Sic for his help the other day and make sure that he hadn't been punished too harshly by Lord Noran. He usually didn't care for the personal lives of others, and only measured them according to their standing inside the hierarchy and their potential usefulness to him, but he did feel a sympathy for Sic he'd never thought possible.

Casto couldn't understand why the young smith was so drawn to Lord Noran, who certainly wasn't the lovable kind. That Sic obeyed the man without hesitation was no surprise and only logical, because the master's foul temper and brutality made absolute obedience a necessity. But why Sic would love him, Casto couldn't grasp. In the smithy, the boy greeted him with a sad smile.

"Casto! Is Lord Renaldo well again?"

"Yes, he is. His wounds healed really fast after all. How are you?"

In light of the countless bruises covering Sic's torso—and his bloody, swollen lip—the question was superfluous. Sic had obviously paid a high price for his friendliness; his expression was grim, yet he didn't utter a bad word about his master. Instead, he blamed himself.

"I disappointed my master." Abashed, Sic averted his gaze. "And I have to ask you to leave. Lord Noran has forbidden me to talk to you until we're back in the Valley. He was really angry."

Casto fought hard against his rising fury. If Renaldo treated him like this, he would never talk to him again. But this wasn't about the Angel of Death, and Sic wasn't Casto either.

"I'm sorry, Sic. Especially since it's my fault. If there's anything I can do, please feel free to ask me."

A crooked smile appeared in Sic's bloodied face, making it look even worse. How Sic managed to see some light in even the darkest circumstances was a miracle to Casto.

"It's okay. It was my own fault. Now I just want to atone for my mistake."

"I respect that." Casto was about to leave when he remembered why he'd come in the first place. "Sic, thank you so much for your help yesterday. Without you, I'd have probably gone crazy while waiting. I'm very grateful."

His unusual friendliness was met with a dazzling smile that felt like a reward. "Don't mention it, Casto. It was my pleasure."

With that, Sic returned to his work and Casto, too, resumed his duties while still pondering the strange relationship between Sic and his master.

Like Casto, the apprentice was a personal slave. He wore a ruby-red collar that told the world whom he belonged to, but he didn't enjoy the privileges that usually went with being a favorite. It seemed as if Sic had gotten the worst of both situations. He was treated like a common slave and at the same time had to answer to his personal master. Why Noran handled things this way, Casto could only guess, especially since Sic was the only one wearing the master smith's colors.

"I CAN'T believe it!"

Speechless, Sindal and Elwan watched as Casto followed the Angel of Death toward the tents where the booty was stored.

"How can this be? What's so special about that little bastard?" Sindal's voice dripped venom. Like Elwan, he hadn't gotten over their humiliation yet.

The scars that were proof of their punishment covered their backs like welts tied from their shoulders down to the hips, not to mention they had been demoted to common slaves again. Their wounds hadn't been healed by the witch, and it had taken a long time—not to mention pain—until they had finally closed. Both Sindal and Elwan agreed that it was all the fault of the blond bastard who seemed to have conquered Renaldo's heart completely.

And so, despite the brutal punishment they had suffered, they still tried to make life hell for Casto. In the beginning they had been careful not attract the Angel of Death's attention again, but soon they became bolder. Since Casto didn't confide in his master, it was easy to sabotage him. When the two former overseers found out about this, their actions became more reckless. They still had to be careful because if one of the lords found out what they were doing, they would face a painful death, but they could rely on the help—or at least silence—of the other slaves.

Casto was not popular. His unique standing in the hierarchy of those serving the masters, as well as the way he dealt with it, made him the ideal target for hatred and envy. Only Sic and Daran seemed to like the blond pest, and they were not what one would call perfect allies. Sic was almost always busy doing his master's will, and he was so eager it spooked the other slaves.

And Daran—he belonged to the desert brothers so completely that Elwan wouldn't have been surprised if he heard that Daran told them his most private thoughts.

Sic and Daran were outsiders, just like Casto, but nobody wasted their hatred on them. For that, they were too insignificant despite their standing as personal slaves. No, it was the arrogant favorite of the Angel of Death who ignited the slaves' animosities and the outright loathing of those ranked lowest in the Pack.

It was a dangerous fire, smoldering silently and waiting to turn into a blaze.

6. INVISIBLE CHAINS

THE JOURNEY back to the Valley was as tiring and boring as Casto remembered from his first trip with the Pack. The snail's pace of the heavy carts pulled by oxen grated on his nerves, almost as much as the humid weather, which led to heavy thunderstorms nearly every noon. Casto was close to asking Lys for help, but the stallion did not want to hear anything about it. He liked the regular cooling.

One of the few bright spots on those boring days was training with Daran. During the siege Casto hadn't had much time to work with him, but now he could resume the task again.

Although in the beginning Casto had resented being demoted to the post of trainer for a slave, he now enjoyed it. Daran was a teachable, friendly pupil who always tried his best. Watching him improve delighted Casto and filled him with a sense of contentment he hadn't known before. It did so to such an extent that he even put up with Aegid and Kalad watching the training.

The desert brothers were as bored as everybody else and truly interested in their slave's progress. At the moment, they were watching how Daran raced his gelding back to the caravan in a series of controlled flying changes. For that, he rode in curves, making Rajan change the leading foot whenever they went in a new direction.

"He's become so good! When I think about how he sat a horse when we first brought him here...." Aegid's voice brimmed with pride.

Casto had to suppress a smile. Now that he knew the giant's story, he wasn't as intimidated by his presence as before, and he liked the way the two warriors showed their affection for Daran so openly. Although he had to endure quite a lot of lovey-dovey sometimes. "Yes, he's very talented. Daran has an amazing physical prowess, which makes it easy for him to communicate with Rajan."

"He does have physical prowess—not only on horseback."

As always, Kalad managed to let this seemingly neutral sentence ring with sexual innuendo.

Casto preferred not to react to the challenge. He concentrated on Daran and his horse, knowing he was about to take a risk with his next words. "How far do you want his training to go?"

"What do you mean?"

The brothers were alert. They hadn't failed to notice the change in Casto's voice.

"Daran and Rajan have reached a point where I could start teaching them offensive actions."

"You mean battle training." Kalad's voice was flat. He didn't seem to be pleased.

"Yes. I could teach him to fight. It's up to you."

"And you say he's good?" Aegid sounded pensive.

"He's very good. He has what it takes to become a dangerous fighter. I don't have to tell you how rare that is."

"Kalad, what do you think?" Aegid looked imploringly at his desert brother, who busied himself watching their advancing slave.

"I don't know. A slave wielding a weapon…? On the other hand, he really is good. Perhaps we should ask him."

Aegid and Casto showed their consent with a nod. They waited until Daran had returned to them, his cheeks reddened from the exertion, his eyes sparkling happily.

Kalad beckoned him closer. "Casto has been full of praise, Daran. He thinks he can teach you a lot more."

Daran's blush deepened. Shyly, he glanced at his teacher. "That's very friendly of you, Casto. Thank you. But it's mostly due to the training I receive."

With a smile that showed his contentment at Daran's humble answer, Aegid caressed the young man's head. "Do you want to learn how to fight on horseback?"

Daran looked surprised. "I'm a slave. What sense would that make?"

"Bettering your skills. That's not a bad reason at all. So, do you want to learn more?"

Insecure, Daran looked down at his hands. It was obvious how overtaxed he was with the situation. He never had a problem acquiescing to his masters' will, but at the moment he couldn't tell what they expected of him. So he settled for the truth.

"I would love to, Master. I really enjoy the training. But I'm your possession. I don't have the right to decide such things."

Kalad placed a gentle kiss on his temple. "If you really want it, then we won't object. Casto, you've our permission to train Daran further."

"How incredibly noble of you, my lords."

Casto's voice was ripe with sarcasm, but the smile on his face showed clearly how pleased he was with the warriors' decision. Daran was kissing his masters' hands and probably wouldn't have stopped anytime soon if Renaldo hadn't chosen that moment to join the small group.

"What're you doing? I thought it was time for training?"

"Training's over for today. We have different plans for Daran." Kalad made a suggestive gesture.

Again Daran lowered his head shyly when confronted with his masters' salaciousness. "Whatever my lords wish."

Kalad laughed. "Isn't he charming? Come on, Daran, show us what you've learned."

The three men left the Angel of Death and his slave alone.

"Did I miss something?"

"No, Barbarian. It's just that Daran's training is going to be a bit more ambitious in the future. That's all."

"So, they've given their consent?"

"I never doubted it. They're so proud of their thief. It would have taken me by surprise if they had resented the further development of his talents."

Renaldo gazed absentmindedly into the distance. Contrary to his usual modus operandi, Casto had sought his advice first before talking to the desert brothers to suggest turning Daran into a cavalryman. The Angel of Death still wasn't sure whether he liked the idea of a slave being nurtured to such a degree, but since he was doing the same with Casto, he couldn't object when Aegid and Kalad asked for similar rights for their favorite. And it meant another task that would bind Casto to the Valley, and therefore, to Renaldo.

Although he knew Casto couldn't escape him anymore, Renaldo preferred rooting him to the Valley in as many ways as possible. The idea of losing Casto appealed to him less and less each day, and since it was out of the question to chain him to the bed permanently, Renaldo had to find different means of keeping Casto bound to him forever. He flashed him a friendly smile. "What about a little scouting expedition?"

Casto's azure eyes displayed unbridled joy, touched something deep inside Renaldo, and warmed him from within.

"Always, Barbarian. Where do you want to go?"

"I'd say we just follow the road, see where it takes us."

EXCLUSIVE EXCERPT

LOVE AND THE STUBBORN

Gods of War: Book II

By Xenia Melzer

All is fair in love and war. By now, Renaldo has found out the hard way how utterly stupid this statement is once you've met your match. And Casto won't give an inch in their ongoing war for love.

After a tumultuous start to their relationship, Renaldo and Casto seem to have finally reached calmer waters. But just when Renaldo starts getting comfortable and thinks he can relax, things get out of hand again. His old enemy, the Good Mother, is dangerously close to defeating the divine brothers by reaching out to what is most dear to him. Casto still clinging to his stubborn pride is all the plotters need to drive him and Renaldo apart. Burdened by the secrets of his past, Casto fights with everything he's got not only to save his life, but also to secure his future happiness. Facing the destruction of everything they have built together, Renaldo and Casto must choose between pride and love.

1. THUNDERSTORM

Kit

DAMON WAS alert when he entered the shady shed. Doron and Sindal, the two former overseers who had hated Casto ever since their demotion, approached him slowly. Damon couldn't suppress a satisfied smile. The two men's hatred wrapped like a warm cloak around his shoulders.

"Damon, what do you want?" Doron was terse. It was late and they still had some work to do.

"I wanted to see how you're doing."

"Don't be ridiculous. You're not really interested in anybody besides yourself. You're here because you need something, so spill."

"Doron, I can't say I've missed your bluntness, but if you must know, I need your help. You do know Casto, don't you?"

Sindal spat out. "As if you didn't know. What do you have to do with him?"

"Well, I guess you could say I'd like to teach him a lesson."

"Forget it. We've already tried, and look where it got us." Doron sounded gruff.

Damon treated him to a bright smile, which didn't fail to annoy Doron. "That, my friend, is because you two are as stupid as the day is long. I, on the other hand, have a perfect plan."

A dangerous glint sprang to life in the men's eyes. It hadn't been a wise move to humiliate them, but Damon hadn't been able to withstand temptation. Now he could feel their hatred bubbling up, swallowing every sensible thought. It was exactly how Damon preferred his minions—easy to manipulate because they were oblivious to everything else around them.

"And what kind of plan do you have in mind?" Doron asked.

"It's easy. I want you to see to it that Casto gets delayed tomorrow noon."

"No chance. He's always punctual for training."

Doron had immediately understood what Damon was aiming for, a fact that didn't escape the priest. As much as the former overseer was consumed by hatred, he wasn't stupid.

"It has to be something pressing, something he can't ignore. He's still riding the brown mare, isn't he?"

"The loopy one? Yes. Although not even the Holy Mothers understand why."

Damon acknowledged this with an innocent smile. Finally his constant surveillance of the blond pest would pay off. "What would happen should she escape from her stall? Of course it would be an unfortunate accident, but once she's outside...."

"Casto will try to get her himself." Doron grinned broadly. "That we can arrange."

"So I can count on you?"

Sindal and Doron shared a long glance. From their own painful experience they knew what kind of risk they were about to take. Because one thing was for sure, should the Angel of Death ever find out about this, they would be denied a quick, merciful death. But the hatred burning in their chests enticed them to give in to Damon's plan.

They hesitated for one more moment, then nodded. "Yes," they said together.

Damon bowed to the two slaves in mockery. He hadn't thought they would deny him, but he was still surprised how easy it had been to win them over. "It's a pleasure doing business with you."

CASTO WAS just about to go to his daily training with Renaldo when he became aware of the racket in the stables. He turned around just in time to see Lord Wolfstan's chestnut mare racing at breakneck speed toward the fields with her eyes rolled back so that only the whites could be seen. It had started to thaw during the past few days, so the ground was frozen over and extremely slippery. At the pace the mare was setting, she would break her legs in no time. Experience had taught Casto that she was too crazy to slow down on her own. Once she started sliding, it would be too late and Lord Wolfstan would lose his most valuable horse.

Casto gave a shrill whistle and Lys appeared at his side. They followed the chestnut mare and finally managed to corner her in one of the paddocks. It took some time until she'd calmed down enough so that

Casto could take her back to the stables. This time he closed the stall door himself before hurrying to the training hall.

Renaldo was waiting for him with a thunderous expression on his perfect face. His right hand gripped the handle of the training sword so hard his knuckles turned white. "Where have you been?"

For once Casto realized it was wise to apologize. He knelt down in front of the enraged Angel of Death. "Please forgive me, my lord. There was a problem at the stables and I couldn't leave."

"A problem at the stables? How interesting. Get up!"

Casto obeyed immediately. Renaldo's tone was icy, his countenance unreadable, but Casto felt instinctively that the warrior was angrier than he had ever seen him before.

Renaldo tossed him a sword with more force than was necessary. While Casto was still busy getting into position, he charged.

If Casto had ever had the illusion of being able to meet Renaldo on equal ground in a fight, it was now shattered. Renaldo was playing with him like a predator might with half-dead prey. He drove Casto through the hall, time and again dealing him humiliating and painful blows while accentuating each one with an angry reprimand.

"You have to be punctual for training!"

"Nothing is more important than your training!"

"How dare you make me wait!"

On and on it went, the blows as well as the scolding coming in accelerating succession. After an especially nasty blow to his knee, Casto snapped. He managed to parry the next strike out of sheer anger. His voice lowered in fury. "I said I was sorry! I apologized! But I had no choice!"

"That's true, you didn't have a choice! But as always, you preferred to deny me!"

"That's not true!"

Casto wanted to say something more, but at that moment Renaldo disarmed him with a quick flick of his blade. He pushed him against the wall, stabbed him painfully in the ribs with the tip of his sword, and looked at him coldly.

"Today was your last training. I want you to get out of my sight, you ungrateful, arrogant little prick. Get lost, now!"

Casto couldn't believe that Renaldo was sending him away. He snapped at him with the ferocity of a rabid dog. "As you wish, Barbarian! I really hate you!"

Trembling with rage, Renaldo watched the retreating shape of his slave. Suddenly a crackling noise caught his attention. The heavy wooden sword in his hand burned to ashes with a blazing flame. Cursing in the tongue of the Ancients, he tossed the blistering remains to the ground, his gaze fixed on the inferno he had just caused with his fury. There was no doubt: since he'd met Casto his powers were getting out of control. The last time he had unconsciously flamed things when he got angry had been shortly after Ana-Isara had taken their hearts, but his slave threw him so off-balance that he was no longer able to contain the powers inside him.

Once again he pondered if it might not be better to get rid of Casto—or to at least discipline him in a way that would teach him his place. Renaldo sighed. A beating wouldn't tame the capricious blond, rather the opposite. And selling him was simply out of the question. The mere idea of somebody else's hands on his slave's flawless skin made Renaldo even more furious than Casto's behavior had done. He would have to find another solution for this dilemma.

CASTO HAD barely left the training hall when he started to realize what a grave mistake he'd made this time. His anger faltered, paving the way for a despair so dark it threatened to consume him completely. Crestfallen, he went to Lys, who greeted him reproachfully.

"I know, Brother. Please, let's ride. I'm afraid it'll be the last for quite a long time."

During the ride through the Valley, Casto couldn't stop blaming himself.

How could he have been so stupid? The powerful Angel of Death, the most feared warrior on the continent, had agreed to train him. It was an honor which only a few elect ever enjoyed and which surely was rarely bestowed on a mere slave. To his amazement, he had taken this generous gift for granted, and, even worse, trampled it underfoot. There was no denying it; he owed the Barbarian a sincere apology. Given how furious

Renaldo had been, Casto wasn't sure whether it would be enough. He didn't want to think about what would happen to him should the Angel of Death decide to sell him. It was difficult enough for him to obey Renaldo, and he wasn't able to imagine doing so for another master.

Glumly he returned to the stables with Lys, said his good-bye to his brother, and lurked back to his master's chambers. Renaldo wasn't there, which gave Casto the chance to prepare everything for his apology. His deed had been so ignominious, so obnoxious that he wouldn't be able to avoid a beating. Sighing deeply, he sat down on one of the lounges and waited for the Barbarian's return.

When Renaldo entered his chambers, his slave got up from a lounge and knelt down with his head bowed demurely. But Renaldo was still furious and not in the mood for games. "I told you to get out of my sight! What do you want?"

"Begging your forgiveness, master. My behavior was inappropriate and lacked respect. I'm truly sorry."

"And you think that fixes it?" Renaldo's voice was pure acid, deep inside he could feel his flame blazing again and the urge to hurt Casto was almost impossible to suppress.

"No, of course not. You've been so generous as to make me your pupil, a grace I took for granted. That alone was wrong, as well as my delayed appearance and my reaction to the punishment you meted out. I'm fully aware that my insolence can only be expiated with blood." Upon these words, Casto held up the leather whip with which Renaldo had punished him after his escape from the Valley.

Renaldo was rendered speechless. He'd never seen Casto so humble, a sure sign of how serious he was about his apology. Against his will, Renaldo felt himself already forgiving the young man. But Casto's behavior had been so unacceptable that he had to atone. With his mind now working clearly again, Renaldo took the whip from Casto's hand and threw it into a corner. "We both know that a whipping will only enhance your defiance. I'm really disappointed, Casto. I'd thought a highly civilized person like you would know better how to behave."

The slave lowered his neck even more but didn't say anything. Renaldo went on. "I want you to go to your room. At the moment I'm too angry to make a decision. I'll tell you tomorrow what I'm going to do with you."

In the oppressive silence following these words, Casto got up. His shoulders were slumped and he was far from his usual overbearing self. All the proud defiance Renaldo loved so much about him was gone. It took all of Renaldo's willpower not to hug and comfort his slave.

CASTO STOOD in front of the bed he hadn't slept in since he spent his first night with the Barbarian. He felt empty and exhausted. Renaldo's disappointment was like a knife in his chest that a cruel torturer slowly twisted. He was able to deal with Renaldo's anger in an offhand manner since he wasn't afraid of him like everybody else, but the mere idea that the warlord could think so ill of him made his stomach turn.

Casto hated himself for making Renaldo's opinion of him so important to him, but there was also no denying that he'd gone too far this time. No matter what else the Barbarian might be to him, as his mentor, Casto owed him respect and obedience.

Frustrated, Casto slumped onto his bed. Even in Ummana, where every one of his teachers had been a cruel monster, he had always shown perfect manners, no matter what he thought about the people entrusted with his education. And Renaldo, of all people, the first person to teach him without trying to break him at the same time, had become the target for his ingratitude.

Casto couldn't escape the insight that should the Angel of Death decide to sell him, it was only just. What use did Renaldo have for a slave like him anyway?

IN THE middle of the night, Renaldo woke. He'd heard Casto scream. He sighed, remembering those first months when the young man woke covered in sweat every night. Since Casto had started sharing Renaldo's bed, the nightmares had stopped, and even when he got restless sometimes, all it took to make him sleep peacefully was for Renaldo to caress him soothingly. He had hoped the evil dreams had been banished, but now it seemed that only his presence had kept them at bay. He wondered what horrors Casto must have endured that they could follow him as far as the Valley.

The scream came again, high-pitched and wailing, and then Casto started talking in a tongue completely alien to Renaldo's ears. He knew it wasn't the language spoken in the area where his slave had come from, but he was unable to connect the quick, melodic stream of syllables to any place on the continent. It sounded a little like Ummanian, but he wasn't sure. Renaldo had never bothered to learn the language of the merchants; Ummana was too far away from the Valley to justify the trouble. And those who came the long way into the mountains were usually fluent in at least four or five different tongues.

Without making a sound, he got up from his bed and moved over to Casto's chamber. The young man was kneeling on the furs, whimpering like a lost child. Casto's azure eyes were wide open but apparently blind. He was fast asleep.

Renaldo approached Casto slowly so as not to startle him. When he reached him, he hugged him gently, pressed him back into the covers, and tried to lull him with soft words. "It's all right, my darling. Shh. Everything's fine. It's just a bad dream. Relax. I'm here."

A last desperate whimper, and then the young man snuggled against his master with a sigh and slept on peacefully.

Once he was sure the nightmare was banished, Renaldo returned reluctantly to his own room. Whatever it was that afflicted Casto so much had to be the reason for his stubborn behavior, his arrogance, and the way he always pushed his master away. But as long as Casto didn't confide in him, Renaldo would be unable to help. The secrets surrounding Casto were stirring his interest more and more, but the young man had to tell him of his own free will. Should Renaldo try to force him, things would most definitely end in tears and misery.

THE NEXT morning, Casto was waiting nervously for his master to call him. He'd had a bad night. In his dreams he'd been back to Ummana, a helpless victim of his father's schemes. But just when his sire had started to humiliate him deeply again, the Barbarian had shown up and saved Casto the same way he'd done during his escape from the Valley. He was still less than happy that Renaldo could follow him into his dreams, but last night he had been glad of it. Casto didn't know what he would have done without Renaldo's help.

As if he'd sensed that Casto had been thinking about him, Renaldo beckoned him to the main room. "Casto! Come here!"

Casto hurried to get to his master, his gaze demurely on the ground. This time, he knew it was better to yield. He knelt down, waiting for Renaldo's verdict and already mentally prepared for his master to sell him.

As if Renaldo wanted to torture Casto on purpose, he looked at him for some time before he started talking.

"I'm still furious, Casto. Your behavior yesterday was unacceptable, but I don't want to take rash measures based on my anger. For the time being, I'm going to keep you. But one mistake, no matter how small, and I instantly sell you to the highest bidder, understood?"

Shocked, Casto stared at the ground. He had been aware that he'd gone too far this time but to be treated so coldly hit him harder than he'd thought possible. All he could muster was a hoarse whisper. "Yes, master."

"Good. Then get to work now."

With this, Renaldo averted his gaze so that Casto didn't realize how hard it was for him to treat him so dismissively when all he wanted to do was pull him into his arms and kiss him. He heard the young man getting up and leaving the room with barely a sound. In that moment, Renaldo felt lonelier than ever before in his long life. He missed their morning ritual, missed the arguments, the passion and, most of all, he missed Casto's pride. But Casto had to learn that his actions had consequences, that he couldn't oppose his master any way he pleased.

If only it weren't so hard to show the necessary strictness.

"YOUR PLAN has worked out perfectly!"

Doron's taunting voice made Damon edgy. His week hadn't been too good so far. He had hoped to get a bombshell from his scheme against Casto, and all that had happened was a faint tinkling. Being mocked by the likes of Doron didn't improve his mood.

"He hasn't even whipped him. The prick has gone unpunished, as usual."

Damon tried hard to hide his anger and highlighted the few positive points. "I admit that things could've gone better, but you're wrong in thinking Casto wasn't punished. His wellbeing is hanging by a thread. Haven't you noticed how humble he's become? I bet you Renaldo's threatened to sell him. Which means there's only one tiny incident keeping Casto from testing his arrogance against a master like Aegid or Noran."

Doron's face lit up in malicious joy. "And you're going to create that incident?"

Damon ignored the mockery and the challenge attached to it. He reminded himself that the man in front of him was nothing more than a gambling piece for him. It didn't pay off to get agitated because of a mere tool. "That's not necessary. Regarding Casto's temper, I don't think he can keep up the humility for more than a few days."

"So we're just sitting back and waiting?"

Damon treated Doron to a smile that made the slave shiver with fear. "That, my friend, is the fun part."

In Wolfstan and Hulda's chambers, Wolfstan was sprawled lazily on one of the lounges, sipping hot tea from a cup and watching his darling wife sharpening her favorite daggers with the ease of practice. The sonorous sound of the grindstone had a meditative effect on Wolfstan and allowed him to let his thoughts go wandering.

He loved this time of year, when winter forced the normally hectic life in the Valley to a halt. It was time to lean back and reminisce about the past year and think about the decisions he had put on hold. When first meeting him, many people underestimated Wolfstan as slow and cumbersome, until time taught them better. The armorer was a thorough man who didn't like to rush things. His never-ending patience also made him the perfect husband for Hulda, whose vivacious nature had drawn in, and then put off, quite a lot of men and women in the past.

Contrary to her husband, the killer couldn't see the benefits of the quiet season. It was the time of year when she was irritable and it wasn't a good idea to challenge her wrath. Now she stopped in her work, her expressive lavender eyes drilled into Wolfstan. "What is it?"

Wolfstan smiled. He knew his wife long enough to know that she wasn't really angry, but bored. "Nothing, my sweet one. I'm just thinking."

"You're doing that all the time, Armorer." Despite the cool wording, there was tenderness in the voice of the mother superior. Hulda loved her husband deeply. She had a strong suspicion that he was the prize Ana-Isara had promised her before the kiss that had changed her life forever. She'd been married to Wolfstan for so long that she knew where his thoughts were taking him. "Don't worry about Casto and Renaldo. They'll make up soon enough."

A fond smile was the answer to that statement. "You always know what I'm thinking. But I'm still worried. Since this unfortunate incident, our leader is as irritable as a whore after an unsuccessful night, and Casto is sulking like a beaten dog. I'd been expecting them to make up after less than a week. If this goes on, I'm afraid Renaldo might lose him."

Hulda cast her daggers aside, snuggled up to her husband, and sipped from his tea. "I know what you mean. They're both so unhappy. Who would've thought it possible that the proud Angel of Death could fall so hard for a slave?"

"You've said it yourself. Casto is far more than a mere slave."

"That's a fact. Although I can't exactly pinpoint what it is about him that makes him so special. I don't like admitting it, but he's almost impossible to read."

"Harder to read than you, my sweet one?"

"Mmm. In comparison, I'm like an open book—for those who can read."

"Are you challenging me?"

Hulda kissed her husband passionately. Wolfstan was never able to resist her erotic assaults, she knew too well how to use her body. He returned the kiss with devotion as he spanned his wife's hips with his hands in a possessive gesture. Suddenly greedy, Hulda started to strip her mate, her beautiful face showing her lust openly. The so-far boring day was definitely looking up.

XENIA MELZER was born and raised in a small village in the South of Bavaria. As one of nature's true chocoholics, she's always in search of the perfect chocolate experience. So far, she's had about a dozen truly remarkable ones. Despite having been in close proximity to the mountains all her life, she has never understood why so many people think snow sports are fun. There are neither chocolate nor horses involved and it's cold by definition, so where's the sense? She does not like beer either and has never been to the Oktoberfest—no quality chocolate there.

Even though her mind is preoccupied with various stories most of the time, Xenia has managed to get through school and university with surprisingly good grades. Right after school she met her one true love who showed her that reality is capable of producing some truly amazing love stories itself.

While she was having her two children, she started writing down the most persistent stories in her head as a way of relieving mommy-related stress symptoms. As it turned out, the stress relief has now become a source of the same, albeit a positive one.

When she's not writing, she teaches English at school, enjoys riding and running, spending time with her kids, and dancing with her husband.

Website: www.xeniamelzer.com
E-mail: info@xeniamelzer.com

Made in the USA
Middletown, DE
05 September 2022

73209782R00166